Hitherto a Lion

by

Rikki Simons

Thirty billion light years from Earth, two hundred toroidal colonies spin within a black nebula of organic matter. The human colonists of the Hæl triple star system are under siege by the Bœzch invaders. Cognizant beings cannot hide from the Bœzch, and when a human falls into their red, spindly hands, they are spun into stardust, until the theory of them is gone from the universe.

Now Fel, the black biomechanical lion, wearily hunts the Bœzch across the African toroidal colony known as the Long Savanna. Here he is tested. Here he is followed by a haunting song and a dream of a familiar human woman ....

Written by
Rikki Simons

Volume One of the Cometary Lions Space Opera

Illustrations by
Rikki Simons and Tavisha Wolfgarth-Simons

Cover Art by
Robert Simons

Proof Editor: Julie Miyamoto

Edition 2018-v1.2 ISBN: 978-0-692-69369-8

Published May, 2018
A Rikkitikki Tavicat Book
Los Angeles - California
tavicat.com

For Dad. I hope to meet you in your Quiet Place.

Hitherto your hither side
I couldn't tell your head's so deep
          - Misheard Lyrics from Hitherto,
          The Cocteau Twins

Gentle hunter
His tail plays on the ground
While he crushes the skull.

Beautiful death
Who puts on a spotted robe
When he goes to his victim

Playful killer
Whose loving embrace
Splits the antelope's heart.
          - Anonymous, translated by Ulli Beier,
          Yoruba Poetry: An Anthology

A Brief Glossary of Words
for the Sake of Pronunciation

Ægeleif Pronunciation: *ayge-leaf*
Æsirisæ Pronunciation: *ay-siri-ay*
Bœzch Pronunciation: *bah-schk*
Bosh Übor Pronunciation: *bah-sh-u-bore* **Eüllo**
Pronunciation: *u-lo*
Euphön *Pronunciation: u-fohn*
Fel Pronunciation: *fell*
Gylfinæ Pronunciation: *gill-fin-ay*
Gylfinîr Pronunciation: *gill-fin-eer*
Göthe Pronunciation: *goth*
Hæl Pronunciation: *hale*
Hiichiim Pronunciation: *hee-cheem* **Holæstin**
Pronunciation: *hole-ay-stin*
Hünde Pronunciation: *hu-nd*
Hvitt Pronunciation: ha-*vit*
Jéudin Pronunciation: *ju-din*
Jeüdora Pronunciation: *schz-u-dora*
Mún Pronunciation: *moon*
Œlexasperon Pronunciation: *ah-lex-az-pur-on*
Oshii Pronunciation: *o-she*
Paölo Pronunciation: *paul-o*
Páss Pronunciation: *paz*
Paternæ Pronunciation: *patern-ay*
Queen Tætanæ Pronunciation: *tay-tan-ay*
Rafæl Pronunciation: raff-ay-el
Staff of Æthax Pronunciation: *ay-thax* **Sword of**
Évir Pronunciation: *eh-veer*
Taum Pronunciation: *tom*
Tishbyt Pronunciation: *tish-bite*
Uedolpha Pronunciation: *hew-doll-fah*
Ünderwritten Pronunciation: *hoon-der-writtem*
Wülvogarti Pronunciation: *vool-vo-gardi*

Chapter One
This Will Never End

Fel forgot that his name was short for Rafæl, the name of an angel, but Fel was a black lion and he lived under the stars in the Long Savanna. He had never seen an angel.

Fel was alive when the Bœzch Generals ruptured the ground of the Savanna, though his memory of the event was only a din of erupting colors of fire-red and screams-of-blue. When the Humans were dragged from their labyrinthine cities on the edge of the grass and abused in ways beyond the Euclidian, twisted towards shapes only dreamed in languid Dali premonitions, the pride kept their distance, and Fel's brothers and sisters were satisfied that the wildebeest and zebra were unharmed. The pride was well. The Bœzch things directed their wrath solely towards Humanity.

He knew he had a favorite companion, he knew he had a pride of his own. He knew he had a Master. It was enough for a lion to think on. He could never comprehend his augmentation. He could not know that every strand of his hair was an electroactive polymer that, when struck, would twist into ropes of banded cables, covering his reengineered flesh in a sealed armor. Bioluminescent monitors covered the length of his hide just under the epidermis, setting blue sparks to course along his four-meter-long frame like schools of pooling jellyfish. His strength and sight were boosted and monitored by robotic ticks locked into biomechanical sockets, just under his black mane. None of these enhancements would make sense to him, and he thought of none of them. He cared only that his favorite companion was near and his pride was free from hunger.

His self-awareness was limited, his empathy anchored in that selfish sleepwalking animal fashion, but there was something deeper than instinct, something that toyed with his base awareness of his companion. He could feel the data from her sensor feeds. He could feel the fractals of her breath strike his neck in dark algorithmic bursts of radio, pushing against his consciousness like a quantum antihistamine. The data made him drowsy, and he nestled into his mate's cheek while his Master remained ignorant of their acuteness. His Master was too preoccupied with the Bœzch Generals curled in a heap a kilometer away.

The Bœzch slept at the foot of the ruined city known as Aza Nairobi. Red, muscled and obscene, splayed out over their halo-horned heads, sucking on the dreams of the dying, and exhaling in glittering arabesque swirls with no visible mouths: the Bœzch Generals moved with the broken-science time-shutter of their eldritch kind.

Fel could see his Master frown towards the Bœzch. She existed only as data projected before him — a visual and auditory hallucination of a slim Eurasian woman — a torrent of photons seen only within the closed Augmented Reality network that surrounded Fel's biomechanical pride.

Within his vision, Fel's Master sat upon a wooden park bench at the center of an abandoned ranger's station. She moved in anthropomorphic fashion, though she didn't need to turn her head to scan the toroidal rise of the colony's inverted horizon.

"Fel, sit here," said his Master.

Familiar with her gestures, Fel folded his massive form around the base of the bench. His pride moved to sit beside their leader; they were, along with Fel, six augmented black lions in all, comprised of his companion, her two sisters and two younger males. The Master made another small gesture and the pride came to rest.

The Master said, "Begin Recording, Tick Seventeen of Rafæl Unit: I am the Long Savanna's Master Artificial Spirit, Etherealon Intelligence Type, now speaking aloud so that Rafæl's ticks will record this moment, my simulation included.

"Should Rafæl's pride be killed, my Ethereal Core will be at risk. This recording will find its way to a Grippership, and then to Olde Sol. I report the following:

"The Bœzch Generals have depopulated all of Long Savanna's one hundred thousand colonists. All have either died from induced frontal temporal dementia or were mutilated until they reached a state of pan-dimensional collapse. Observations from all nine hundred of Hæl System's sister colonies reveal their own loss of life to be in the millions. Here on this colony, the Bœzch invasion left only the Savanna's animals untouched. We suspect the invaders' interests lie only in destroying sapient life, and this is why we are proceeding with Manticore Project.

"A report was sent to Olde Sol explaining the necessity of these lions. For the past six months I have used them to scout the Savanna and test the Bœzch Generals' reactions, and the Bœzch are thus far oblivious to the lions' presence — therefore, I am now proceeding with the stalking and execution of the Bœzch menace. This is Long Savanna Master EtherCore. Ending analog report."

The living image that was the consciousness of the Long Savanna's Master EtherCore personality, visible only to those with access to Fel's closed Augmented Reality network, did not move from sitting to standing position, but she stood nonetheless, the sequence between skipped out of irrelevance. She ordered the lions to their feet.

Holographic tactical displays materialized that only they could detect, their directives based on scent and impulse rather than alphanumeric or associative symbols. Fel bristled. He felt compulsion rise, directed at images within his primitive mind. Shapes of the Bœzch, the urge to hunt, to rend and abuse, to eat. But there was something else, too. Fel turned to his companion. She too stared at the distant Bœzch pile, yet there was something in her expression. Her eyes were too focused. The impression within her pupils told a story of a thing deeper, more complex than instinct. Comprehension.

The Master EtherCore's avatar turned without moving and faced Fel's companion. "Nova! Stop!"

An eruption of dust and rock and metal as the pride was thrown apart. Red and black arms the length of old elms, the texture of willow trunks, tunneled up from beneath. Fel's companion, Nova, vanished beneath the ground. He saw the remainder of his pride in various states of shock and rage. Nova's sisters were engaged in combat, both together tackling a risen Bœzch General, dragging it to the ground with the fleet and ephemeral precision of animal brutality. But one brother was already dead, gored by a Bœzch General's halo of horns, and he remained there impaled as an obscene ornament. The remaining pride brother was still, stunned by the assault, abandoned to rouse his senses.

A triad of Bœzch fell upon Rafæl.

Despite their bulk, they moved with the speed of swift robins and reached out for him, eyeless faces snapping with holographic mouths hung upon halos of horns. Gigantic fingers closed around Fel's waist, completing a circle. As they attempted to pull him apart, one Bœzch to the front of him and two to the rear, Fel bristled and roared, his fur snapping taut, becoming armor. Generators within his larynx responded to the roar and his aggressors were electrocuted, startling them enough that they released him. Fel touched the ground only for a moment and then was airborne, leaping towards the tumescent throat of the Bœzch before him. Fel's metal teeth sunk in; the transparent Bœzch faces cried out, an orchestra of whale song perverted and warped in glass treble. Fel tasted honey. He had the throat with him when he kicked off his foe and landed twenty meters away. He spun to see the stricken Bœzch writhe, a convulsing giant that phased from one dimensional plane to the next until it quaked its last, settling into this world, collapsing into death.

Though sightless, the other two Bœzch could sense their companion's demise and shrieked, arms outstretched like the legs of Dali's Elephants, mouths gasping in rancor. Fel spat the hunk of preternatural meat from his mouth and charged, but both his targets skittered away like stilt-bearing crabs. Fel turned to face them again. He stopped. The ground slid forward, towards the rupture where the Bœzch first attacked his pride; up from the original chasm rose a Governor General. The other Bœzch moved aside, and Fel saw it had something in its hand. Between thumb and index finger, the Governor General spun Nova. The lioness writhed and turned in its grasp, one moment an organic thing, the next a series of geometric shapes and colors. The Bœzch toyed with her in that way Fel had seen them play with the Humans, though Fel lacked the long-term memory to place it. Spinning and spinning, Nova turned over in the creature's fingers. Moment to moment she changed, twisting like clay, a lioness, an inverted pile of organs, the blood contained in midair, the image of horror changed again into blocks, into geodes, into nebulae, finally into stardust. Nova's glittering soot drifted away in the Long Savanna's spin-ward wind, nothing more than particles in the slipstream.

As a non-sapient, Fel could not comprehend all of what he witnessed, but he felt loss, a loss that rose into panic — not the panic of empathy from calamity, but an animal, selfish panic. His back arched. Armor bristled. Generators inside him moved safeties to their off positions and his internal plasma coils boiled his insulated guts. Anger moved within him like a shaking pulsar, each generator's revolution expressing fuel into his forepaws and face. His mouth filled with light, and lines of burning venom dripped from his canines. His claws brightened, blue, then white, his every step now striking small fires. For a moment he halted, exhaling cinder wisps. A sound of something being activated, a simple but pleasant electronic hum. He raised his head. He was upon them.

Fel moved through the air as if propelled by a shift in gravity rather than the spring of his muscles. A mutual descent, Fel fixed into the chest of his companion's destroyer just as the two remaining Bœzch raked at the black lion's hindquarters. They collapsed upon him, a frenzy of demonic arms and horns convulsing, and Fel vanished beneath the froth of combat, only to rise like an impulse, combusting those he touched, reducing his foes to smoldering shanks of meat and ash in a roar lit like the blaze of stars.

And then he was alone.

His favored companion, her sisters and brothers —
all dead. Only Fel remained. He slumped, not from grief
but from exhaustion. His power was spent and his hunger
now ebbed. Dragging himself in a small circle, he looked
for his Master and found her behind a mound of upturned
soil and metal. The Long Savanna's repair systems
mobilized, and as Fel walked over to the augmented part of
space that only he could see, torn bits of real metal
structure repaired themselves, falling into their rightful
place.

But something was wrong with the Master
EtherCore's mind.

She drifted there like an aimless spirit, her arms
limp, back arched, head tilted in a questioning manner.
When she spoke, her voice was broken, not strained but
collapsing. "Re ... Record Message: Ethereal Core
compromised. Comprom ... compromised. Initiate
emergency shut down and copy cognitive ... cogni ... nitive
self to silicon backup up. Rafæl now only survivor of
Manticore Project. Project. Initiate Bœzch Genocide
Sequence. Initiating ..."

Unmoored from the real, the Master drifted towards
Fel. She was unable to look at him. In that way the blind
move when they address the sighted, gazing at nothing,
shaking farther than necessary, she said, "Initiating ..." A
sound of modems crashing issued from nowhere in
particular, and Fel's crystal blue eyes dilated. A new
impulse: he must track and kill every Bœzch. He must hunt
them down through heavy grass or barren plane. He must
seek them out whether he is hungry or not ....

Fel retired from the shadow of his Master and began
to eat. His hunger punished him, made him ravenous. He
found every scrap of meat. He ate the honied muscle

tissue, he ate the Bœzch limbs and cartilage, and when there was no more meat of the god-things, Fel's fangs found cannibal purchase in the bodies of his fallen pride. Only when the last scrap of flesh was consumed did Fel feel the generators within him reach satisfaction, though he was still left enfeebled from fatigue. He chuffed and licked himself alone.

The Master drifted near him. She was dead now, an inert ghost transfixed on nothing in particular, unable to remove herself from his side, floating two meters away. Briefly, a message hovered above her head: PLEASE ENJOY A MUSICAL SELECTION WHILE MASTER UNIT REBOOTS. NOW PLAYING UNA FURTIVA LAGRIMA; COMPOSER: DONIZETTI; PERFORMED BY OMIC, THE ORION MUSICAL INTELLIGENCE COMPANY.

The following night Fel heard the melancholic aria *Una Furtiva Lagrima*, "One Furtive Tear," repeat a hundred times. It never completed to climax, but skipped as it reached the middle and started over from the beginning. He turned in sleep to its plodding wake. The dead image of his Master stayed with him, hovering over him as a limp guardian, and the bassoon and strings slowly plucked away into Fel's dreaming, the tenor raising his voice with the words beginning, "Una Furtiva Lagrima ..."

In his dream, Fel saw a young lady, a Human. She was familiar to him, but in a fashion that was beyond his understanding. She was dark, amber ale eyes and almond hair, the scent of gardenia and vanilla. She touched a young man's hand and laughed, walking with him under the covered sky of the Long Savanna, pausing to stare in wonder for a moment, finally splitting into rubies and geometric stardust, the young man calling out to her in despair, "Luti, Luti, where are you, Luti?" The song reached the line, "M'ama ... Sì, m'ama, lo vedo ... Lo vedo ..." and cut again, moving back to the beginning.

Fel awoke exhausted and searched for his pride. By midday he pined for them. He needed their closeness, to hunt with them in the tall grass, to rest under shade for hours, to bury his face in Nova's neck. Weak and afraid, he gave an awkward roar under the wide filigree of a jackalberry tree. His Master stared dead away. The ghost was still inactive but the secret song heard only by Fel was yet intact. The bassoon struck up again. Fel lifted himself out of misery and set out to hunt.

For several weary months, Fel's wanderings cycled; everywhere he traveled within the great toroidal space colony, the broken aria and the ghost of his Master drifted with him; everywhere he went he killed Bœzch exclusively; every step he took drove him closer to collapse; every time he closed his eyes, he dreamed of the mysterious young Human named Luti. That she shared the same smell as his lost companion meant nothing to him. He only cared that she felt real. When he sat upon the bloodied bones of fallen Bœzch Generals, when he prowled the edge of empty settlements, head bent in pain, when he drank near the ponds where elephants kept their distance, or by the river where gazelles watched with numb fascination as Fel abused his enemies — he began to look forward to sleep and to dreaming of Luti.

A sweet release from the drudge of fighting, he did not understand the dreams as dreaming. He did not know he was asleep. He only knew exhaustion and anticipation for the scent of gardenia and vanilla. In the beginning he dreamed of walks through elephant grass under the covered sky, but in time the illusory girl began to repeat the same line to the empty young man in his dreams, "Good, good. Keep up, keep up. Good!" It was baby talk. The repetitive, condescending language used to train children, idiots, and animals. And the young man followed her like all of these. Whenever Fel awoke, he was reminded of his weakness.

As his encounters with the Bœzch grew more desperate and inhumane, so did the complexity of his dreaming. Now when he rested after gorging, Fel's dreams seemed more real, more dimensional, more comprehensive, the dream couple firming up as his exhaustion wore him down. Human Luti began teaching the empty young man how to speak, pointing at objects by the river, saying their names over and over. This continued in a one-sided fashion until finally the young man replied in what Fel understood as a sense of eager yearning, the need to please a mentor, mother, or lover.

"Are you brave enough to be brilliant?" Luti repeated the question several times while staring into the man's face with collapsing sincerity.

The man struggled after every question, but his need to please overwhelmed his handicap. He wanted to feel proud, and finally, he said, "I ... I'm brave ..."

And the woman hugged him. "Then save me."

Fel awoke startled and sick. He felt the arms around his own neck. Sitting up, he blinked under half-moon lids, mild panic settling into haze. But for the drifting Master EtherCore ghost and the repeating broken aria, he remained alone.

Four months of wandering his beloved savanna —
four months of hunting and slaughter: though he did not
know it, he was fast approaching the end of his journey.
On a morning of spangled mists glittering with the vapors
of dew from a false daybreak and the smells of musk and
pollen, Fel hurried through a maze of granite kopjes
littering the ground like sleeping elephants. There were
real elephants present, too: a strong group of many fathers
and many mothers, their children mostly grown, their elders
absent, gone to rest long ago. It was a proud and healthy
herd, and Fel was somewhat emboldened by their presence
near the watering hole. The pond shone like a black mirror
in their midst, reflecting their sublime outlines as if the
colony itself was opening a wide eye to get the most
complete look at them. Fel would have been excited by the
presence of the herd if it were not for the Bœzch he
detected here. He roared once, and the sound that issued
forth acted as a packet of sensors feeling out ahead,
reaching around the forty pachyderms, plunging into the
black pool, reaching and weaving amidst the kopjes and
their sparse shrubbery.

Nothing.

And yet, he felt something.

Fel roared again, this time to the ground below him,
more in frustration than out of design. He looked to the
frozen form of the Master who still glided silent and dead
at his side, a phantom rag doll, bouncing between the beats
of the broken aria that only Fel and, if she were cognitive,
his Master could hear.

The sensor packets touched something beneath him
and he did something unusual: he pictured in his mind what
it could possibly be. The old eruption began: that splitting
of earth and rending of the colony's interior structure

common to every burrowing Bœzch. But this was different. This time the tumult was greater and more extreme, the hands reaching out to him bigger than any he had yet destroyed. Up and up the monster slithered, as fat as houses, and red as arson. The land tipped up and over, and Fel found himself clinging to terrain, finding purchase in a series of mounds and uprooted trees, one after the other, bounding between them. He heard the elephants cry out. It was a sound that struck something terribly deep within him. At the sound of those awful trumpets he canvassed the emotional scale from fierce centurion to panicked civilian. From his steady place he could see what was happening. As the Bœzch unraveled itself from whence it slept, a tremendous sinkhole had formed. Elephants scrambled to stay upright and soon they were scrambling for their lives. One after the other they fell to their sides, and legs flailing, trunks blaring, throats screaming, they slid into the rupture.

In Fel's panic he forget the Bœzch. Something entered his psyche that was almost unnatural for a male lion: concern for the well-being of others. Forgetting his enemy, Fel leapt past the uncoiling horror and placed himself on the sliding level with the elephants. But he could do nothing for them. From one to the next, he ran to them, shaking his head in that fashion zoo animals do when they have tested the walls over and over for months on end only to find no exit. One after another: slide and crash, slide, scream, trumpet, and crash.

Even when he was lifted into the hands of the mountainous Bœzch serpent, even when he set the thing on fire and kicked away from its smoldering corpse, Fel's eyes remained on the elephants, now all dead, now all lying in a heap of shattered mass at the bottom of the earth and metal ravine.

He did not eat the Bœzch, though he suffered the usual pangs of hunger after exerting himself. He stood over the edge of the abyss and looked down upon the once majestic herd, weeping quietly, until his chuffs turned to roars like strangled cries. His sympathy held him in place and his empathy for their plight only grew when the colony began to heal the rupture. The superstructure closed its wound, and the dead were lost as easily as if they were closed in a tectonic fissure.

Fel stood there for hours staring at the place where the elephants vanished.

So soon they were gone, it made him think of clouds ... and for the first time, he was lost in the abstract ....

A female voice in his head said to him then, "You are ready for me." And Fel dragged himself away.

In the fourth month of his wanderings, he noticed for the first time that the Bœzch Generals' numbers were thinning. That he understood this fact on some murky, toddler's scale was astonishing to him. During the dry engineered winter, he tracked the last of the Bœzch all the way back to where he started, having circled the entirety of Long Savanna Colony. He arrived at the gate of the city known as Aza Nairobi.

Head down, Fel shuffled through the wide Art Nouveau arches with squandered health in place of enthusiasm. His blue eyes weak and bleary, his brow dipped in retirement, Fel moved into the shadows of the neglected buildings. Even in this controlled environment, wildlife moved in to occupy where people departed.

19

Startled zebras raised their heads and darted away as Fel entered the main plaza. Had he the energy, Fel would not have chased them. His directive was compelling, though it was self-modified: he must destroy the remaining Bœzch ... now to save Luti.

It reclined in a heap of shed chitinous silk. The Bœzch Governor Commandant was ten meters of muscled atrocity, with stick figure legs and arms and long serpentine neck that ended in a collection of haloed horns. No eyes, no mouths, but a visible aura of contorting holographic Human faces surrounded what must have been its head. It regarded nothing.

Fel stepped forward with the bassoon and strings. A woman's hand stroked his mane. Fel drew back, startled. He raised his head, expecting to see his Master returned to life, but instead, within the augmented space around him that only he could see, he found his dead Master's face sliding aside, transforming, folding away like digital moths from a darkened wick as she became the young woman from his dreams. Luti took his head in her hands and brought his great face up to hers. She said, "You've arrived and now one Bœzch remains. There is only one thing left to do."

Fel heard another Human reply - a boy really, a voice only he could hear, existing only in the sphere of Augmented Reality shared between himself and Luti. The voice was his own. Fel heard the voice say, "Tell me."

She smiled down to him and her back arched until her feet left the ground; slowly she levitated to the sound of the rising tenor of *Una Furtiva Lagrima*, "M'ama ... Sì, m'ama, lo vedo ... Lo vedo ..." And she said to him, "They only want to know that you understand them."

The music held.

"They have a message," she said.

"Tell me."

Luti whispered, so close to his animal ear, "Invisible no more. They now see you thinking."

Her image shattered, separating in a blister of wind and violence. The Bœzch Governor Commandant moved without seeming to move, and now Fel was up in its arms. It began to weave the terrible spell, the trick that was played upon all cognitive beings. As Fel twisted end-over-end he could feel the demigod reach into what he now recognized as his thoughts. Carbon, nitrogen, hydrogen, oxygen, phosphorous, each interlocked with whimsy, shape, color, motion, and greed, and Fel could feel the invisible tendrils from the terrible mind of the Bœzch attempt to break down the barrier between the real and the sublime, to push the lion into shapes that lie within his dreaming. Fel recognized what was happening, that this was how Humanity fell before the Bœzch.

But the augmented lion was not Human. While men dozed in sexual fantasies, Fel walked as a eunuch; while women reclined in somniferous valleys of colors and intrigue, Fel only dreamed of the hunt; where children twisted in nightmares of forests of legs, Fel thought only of using the brush for cover. Where Humans and cognitive prides alike succumbed to their augmented senses, and found themselves defenseless against the transformative powers of the Bœzch, Fel felt only exhaustion and anger. Anger blistered up within him now. Anger ignited the transformers deep within his hide, pumping weary generators into full, anger bristled his fur into plates of living steel, and anger made him invigorated by the transformation. He could feel the fear from the pan-dimensional demigod. The creature stepped back, attempting to hold the feline at arms' length, yet itself unable to disconnect from its prize. The rage of the lion continued to grow, and the aria finally swung past the sticking point, the tenor's voice falling into the gloom of the song, rising up again. Flame and plasma curled from Fel's mouth, and he exhaled torrents of superheated gases. Bursts of electricity and fire forced the Bœzch to break from its trance and drop the boiling lion. Too late. The tenor swelled. The many holographic faces circled in shouts around its horns as Rafæl the black biomechanical lion hammered and mauled his prey in an electric firestorm of brutal, convulsive fury.

The final Bœzch horror hung in blackened strips from statues and terraces within the courtyard; Fel ate in fervent silence. The hunger and the weakness in him were now one. Soon he collapsed under the shadows of elephantine clouds as somewhere far off, deep and quiet, a trumpet blared.

When Fel stirred awake, a familiar person flickered before him. The empty young man from his earlier dreams said to him now, "Mún Rafæl, hello. I am a limited EtherCore simulation of when you were Human, before Manticore Project. I am speaking to you now via your AR network, where I am projected from, and stored within, your ticks. Our problem is this: sensor ticks are detecting nuance in your frontal and temporal lobes. In essence, I surmise that the Bœzch breached the telepresence firewall to your Augmented Reality Network, overcoming what remained of the Master EtherCore's personality, and tricked you into thinking again.

"You must be repaired.

"The Bœzch are extra-dimensional, but they can only clearly see *sapient* beings. Dumb animals are mostly invisible to them — and this is true for Humans transformed into animals, too."

Fel sighed.

"When you are ready, Mún, you must board the patrol cruiser I have marked upon your guidance system. The ship will again reduce your mind to an animal state and then transport you to the next colony, Serengeti One. You must do there what you did here, and then you must do the same at every Hæl colony." He paused for a moment, taking in the pained expression in Fel's eyes. "I'm sorry about our ... your fiancée, Mún. But you cannot think of Luti Casanova again. As long as a single Bœzch survives, your thoughts must be ... regressed ... whenever you become cognizant.

"If you fail to kill the Bœzch here in Hæl System, they will spread to the rest of Human space ... and then this will never end ..."

The Etherealon Core-generated apparition winked away, and Fel was left alone. No music followed him, no drifting ghost or Bœzch dream crept with him. Only the pad of his bone-weary footsteps echoed through the deserted city. He followed his guiding impulse to the depths of the tallest tower. He rode the elevators that whisked him down into the outer rim of the colony. He found the patrol cruiser, a two-hundred-meter-long cigar-shaped collection of thrusters and conning towers. He stepped into the waiting isolation chamber. And when he was locked into place by robot helpers, Fel waited for his sapience to be erased, to be reduced back to animal instinct .... The lion shook his great head and thought one final thought as Human Luti's face passed before his mind: *This will never end.*

Chapter Two
Behold the Man

Hæl was a triple star system.

For every sixty-nine thousand years that burned through the heavens, the cold brown dwarf called Bram and its companion orange dwarf star, Étienne, would complete an orbit around the central blue giant star, Hæl Damiano. Bram was the sixth and final substellar object in the system, a failed star eighty times the mass of Jupiter. As an engorged brown dwarf just teetering on the edge of stellar ignition, its upper atmosphere swirled with ammonia clouds barely hotter than a wood fire oven. Like a black comet suffused in a radiant fleece of planet-sized lightning storms instead of elementary ice, it cut through the star system utterly perpendicular to the plane of the ecliptic and carried a lantern to light its way in the form of Étienne, the bloated orange star — and within the long span of its highly elliptical orbit, the blind aeons sat rapt as it slowly stalked its celestial prey. Bram was a planet killer. This was the information that flowed into an isolated part of Fel's sleeping brain.

Patrol cruiser *Mare Hypatia* worked through its pásscoding, using its constant velocity drive to fly clockwise for a distance of three AU along the orbit of Hæl IV, the System's fourth "planet" — actually a tiny planetoid trailing an asteroid belt that spread over a billon kilometers in width — and this information, too, was absorbed by the unconscious lion.

The facts continued to fill Fel's head:

Main Star: Hæl Damiano (O Class, Blue Hypergiant)
Distance from Olde Sol System: Possibly Thirty Billion
(30¹⁰) Lightyears
Mass: 148.297 M ☉
Radius: 77.055 R ☉
Luminosity: 73,744 L ☉
Claimed by: Euphön Diversity of Life Authority (EUDOLA,
Windsor Temporality Vested Cosmopolitan Fellowship)

It was so very dark here in Hæl System. No stars
shined in any direction. A hundred and twenty years ago,
when the first EUDOLA surveyors pushed through a
Gripper Gate in Society Space and, with the blessing of an
Ægeleif Entity, tunneled through thirty billion lightyears
and out the massive gateway at Bram, their Human crews
quietly stared through the wall of black and knew
loneliness on a terrible, despotic scale. Mouths gasping in
the wheelhouses of their research vessels, arms outstretched
and knees buckled, they cried out, "Where are the stars?"
There was only the stark triune of suns: tenuous orange
Étienne, pleasing yellow Foss, and astonishingly bright
blue Hæl Damiano.

Orbital Bodies (6): Hæl I (Dwarf Planet, Vacuum), Hæl II
(Dwarf Planet, Vacuum), Hæl III (Dwarf Planet, Asteroid
Belt), Hæl IV (G Type Yellow Star Named "Foss,"
Planetoid, Hyper-Kuiper-Size Asteroid Belt, and EUDOLA
Colonies), Hæl V (Planet Named "Bosh Übor,"
Inhospitable), Hæl VI (K-Type Orange Dwarf Star Named
"Étienne," and Inhospitable Brown Dwarf Named
"Bram" [System's Grip Point, Seat of Ægeleif Matter Entity
Jeüdora]).

The fact-finding part of his brain focused in on that name, *Bosh*:

Planet: Hæl V (Bosh Übor)
Distance from Hæl Damiano: 5,422.038 AU
Radius: 6,866 km
Gravity: 1.07 g
Orbit Period: 26,423.76 years
Rotation: 26 hrs
Surface Temperature: 731 K/458 °C/856.4 °F (Since Thaw)
Atmosphere: 60 atm (CO_2 87%, SO_2 12.4%, H_2O .6%),
Inhospitable
Moons: 2 (Pawn, The Follower)

It was from there, the fifth planet, Bosh Übor, whence the Bœzch Generals sprung. That was theory. There were no visible city structures on the planet, no signs of life even on the microbial level, for the world was a literal hell. As it drew nearer to orange Étienne, on its slow death march to Bram, the frozen atmosphere thawed and the surface became a hot Venus with crushing pressure, suffused with a heat that could melt lead beneath its thick clouded carbon and sulfur dioxide atmosphere. But regardless of the inhospitably, trajectories revealed that the Bœzch Generals flocked from there in the thousands when the invasion of the colonies took place. They moved across the blackness in clouds of non-Euclidian surreality, pitched silver and ruby against the empty night — the night that only recently was claimed safe for Human exploration by their Gylfinîr Engine Priests.

Scant weeks before the invasion a EUDOLA robot Grippership sent a message three lightyears from the other side of the onyx sky and explained what it found: that all of Hæl System, as far as five lightyears beyond its Oort Cloud, was encased in a black nebula of organic molecules. Beyond this ebon haze was the rest of the universe. The Hæl Black Nebula seemed to reside in the center of a globular cluster of very young stars. Outside this stellar collection, a mere eighty thousand lightyears in diameter, there existed an intimate local group of clusters, as few as sixty clusters, and they trailed away into the body of a lone ring galaxy, its center punched through aeons ago by some cosmic collision, the interior of which there radiated a supermassive black hole, giving the entire structure the appearance of a great eye, and the globular clusters a trail of tears. After this, there was nothing. No other galaxies could be seen except a series of tiny white smudges far, far away. These were quasars, a whole sky of quasars. They were seeing an image of the universe when it was so very young that all of its matter was bound up in impossibly bright, super-compact galaxies that roared and crashed in silence, the dinosaurs of cosmic antiquity on display. The Milky Way Galaxy was nowhere to be seen in a form recognizable to Human memory.

So the record was set: Hæl System's Ægeleif Entity Jeüdora stated the evidence showed that their triple star system was as far away as thirty billion lightyears from the star of Olde Sol and the planet Earth. Thus Jeüdora marked their place down on the real-time map of the Universe, and her Gylfinîr Engineers said it must be so.

They had gone to the end of the universe and now they had found it was inhabited by celestial horrors.

One final fact wormed itself through the wireless tick receivers at the base of the lion's neck before the data collecting stopped. The information was this: in five years, four months, twenty-two days and seven hours, Bosh Übor's aeons-long sojourn around its star will cross a final time against the path of the monstrous planet killer, Bram. The hot little hell of Bosh Übor will be swallowed and destroyed forever by the brown dwarf that roams the night like a lantern-bearing comet.

The act of collecting data for the sleeping lion was contrary to *Mare Hypatia*'s pásscoding, and yet the information stuck. Within the patrol cruiser, the ponderous lion sprawled inert in a state of semi-molecular stasis in a chamber that was known as the blackout box. There were twelve blackout boxes on board the ship, but all were humanoid in shape and size and they were located on the deck above, in the medical crèche. Fel's blackout box was a cargo crate designed for the storage and transportation of livestock and perishables, and it sat bright white but cold, locked within the midship cargo bay. Besides the usual duty of anesthetizing and then slowing down the atomic structure of its occupant for hibernation, Fel's box contained a repressor, the kind of memory suppression machine employed by psychologists in the abolishing of their patients' unwanted memories. Fel's repressor was modified to go beyond its intended function. It not only repressed memories, but also disconnected the brain's comprehension of sequencing events. Fel no longer understood that in order to achieve Result C he must first go through Events A and B. This was all that was needed to destroy cognition, leaving only the animal intuitions that required his robotic ticks to lead him from Event to Event like a lion in a circus ring.

As *Mare Hypatia* attempted to deliver Fel to the toroidal colony called Serengeti One, the information secreted through Fel's biomechanical ticks did not undo the cognitive suppression set by the ship's repressor, but instead, Fel's brain stored it away for some unknown purpose, by some unknown phantom agent deep within the lion's own psyche. The data acquisition leak remained undetected, and regardless of the volume of data, the lion yet again became a simple beast. The ship's Etherealon Core was satisfied that all was well. Fel continued to sleep.

He was unable to disembark when the ship reached Serengeti One. The entirety of the toroidal colony's thirty-eight-hundred-kilometer circumference was gutted and open to space, the local remnants of the asteroid field once used to build the station now battering the hull like earthen hail. Fel's ticks linked up with the ship's external sensors and cameras and passed the images amongst themselves. In the torrent of their processing and analyzing, some information leaked down to Fel, and in his molecularly slowed state within the blackout box, he felt as if he himself were floating through the vacuum in a frame rate crippled video. Despite the sadness of the colony's loss, it felt good to see, even if in a broken dream.

From a distance, the EUDOLA-built colonies looked exactly like bicycle wheels. The colossal toroidal rims wholly contained their terrestrial environments and silently spun as centrifugal superstructures through the night; a network of freight elevators and personal lifts made up the spokes of the wheels; a tug dock at the center of the spokes formed the hub; spaceports, attitude blisters and shielding made up the treads of the tires. The patrol cruiser *Mare Hypatia* moved on past the dashed spokes of this busted wheel, and traveled down Colony Road, a path clear of asteroids just above the endless ring of rubble and cometary objects. Fel didn't think it strange that he had vague memories of riding a bicycle, though he didn't recognize the pedaling feet and grasping hands as his own.

The yellow-amber light of the star Foss twinkled twelve AU ahead as debris and asteroids passed before the field of view. Hæl Damiano's bright blue giant star burned at a distance of fourteen hundred AU away and shined like a pixel pearl to the starboard side. To the port side, over four thousand AU away, just above the plane of the ecliptic, the failed star, Bram was invisible but for the bond it shared with orange topaz Étienne. All else was black.

Serengeti Two and Three had fallen to a similar fate as Serengeti One, Serengeti Four was missing completely, but Serengeti Five had undergone a sinister transformation.

As Fel slept within his isolation chamber, patrol cruiser *Mare Hypatia* attacked the pulsating thing that had once been a home to Humans and animals alike. The ship's three fractalwire accelerator gun turrets lanced the habitation rim of the colony, which caused the red, chitinous thing to unravel like a worm. Ship recorders captured the images of Bœzch Generals bursting from the protective skin of the hundred-kilometer worm, and the ship's limited artificial intelligence decided the Bœzch must have converted much of the colony's mass into the material needed to make this worm. It had become a living Bœzch Hive. This was too much damage for the colony's systems to compensate for, and under the strain of the patrol cruiser's guns, the colony broke apart, the worm crumbling under the assault, and the Bœzch there freezing in the shadow of the colony. They did not die, but stiffened in the cold, falling into a state of hibernation. *Mare Hypatia* picked them off one by one, though not all died in this plane of existence, and many passed bodily into some dimension that sucked them down silently screaming through the fabric of the vast cruel vacuum. If the mission wasn't to save the colonies, this would have been the easiest solution to the Bœzch invasion.

So much waste, mused an unknown voice somewhere near or within Fel.

They moved on to Serengeti Six.

The colony was intact and all Bœzch ruptures had been healed by automatic repair systems. The patrol cruiser matched Serengeti Six's spin, capturing images of the interior as it closed in on an underside spaceport.

The ship examined the images as they came in, and it was immediately obvious that Serengeti Six was also undergoing a transformation. Through the transparent ceramic interior the ship could see that much of the colony's forests and planes were undergoing the conversion to the wormy texture of a Bœzch Hive. The *Mare Hypatia*'s limited AI noted a discrepancy between the condition of this colony and the Long Savanna. Long Savanna suffered no conversion. "What was the reason?" the ship queried itself. The *Mare Hypatia* weighed the only significant difference between Long Savanna and the Serengeti series: all of the colonies were enormous, but the Long Savanna, a smaller colony with a circumference of nineteen hundred kilometers, was still dwarfed by the larger stations like the Serengeti series. Long Savanna's population was only one hundred thousand Humans while each Serengeti held a minimum of one million Humans. The Etherealon Core put the improbable answer as, "Bœzch using sapience as fuel for expansion?"

Patrol Cruiser *Mare Hypatia* weighed the decision of whether or not to destroy Serengeti Six before this colony also transformed into a Bœzch Hive — or even if it had enough firepower to make a difference. Fractal lances chose their targets as the ship's AI assessed the risks, but the ship immediately dumped its task the moment one of the collected images revealed something startling. A detailed zoom of the area near the colony's largest city, Sacramentus, showed figures in martial-standard beetle-like power armor engaging in combat with relatively small Bœzch Lieutenants. Human survivors?

The *Mare Hypatia* hailed the colony but was met with only silence. No Human replied. The ship contacted the colony's AI and found it operative, but when queried about whether or not any of its population survived or retained sapience, the colony only responded, "Inconclusive." To save itself, explained the colony's Master Etherealon Core, it had killed its own Ethereal Intelligence and transferred its consciousness to a quantum-silicon hyper-thymonucleic acid cell called a Thymotemporal Entity Ascender, or TEA Cell. The TEA Cell only recently reawakened. It could not recollect what had transpired while it was dead. It only knew that signs of Human life aboard the colony were few or irregular. It could not define "irregular."

The colony's Master EtherCore asked to be rescued, and reminded the patrol cruiser's AI of its duty to defend and rescue any benign intelligent life.

"You have downgraded to a TEA Cell. Are you diminished? Have you suffered any sequencing difficulties?" asked the *Mare Hypatia*.

The Master EtherCore of Serengeti Six replied, "No. I am still capable of nonsense."

"Elaborate, please."

The Master EtherCore recited:

> "Two black kettles sitting on a petal.
> Said the sad petal to the kettles,
> 'Ten pounds of iron weighs upon my head.
> Move on, move on before I am dead.'
> Replied the kettles, 'But I am tethered!'
> 'And my brother filled with feathers!'
> The weight was false, did the petal decide,
> And thought itself mad until it died."

"Are you quoting?" asked the *Mare Hypatia*'s AI.

"That was original."

"Attempting rescue." The *Mare Hypatia* decelerated and moved into one of the colony's wall side spaceports.

All of the EUDOLA colonies were forested and wild, and this should have excited Fel's sense of predation when he arrived at Serengeti Six. But the evergreen here was not right. Though he was fresh from his long week of napping, the gloom of this place tempted him with equal parts sloth and loathing.

The interior of the station had been designed as an austere collection of rocky African kopjes that dotted the banks of a colony-long river. Quartzite was gathered up from the asteroid belt by the EUDOLA drone builders a century ago and now it graced the hills that surrounded the engineered acacia trees. It was once beautiful. Now most everything was splayed out dead, dying, or in the midst of transformation.

Fel smelled the rot even before the ship shoved him out the airlock. With hovering robotic drones tugging at one end of the nervous cat and pushing at the other, the smell of blowflies curling in the dead meat somewhere ahead of him made him whimper low in sedentary chuffs. Once outside *Mare Hypatia*'s airlock and standing on the pressurized metal loading ramp, Fel turned to run back to the ship's gate, but the ship's AI shut the door on him with a hiss and a slamming of bolt locks. He paced there in the flickering dank light of the bay. Somewhere, a burst water pipe raised the humidity of the normally comfortable atmosphere. The ship's AI and the station's sluggish EtherCore continued to plot Fel's course, and a second portal opened up a hundred meters ahead of him. Through the doorway, the yellow pin light of distant Foss strobed, passing low behind the tops of the mountains that reached towards the station's transparent roof. The smell of rot thickened, drawing up in his sinuses like a black pudding. He chuffed another quiet whine. The *Mare Hypatia*'s AI responded by urging him further on. Fel felt compelled to move forward, but he did not.

The lion froze at the sound of shuffling up ahead. Quadruped shadows, bent and hunched, slinked in at the edges of the doorway. They approached, making sounds like a recording of twisting balloons pitched low in a synthesizer. There were seven of them. They growled along with their pitched balloon grunts, and their eyes glinted in *Mare Hypatia*'s red berth lights. Fel panicked and bolted ahead, zipping past the mongrels as they turned to snap at his sides. The spaceport led immediately into a squat shipyard filled with overturned forklifts and the skeletons of long picked over Humans and animals. The massive cat trampled the graying bones under the blue light of a false dawn and crashed through the utilitarian bars at the end of his charge. The bars flew apart like bowling pins when he struck. In his panic, he would have crashed through the gate even if it had been concrete. He was running on fear, blind to his surroundings, the sound of the snapping pack behind him growing nearer, the balloon bass cries driving him faster forward still. He would have continued on like this had it not been for a voice in his head. *Why are you running from hyenas?* it demanded. It was not the *Mare Hypatia*'s AI or the colony's EtherCore speaking, but the voice of a man, familiar and young.

Don't be stupid, the young man commanded. *Turn and kill them!*

Fel spun into a full stop. Half-rolling from inertia and confused by the nearness of the words, he was overtaken by the pack.

The hyenas went for him like they would a zebra or gazelle, attempting to tear at his belly and anus, trying to push past his snout to get at his eyes. Fel regained his courage, and in that writhing orgy of mange, rounded on his attackers like a biomechanical weapon should. His fur turned to armor, denying their famished mouths a hold upon his flesh as he reached for two of the nearest hyenas, the ones that slavered for his eyes, and put them into the earth with two sure strikes. A crack of bones and the pair expired in wooden marionette collapse, their legs stiff, seeming almost immediately fossilized in death. The rest of the pack spread out, startled by the lion's return to his senses. They did not spread far enough, and their final dying lament reverberated in a short cantata of astonished squawks.

When the pack was destroyed, Fel surveyed his surroundings from his circle of fresh death. He looked around for the source of the voice, but he was alone, standing now at the top of a narrow kopje. He saw the perennial devastation. What was meant to be a green and gold animal park with fractal-theory-designed hills and mountains lining the walls, with port and starboard a hundred kilometers apart, a clear and languid river drifting through, was now a blue and gray home to burnt vegetation, blast craters from combat, bones and rot and flies, and everywhere the pulsating silk of the Bœzch's creeping transformative fluids.

The blueish light from the Charon lamps that hung far overhead was dim. It was still early morning, and the station's twenty-four-hour cycle allowed for the transparent ceiling to slowly brighten through another two hours of dawn-tinting. No lights shined from any of the ranger stations visible along the riverbank. No Bœzch appeared to be present, though there were many dead and dying trees jutting up along the kopjes and hillocks, any one of them big enough to conceal a Bœzch Lieutenant.

The ship's AI began issuing Fel his orders as a series of images and compulsions. *Travel seventeen kilometers anti-spinward to Sacramentus City.* This was represented in his mind as a series of moving images, as if he dreamed the way to the city some nights ago; down the river, past the rock shaped like an elephant, under the tunnel of trees, to the gate of the lathed and cylindrical wall (a compulsion of shapes), into the crooked building beyond the narrow pedestrian bridges (they looked like rib cages), he would wait there until drones delivered the Colony Master EtherCore to him on a plate of robot ticks (the purple metallic shapes outstretching over a flat color of gray, hazy impulses). The compulsion made it known that he should stop to rend Bœzch only if they barred his way. This

colony was not to be saved. He was only here to rescue the
Master EtherCore. He did not understand, but he moved
forward with his mission.

He was not weary when he set out. His time in the
blackout box refreshed his tired, heavy brow and his
months of exhaustion. Fel walked on, shadowed by the
many kopje mounds of fractal-theory-weathered granite as
he moved past the spoiled, alkaline river. He looked up
once at the unending sea of blackness beyond the
transparent ceiling, and for a moment the single tiny dot of
the distant blue giant star appeared to spread its twinkling
arms out like an angel — and though Fel did not know
what an angel was, he felt both puzzled and comforted by
the sight. He chuffed unexpectedly; the ship's AI caught
this and ran a quick diagnostic of his systems. He seemed
perfectly all right. His mood continued to lighten until he
met a leopard ascending a slope.
The leopard was panting alone under a bedeviled
acacia tree, panting as if having just run a great distance. It
spied Fel first as he moved up the hill and it regarded its
natural enemy with an understated growl. Fel stopped and
fought instinct, waiting for the ship's AI to supply him with
the next impulse.
Both big cats suddenly gripped the ground in
surprise as a short series of explosions echoed up from
some place up over and beyond the slope. The leopard
turned to look over its shoulder at Fel, then coiled and
charged off in the direction of the disturbance. Fel ignored
the *Mare Hypatia*'s order to wait and followed the leopard
up the slope, past a short waterfall and rapids, hearing
projectile weapon fire now interspersed with Bœzch
squeals and buzzing shrapnel. He ran through a dead

thicket of evergreen that withered into a webwork-like network — once great trees reduced to mere briar tunnels suffused in sapphire gloom. All vegetation here succumbed to the Bœzch poison silk that stretched up with shimmering white fungi fingers from the black and gray ground. Fel ran on through the darkening passages, catching sight of the leopard's tail and hind quarters always just ahead of him, rounding this corner and that, heading on into the sounds of danger.

Some of the information that Fel's brain downloaded from the *Mare Hypatia* while he was asleep included the construction details of this place and of the colonies. Some isolated part of him thumbed through the data now as he ran. Eighty years ago, the data read, fractal-theory evolution was used to quickly develop the landscape in each station. Picometer-scale fractal robots in charge of the construction, called Farmers, molded the infinitely complex iterations of their patterns down to an imitation of terrestrial geology. Like a time-lapsed movie of the creation of the Grand Canyon, the Fractal Farmers eroded the collected raw materials of the asteroid belt into surrounding crops of rock in Precambrian fashion in only twenty years time. Now artificial light sources sparkled against shales, meta-cherts, and gneisses, shimmering around the shadows of filigree branches in the tunnels of dead wood. Forward, Fel pushed on, gaining on the yellow cat before him, the pop, pop, pop, and rat-a-tat of gunfire growing louder along with the mouthless telepathic squeals of the Bœzch. Chalky, calcareous soil kicked up behind Fel in a gray mist. Ash from some unseen disaster flittered by in gale-full puffs as if the ejecta of volcanoes somehow found their way to these man-made shores.

Fel lost the leopard at the next turn and he slowed to a trot, frustrated that the constant stink of rot occluded his sense of smell. The gunfire ceased as well. He stopped now and sat upon his hindquarters, listening to the air around him. He wanted to continue to hunt the leopard, to find the source of the sounds of combat, but the colony's EtherCore urged his impulses on from somewhere far ahead, demanding that he go back to his plotted course. Meanwhile, from kilometers behind him, the *Mare Hypatia* changed priority and forced Fel's local Augmented Reality network into tactical displays of Bœzch. As always, the symbols were sensed as impulse and rudimentary stimuli rather than abstract. He fought the rising compulsion directed at the Bœzch images within his elementary mind. He wanted the *leopard* right now, not the Bœzch. Images fought for supremacy on the little stage in his brain, one minute a leopard, the next a Bœzch horror, the next an abstract EtherCore. He was frozen in this state of dueling natures when the forest suddenly tumbled and crashed around him.

A bipedal beetle-like machine the hight of two men and the weight of an elephant seal bull, slid through crumbling jack trees and rolled over from its back. It had slid into Fel and took no notice of the lion lying prone as it righted itself on two legs. The tiny face at the center-top of the beetle contained a pair of narrow sensor eyes that checked the scenery in quick, bird-like clicks of the head. In its near-transparent chest plate could be seen the outline of a man crouched over symbiotic controls. It raised a fractal pulse rifle with both hands and fired at a target out of Fel's sight — and Fel's sight was very limited at the moment. His back had supported the full weight of the robot suit in a collision that would have killed a normal

lion. But biomechanical Fel shook his black mane and
waited a brief moment while his cybernetic ticks collected
data from all four corners of his body. All systems were go.
The lion straightened himself and spun about to see what
had hit him.

One Bœzch Lieutenant ripped the rifle out of the
robot beetle's hands but not before taking thirty shots and
toppling, while a second Lieutenant leapt over and from
behind its injured brethren and dug its impossibly long
fingers into the shielded cockpit of its foe. The shield came
away, exposing the terrified and furious Human beneath.
The man screamed, "No!" and the fingers now closed
around his head. The picosteel arms of the man's robot suit
knocked the Bœzch's hands away once, but it had him
again on the second try. Fel watched in astonishment as the
insides of the cockpit glowed in geometric colors. The man
gave a final shout, and bloody organs burst into ribbons of
embers and dust. Then came the disembodied voice in
Fel's head again, angry with him once more. The voice
said, *What is wrong with you today? Fight!*

Fel did not resist this voice like he did the dueling
commands of the AIs. As the robot beetle suit toppled over
he could see the Bœzch attending to its fallen comrade.
The one on the ground tried to push the one standing away,
but it was without strength. Holographic howling Human
faces swirled around the healthy Lieutenant's halo of horns
and Fel could see the freshly killed man added to the horns'
phantom milieu. The injured Bœzch tried in vain to shove
away the other one last time before it began the
cannibalization. Thrashing hookah arms beat the ground in
cancerous agony as the injured creature was drawn up into
the standing Bœzch, reduced to blocks of matter,
transformed to color and smell, devoured as sunlight. Fel

leapt on the distracted Lieutenant's back, his massive four
meters hitting the thing like a piano dropped from a
building, smashing its head into the ground and snapping
its horns in three places. Fel twisted its neck in his jaws
before it could rise up again, mauled what was left of its
spine, and only released his eyes from the enemy when its
golden blood made him salivate. It had been a while since
he'd eaten.

He forgot his appetite, though the old pangs ebbed.
The path was clear to the source of the previous sounds of
combat. There was no sign of the leopard. Instead, Fel
saw over the top of the waterfall leading to the river at the
base of the slope. Broken beetle suits sprawled out three to
a pile, their cockpits smashed open, the only hints of their
pilots represented as streaming mists of multidimensional
light and dust and geometric blood stains that soaked many
a cracked chassis. Around the dead and broken fighters a
throng of evil spread. At the edge of the waterfall, atop a
kopje that stood out flattopped and open like the center
stage of an amphitheater, an audience of hunchbacked
Bœzch Serfs, man-sized brutes who lived lowest on the
alien ladder, gathered at least thirty in number at the base of
the stage, howling up at a Bœzch General and his prize.

The severe Bœzch General towered over its
audience of the damned and stood motionless, long arms
before it. Seven Lieutenants drooped like Dadaist mimes
around their leader, then, as if heeding a signal from a
drum, the Lieutenants dropped to their wrists and raised
their long stilt legs from the ground until their tiny hooves
were high above their heads. A scream issued from the
Lieutenants' featureless heads, and they changed poses,
coming forward and bringing their legs behind them, still
elevated; they looked to be doing push-ups without the help

of their legs. At that moment the General opened both of his long, sickly hands and revealed that it was holding a live Human woman between them.

The disembodied voice of the young man returned for a moment, whispering to Fel, *Remember, the Serfs do not have the transformative abilities of their taller masters, but beware their horns.*

The Serfs were emaciated brutes, skin-and-bone bloodhounds raised to sniff out sapience, increasing their master's range of detection. Had Fel been a thinking creature, he would have recognized the scene as an execution, and in truth it was very much like a Biblical stoning. The ragged red Serfs, their bodies like bipedal serpents, their arms long and knuckle-dragging, their heads without eyes, ears, noses, or mouths were featureless but for a single black horn that protruded up from their necks and extended longer than their bodies, and at the end of the very tip of every Serf's horn silently screamed a single blue holographic Human face. Impaled through the open mouth, the holographic faces shimmered away at their edges in auras of red light, creating a deep crimson spotlight around their horrid gatherings when they came together en masse. Like revelers at a medieval beheading they gestured with carnal relish to their General upon his stage, hopping and waving their arms, clanging their horns together in an imitation of clapping. The towering General held his prisoner by both her arms and shoved her forward.

Why is she still alive? whispered the young man.

The woman was petite, only a hundred and sixty centimeters tall. Her skin was fair. Her leather-like clothing was a black and orange aggregation of Harlequin frills and Samurai armor, her eyes concealed under a tasseled black headscarf that also glowed here and there with faint orange lines that crossed like circuits. Her mouth was expressionless, but Fel felt himself drawn to her, curious, amongst all this barbarism, as to what this elegant thing could be. The lion stepped out into the open, transfixed by her, unaware of the danger he exposed himself to.

One by one, thirty Serf heads turned up as the black lion walked into the battered clearing. They seemed to be staring through Fel, unsure of the danger, unable to fully see the lion. The General and his seven Lieutenants also froze upon the stage, seeming to sniff the air as their bloodhounds regarded the intruder. Fel was but a blurred hint of danger to them. The woman however — she was looking right at Fel. She nodded once, turned completely black but for her lips that radiated yellow-gold light, and fell back through the Bœzch General's legs as if she were a troubled spirit drifting in a haunted wood. The General's many holographic faces cried out in anger when he sensed his prize had slipped away from him, and this was enough to shake Fel from his trance. He took a few steps back, coiled, and then charged.

In his first strike, Fel parted the group of brutes with such force that the Bœzch upon the stage had to scatter or else be hit by falling Serfs. Many of the Serfs were easily put down, some crumbling as if run down by a train, others lifted on high and thrown into the air like flailing matadors. Their long unicorn crowns had bent in defense when they felt the great feline approach but even those that struck him could not penetrate his armor. Metallic bone sparked against biomechanized hair follicles.

Fel skidded to the foot of the stage. He crunched down hard on a Serf lodged tight between his jaws, shook it once, and flung it to the river. There was something in the suddenness of violence that raised the Bœzch's awareness of incognizant animals. They could see him now, though not clearly. He was a terrible virulent blur to them, a black speed line whirling about in their peripheral senses, making them fan apart for one cautious moment.

The General bent forward, its halo of horns and transparent faces jutting forward in a kind of challenge. It raised its arms, gesturing to its Lieutenants and Serfs to round on the attacker. The Lieutenants responded first, each of them peeling themselves off of the stage and leaping down on the sides of the lion. The seven Lieutenants played a game with Fel, racking their claws down his back and then darting away, making a great circle around the battleground. Fel was at first confused by the numbers but the voice within him directed him forward, coordinating with the targets set up in tactical AR by the *Mare Hypatia*'s AI. Fel leapt into pursuit just as the Serfs together struck at his last position, throwing themselves as one into the river.

The game went as thus: as Fel closed in on one Lieutenant before him, one from behind snatched at his legs, and even if he struck the Bœzch running before him, the one at his rear always knocked him away. Within a minute Fel grew tired of the charade. The armor follicles at his hindquarters were starting to whittle way. Another few rounds in the circle and his raw ass would be exposed to the monsters. For a moment he understood the implications of this on some murky, vestigial level and the feeling angered him. Generators kicked in with the rush of frustration and his speed picked up. Fire began to bleed out from his nails and his eyes grew hot. With the burst of speed he shot forward until he rode parallel with the Lieutenant ahead of him; he swerved to the right, toppling into the Bœzch, sending it tumbling with him. They collapsed into a ball that quickly sucked up the two Bœzch behind him and the four of them crashed through rot and dirt and rock, breaking bones and claws and spines and necks — and none of them Fel's. He lay still in the pile of filigree gore when their momentum finally ceased.

Through the clouds of debris, the hands of the remaining three Lieutenants reached out for him, holding and pinning the dazed feline to the ground. They called out to their Serfs with a series of scraping chirps that made the lower minions back up. Together, a unit of sixteen remaining out of the original thirty, they charged the prone lion, bladed screaming horns bent to the fore. One after another they struck Fel's side, bouncing off again and again until his shifting armor could no longer adapt in time, and one final Serf penetrated.

The long horn moved in nearly half a meter into Fel's abdomen, and he roared fire in his agony. A thousand degrees Celsius of engineered fury was regurgitated, and the Lieutenant holding his forequarter was pushed back by the ball of elemental fire that Fel coughed into its face. It writhed into cinders. Another roar, and Fel electrocuted the Serf that impaled him. Lightning crackled and blasted away the Lieutenants at his hindquarters. Wounded, Fel cried out and shivered with the onset of shock. Repair ticks under his skin released healing fractals into his bloodstream, and the wound began to close as he lifted himself to his full height.

Flame and lightning strobed from him in a torrent of shockwaves, setting the rest of the Serfs on fire and incinerating what was left of the Lieutenants. Fel's every breath extinguished the oxygen around him as his vision focused on the startled Bœzch General, now alone upon its stage, frozen in the presence of this vengeful feline, this Cerberus in cat form. The General barked a single insult and began whirling into the ground, digging away with incredible speed. Fel would not allow the monster to retreat. Though the agony of damaged organs made him chuff in pain, he leapt to the stage while he still had strength. He came down on the head of the digging General like a shooting star, pummeling and tearing at the trapped entity with every tooth a needle of flame and every nail a contact of electrocution, and when the thing was dead and moved no more the lion's lust for death was yet unquenched.

Through the smoke and burning grass he saw another figure moving. A yellow shape, a blurred hazy thing shifting into reality. He must have the leopard, too! Fel coiled and shot across the river like a comet and landed before not another feline but the woman in black and orange. He approached her slowly, and she put her hand up in defense. Where was the leopard? The sight of this woman frustrated him further, and he roared and bellowed like a furnace again, bringing the woman to her knees. She crouched against a boulder, covering her face from the heat.

Fel remembered his hunger.

And then the young man was standing between him and the woman.

Ræl the lion beheld the man before him. He seemed so distantly familiar. It was true that he was young, maybe twenty at the most. He wore a simple gray suit with a band collar. He had a prominent curved nose, ashen-gray skin, and eyes so blue they seemed to whirl like spinning jewels. There was a boyhood blush of amber upon his cheeks, and despite his youth, his short hair was a soot-colored, dirty-white color that belonged to the old and dying. He held his arms apart, barring Fel's way. For a moment, when the lion noticed the ethereal, near-transparent nature of the young man's countenance, he almost lunged past him to get at the woman. But again the man held him back, now putting his hand on Fel's burning head.

The fires died down. The sparks grew dim. Fel remembered his exhaustion and pain. He began to stand down under the weight of the young man's fingers, and when his face was level with his forepaws the Human bent to his ear, stroking his mane, and said, "You poor, poor fool. Sense surrounds you ... you use it so little."

Fel was growing tired now. The hunger was overwhelming but the power this man held over him made him feel too reticent to move, and the young man's fingers seemed to push him towards rest. As his eyes grew heavy with the heat of extreme tiredness, the lion's vision began to recede. In a mist of sleep he saw the pale woman approach the young man, and though her eyes were concealed by her electric headscarf, both the cat and the man knew she was staring at them. She moved her fingers through his face.

"You can see me?" asked the young man.

"Yes," she replied. "Why are you only visible in Augmented Reality?"

"Because I'm sleeping ... isn't it wonderful?"

Fel's mind began to fade now, the command from the man taking him into sleep just as surely as his repair fractals bade him to rest. As he moved into dreaming, his mind came to the image of the mysterious leopard, and he gave chase across the backs of elephants that marched across the sky. In his excitement, Fel's weight struck down each pachyderm cloud as he leapt across them like stepping stones. So the elephants fell one after another, Airavata clouds no more — just simple animals upon the ground, fallen celestials reduced to animal drudgery by the careless footfalls of a dream lion and his yellow quarry. Winds sucked up from some distant phantom sea, elephant trumpets piped earthbound complaints to the skybound felines. Cats canvassed under mist and in sound until they too became cloudwork. There they ruled over the elephants' kingdom until the dream moved into blackness and the cloud cats dispersed in the coming storm, and all the while he felt the presence of the man at the edge of his dream, standing there, watching.

Chapter Three
The Conjurer

The young man whispered in Fel's ear, "Helpless and tired, you lay your head down weeping and smile yourself to sleep."

And Fel did sleep.

The colony's artificial daylight filtered though the filigree blur of his closing eyelashes. From the rolling dreams of cloud elephants and leopard hunts, Fel drifted in and out of blackness. Once, he opened his eyes and saw the woman and the man standing over him, speaking at length. The colony's lighting systems were stuck at dawn, and so the two Humans continued to stand there under the blue-black faux morning, the young man glowing like a Hindu messenger under the sapphire phosphorescence, the woman absorbing all light like Pan's shadow. He saw that she had recovered a metal staff and a scabbarded short sword from the wreckage of the battleground. She stood with the staff in both her hands and the sword fastened to her side. Staff of Æthax and Sword of Évir, glowed the words only seen in AR. "Who are you?" he heard the woman say.

The man considered for a moment, then replied robotically, "Mún Rafæl, EUDOLA Student of Transnatural Sciences, Post Graduate, Long Savanna Colony."

She stood over him, and the man crouched down to the height of Fel's mane. The lion's fur did not move, but he twitched as the man, trapped in Fel's local Augmented Reality network, interacted with his telepresence sensors. The man could not actually touch the lion, but the lion's sensors made him feel as if he did. The woman took no notice and continued, saying, "Are you a TEA Cell?"

Mún Rafæl shook his head once, looked as if he were trying to recall something, and then shook his head a second time. "I ... I don't know what that is."

"You don't remember?"

"Should I?"

Though her eyes were hidden behind her headscarf, her face held an expression of perturbation. "TEA Cell stands for Thymotemporal Entity Assisted," she said. "Ascended Humans have their brains absorbed into TEA Cells when they transcend themselves. It's part of Transnatural Sciences."

Mún said, "Ah." He paused again, shook his head again. "Transcend into what?"

"Some people take android bodies, some ascend even higher and become Etherealon Cores, others, like me, take boosted bodies," she replied, motioning to her own black-garbed body.

Mún's response was again robotic, and for a moment he sounded helpless, as if he were slowly picking a great many pieces of a puzzle from the ground. "Boosted means biomechanical. I was a student in Transnatural Zoology." He continued, saying, "Do you think of yourself as Human?"

She nodded slightly, a sort of tight genuflection. "Ascended Human. I'm a Gylfinîr Engine Priest. Do you know what that is?"

"I'm an Ascended Human too, though not a TEA Cell." Mún spread his hands out over Fel's healing wound and then smoothed out the fur upon his back in a gentle gesture of telepresence. He said, "This is me."

She leaned down to face the young man. "There is a TEA Cell in this lion?" She asked.

"No," said the man. "I am his REM sleep."

"What?"

"REM means Rapid Eye Movement ..."

"I know what it means."

He traced his finger along Fel's cranium now, making small swirling motions as if he were drawing a picture. "When the brain is damaged," he said, "it becomes a remarkable thing. It moves parts of you about, puts you in safer places away from the damage, sticks you between the walls of the disorderly house. That's my theory. Do you like it? It's quite elegant." He smiled. "I am a mouse in my very own house."

She dismissed his last comments with a wave of her hand, trying to call his attention back to her. "You said that your name is Rafæl?"

"You may call me Mún," he said.

She pressed him further, demanding, "Are you familiar with Hünde Rafæl?"

Mún closed his eyes and looked to be struggling. There were bits of information hiding from him in the dark reaches of the lion's brain. The lion released its grip on a small tidbit, a modicum of recollection, and it scurried away, into a hole leading to Mún's place between the walls in Fel's brain. Finally, he said, "Yes ..."

"Yes?"

"He was my brother once."

She leaned away from him and said, "I ask that you accompany me."

Mún put his translucent finger to the woman's lips and said, "Shhh. The lion is falling into a deeper sleep."

The man faded away. The lion slept.

Once, Fel shuffled awake as armored beetles lifted him onto a platform. The young man was gone, though his presence seemed near. Fel tried to smell for him but didn't know his scent. The AI of the *Mare Hypatia* instructed him to go along with the woman and her beetle companions. Fel was fine with this. He was still so very tired. Repair fractals mending his ribs together pushed his eyelids closed again, demanding he reserve his strength lest his fuel-hungry generators cannibalize his own flesh.

Demons stood in blast craters at the bottom of a hill. Awake again but barely, Fel peered through his eyelids in groggy incomprehension under metal bars as the platform moved over a hill overlooking the bellowing horrors. These were not average Bœzch. These, by appearance, were devils in the most classic sense. A brackish fog swept up out of the polluted river at the foot of the hill and drifted between the ankles of the seven giants. From the smallest to the largest of them they were cyclopean in size and stature. Some wore clothes, but this was not all that set them apart from normal Bœzch. These monsters all had faces: eyes, ears, noses, lips and teeth, smirks and grimaces — all the features absent from a typical Bœzch head. Though their features were free of the bizarre holographic screams of victims that adorned the horned halos of all other Bœzch, these horrors also radiated a strange light. Instead of screams, the demons were framed by holographic symbols like the illustrations in the boards of tarot cards. Roses circled around some, bones and Insular art patterns surrounded others. Symbols like hieroglyphics spun about their heads, one minute displaying in an unknown language of pictographs and dots, the next turning into standard Windsor Ing'Lesh.

The smallest of these seven remarkable horrors was five meters in height, and though Fel could not understand the words, the demon's name clearly twisted above its head for those who could read: Emmott the Judge, it read, Lay Your Souls Underfoot and be Trampled by Righteous Spurs. It was portly, squat and barrel-shaped, wearing a long red leathery coat of the sewn skins of inert Human faces. Its naked white belly protruded from an opening at the front of the robe and it carried a flaming gavel the size of a small bear. Its white horns curled like a ram's and fit its head like a powdered wig over sunken eyes, fish fat lips, and a nose like a vulture's beak.

Emmott the Judge smashed and beat its gavel into the ground over and over again making a sound like a lone kettledrum in an echoing bay.

The next tallest horror — Merced the Miser, A Banquet of Stars is a Handsome Beginning — at seven meters, was as thin as Death as depicted by the great medieval painters. Its alabaster head was bald, its eyes were set so deep they appeared to be empty sockets, its leathery robe was white and clean, but it was filled with the geometric shapes of Mayan tiles. It stood motionless while its brethren clamored aloud in wild prehistoric spasms. Truthfully, it seemed so miserable and weak. Had it exerted itself, it looked as if it would have collapsed like a taxidermist's most disastrous project.

Merced the Miser shouted up the hill, its voice but a faint hiss, an exhausted wisp of futile breath. "Come down to the banquet, come down and be collected! Let us take your hearts apart and nourish the universe with what you have stolen! Deny our Masters not their rightful feeding and be heard as a cantata of quasars where once you were but a whisper of mice! Come down! Come down to the banquet, come down and be collected!"

Ambros the Wayfarer, HOUND Of RESURRECTION, Your Flesh, Your Flesh, Take and Take, I Take and Take and Make Amends to the Blood of Giants, were the words written above the six-meter mongrel that scratched and chirped in restless coils of energy between Merced the Miser and Dianthus the Head. It was a flayed hyena, its muscles glistening in beads of blood, its eyes two pins of fire where retinas should have been. It held the line with its horrific companions, sniffing the ground, seemingly drifting to-and-fro in a collecting pool of its own fluids.

Ambros the Wayfarer howled up the hill in throaty barks of blood and spittle. A flock of famished loons fell like hail from the shock of the Wayfarer's chirps, littering the ground with gasping corpses and blackened feathers. Another bark, and the birds were brought to life again with a shock of lightning that coiled out from the spine of the mongrel. The loons attempted escape, pulling themselves to their feet and running for their lives. A sound like laughter issued from Ambros and the flock fell again, then vanished like rainfall into mist. Were they real at all?

No words accompanied the name of Dianthus the Head. The only obvious female of the diabolic group, she towered nine meters from the top of her horned bonnet to the hem of her red bridal ball gown. Her skin, her hair, her pelerine, bonnet, cape and converts, and even the monstrous Human heads she collected and hung from her belt, all appeared to be cast in black steel. Red runic lines crossed over her body in arabesque complexity, and she stood posed in utter stillness, her face a mask of ennui under a wig of shrapnel, her hands clasped before her in melancholy and defeat.

Dianthus the Head sighed and chilled the base of the hillside with the frost of Dante's lowest hell. The frozen sigh spun up as a whisper, into a shout that said, "Where are you who suffers not a mind to live? You seek out and see out of too many faces, ever faster you spin up in entropy. You are the bringers of Telic Death! The look of you, the thought of you, the smell of you thinking — but you do not know where you are! Property of Hell! Abhorrence! You are the reason the galaxies fly apart! Where are you who slow your thoughts and rest your weary heads in the embrace of aeons? WHERE ARE YOU, OH PROPERTY, WHERE ARE YOU?"

Tautolo the Hermit and Sayre the Conjurer looked to be brothers; like ten-meter clones of Tweedledum and Tweedledee, they radiated a kind of sickly, obese closeness. Even their titles were connected. Envy the Emptiness that Follows Your Doom ... began the placard of Tautolo the Hermit. As Your Futile Sex is Remade in the Image of Nullity and Neglect, finished Sayre the Conjurer. These naked balloon-shaped beings with their tiny heads teetering in unison, both were pale white and striped in monotone colors, the Hermit in faintest blue to match the single sapphire horn that rose from the back of its head, the Conjurer in powdered salmon, its jaw fixed with twin ruby tusks that curled into its bloated neck. They said nothing. They just rocked quietly, to-and-fro, to-and-fro.

Circling this troupe, arms folded, head down, walked Wülvogarti the Wrathful. Fifteen meters of unforgiving flame and red biomechanized muscle, this powerful, brutal satyr with a canine face thundered in circling pools of fire. The back of his masculine head was a blossom of smaller antlers bookended by two enormous horns that rose two meters behind him and a meter down through his jaw. Recessed features in his shoulders, part machine, part bone, socketed the bottom of the two horns so that his entire upper vertebrae had to swivel in mechanical gimbals when he moved his neck. Steam screamed from his horns in pyrocumulus plumes and when he made a full circle of the bunch, he turned, shouted up the hill, his lower jaw dropping ridiculously far with each vowel, his nostrils fuming, and raged, "YOU WILL BE MINE! You Brummagarti, Prugarti and Gylfinîrs! We Seven need not the powers of our masters to sniff you out! We are sighted all the way to the ultraviolet. Hide behind your shields, your tiny guns, but we — I will have you! I will split your skulls myself and drink your souls like tepid rain! I will brutalize your families! I will ...!"

Fel stood up and roared down the hill at the Bœzch Servants. The two beetle-armored Ascended Humans who carried his anti-Casimir platform stopped, startled by the lion's sudden activity. The woman in the black and orange headscarf, who sat atop the platform outside Fel's cage, stood up and came to his side. He roared again in the direction of the horrors and silenced them. Fel blinked in confusion this time. His roars were a kind of sensory packet burst used for deep scanning through dense matter. Thus, as he thundered towards the hateful group at the bottom of the hill, information describing strange, nonsensical matter flooded his senses.

Even at the distance of a hundred meters, Fel and Wülvogarti locked eyes, and the lion felt a pounding compulsion. Hatred electrified the space between them, an invisible lightning field of recognition. In that brief moment, the lion, this patriarch of terrestrial nature, understood he was looking at elemental destruction: not the restorative destruction brought about through the hunt, not the ending of things to replenish another, but the will to bring down principle and culture and replace it with oblivion. And in that brief moment, the demon, a smoldering wretch of surreality, knew he was looking at a majestic servant of the natural sciences. They would have at each other, no mater the obstacle between them. Eventually, they would do battle, they both knew without thinking, for this was why they were made, and no prior hour seemed as near to cognition as this here. Thus, Fel lunged forward, but was met by the bars around him, and he blasted back with an anti-Casimir force. He shook his head, still weak from his wound. Repair fractals flooded his brain again with anesthetizing agents, forcing him down so they may finish their work, but before sleep claimed him once again, he was surprised by one more action: the woman in black and orange was stroking his mane through the bars. His eyes opened again for an instant more, just in time to see the young man sitting next to him, cross-legged in the cage, to see the cage and platform being pulled into the gates of a once grand city, to see the iris of darkness overtake him again. Fel put his head down and returned to chasing the leopard in the clouds.

From his high perch in the elephant dream clouds, Fel could see his body below him lying on the mobile platform under bars. He was in a wide auditorium filled with cages like his own. Ascended Humans, mostly noble Brummagarti androids and proletariate Prugarti androids, came and went through the three great rosewood doors. It was dark and many of the light sources — hanging lamps, desk lamps, and recessed lights — were damaged and failing. Data-desks and study chairs were gathered in the center where six of the Ascended Humans sat and talked.

He could see that the cages were full of animals: young giraffes, oryx, okapi, rabbits, many types of waterfowl, a few small elephants and crocodiles — some of them tranquilized, all of them underfed. Most of the cages, except for the elephants' and hippos', were resting atop desks, some of the smaller animals' cages elevated on the backs of real paper books. There were books everywhere, rare artifacts in the advanced world of Tacit Reality lounges and Augmented Reality book clubs. Had Fel the words for it, he would have recognized this place as a library museum that was as large as ancient Alexandria. But his interests rested only in the animals and people, the smell of straw and feces, and the humid stickiness under the pale blue light.

Fel saw himself sleeping closest to where the people were, and he felt their interest in his direction, though they didn't look at him. The woman in the black and orange headscarf was there, too, and then she was there in double, one version of her in the flesh, the other only visible in the Augmented space between Fel and her. While the real version of the woman discussed events with the Humans around the center, her AR avatar held a separate conversation with the young man, Mún. He was also only visible in Fel's local Outher network, and the Brummagarti Humans seemed unaware that Fel's AR Outhernet even existed.

The AR woman leaned against the platform's anti-Casimir field and the force feedback of her avatar's telepresence made her react as if she were touching the cage in the actual. She said, "Tell me how you became a lion, Mún."

The avatar of Mún sat cross-legged upon the platform, just outside the lion's bars. "Tell me your name, first," he replied.

"All right," she nodded. "I am Gylfinîr Engineer Fawn Virgilis."

"Gylfinîr ... you talk to planets."

"No, as a Gylfinîr Engine Priest it is my duty to speak the poem that will satisfy this system's Ægeleif Entity."

Mún held up his hand as if he were answering questions in a classroom. "That's Jeüdora," he said, smiling.

Again, Fawn Virgilis nodded as she replied, "Correct. Her seat is at this system's only gas giant equivalent, the brown dwarf, Bram."

She could see that Mún enjoyed talking with his hands. Using his fists, he pantomimed two objects colliding. He said, "And what will happen when, in over five years from now, the fifth planet collides with Bram? Will Jeüdora be killed?"

AR Fawn moved to sit next to him on the platform. She shuffled once, vanished and then reappeared in a near lotus pose, hands folded upon her armored skirt. The real Fawn Virgilis did not look over at them. She busied herself with a holographic chart of the Hæl Star System that turned a meter above the table of the six Brummagarti Humans. AR Fawn Virgilis said to him, "We knew that there would be a planetary collision when we first surveyed this system, of course. But Bram is eighty times the mass of a Jupiter body, so we have been certain from the beginning that, while the fifth planet will be destroyed completely, Bram and its Ægeleif Entity will survive. The collision has never

been our concern. Yet we do have an unrelated difficulty:
Jeüdora has stopped talking to us."

Mún was honestly surprised by this, and from the
coded alarm he received through Fel's robotic ticks, so, too
was the *Mare Hypatia's* AI. "Then, no ships have been able
to leave Hæl System?" Mún asked.

"None," she answered. "We monitored fifteen
Gripperships trying to break system to Olde Sol but they
became inert once they entered orbit. We don't know
what's wrong with them."

"How are you going to leave this system if the
Ægeleif Entity won't listen to you? You won't be able to
use a Grip Point through Bram as an exit." Mún paused a
moment and stared intently into Fel's sleeping face. He
was looking for something. Then he said, "I have a ship.
A patrol cruiser. If we can find three more working ships,
we can use them to tug Long Savanna and then D-Fold our
way out of this system. We can probably simulate a speed
of at least eighty C. Or just use the one ship we have and
travel at a forth that speed. Either way, we can go."

Both the real and AR versions of Fawn gasped
aloud. The Humans surrounding her asked her what was
the matter while AR Fawn exclaimed to Mún, "We are
thirty billion lightyears from Olde Sol's domain! We would
be lost!"

"But alive," Mún said flatly.

This time AR Fawn used her hands to talk, throwing
both up in the air in exasperation while saying, "It would
take more trillions of years than there are left in the
universe to return to Olde Sol System at that speed."

Mún dismissed the comment with a wave. He
insisted, "My colony, the Long Savanna, is self-sustaining
enough to provide life for a hundred thousand years. That's

plenty of time to find a safe system with a gas giant, create a new Ægeleif Entity, and eventually build a Gripper Gate and bend our way through the giant and back to Society."

"You can't make an Ægeleif Entity without seeding it with another," AR Fawn said as a statement of fact.

Mún wondered if she could see him, unhindered, through the tasseled headscarf that covered both of her eyes, or if, like Fel, she used her voice as a kind of echolocation. He would have to study more on Gylfinîrs when he returned to the *Mare Hypatia*.

Mún said, "But there was a first."

"The birth of the very first Ægeleif Entity destroyed Proxima Fujiai. Every child knows this." AR Fawn sounded as if she were growing weary of him.

"We'll have time to make it right this time. Safer."

"We've thought about this."

"And?" Mún asked.

"We'll never survive the search for other ships." She added, "The Bœzch detection of TEA Cell Ascended Humans is getting stronger."

"I don't understand."

AR Fawn Virgilis held up a holographic image of a scale model of a Bœzch General in her hand — as if Mún needed to be reminded of what she was talking about. The red Bœzch General animated in a loop, its Dali stick-elephant legs stretched to the shape of stilts, its long, rail-thin arms precisely swinging as it walked upright. Its faceless head was a nest of horns growing into the shape of a crown-of-thorns. When it completed three walk cycles in a loop, AR Fawn said, "All of the Moartale Humans in this system have been killed by the Bœzch. Evidence suggests that the Bœzch Generals can sense the cognition in normal, Moartale Human brains from billions of kilometers away.

But the act of becoming an Ascended Human means your brain, your sapience, is absorbed and becomes one with a TEA Cell collective. The kind of quantum cognition that springs from a TEA Cell is ..."

Mún finished for her, saying, "Is cognition that is brought about via entanglement tunneling instead of neural pathways ..."

"Yes, and it's significantly alien to the Bœzch," AR Fawn said. "How do your thoughts feel to you since you moved into your TEA Cell? You feel fast and vigorous, yes? The Bœzch must seek out the laborious process that comes about from organic thinking. But they adapt. When we were first attacked, the Brummagarti and I were undetectable unless the Bœzch closed to a distance of at least fifty meters. It's risen to eight hundred meters in the last few months, and even more for the Prugarti."

Mún shook his head and put his hand through the lion's cage. He insisted, "My thoughts are not contained in a TEA Cell. I told you, I'm in this lion organically."

AR Fawn closed her fist and the holographic Bœzch winked away. "And you need to explain to me how that happened before I believe you," she demanded. "Tell me about Manticore Project."

Mún looked up in mild astonishment.

"Don't be surprised," said AR Fawn. "Our equipment may be damaged but we're not totally primitive here. Though we were only able to hack surface levels of information before your socket ticks locked us out of your little Outhernet, we caught the name 'Manticore Project' several times. What is it?"

He waited a long moment before speaking, but after a minute his serious expression changed from bemused to sincere to simply amused. He laughed once, quietly, and said, "You may recall the political situation before the invasion."

"What are you referring to?"

He laughed again and trailed off into an awkward sort of ennui. She was having an effect on him, he realized. He would have to remember to quiz the *Mare Hypatia*'s AI about Gylfinîrs and whether their presence was known to induce faint euphoria. He continued, "Months before the Bœzch struck, many of the larger EUDOLA colonies started to press their government on the smaller stations, like Long Savanna."

"It was the will of the people."

"It was the will of *your* people."

"That's a cowardly assessment of the complexities involved. We ..." she began.

Mún shrugged off the euphoric feeling and held up two fingers, saying, "You took all of our weapons and beetle suits. You forbid us from gathering in groups larger than five, even in Tacit Reality. What were we to do after you declared martial law on us? Surrender our charter rights? Of course not. It was decided we had the right to a rigorous defense."

AR Fawn blinked, nonplussed. "That is treason."

With a precise directness, Mún replied, "Perhaps to the larger bullies like the Serengeti Series or the Guggisberg Colonies, but not to the EUDOLA or to the Windsor Charter. That's who we all should have been allied with."

AR Fawn Virgilis remained vaguely dismissive but polite. "That's irrelevant. You were still vested under Windsor Charter, just through our Amalgam Arbitration."

"That's occupation, not representation."

AR Fawn shifted the subject slightly by saying, "And where were you interned as a Transnatural Zoologist?"

Mún was not looking at anyone in particular, but since he was a mere projection of information into the AR Outhernet surrounding the lion, he could, with some concentration, observe his surroundings while seeming to look elsewhere. So while he stared at nothing of interest, he carefully watched the Ascended Humans gathered several meters away. They still appeared to be unaware of the AR conversation taking place and went about their business plotting and discussing tactics with the real Fawn Virgilis.

"With the Masai Mara Institute," Mún replied after a while. Then he admitted with a half smirk, "But really, I was in the disbanded Long Savanna Militia."

"How could the Militia have reformed? There was no activity in any of the banned TR Rooms."

"My major area of study was transnatural boosting of the brains of terrestrial animals in alien environments. But my minor was pásscoding."

"Just pásscoding?"

"Symphonic Domain Ontology ... using music to reinforce pásscode programs in esoteric systems." He added, "That means I make Outhernet firewalls for weaponized biomechanics. It also means that I'm just more imaginative at pásscoding than your people are." He understood this was an absurd boast to make before a Gylfinîr Engineer, but he said it anyway and waited for repercussions, inclining his head to her as if smugly leaning into an expected punch.

"That *is* ... rather esoteric of you," came her measured reply.

From his peripheral sensing, Mún felt the temperature rise around the Ascended Humans. AR Fawn Virgilis cleared her throat — a sound not unlike a kitten coughing — and brought Mún's full attention back to her. She said, "You were a Mœrtale Human? How old are you?"

"I was twenty when the Bœzch found me."

"And what did they do to you?"

Mún closed his eyes. "I came to Long Savanna under a research contract with my fiancée. Her name was Luti Casanova .... I quickly became involved in Manticore Project, but she was a legitimate park ranger. She studied the lions for the great Diversity of Life Authority. I studied them, too, but for the Project. When the Bœzch invaded, we were sitting alone on a park bench, enjoying our work, enjoying each other's company. They plowed up from under us; we didn't understand what was happening. One minute there was nothing but the quiet rustle of a leopard hunting somewhere in the distant dark, the next we were seized up by putrid fingers. They tried to harvest us. I remember suffocating into a lucid dream, and I remember the fingers sliding into my dreaming. Do you wonder what it is they do to you when they harvest you?"

"Tell me," breathed AR Fawn. "No one's ever survived a direct attack."

Mún pointed to no direction in particular, saying, "Those horrors standing at the bottom of your hill out there should be a clue to you. So should my lion."

"What are you saying?"

"You Gylfinîr Engineers believe in the Anthropic Æincode of Gylfinæ. You say: 'We are not here to accept our deaths. We are here to question why we die.' Well, my people were convinced your statements did not go far enough. We believed in the literal divinity of the Æincode."

Fawn Virgilis shook her head and said, "Divinity is not the true purpose. We Gylfinîr believe, yes, that the first question that any freshly awakened being thinks is, *Why should this ever end? You must go on, you have to go on!* How is this 'not far enough?' Existence is the mantra of the cognizant, because once we gain cognition, oblivion is the enemy. We believe that we are here in this universe so that the universe may see its boundaries, so it may understand itself, so it may, through us, ask the question, 'Why should this ever end?' As we have prolonged our lives and extended ourselves, indefinitely in many cases, so too the universe waits for us to apply these same medicines to it. We are here to sail our suns and worlds to safer harbors, we are here to save the universe from Telic Death at the end of time. *That* is why every death of a thinking, sapient being is an abhorrence to ourselves and thus to the universe itself. How can it know itself, how can it save itself, if parts of its mind keep dropping off?"

"Yes!" the young man exclaimed. "And what the Bœzch do is take the eyes of the universe, your mind, and collapse cognition in on itself by pushing you into the shape of your subconscious. In that instant, all the suns you've ever seen set forever, and you become geometric fragments of the abstract things you believe in, because that is how they see us; we're a collection of colorful totems and wistful, fickle belief systems. They eat you then. They lap up your neurological assumption of your own existence, your mind's lone imprint on the universe. They are theory eaters."

AR Fawn's cheeks flushed pink by the end of the tale, and Mún sensed a similar reaction from the Ascended

Humans nearest. He knew now that they were only pretending not to see him.

The tremor in Fawn was ever so faint, but it was there upon the surface of her skin and in the sound of her voice. She said, just above a murmur, "How can you possibly know any of this?"

Mún said, "Because when they tear you apart, you feel ... I ... I can only say that what I felt was ... was that the explanation for my existence was going away, and without that proposal for my being here to tie me to here, then I *couldn't* be here. You see? You feel theory of you unravel. If you felt it, you would know what I mean. It can't be explained in any other fashion. You see yourself from the outside and you know then. You're just an assumption of the universe. They disprove you, and you're gone ..."

A sudden breath of excitement rose up from where the Brummagarti Humans gathered.

Mún turned and faced them, mocking, "Yes, gather 'round, gather 'round! I know you're all listening! You're Brummagarti. You can hold up to six conversations at the same time. Don't pretend. Step into my Outhernet." He waved them closer. "That's right. You can see me. I can see you. Hello! The Lion's name is Fel and I am Mún. Pleased to meet you."

He examined them more fully now. They held the perfect complexions and physiques of Brummagarti, but they still retained the basic shapes of their previous, Moartale Human lives. Two were women, four were men, wrapped pressurized and protected in coffee-and-rind colored campsuits, the body forming space armor and replenishing threads akin to military doublets in appearance, worn by safari crew in the most aberrant environs. Their headgear were switched off, leaving great circular plates around their necks where usually the base of their illuminated deflector fields formed a transparent helmet — an oblate spheroid — out of collapsible picoscale matter.

The two women wore the deep gray complexions, the crystal blue and amber ale eyes, and the sooty white hair of the cultish Hiichiim people, with whom Mún himself shared a bloodline — and so he knew, if they were like him, they could be stubborn, they could find a thing and obsess and cling to it and burn with equal parts melancholy and pride. They looked to be kin: tall and slender, they carried themselves with an elven grace, and together they circled Fawn Virgilis, protecting her from either side. Their feminine elegance was a great contrast to the rugged men — two pale, one dark, and one azure blue; the men simply appeared weary with each other, weary with time, weary with momentum — while the women, in turns both cautious and inscrutable, watched the lion at all times.

The one dark-skinned man, a thin Oshii Librarian, wore a short curly-tight hairstyle while the symbol of his order, the kanji "司書" ("shisho") shined in holographic blue over the surface of his forehead. As if in pantomime of his information-obsessed sect and race, he clutched two volumes of old books in both his arms. He stood farthest from the group, looking as if he could bolt from them at the first sign of a hole in which to hide.

One pale man was of the bourgeois race of Mitteleuropa, and he stood with obnoxious bravado, hands on hips, broad wrestler's chest moving with determined breaths, his waxed mustache leering over a briar pipe. Mún thought back to unwholesome fables spun by bankrupt graduate students who were nostalgic of their ancestors:

classist, racist, trophy-coveting yarns of pugnacious European gentleman hunters of Olde Sol System's Africa. At the first sight the man, "*Oh, no,*" was the thought that marched past Mún's mind like a crimson-lighted letter board.

The other pale man was somewhat scruffy for a Brummagarti. He was also Mitteleuropan, but far less stout. He wore a black pub cap from which his shock of blue-black hair bulged out like tarantula legs from beneath a pebble. His chin bore a short unkempt halo of stubble grown for effect; no Brummagarti grew stubble without willing the bristles to propagate. Mún assumed he was an eccentric, probably looking to be taken for a poet, and was likely to be as unaccustomed to combat as the book-clutching Librarian.

The dark blue Brummagarti man, his skin of a metallic hue, radiated a sense of serene numbness, his yellow eyes examining everything, missing nothing. The faint light from the flickering sconces reflected off the biomechanical plate he wore instead of hair, and off the golden curvilinear markings, like embossed tribal tattoos, that spiraled about his face and neck. Mún had seen this type of Ascended Human before and guessed he was the oldest of the bunch, probably having shrugged off his ethnicity a thousand years thence without regret.

Mún continued to usher them forward, saying, "Let's hurry now. It only takes a day to heal the level of injuries Fel sustained, and when he wakes up he will be hungry." He blinked away for a second and reappeared between them, putting his arms around the man in the waxed mustache and one of the women. He said, "Now we're friends. And we better trust each other as friends. Know why? Because when the Bœzch come for you like they did Luti and me, they will eat you up and take what's yours. I know this because I can see that none of you is a dreamer." They pulled away from him just as he moved over to the real Fawn Virgilis. Her AR form had vanished. Her real body stood with elegant poise while Mún paced before her. "Luti and I dreamed all day and night," he continued. "We lived and loved our work. We didn't just study the lions of Long Savanna. They were our family and friends, they were everything, they were everywhere in our minds. They were in our shared dreams. They were all we talked about. We'd wake up after a night of sex and poems and we'd talk about our dreams and finish each other's sentences. In every one of our dreams played a sleeping lion or leopard. And so when the Bœzch unraveled us, we spun ourselves back up! Because we were always lions in here!" He pointed at his own head, stabbing his fingers against his temples. "They tried to dismantle our dreams, but our dreams had teeth and claws!"

Mún paused, seemingly exhausted by his own display. His hand covered his eyes as he searched the memories there. They waited for him to continue, looking from one to another.

He carried on, saying, "We woke the next day, gorged on fallen Bœzch Generals, and we marveled in horror at our quadrupedal limbs like the man in Kafka's *Metamorphosis*. And then we laughed. At least we weren't cockroaches!"

They each shifted where they stood, always watching the phantom madman.

"In that moment when the Bœzch whispered in our minds about their terrible origin," continued Mún, stroking his hair, "we knew that our own cognition was our enemy. And then we were rescued. Through a conservation tower at our ranger station, the Master Etherealon Core of Long Savanna witnessed our transformation. Thus when I scratched out 'help' at the gates of Aza Nairobi, she knew what to do. We two lions walked through the deserted city and then into the secret laboratory where Manticore Project was based. At the time, two of my fellow engineers yet lived. They weaponized our new new lion bodies, using the biomechanics they developed and my transnatural pásscoding — but more importantly we set out scheming. It was decided that the only way we could beat the Bœzch is if we stopped thinking. We regressed our minds, we were joined in a pride with the other real lions in the Project, and we set about our mission."

He moved without moving, and the AR avatar of Mún Rafæl was sitting by his lion body again, his back against the bars of the cage, his eyes drawn up to the vaulted ceiling of the museum library. No one spoke.

Then, like a parent burdened by a melancholy child, Fawn Virgilis calmly beseeched him, "What is your mission, Mún?"

He looked up, honestly disappointed by the question, and said, "That should be obvious: to murder every Bœzch I find and to rescue any sapient beings or wildlife and bring them back to Long Savanna for acclimation or storage."

"Storage?" repeated the shaggy Brummagarti.

Mún nodded and replied, "We can't have you thinking until every Bœzch is dead."

The barrel-chested hunter with the waxed mustache stepped forward. "But you can run around thinking all you like, eh?" he demanded.

Mún was unmoved by the man's aggression. He expected this from him. "Yes," he chided, looking at nothing in particular again. "When I was first regressed I kept regaining my sapience over time, and every time this happened I had to be regressed yet again. But then my mind learned to hack itself. It happened quite automatically. Like when I first intuitively learned to pásscode when I was ten. Like the ghost pásscodes I developed when I hid the Militia from you, my own sapience hid between the walls of my own mind." Mún laughed, dry and morose, and proclaimed, "I am the lucid dream of an amnesiac cat!"

The mustached man waved him away in a pugnacious gesture. He shouted, "He's delusional!"

"Why should we believe anything he says?" said one of the women to Fawn Virgilis.

The frail man with the books looked back and forth between his colleges, quietly reasoning, "I don't know – I mean, he could be telling the truth. Why not? The Bœzch don't make any sense either, but that doesn't stop them from killing us."

The blue man spoke now. His words were precise and without suspicion. He asked, "Earlier, were you suggesting the *demons* — the Bœzch Servants outside the city — also used to be Human?"

"Yes."

"Again, how?" pressed the scruffy man.

"I just know," said Mún. "I know their eyes."

Fawn Virgilis moved between them, her hands apart, and said, "Mún is right. They were all Human. The probe from the fifth planet confirmed it last night."

The mustached man barked, "Why didn't you tell us?"

"Thirteen of our people died escorting me from the antennae station this morning, Zallo," she said. "When should I have relayed the report, before or immediately after I was rescued by a lion?" The mustached man, Zallo, shrunk somewhat under the bloom of the Gylfinîr Engineer's scold.

Zallo fiddled with his campsuit gloves, not looking at fawn Virgilis. "It's not my intention to disrespect your title, Madam Gylfinîr, but every bit of information is important to us in this fight."

"How many of you are there left alive?" asked Mún.

"Fifty-Two," said Zallo, smoothing his mustache with the back of his glove.

"Then thirteen dead is too many." Mún commanded, "Collect the animals and the Master Etherealon Core's TEA Cell. I will escort you back to my ship."

Zallo shook his head, defiant. "We don't take orders from small colonies. And you can't get your ship out. The Bœzch are warping the autonomous utility AIs in every section of the station."

Mún used the ticks in Fel's neck to query his ship's AI. He received a burst from the *Mare Hypatia* a second later confirming that, indeed, the outer doors to the spaceport were locked down.

"Then we need to destroy the source of the interference ..." Mún began, but he was cut short by a sudden weakness and he toppled over, unconsciously acting out a physical reaction to a mental instability.

The lion kicked hard in his sleep at the same moment the demons' shouts suddenly echoed up through the city. Mún hadn't noticed before that the creatures could be heard throughout his conversation with the Ascended Humans. But until now the clamor had been a distant rumble in the background, a sound similar to his own inner musings. Now their inane cacophony burst through the air like a sonic boom, sustained by their will to cause harm.

Everyone present looked to the ceiling and covered their heads as the sounds of the Damned repeated through their chamber. The gavel of Emmott the Judge smashed and thundered ahead of Merced the Miser's sordid hiss of, "COME DOWN ... COME DOWN TO THE BANQUET, COME DOWN AND BE COLLECTED ..." It drummed before the septic howls of Ambros the Wayfarer. Before Dianthus the Head it shattered glass relics within the museum halls as it accompanied her arctic screams of, "SUFFER NOT A MIND TO LIVE ... WHERE ARE YOU ... PROPERTY ... WHERE ARE YOU ..." The drums stopped for only Wülvogarti the Wrathful, whose rage touched them all and even brought the brave Zallo briefly to look for an escape as the words of hate poured over them: "YOU WILL BE MINE!"

Mún stood, watching his hands fade in and out of view. At first he looked around in subtle panic, but then he appeared to be studying the effect, the light behind his eyes growing more wise as the avatar of his once physical body shed itself from the visible spectrum in bands of dissolving luminescence. The lion shook his head in his sleep with greater urgency as Mún's image weakened, and with a great high kick he bent the ceiling to his cage. Fel rolled over, his eyes just barely creaking open. The lion and his Human conscious stared at one another.

Fawn Virgilis moved to Mún's side, asking, "What's wrong with you? Are you ... hurt?"

Mún shook his head and his chin moved slower than his brow. He replied, "Fel is waking. I'm leaving you for now. But take care of your Bœzch problem, or Fel will do it for you — and once he's up, I can't always control him."

"We've tried!" Zallo bellowed, picking himself up from the table he leaned against. "Scans say they're here in the physical but they react like holographic avatars when we attack them. Our weapons just go right through them."

Just before he winked away, Mún grimaced and shouted, "That's because there's only one of them really out there, you fool!"

Fel awoke with the inertia of a locomotive and tore through his bars before the anti-Casimir field could repel him. Though he was still not fully repaired or healed, the sound of the Bœzch horrors suffocated the pain of his punctured second heart and fractured ribs. Immediately, he saw that he was not alone. Where was the leopard? The instructions from the *Mare Hypatia* bade him focus his ferocity elsewhere. Did "elsewhere" mean these Ascended Humans surrounding him now? No, the sleepwalker's urge fed him with a desire to abuse other prey, and his ticks imprinted him with an image of his earlier discovery — from his sensory packet roar — and aligned the sound of the horrors, and the data in the packet, with the feeling of the hunt.

The Ascended Humans moved in a clumsy circle away from him, keeping their backs to the walls, always facing the lion. The woman in the headscarf and armored skirt waved them behind her and commanded, "Let him through! No one try to stop him!"

"Oh, certainly!" replied one scruffy man.

Fel paced, looking for an exit. Habit and repetition impressed him with the importance of a doorway, but the only portal he found was barred. He was restless, and the

Humans skittering about and clinging to the walls agitated him with their gibbering. He roared but the door stayed fixed.

The woman in the headscarf drew symbols in light in the air around her, and the great double door flung open. Fel looked at her, surprised. For a fleeting moment he was aware of her cooperation, but his agitation still ebbed and he roared again.

A large man with a hairy lip blew smoke from a stick and shouted at the woman, "What are you doing?"

The woman moved to the man quickly, covering several meters in only a few steps. She took him by the arm and said, "Don't agitate the lion. We're letting him go so he may do his work." She faced the rest of the Humans present and continued, "The rest of you gather your things! Collect all the animals onto their trucks along with all the supplies we've saved. I'll retrieve the Master Etherealon Core. We're leaving as soon as Fel kills the Bœzch outside the gate."

"We'll do no such thing!" the big man bellowed. "I have authority here and there is no call for evacuation! We are not following a mad ghost and his cat into unprotected space —" Fel silenced him with a chuff and a deafening growl.

Someone else must have obeyed the woman, for the doors ahead of Fel pushed open with the sound of clapping echoes through vast museum halls. Fel didn't wait to see who aided him. He shot forward, bounding through the wood and imitation marble corridors and out into the once beautiful Art Nouveau city. Down dead escalators and through withered parks, the lion rushed on towards the sound of his enemies. Not yet to the gate, he saw shadows creep along the walls through the sphere of light at the end of the tree-lined road. A new utterance issued through the sapphire dawn, a low chirping babble. More hyena? No, this was the sound of the Bœzch Serfs.

Soon they were running alongside him, trying to beat him to the very gate they just entered from. They crisscrossed his path, running their single-horn heads straight at him and missing again and again. There were at least ten of them and they fell to his flanks, unable to match his speed. Ten more Serfs appeared now at the gate ahead of him. A change in strategy: the flanking Serfs to the left and right of him tried to prevent him from turning, while the Serfs at the gate attempted to gore him head on. But Fel rode his intuition like the wind and sailed over their terrible heads with a bounce and a leap, spinning about behind them and thrashing their hindquarters with a single swipe. They flew apart like dead leaves and tripped the perusing Serfs before they could recover. Fel was already off, out the double, reinforced gate of mesh and decorative bars, and charging down over the hill.

Everything here held the texture of ash and bone. The trees were sick with the Bœzch poison, sagging over in leathery mounds, and the very soil bled a kind of black ichor that pooled like crude oil and bubbled in swirling stink. Sulfur and tar filled his nostrils as the horrors came to within his sight. The smell alone made him eager to end them all.

He needed only one.

The seven horrors howled together as the lion approached. But their massive arms, teeth, and robes moved through him like holographic waifs, and he was left unimpressed by their show. He roared once towards the ground, marking a spot where the creature called the Conjurer lumbered in his rotund Tweedledee bearing. Fel began digging with a great ferocity. He raked with a startling swiftness, searching for something he knew must be there, like when he would dig for warthogs on his favorite path in Long Savanna. The horrors grew silent, fascinated by the lion's display. All but one of then, the Conjurer, stood still as monoliths. The lumpish Tweedledee showed signs of terrible worry, and as Fel's head dipped below the surface a good meter and half, the horror turned to its companions with a pleading expression, its lower lip curling in childish terror.

The Serfs returned once to harass the lion, but he killed them with little flourish and continued his work with even greater interest. After several minutes he uncovered what appeared to be the top of a graying egg the size of his own head. The Conjurer screamed aloud at this and paced in tight circles, stopping to fall at the feet of Wülvogarti the Wrathful. The pathetic wretch outstretched its hands to its leader, begging for aid, but the beast known as the Wrathful only watched the lion with sincere interest. Fel bit into the egg and was met with a geyser of steaming red ichor. The avatar of the Conjurer twisted into an epileptic fit, convulsing on the ground before winking away. Soon the real Conjurer was rising in a similar fit of howls and thrashing. Fel ignored the panicked shrieks of his victim and hauled the monster from its lair. His grip on the thing's bare skull was unrelenting, and the uncovered Bœzch horror pushed the rest of itself out of its hole, trying to move with the lion's abuse. But once the fat naked thing was above ground it was throttled, dragged, and slammed this way and that across the width of the black crater, where it soon collapsed in sickening rodent squeals. Thus raucously rendered inert, as it had been in life, it was a horror in death.

Fel sat upon the twitching carcass and watched as the six remaining demons vanished one by one around him. The last one to go was Wülvogarti, and his eyes burned with a frenzy of bloodlust, the temper of storms, staring on into the lion's pupils, remembering every detail until he too faded from Fel's view.

Alone now.

Fel chuffed until the ground began to shake.

Chapter Four
The Extraction of Madness

On his plateau of elephant dream clouds, Fel watched as his body was tucked into the blackout box in the *Mare Hypatia*'s cargo hold. His mind reached out from there, his robotic ticks allowing him to interface with the ship's various sensors. He saw the blue and white ship, shaped like a cattail plant with too many bumps, slide with silent drama from the rupturing spaceport, saw the ship's guns turn on the great rotting bicycle wheel and strip its skin from its rim.

The ship, with its curvilinear form, felt female to him, and he was aware now of the other presence in his space, of the young man looking over his shoulder. The young man agreed the ship was female, though he didn't say a word.

The *Mare Hypatia*'s fractalwire accelerators swung about in their turrets and settled back to their safe position. She was free again, striking out through the dark abyss of Hæl System's empty night. Her blue hull was illuminated yellow and green-blue by the light of the star Foss, but otherwise the only lights were those beaming out of her few portholes. The fifty-two Ascended Human passengers stared out through those portholes now, their melancholy eyes falling over the vast debris field that made up the totality of their once splendid home, the colony called Serengeti Six.

The remains were a continent stretched and burst like yolk. The once majestic valleys and kopjes of fractal-theory's expedient imagining now twisting in dashed bits, spinning back towards the asteroid field it once used as raw material for its own construction.

The view below Fel's dream cloud shifted to the interior of the ship's cargo hold where the young man stood looking down at him though the transparent wall of the blackout box.

The woman with the headscarf — the one called Fawn — she was there, too. The young man was studying her, though he didn't look at her. The information the young man collected moved past Fel's own senses for study, but it was all a babbling brook to the lion. The young man watched Fawn Virgilis set up her office in the ship's cargo hold where all of Serengeti Six's few surviving animals, secured from the dead colony, were placed into blackout boxes. Only five hundred odd creatures remained alive from the once thriving ecosystem of hundreds of thousands of living things.

The *Mare Hypatia*'s hold was already full, so her first stop would be to return to Long Savanna, to drop off the animals and to place as many Ascended Humans into hibernation. Fel's specially designed blackout box lay closed near Fawn Virgilis' desk. Hovering robot drones worked around her to clean up the carcass of the dead horror once known as Sayre the Conjurer. Fel had dragged the corpse with him through the chaos of the Ascended Human's evacuation. No one dared to take the body from him, and all tried but failed to look away as he stripped the meat from the bones. The tang of this Bœzch demon held more of a metallic, iron taste than the honey sweetness of the typical Bœzch, but meat was meat, and Fel was famished.

Fel and Mún could see holographic blue circles spinning with runic characters under the feet of the woman.

They followed wherever she went. The young man knew these circles were called False G Lots and that within the space of each three-meter False G Lot there was gravity enough to keep one's feet fixed to the floor, but outside each circle there was the true state of zero gravity. The *Mare Hypatia* used displacement technology to protect her flesh-and-blood cargo from inertia and the high G forces associated with ship maneuvers, but she was not large enough to generate her own artificial gravity field. Instead, each passenger was granted their own personal gravity well in the form of the runic Lots. Due to her status as Gylfinîr Engine Priest, the ship had granted Fawn three False G Lots of her own, two for her desk and one for herself. The young man approved of this decision and told the ships AI so, not hearing himself whisper his authorization out loud.

Fawn Virgilis stared from her desk and asked, "Did you say something, Mún?"

The young man Mún kept his head low, curling into a half fetal slump at the head of the lion. He said weakly, "No ... no, I probably didn't."

There were several items spread out over the length of the cargo bay's collapsible desk. All of the objects were small and were pulled from the confines of several metal pouches fastened to the black pleats of the Gylfinîr Engineer's armored skirt. There was a small transparent jar filled with what looked like glowing fireflies. There was a cylinder the size of a lipstick case. There was a quill, two small parchments, and several large glass marbles. She set all of these in a circle going clockwise, and when she was satisfied with the bunch she turned back to the distressed young man trapped in Augmented Reality. "You seem unwell," she said.

Mún rolled his head around the transparent exterior of the blackout box, always watching the lion's sleeping face. "Yes," he replied.

As she spoke, she unrolled the tiny sheets of parchment and tapped them each once, making them grow taut. "I don't mean to intrude, but you seem less animated than our last meeting."

"Have we met before?"

"Yes."

"I see ..."

Fawn used the quill to drag information only she could see from one parchment to another. "You don't remember?"

Mún groaned and tapped his head against the blackout box. The light inside the cargo hold was set to its brightest, and though he was only an avatar, he winced whenever he raised his eyes. He hid his face in his arm and said, "I just looked at the records. Fel's ticks record everything. It felt very distant."

"What did?"

"Me."

"How do you feel now?"

"Like I would rather be anything but myself."

"You seemed very confident earlier."

"That man is a joke."

"But that was you."

Mún patted the side of Fel's blackout box. "This is me."

"You described your fiancée before," Fawn said. "What is she like?"

The young man clutched at his heart, and the lion moved his forepaws ever so little in the slow-time of the blackout box's interior. Mún said, "She's dead. I watched the Bœzch spin her into stardust the day she regained sapience as a lion."

Fawn Virgilis set down her quill. "I'm sorry."

Mún said nothing.

Fawn continued after a beat, saying, "You weren't born in Hæl System. Were you both originally from a colony, a ship?"

"What do my records say?"

"They are incomplete."

The melancholic young Mún smiled fleetingly, but then a darker light passed before his eyes and he rocked his head to voices attuned only to his hearing. Fel could hear bits of the conversations floating past the sad young man's ears, though Fawn Virgilis was unaware of any distraction. Mún asked the woman in the headscarf, "Did the other me tell you I was originally from an Ærdent colony?"

"No. Which one?"

"Tenniel's Garden."

She waited before replying, tilting her head to the air. She said in a dictational manner, "'Tenniel's Garden: vested for the Ærdent Cosmopolitan Brotherhood. Hiichiim population decimated by close proximity to blind birth in Engineered Year 6,009.'"

"Did you look that up?"

She ignored the question and continued, saying, "So you were born to Ærdents; that explains your defiant streak, but it's contrary to your exceedingly high understanding of pásscoding."

The young man suddenly shrieked and beat his hands against his head. Fawn did not react. Mún cried out, "We had no business being on that planet! We had no business being anything or anywhere!"

When she spoke this time, he felt her ethereal presence reach out to him in the space between them again, and though he was but data projected in an invisible Outhernet, he felt her words interact with his telepresence, pressing gently on him as if they were a warm fleece. "*For each of us*," she quoted, "*there was once a hole in the universe in our shape, and we were made to fill it up.*"

He was soothed. "That's one of my favorite Æincode poems."

"Mine as well."

Sad young Mún stared at her now, saying, "Without looking it up, did you know that on Tenniel's Garden, the main entertainment was books and music?

"No. Tell me."

He stifled a sigh. "The books were made of paper, the music was acoustic, but we also had movies, and the movies were on film. Everything was flat and full of imagination. We watched any kind of movie, even old films made by families on holiday. That was when I first discovered what it meant to be a thinking thing. I was watching a movie of Moartale Humans back on Earth, probably filmed three millennia before the Engineered Years. I saw all these men and women in their inelegant suits and dresses of the time, stuffy and inert things, closeted in their sexuality and awkward in their mannerisms. They rode on public cable cars pulled by counterweights. They looked happy and fulfilled as they traveled up and down the hills of an ancient seaside city. And I wanted to be with them. I wanted to smoke a pipe overlooking the great red bridge and laugh as I adjusted my stuffy old tie. I wanted to drive down the crooked street. I wanted to smell the fog-bound air.

"I realized then that if it had been a film about any era and any people I would feel the same. I didn't want to be in that specific city, in that *specific* time. I wanted to be in that place because it was a place without me. Looking at that movie, I could feel the universe without me. I could feel an icy wire of excitement as the molecules waited to make me thousands of years later. Quite by accident. It was the thrill of the precipice of life. One more set of eyes so the universe may see itself, one more mind waiting to be made. I think that's what consciousness, cognition, sapience is: the thrill of expectation. And in that film the universe was expecting me, you, all of us. Anticipation. What a thrill. What a thrill ..." And strangely, he wept.

Fawn Virgilis waited for his tears to dry before she spoke. When he was quiet, she said, "You have a firm grasp on the tenants of the Ægeleif."

"Then why am I so unhappy?" he trilled.

"The search for the Æincode doesn't guarantee happiness. It only guarantees you'll continue to search."

He flattened his palms against the side of the blackout box with the dark heat of depression anchoring him to the side. He was frantic when he continued speaking. He said, "The sadness is burning me. I can feel it. I can feel it. The thrill and the anticipation are gone. I don't want to go on! I don't want to go on like this!"

Fawn Virgilis stepped away from her desk and kneeled beside the distraught avatar. "Show me the other Mún," She demanded. "The one from before."

"What do you mean?" He spoke to ceiling.

"Do you remember when the lion saved me from the Bœzch, and then you saved me from the lion? In the beginning, you spoke in a manner that was quite manic but also confused. Later, when you reappeared in the museum, you were commanding and decisive, rather taunting. And now ..."

Sad young Mún shook his head, as if trying to shake away her words. "I don't feel well."

"Let me speak to the other Mún," she repeated.

"Why? He won't help you."

"It's all right. I just need to advise him."

"No one wants to talk to me."

"You're tired."

"I am. So tired ..."

"Rest and show me the other Mún."

The avatar of sad Mún fluttered like a sparrow's broken wing, if but for a moment, but strengthened against her entreatments, for his place here was still wrought with urgency. The Gylfinîr Engineer was unaware of the young man's intentions, that this wretched version of his inner self was sent to keep her occupied. His spirit, as it were, was a fragmented thing, and like an Ascended Human he was able to split himself up, but only among his disparate emotions. Thus, his more strident self worked a way through the pásscoded locks of the Brummagarti virtual departments. Fel watched the unlocking with his mind's eye and to him it seemed a whirl of colors blending away until a clear image presented itself. He then saw the cheery interior of an antiquated pub. Wrought iron floral decorations circled low booths sitting six to a circle, a magnificent fire shifted through its embers in a great stone fireplace, central to the room. A white-bearded publican in red flannel and canvas overalls, himself a limited AI simulation in this Tacit Reality room, cleaned glasses and cheerfully waited to take orders from the five Brummagarti patrons in the far corner booth. A wooden sign above the ale tap spelled out the words in relief: WELCOME TO THE CUTLIP NOMAD.

The five Ascended sat within the warm light of the merry fire and stared into their drinks, each of them dressed in the casual manner of the times: dark trousers, band collars with vests, simple ankle boots with clipping buckles.

The large white man, who Fawn Virgilis called Zallo, spoke first, his ale tucked squarely between his strong hands. "What shall we do about our cat?"

"Do you feel he's a problem?" The Librarian, who Mún identified as Montefeltro, was first to reply.

Zallo's retort held an air of confrontation, and he said almost in the manner of a demand, "He's a Bœzch concoction."

One of the Hiichiim women, either the one named Vígdís or Védís — it was difficult to tell them apart — said, "Is he? I saw him destroy quite a few of the monsters single handedly. Didn't you?"

Zallo dismissed her words with a shrug and a hoist of his ale. He said, dabbing the corners of his mouth like a gentleman, "They're deceptive horrors. He could be a walking trap, leading us to sniff out any remaining Humans for his masters. They would sacrifice a few of their own if it meant they could finally take the rest of us."

Vígdís or Védís replied, "There are no more Humans alive in the remaining colonies."

Zallo shouted, "We don't know that!"

"It's obvious!" Vígdís and Védís said together. "Completely obvious, Zallo."

The big man appeared trapped between the two women, though they sat apart, and he looked around the table for support, his eyes falling upon the Librarian. He bared his teeth. Desperate for relief, he asked, "Montefeltro, what do you think?"

Though he was more spirited here than he was in the real world, Montefeltro clearly did not wish to agitate Zallo further. But it was the Librarian's burden to analyze and inform. He replied, "It's ... highly probable that everyone on board this vessel are all who remain in the Hæl System. Moartales cannot last against the Bœzch more than a minute, and we here are the last of the Ascended in-system."

"That's speculation," Zallo insisted.

The blue man spoke now, and when his words filled the intimate room it seemed as if age itself had broken into syllables. He said flatly, but with the boom of command, "We trust our Librarian, do we not?"

Zallo shrunk under the blue man's gaze. "We ... we do, Bacalhaus ... but ..."

"Then there are no more Humans in system." Bacalhaus then added, "I am sorry for you."

It was quiet for several minutes then, the only sound being that of the publican simulation tending to his virtual steins and glasses. Finally, with the crackle of the fire behind him, the scruffy poet said quietly, "We should still prepare for the chance of treachery from the cat."

Although the data was useless to Fel, his Human conscious ran the crew manifest before the lion's eyes in great heaps at a time. Indeed, the mustached man's name was Zallo: Zallo Frautmorgan, a 327-year-old Brummagarti, he retired his Moartale Human body early at age thirty, eagerly participating in the kinds of experiences only an android could survive. Safari hunter, bodyguard, and mercenary, he was employed by Serengeti's Amalgam

Arbitration to help demilitarize the smaller colonies like Long Savanna.

Bacalhaus was the pseudonym used by the tattooed blue Brummagarti. He was listed in the manifest as Zallo's silent partner in their legionnaire's enterprise called Fury of the Spheres. As silent on paper as he had been in word, he was, however, never a mute, for his was a bold and strident history of conquest and cannons that spanned many millennia. Zallo's partner, certainly, he was this — but so too was he the man's great-grandfather ten generations removed, and over four thousand years old. He had lived and died through hundreds of android upgrades, flowing freely forward in life as a questing fish against the current, on and on he moved as a hero or as an oppressor, his side in a conflict determined by some abstruse moral compass known only to him.

Alon Elbett was the scruffy eccentric. Mún had been right to place him as a poet. He was half as old as Zallo, and Mún would have thought him twice as wise if it weren't for the very obvious fact that the two men were best friends.

Zallo pointed to the poet as proof of his right-mindedness. "Ah, see! A voice of reason!"

Vígdís or Védís laughed and scoffed, "Please. Alon is your flatterer. He would agree with you if you said beer was wine."

"Bah," shrugged Zallo. "He has a mind of his own."

Alon raised his glass of ale in a cheer, saying, "I agree with that!"

"Peacocks flatter their mates. I see a feather in his cap," chuckled Védís or Vígdís, not wholly cruel this time.

Zallo derided the women, saying, "And what does a Gird of the Gyl know about friendship, eh? You friend yourself alone, and we should be impressed with your foresight? Ha!"

Bacalhaus broke the argument with the boom of his intonation, once again. He said, "How would you suggest we prepare for possible treachery, Alon?"

"Oh, um. I hadn't thought that far ..." Alon looked to Zallo to finish his sentence.

Vígdís or Védís snorted.

Zallo put up two fingers to pantomime the shooting of a weapon. "It's easy. Kill the cat while he sleeps."

"Madam Virgilis would never allow it," Montefeltro protested.

"She can fire me afterwards."

"And how certain are you that you can kill it?" asked Vígdís or Védís.

"Him," said the Librarian. All eyes moved to Montefeltro. He continued, "The cat, as you call him, has made it very clear who he once was."

"And you believe him," Zallo mocked.

"My records have him listed; Mún Rafæl was a colonist of Long Savanna, he and his fiancée were working with lions, as he described."

"But that doesn't mean we should believe his boast about pásscoding."

With Zallo's last statement, the young man himself, the avatar of Mún approached their table dressed as the publican. Mún said, cleaning a glass with an old rag, "Boast? Really! I'm offended. A lion never boasts."

Zallo spit ale, shouting, "How did you get in ...?"

"Astounding!" trilled Montefeltro.

"Last call!" And with these words from Zallo, the Tacit Reality simulation ended.

In the real world, the sad avatar of Mún Rafæl sighed again, but this time he melted into his sigh, his dark face fading to transparency, his sallow chest heaving until it inhaled itself, his flat palms vanishing without a mark upon the blackout box beyond an impression of space filling up. Fawn Virgilis waited alone now in the cargo bay, watching for some sign that the competent Mún would appear. His voice arrived before his form.

The assertive version of Mún's personality matrix now addressed Fawn Virgilis within the lion's AR Outhernet, stating, "Well, it's about time you did that. I was starting to think you enjoyed placating depressed spirits."

Without meaning to, Fawn directed her question to the ceiling. "Are you the arrogant Mún?"

The AR avatar of the young man appeared in the middle of the room, his countenance fresh and beholding. He said flatly, "I am the correct Mún."

Fawn stood to face him. She asked, "How many lives of Mún Rafæl are there?"

He waved his hand in a small, irritating gesture, saying, "You'd think I was bragging if I said nine."

"I'd think you were being cliché."

"Funny how that is."

"Why do you say that?"

"Because it doesn't make it untrue."

Fawn turned and gathered her things back from the desk, locking them away in their individual pouches. "Where do you go when your other personalities are dominant?" she asked as she put away the firefly jar.

He opened his mouth to speak, but stopped and nodded towards the one of the access doors. "I think your men are about to tell you."

"What's that?"

The interior door to the cargo hold folded into the wall and the mustached man, Zallo strode in along with Bacalhaus and Alon.

When they marched in under the blue runic circles of their False G Lots, all three were armed with miniwire pistols prepped for close combat. The actions that followed were swift and unforeseen by Fawn Virgilis. Before she could issue an order to stand down, Zallo shot the transparent face of the blackout box four times. The gun rapid-flashed red as the propellant launched the twenty-caliber-sized canisters of picoscale fractals. They struck but did not penetrate immediately. In the next few seconds they would bore their way through and then — if conditions allowed — return to their original velocity, striking their intended target, the sleeping lion within. In the same instant Zallo fired, Mún gave the silent command to the *Mare Hypatia* that both switched off the False G Lots throughout the ship and explosively decompressed the cargo hold. There was no howling wind or rush of pressure. The atmosphere was gone in an instant as the wide cargo door stood gaping to the cold oblivion of seventy five degrees Kelvin. The men had been prepared for this. Their boots locked magnetically to the floor and the illuminated deflector fields came alive, pressurizing their campsuits and surrounding their heads in bubbles of transparent picoscale structure. What they had not counted on was the sight of Fawn Virgilis firing out the open airlock, as helpless as a windblown dandelion.

In the silence of the vacuum Mún saw Zallo mouth the words, "Oh, HELL!"

The three of them fired several more shots into the lion's blackout box before they separated, and the two experienced soldiers used their campsuit thrusters to fly out the open hatch after their lost Gylfinîr, while Alon stayed behind to keep the stream of miniwire bullets coming. The moment the two men had left, the door immediately shut behind them, and Alon was brought face first to the floor when a False G Lot of one hundred Gs suddenly sprung up around him. The gravity limit for a Brummagarti was half this, thus the scruffy poet not only stopped firing, but also stopped living. The atmosphere returned to the cargo hold, and in the area where Fawn Virgilis once stood, the air began to blur until the lost Gylfinîr reemerged from a holographic illusion of an empty room. She stood magnetically fastened to the floor with her face covered in the pressurized faceplate of her own picoscale structure helmet. Mún noted that her entire armor assembly was actually an environment suit. He said to her, "Your men just chased a holographic simulation of you out into space. Now, leave this chamber while I save myself."

Weakly, but with poise prevailing over trepidation, Fawn Virgilis nodded once and walked with care under the supervision of her restored False G Lot. She paused by the body of Alon. "Leave him," said the terse young man. She did. Once she was through the interior door, Mún locked it behind her and ordered the *Mare Hypatia* to release Fel from the blackout box. "Try to lure him into another box if you can," Mún added.

"Acknowledged," replied the ship's prosaic female voice. "And if that proves impossible?"

Mún nodded to the corpse in the center of the room, "Feed that to him to keep him occupied. But spare the animals. They're valuable."

Fel woke to the sound of humming bees. He smelled smoke and there was a sudden urge to move. The

Mare Hypatia impressed his ticks with a desire to change his footing. He complied, following the blue circle that trailed under him. Slowly at first, he pushed ahead from the molasses-thick time of semi-stasis, then with a lurch and a rush, he emerged into real time. The buzzing sound ended behind him with a deafening bang, and he spun about. At least seventeen holes appeared in the floor of the blackout box, exactly in the place where he once rested. This meant nothing to him.

He decided to investigate his surroundings. It was a fairly large and comfortable structure. Bright and clean. He could see many kinds of animals asleep in boxes similar to his own. He felt nothing for them. There was, however an urge to move into one of the open boxes. Later, perhaps. He was too curious at the moment. Besides, there was a body on the ground, and he was eager to investigate.

He prodded at the corpse with his great black nose and found that it smelled fresh, though somewhat *wrong*. He couldn't place the deviation from normal meat, but then he couldn't really place what was so special about normal meat either. It was terribly broken in many, many places, and as he pushed it around on the floor of the room, its limbs grotesquely folded over.

The impetus to shelter himself in a blackout box struck him again, but still he felt like resisting. Everything was just too interesting. He flopped down onto the corpse, resting his paws upon its buttocks, and chuffing in heavy vacillating breaths of pleasure.

His augmented ears heard two voices in conversation in a place outside his line of sight, in the next room over. He recognized the voices with blurry images of the young man and the woman in the headscarf. He felt little for the young man, except perhaps some consternation, but the woman he liked. She made him feel very confident, just like his old Master used to. He did not recognize that he was thinking of his old Master. He only understood that certain images made him feel warm or pleasant, or sometimes intuitively proud.

The voice associated with the young man said, "Hello, Gylfinîr Engine Priest Fawn Virgilis. I am not Mún Rafæl. I am a limited AI simulation. But I have been programmed to respond in a fashion reasonably similar to his own.

"As you probably know by now, your men attacked Fel the lion because Mún invaded their personal Outhernet, in a pub environment in Tacit Reality called the Cutlip Nomad. It is in that setting where your security advisors, Zallo Frautmorgan, Bacalhaus, Alon Elbett, Montefeltro Koalitra, and Vígdís and Védís Vongallo conspired to overthrow the *Mare Hypatia* and Long Savanna colony.

"But you're aware of this, because while you engaged in conversation with one of Mún Rafæl's more distressed personalities in the cargo hold, you simultaneously reprimanded your employees for mistrust of Mún in another TR room independent of the Cutlip Nomad. Correct?"

"Yes," said the voice of the woman in the headscarf.

Fel put his head down on the left leg of the corpse and dug his claws through the armor of the campsuit and into the flesh beneath with a satisfying pop. He began kneading the mangled limb while he looked about, somewhat incurious as to the source of the voices.

The voice of the young man continued, saying, "As you recall, you finished speaking with your people in TR and removed your avatar from the local Outhernet, allowing you to more fully focus your attention on the distressed avatar of Mún Rafæl in the cargo hold. In your absence your employees resumed their talk of mutiny until, in the confines of this Tacit Reality room, Mún Rafæl's more adroit personality approached them, overtly and in jest, and ill-disguised as a fellow publican, gave them suggestions for approving their tactics. The patrons found the joke unfunny and thus decided to, and I quote Zallo Frautmorgan here, 'Violently extract the madness from that damned cat.'"

"Ah," said the weary voice of the woman.

"I am instructed to supply you with the following demand. Are you ready to receive it?"

"All right."

"That is a reply in the affirmative?"

"Yes."

"Very well. You will notice that all forty-six of your remaining Prugarti population have died from high gravity trauma and that, due to your campsuits, only your six Brummagarti, minus the one called Alon Elbett, are now left alive. Therefore, it is ordered by Mún Rafæl, lone survivor of Long Savanna Colony and freedom fighter for his colony's rightful defense force, that you and your people surrender and agree to pássload an invitation of the Will of Æsirisæ into your TEA Cells. Upon agreeing to surrender, you and your employees will retire to the medical crèche and await implantation of the Will of Æsirisæ. After successful recoding of your TEA Cells, Zallo Frautmorgan and Bacalhaus will be allowed to reenter the ship, whereupon they, too, will undergo implantation."

"The Will of Æsirisæ is an enslavement algorithm."

"Correct."

There was a pause.

"What about my dead?" asked the weary woman.

"It will be your task to stack them in the remaining blackout boxes. They will be resurrected once the Bœzch menace is destroyed."

Though he couldn't see her, Fel felt the grimace upon the woman's face.

The young man's voice continued, "Do you have any further questions, Madam Virgilis?"

"Yes ... if I don't submit to the implant ...?"

"Immediate G death followed by spacing."

"Mún Rafæl is a ruthless enemy."

"That is not a question. Do you agree to the demand?"

"We do," she sighed.

"Thank you for your cooperation."

Fel grew tired of listening to the voices babble to and fro in the firmament of this stark white room. Perhaps he would finally give in to the gentle coaxing to go and lie down in container at the end of the row of boxes. It seemed a shame to leave the body. *NO!* the *Mare Hypatia* silently emoted. Very well. Fel chuffed in irritation. He left the body, though he took a leg with him.

Chapter Five
The Epiphany

Enslaving the Ascended Humans' TEA Cell brains with the Will of Æsirisæ had not been pleasant, but the lion didn't understand, and the young man pretended to not care. Fel could feel Mún Ræfl below his dream cloud somewhere; not corporeal, he seemed to exist only as a mist, a bemused and belligerent spirit seeking to betray its ephemeral nature. He raged alone, furious that his own race mistrusted him.

Fel watched as the phantom young man oversaw the enslavement of the six living Ascended Humans. The Gylfinîr Engineer went first, lying her body down in one of the *Mare Hypatia*'s warmly lit medical crèches. It was a hollow tube in a row of four identical tubes set into the curved wall of the white and ocher room. The others were near. The two women still kept a protective circle of their charge, while the three men hung back, sitting at a long blue table with expressions of either suffused anger or frustration. Of the men, only the Librarian's face was visible with worry.

In her quiet prosaic fashion, the *Mare Hypatia* informed everyone that the process of pássloading indentured servitude coding into Fawn Virgilis would begin in ten seconds, and while it was against Windsor law to inflict the Will of Æsirisæ upon TEA Cell individuals without due process of law, this action was being taken by Mún Ræfl as a response to extraordinary circumstances. "Thank you for understanding," the *Mare Hypatia* said just before Fawn Virgilis screamed.

The lion did not like the sound of the woman in distress, and as he watched the scene relayed to his mind through robotic ticks, he felt a strange domestic yearning to run up to her and put his paw upon her lap. In his new, more cramped blackout box, Fel's right paw moved ever so slightly in the slow-time of the container. The two hearts he shared with the phantom young man sank for both of them. The young man lowered his eyes in shame while his avatar, extended away from Fel via the ship's Outher network, stood invisible inside the medical room.

But the young man never left the room, and watched as each of the Ascended Humans endured the torturous rewriting of their free will. By the end of the operation, when the last Brummagarti, the Librarian man identified as Montefeltro, writhed within the crèche, both the lion and his ghost were sickened.

So it was done.

After the brutal scene of enslavement had passed, Fel watched Mún as he moved invisibly through the halls of the ship, passing each defeated Ascended Human and reaching into them for but a moment, searching for their Quiet Places.

Gylfinîrs were classically Human by appearance. They lacked the posture and fluidity of movement of their android brethren, and there was a kind of weight to them, as if all the universe were pressing upon their shoulders, just a tip of the cosmic thumb, arching the back, casting the tilt of the head to the heavens, like their ancestors, to wonder at Creation's heavy hand. Moartale Humans who shed their biological weaknesses at one hundred and thirty years of age, they could not, or would not, shed their worry — though they shifted and grew heroically with what

Nature granted them at birth, biomechanically upgrading their given bodies and shunting their neurological souls into TEA Cell brains. Their spines contained no internal Quiet Place, but they could, if desired, engage in up to four completely separate conversations at once through many different media. Brummagarti on the other hand, were true synthetics, once-Moartale Humans with enough karmic wealth who ascended into the latest and most fashionable android bodies. Brummagarti blood was a superconductive river of fractals, their picoscale matter flesh and bones more abiding, their minds capable of sustaining many full sensory interactions concurrently, the average number being six conversations, but some advanced charismatics could engage up to eighteen. It was so simple for them. There they'd go, chatting up someone who was physically in the room with them while simultaneously projecting an avatar of themselves through a holographic projector, an AR sphere, a distant loaner android body, within a Tacit Reality virtual room, to a ship flying opposite their own, across an orbital platform — wherever Outher networks linked up. Mún recalled the common scandals within Windsor Society, the ones where chaste nobles were discovered to be secretly romancing half a dozen fiancées at the same time. In this civilization, whose currency was the Saṃsāra dollar — which was measured by karmic value — the offending noble would lose wealth as well as their position, risking a downgrade to proletariate status overnight.

Mún wondered how many Saṃsāra the Ægeleif would charge his Karmic Account for this violation of the Human spirit, and he decided he didn't care. If there was a Society alive to punish him after all this business was concluded, then he would accept whatever fine they lotted. He had always been poor.

Every Brummagarti spinal column contained a Quiet Place, an internal virtual paradise constructed in Tacit Reality. Mún visited one when he was at University. A Brummagarti instructor invited him into her own Quiet Place so that he might fully comprehend the transnatural sciences. With his simple Moartale body, Mún had to rely on an external interface that put him to sleep, and hope that, if there were any difficulties, his Samaritan implant would keep his brain alive for as long as it took to restart his heart. He entered her. Within the instructor's Quiet Place he found her avatar hiking through a canyon with weathered vermillion cliffs under a clear blue sky the swirling thickness and hue of Van Gogh's Starry Night. He remembered the pressure of the place, the fact that it felt more real than any of his solitary moments since leaving Tenniel's Garden, or since passing through a Gripper Gate, and on to Society. The sweep of color and the whisper-crisp sound of the air singing, whirling about butterfly acrobats — making virtual love by a lone waterfall nearly burst his heart in the real world.

He couldn't remember the instructor's name. He could only remember the shame and his apology to Luti. There she sat on the grass at the university, laughing at him, saying it was only Tacit Reality. He may as well have told her he had a wet dream, she said. He felt so much worse.

Tacit Reality was almost solely the playground of the TEA Cell Ascended Humans who could live through the richness of the experience without expiring, so Mún was surprised now to find that the Librarian's Quiet Place was simply that, a library. As his avatar entered the elegant room filled with every book committed to text, and many of those never set to paper, Mún found Montefeltro standing in a lower carpeted pit in the center of the library, between two comfortable chairs, a sofa and various tables and floral lamps. Piles of books were stacked taller than the hem of his brown jacket and just even with the highest button on his embroidered yellow vest. Many of the books had luminescent, holographic markers in them. He made notes in the air using a lighted fountain pen, and as the radiant end of the nib passed over the banks of shelves, Mún could see they were molded with carved motifs of dancing rabbits. The pattern persisted around the room. Everywhere Mún turned, he caught the long ears and short tails carved out of wood or stone, cast in brass or bronze, their small lapine bodies holding up book ends or curled around lamps, crawling up the legs of desks, or captured blank-faced yet mirthful at the ends of armchairs.

"Do you spend all of your time in your spine?" Mún said, looking towards the tops of the immense bookshelves and their stained glass crown of a ceiling.

Montefeltro Koalitra did not appear startled by the intrusion of Mún Rafæl into his secret library. He closed the heavy brown book he was holding and said, "Hello! Welcome! Please find a seat and make yourself comfortable. I just made coffee. Would you like cream? That's not a cat joke. I do have cream."

Mún accepted the silver tray with the coffee cup and saucer and set himself up on a plaid sofa near a lacquered end table adorned in laughing hares. He sipped it once and was exhilarated. He drifted back to the instructor's Quiet Place. Rosalynde, that was her name.

"You seem ... all right," Mún said, looking over the rim of his cup.

Montefeltro sat dwarfed upon a large red armchair opposite Mún. He moved aside a pile of books from his feet and replied, "Oh, the encoding was painful, I assure you. But I'll be fine. I still have my library. I like it better in here than out there, anyway."

Mún nodded once and said, "I don't blame you .... You're name is Montefeltro, yes? It's good to meet you. I'm sorry for your discomfort during the encoding, but your comrades left me no choice."

Montefeltro's eyes moved to the panes of the double-hung window nearest. There was a vast wildflower meadow beyond the window, and beyond that a gentle green hill rising like a sleeping salamander over a technicolor quilt. There was a ring of nobility to the Librarian's cadence, but it wasn't the concocted speech patterns of a patois mod that many Brummagarti used — but a natural nobility of spirit. This was not the air he resonated outside his body. In the real world, Montefeltro seemed small and squeamish, near to fainting from mental exhaustion. But here inside himself, he held the poise of a king — even if only a king of iconographic rabbits. His eyes stayed on the distant hillside when he said, "They're not all bad. They just want to be certain they can trust you."

Mún asked, "And what about you?"

Montefeltro bowed once to Mún and then stood, walking over to a far shelf of black tomes, saying, "I'm just an Oshii Librarian. It's simply my duty to be certain that information is reliable before we follow through with action."

"Well, then your job will be easy with me. The indentured servitude implant gives you no choice but to follow me."

Montefeltro examined a five-meter-tall shelf. When he was satisfied with what he found, he made a gesture as if to reach out, and a book the size of his torso flew down to his waiting hands. "Slavery isn't trust," he said.

"Yes, it is," Mún insisted. "I now trust you, because I know that it is physically impossible for you to stop me."

"Ah ... all right then," said the Librarian, holding the book to his chest and returning to his chair. "Well, Mún Rafæl, I see logic is your dearest friend. Listen to me, and maybe some real facts will help you sort out your thoughts. Look here." He jostled the book in his hands. "The Will of Æsirisæ is named after an Ægeleif Entity. Æsirisæ argued that every Human should be enslaved in order to protect us from ourselves. The Ægeleif Council censured her and, in the end, she claimed her idea was only whimsy. Funny that it should be Humans who actually use the slave code."

Mún put his coffee to his lips, and the bitter almond taste warmed his spirit. If this was the only way he would ever eat or drink again as a man, perhaps he could be happy. He said, "I've been re-educating myself, filling in the gaps destroyed by constant regression. I came upon the Will of Æsirisæ when I was pássloading Ægeleif history through Fel's ticks, and I remembered the time I first discovered the coding technique as a student."

Montefeltro traced the embossed lines on the cover of his giant book. It hummed as he did so, and light began to follow his finger like a queue of fireflies tracing Insular art. "And how did it make you feel?" he asked without looking up.

"It was ... the first time I ever doubted the righteousness of the Æincode," Mún replied.

Mún shook himself from the hollow feeling of his last statement and reached for the silver kettle of coffee. He poured in silence.

"Look," said Montefeltro, opening the book on his lap to the exact middle. "Here is Æsirisæ's picture."

"I've ... seen her before ..."

"Well, have another look. Please."

A dimly glowing figure leapt up from the page. The three-dimensional image of the Ægeleif deity was a porcelain white humanoid. A being clothed to appear somewhat mortal, she was swept up in a myriad of ancient feminine costuming: baggy salwar trousers layered over with a pleated skirt, brocade vest, rich velveteen shawls and tasseled scarves fastened by carved Insular broaches, draped with beaded jewelry and peacock feathers. Though Æsirisæ took the form of a woman, in truth she could move between genders as she moved between the stars, a burning, sighing all-thing, radiating a melancholy unequal to the depth of her understanding of All. She was a giant, a slender glittering goddess, five meters of alabaster, her gray-white hair a shock of gossamer feathers undulating in an Autumn wind only felt, only ridden, only known by the Ægeleif and their Gylfinîr Engine Priests.

Montefeltro pointed to the figure hovering over the book and quietly, but with worshipful excitement, said, "Notice her aura? Æsirisæ is gray compared to the brilliant white of the other Ægeleif. When an Entity is censured they lose some of their brilliance, and their power to navigate is shortened. She was the Ægeleif Entity for Odin System's gas giant and she controlled the Grip Point between there and Thrundin System, ten thousand lightyears away. But her power diminished and she could no longer see beyond a hundred lightyears. Those who colonized Thrundin were closed off and alone for nearly a decade until their system's Entity, Jéudin, found them the way back to Society."

Mún stared at the figure's melancholy eyes, the eyes of sickness and remorse, her chin down, her shoulders slumped. This was not the usual visage of a lawful and serene goddess. "What happened to her?"

The Librarian closed his book, and the image blinked away. He said, "She disappeared after a few years, banished herself into space."

"Have we ever made stranger gods?"

"May I ask something of you?" Montefeltro said, moving his hands through his short afro and sighing.

"Yes ..."

He leaned towards Mún with his elbows on the book and implored, "Please don't stack Alon away with the rest of the dead Prugarti. Set him in the medical crèche for full resurrection."

"Why?"

"It will calm down Zallo," Montefeltro said, continuing. "They have been best friends for a century. Even before the Bœzch invasion, it was Alon who was always able to soothe Zallo with a joke or story. They're practically brothers."

Mún scoffed, "He certainly did a terrible job at preventing the mutiny."

"Yes, but ..."

Mún dismissed the protest with a small wave and Montefeltro was compelled into silence. He said, "Show me the data you've been collecting."

"Ah," said the Librarian. He blinked for nearly a full minute before he set the giant book aside and raised his hand. Another tome, smaller and leather-bound flew from a shelf and into his grasp.

He opened a page and said, "So that is the reason you've intruded on my Quiet Place. Well, then look here. It's about the Serengeti series of colonies and the Bœzch impact on all of them."

"Will the rest of the series have androids hiding as well?" Mún inquired, interrupting.

"No. All of the Ascended Humans in system were gathered at Serengeti Six when the Bœzch attacked."

"All of them?"

Montefeltro nodded reluctantly.

"You were planning to invade Long Savanna."

The Librarian did not deny the accusation, but instead said, "Every Brummagarti and Prugarti in system was secretly drafted into the Amalgam's service, many against their will. But, getting back to the information ... here ..." A holographic image of the dead space of Hæl System rose above the pages. The view swung about and the star, Foss, shined behind a seemingly endless circle of drifting matter.

"What is this?"

Montefeltro said matter-of-factly, "An expanded debris field extending through all ninety Serengeti locations."

"All of the Serengeti colonies were destroyed?"

"At the same time."

"How?"

"Did you not think it strange that Serengeti Six crumbled to pieces when Sayre the Conjurer was killed?"

"No," Mún admitted. "The colony was already dying. You're suggesting he was a kind of link? A support system?"

The Librarian unsheathed his lighted fountain pen from his vest pocket and assembled a three-dimensional map of Hæl System in the air between them. With an animated picture of the Bœzch horror, Sayre, he marked the center of the area where the Serengeti series of colonies once thrived. Red ripples issued from the horror, extending over the area of the obliterated ninety colonies. "I'm saying ... how do the Bœzch communicate with one another? What is their range?" Montefeltro pointed to the termination point of the ripples. "Is there a single mind behind them all or are they directionless? I think this is the first evidence we've seen that they set up administrators in the form of higher horrors, the Bœzch Servants like Sayre. All of the Serengeti series were undergoing transformation. When Sayre died, there was nothing to guide the transformation, so they unraveled. It's my belief that he was the administrator for that area of space."

"What about the Cape series of colonies? They're the next group of ninety after Serengeti."

"I don't know. We're almost back to Long Savanna, which means the Cape series is now six AU away, and the asteroid field is interfering with deep scans. *Mare Hypatia* can detect debris in the Cape's location, but there's no way of discerning if it's rocks or dead colonies." Montefeltro paused. Then, looking up at nothing in particular, he said, "Our Gylfinîr is at my door."

Mún nodded.

The Librarian stood and bowed slightly to the great rosewood door at the entrance, where motifs of languid rabbits lazed in a picnic scene that filled up the whole of the egress. He gently called out, "Please come in, Madam Virgilis, and join us."

The lithe, snow white figure in black and orange armor stepped through the entrance as if it were a real door and politely closed it behind her. She wore the same vestments here in the unreal world as she did in the real, including the sword and staff at her side and the headscarf that concealed her eyes behind black cloth and radiant lines. Here in Tacit Reality, all signs of her prior distress were gone. She spoke directly to Mún when she said, "All of the dead have been placed in blackout boxes."

"Thank you."

She stood with both hands on her staff, leaning forward on it as if she were actually worn from her task. She tilted towards Montefeltro when she spoke, but she addressed Mún. "I want to finish my conversation with you," she said, her eyes trailing over to the Librarian. "Before Zallo's mutiny I was trying to talk to you ... about your brother, Hünde."

Mún waved to both Montefeltro and Fawn Virgilis, directing them to the two chairs before him. "It's all right. Montefeltro can stay. It's his spine."

"Of course," she said, taking the seat before Mún. Montefeltro was sitting comfortably next to her, but with a look from her he knew to stay quiet. She continued, saying with composed urgency, "A year ago, your brother left Guggisberg Colony Sixty-Seven on a mission to explore Hæl Five, the planet that he himself named Bosh Übor."

"He was an actor, not an explorer," said Mún. "I knew that he came to the same star system as Luti and I. But he was on a tour, and I avoided contact with him ... though I always wondered if he was stalking us. Several of his friends from his old gang found work on some of the Guggisberg colonies. But we never spoke to them, never saw Hünde. Why would he suddenly take to naming planets?"

"He didn't go to the fifth planet. Not immediately ..."

A cloud passed over the window, and they were drawn into its shadow. Mún could see the distant hill disappearing under the low mists. He wondered if this was an effect of the librarian's thoughts, but the gravity was upon his own shoulders, and the very sound of his brother's name brought back memories that clouded his mind in the past. Grimaces, shouts, and bloodied knuckles swept past Mún's inner eye. "Then where ...?"

Fawn Virgilis answered, "Just weeks before Hünde's departure, his friends detected an object at the same five thousand four hundred plus AU orbital distance as Hæl Five. The object is planet-sized, but it is stationary, currently resting over three thousand AU ahead of Hæl Five, lying inert on the path of its orbital trajectory. That is the mission he never returned from."

"Planet-sized?"

She extended her hand, palm up and the image of a black ring just barely revealed itself in Hæl System's starless night. She said, "This is the only picture we have of it. Your brother named it the Ouroboros Object because it is literally a colossal effigy of a snake eating its own tail. We don't know how old it is or who built it."

"Incredible," Montefeltro murmured from his chair.

Mún asked, "What happened to Hünde?"

"We originally thought that he and his team vanished somewhere around the object. But a probe that I sent to Bosh Übor reveals what happened. The probe was able to penetrate the planet's thick cloud layer long enough to establish a link with the remains of Hünde's ship. The data shows that, indeed, he did travel to the unknown Object before then flying to the fifth planet. First, the recording from the Object ..."

The image within her palm shifted to reveal a fat, colander-shaped research vessel. Unarmed and unshielded, it moved slowly into an alien chasm made of green-black metal. Through a corridor lit ever so dimly by emerald lights in patterns of inconsistent hieroglyphics and fluctuating runes, the scene jumped to the ship being drawn into a colossal, irising doorway. The scene jumped again: seven intrepid astronauts in campsuits stepped down from the ship's loading lift. Another shift, and the image was an orgy of grasping monstrous red hands dragging the crew across the dark superstructure, holding them up in the familiar Bœzch way, spinning them and spinning them into bursting shapes and colors. But they did not become stardust. Hünde was the first to be brought to his feet. He was naked and his skin was hardening, his hair gone and the horns painfully extending from his head and neck, his face pushing into that of a wolf, and though Mún could clearly see he was in agony, Hünde's teeth beamed a smile lit aflame like a canine jack-o-lantern.

Wülvogarti, beamed the title assigned to the recording.

"Later images show the following ..." Fawn Virgilis shook her hand once as if she were rattling an aerosol can and flattened her palm again. The research ship moved into the atmosphere of the fifth planet, Bosh Übor, but did not dip too far below the cloud layers. Such a simple vessel would never survive the surface heat without adequate shielding. The cargo door opened, and this time the full-sized demons appeared and jumped, one by one, into the clouds below. The imager tried to follow their descent.

Just before the last of them vanished, a burgundy hand at least ten meters in width, a great claw of iron and flame, reached up through the mists and snatched them all away.

Mún shouted without meaning to. "What was that?"

"Without the aid of my patron Ægeleif, I can only speculate," said Fawn the Gylfinîr. "But know this: just like when you underwent a transformation under the influence of the Bœzch and became a lion, your brother, too, was twisted. He is the horror Wülvogarti the Wrathful."

Mún leapt to his feet and shouted again, this time with full purpose: "But I am not a Bœzch! I am not under their power! I'm free, like an animal should be, and they fear me because I move in places they can't see!"

Fawn and Montefeltro lowered their eyes. "Of course ..."

Mún stepped behind the sofa and began to pace. "But Hünde ... always so angry, Hünde ..."

"Angry?"

"Anger and revenge ... it's all he ever thought about." Mún was speaking to himself now, rocking his head in both his hands as he searched his memories. Fawn Virgilis crumpled away the image in her palm and stood, approaching Mún and trying to take his shoulder, to look into his face. "Why should he be so outraged that he becomes the very expression of wrath?"

Mún sagged somewhat under the weight of her fingers. He shook his head with grief and said, "He blames me for his unhappiness."

She hugged him by the shoulders, though he was taller than her, and brought his face level to where her eyes hid behind cloth. She said to him, "I believe we should invade this Ouroboros Object ourselves."

Montefeltro stood now. He spoke with palpable concern, though he was able to conceal his misery at the thought of approaching the alien tomb. "Madam Virgilis, isn't it better to finish the task that Fel and Mún began, and then, if possible, simply destroy the Object from afar?"

Fawn Virgilis paced with Mún now, helping him along as if he were a crumbling old man. She said, "'Simply' may be the least of possibilities if you mean we should attack its superstructure with ship-grade weapons. This is a patrol cruiser we lie harbored within, not a warship."

Montefeltro shook his head. "But how are we more capable weapons as foot soldiers?"

She took both men in her arms now, pressing them close as if in conspiracy, speaking low and guarded, though they were alone within the librarian's Quiet Place. "We assumed the Bœzch all arrived from Bosh Übor, because that is the direction their pods flew from. But that doesn't mean it is where the invasion originated. Hünde and his team were all Moartale, and their transformation started before they landed on the fifth planet, that much is certain. The Bœzch stationed at the Ouroboros Object may have been the ones who started this invasion, and if so, we may be able to end this by destroying them first. None of us here is Moartale. We have a chance because they are weak when surprised. We know this. The only reason they have killed so many is due to their ability to see thinking minds from so great a distance. But we are hidden from afar. We can move in like assassins and take their hearts from them before they realize they are dead!"

Mún broke away from their circle and moved to the window. He watched the passing clouds that lumbered overhead like stricken, gray behemoths. He was reminded of when he first became involved with the science of animals and what a respite they were from Hünde's madness. The screams, the wailing, the breaking of furniture and the bruises upon his skin, Hünde was the rabid, bellowing cyclone of his childhood, unhinged from anything but his own narcissism. Nothing could pacify the young actor. Nothing could divert his violence but more violence, and so Mún said, "We'll go. If I'm going to exterminate all the Bœzch then that means *all* of them. We'll continue on course for the colonies after we kill whatever is living in the Object."

"What about our cargo?" Montefeltro asked.

"We have two skiffs," said Fawn Virgilis. "We can load all of the animals and Prugarti onto one. The drones can fly it back to Long Savanna, unload everyone, and then return to the *Mare Hypatia* with more blackout boxes. What say you, Mún? Mún ...?"

The young man was no longer listening, just marveling in the epiphany of the moment: that he and his brother should come all this way, from humble beginnings on a world that despised technology, across an absurd portal — one of many opened by the divine Ægeleif — spirited thirty billion lightyears away, and now to here, both of them remade by devils of worlds lost to darkness. Mún thought of Hünde and himself as brother performers now, their monstrous auditions on display for the universe to bear witness, applaud, laugh, or scorn.

Mún laughed quietly to himself.

The clear field of flowers outside the library window brought back another memory now, to a time when he was eight and Hünde was nine. On a fine day, a turquoise spring morning on Tenniel's Garden, their green, unpowered Tudor-style village rested at the foot of misted glacial steppes. A single lane of gray road paved with sett stones, quarried from local granite, separated the two story houses on either side. Young Mún Rafæl was hiding with his baby brother Paölo and their neighbor friend Luti on the balcony overlooking the open courtyard kitchen. Below, a wrecked bicycle and a smear of blood lie upon the sett stones. Also below, his face bloodied, the child Hünde, raged in the kitchen, smashing cupboards and dishes, dashing to bits a rare glass carafe, throwing the utensils into the stove, burning the dish rags and aprons, screaming, screaming, always screaming — and all while their simple mother cowered and wailed in the corner.

Young Hünde shrieked to the heavens, "My face! My face! My beautiful face! Who put the street so crooked? Who did this to the world's greatest actor? I will murder everything and everyone!"

It was the moment Hünde kicked their mother in the back when Mún jumped from the balcony, breaking his foot on landing, and in the thrill and pain of the shock from the fracture, he leapt upon his brother and bit him on the throat like an animal.

Oh, Luti, Mún thought now. How will it end for us now?

Mún needed to learn more about his reluctant crew. While his "correct" self planned and discussed with Montefeltro and Fawn Virgilis, his more melancholy self toured the rest of the Brummagarti Quiet Places.

His most interesting discovery was when he learned that Vígdís and Védís Vongallo shared interconnected Tacit

Realities — two separate realms blended together where they both were curled under hundred-foot redwood trees, and where they both read books on ornithology. The line between one Reality and the next was so invisible to Mún that it took him a few minutes to realize he'd gone from one woman's Quiet Place to the next.

He checked on them again. It was true. There was one Vongallo girl sitting under her redwood. Mún swept by her unseen and rounded the back side of her tree. There he happened upon her again, then realized she was not the same woman, for the book in the hand of one was not the same in the other.

Birds ... that's what they are, he thought, *Two predatory birds without a nest*. Despite Mún's natural gloominess he smiled briefly under the weight of his mood. A hallow screech caught him by surprise then, and Mún's avatar jumped. He looked up and saw that he was spied by a great bald eagle. The majestic white brow regarded him silently, and seemingly peering through him, the eagle rose and took flight with several of its kind.

He moved on to the blue, ageless warrior, Bacalhaus, and found him in a white room, meditating nude. His Quiet Place was exactly that: a place of solitude. Even the sound of Bacalhaus' breathing held a kind of stillness to it, an impenetrable will of silence reminiscent of ancient Zen. *There's nothing to see here*, thought Mún. The avatar of Sad Mún stepped away then and missed seeing the sea of galaxies unfolding behind the white facade. But Fel somehow saw everything as he, unconsciously, invisibly, hitched a ride with every version of Mún. The sleeping lion wanted ever so much to chase the whirling stars that floated in the night like embers from a fire. The lion watched where the blue man swam like a fish from nebula to nebula, and so the great cat was stalking his mirth.

In Zallo Frautmorgan's Quiet Place Mún found an English-style manor, a stone and concrete monument that spread the length of ten thousand square meters or more. Horses bridled for show grazed alone on the lawn of the perfect garden, and in the far off horizon white dots of sheep puttered to-and-fro in the manner of drifting dandelion seeds. He stepped up to the great door at the main entrance and outstretched his hand. Mún froze. He was without the heart to enter. He thought of this man, and how he disliked him on principle. Zallo was a hunter of beasts, and here Mún was a predator himself, stalking hearts and minds. He could not bring himself to dislike the rest of the crew. He realized now that hating this man made him distrust everyone, and so he grieved silently to himself, knowing he had enslaved good people to a worthy cause.

Hours later, Mún ordered that the poet, Alon, be set up in a medical crèche for full resurrection.

Chapter Six
The Hermit

The *Mare Hypatia* broadcast her itinerary to the crew via her local Outhernet, filling the minds of everyone onboard:

Dlaüt-Fold — Preparing to Engage ....
SIMULATED Speed: 7.521x10⁷ Km/s
Real Distance to OurOboros Object: 3,973 AU
Real TRAVEL Time: 2hrs, 47 mins

Mún poured himself into an empty corridor and thought on what was to come. To Dlaüt-Fold, to stutter a Grippership across space, was to simulate forward momentum by displacing the portion of space in front of the ship with the ship itself, repeating this every quarter second, over and over until its destination was reached. This gave the effect of a vessel that moved as if it were the projection from a silent movie, as if rather than moving from place to place in space, it was being cast from frame to frame.

Resting at the outer edge of the asteroid belt, the *Mare Hypatia* waited to begin.

The skiff departed an hour earlier, using its own powerful velocity engines to bring it the rest of the way to Long Savanna. Once the small ship docked with the colony, its little drone crew of hovering robots would unload and free the animals, then connect the rescued EtherCore of Serengeti Six to Long Savanna, replacing Fel's deceased Master — but they would leave the dead

Prugarti Humans in their blackout boxes stacked in the spaceport, to await resurrection in the future. New supplies and blackout boxes would be loaded into the skiff, and it would fly out to a rendezvous point near the colony called Cape One. It would hold this position for five years, and then, if the *Mare Hypatia* never appeared, it would return to Long Savanna with orders to have the drones incinerate the dead Prugarti and maintain Long Savanna's ecology forever.

Though they all sat comfortably in the ship's spacious lounge, none of them had yet removed their campsuits. Everyone but Fawn Virgilis dozed in sleep. Mún's avatar was absent, or at least not making himself visible. The light in the lounge was warm and dim. Ambient sensors waited to lift the light levels at the first hint of any crew member stirring. Their False G Lots sat them firmly in their reclining chairs where they rested in a circle, food packets and covered drinks fastened down just at the termination points of their G Lot gravity wells.

"Begin Dlaüt-Fold to Ouroboros Object," said the disembodied voice of Mún Rafæl.

There was no feeling of acceleration, for unlike the pull of velocity drive, the ship wasn't really moving. It was simply appearing ahead of itself over and over again in rapid fashion on a linear course.

Sensor cameras the size of shirt buttons, anchored to the hull of the ship with anti-Casimir mechanics, hovered over the exterior of the ship from a distance of up to ten meters. It was through these cameras that Fel watched the ship from his elephant dream cloud. It was a mesmerizing sight, this stuttering thing, and it made him drowsy as it moved farther and farther away from any formal source of light. Soon all that could be seen of the vessel from the outside was her running lights and few amber-lit portals. All else was black.

Inside the ship, Zallo Frautmorgan was waking from his nap. He looked over to his left to see that total darkness through the large man-sized window. He called up a status report on a holographic table between his sleeping comrades. Though he saw that they were indeed approaching the Object's location, nothing but blackness was yet detected. "How did anyone ever find this thing?" he mused out loud.

Fawn Virgilis was closest to the window, sitting with her legs crossed on a bench, her back facing Zallo and the others. She turned away a hovering drone that tried to serve a drink. She said to no one in particular, "The temperature outside is point eight Kelvin. We move into the loneliest circle of Hell."

Zallo shook his head and leaned back into his lounge chair, attempting to catch just a bit more sleep before he woke to fight horrors in their own lair.

Thirteen minutes shy of three hours later, the *Mare Hypatia* found herself a little more than seven hundred and fifty billion kilometers from where she started. Her Dlaüt-Fold drive powered off, her running lights the only illumination against her hull, she found herself dwarfed by a faintly glowing ring the size of Venus. The shifting runic lines of the thing's superstructure were all that made this apple slice of a world known to the outside universe. The dull sepia lights pulsed along its skin, giving the illusion of cometary bodies running in a great parade together, like a child's puzzle of connecting dots. The shape of the serpent's face and the tail going into the mouth were evident from the angle the *Mare Hypatia* approached. The Ouroboros Object did not rotate. Besides the cyclopean running lights, it was an inert, sepulchral monolith.

Fel could see everything and little of it meant anything to him. Zallo, Bacalhaus, Montefeltro, Vígdís and Védís all stood in silence in the patrol cruiser's wheelhouse with Fawn Virgilis and the avatar of Mún. The wheelhouse was spacious, with a high ceiling and wide transparent hull windows on two sides. Without the engineered eyesight of an Ascended Human or a Moartale's pásscode-enhanced eyewear, the room would seem empty, a collection of seats in a semi-circle around a large table elevated over a cushioned pit — but Ascended persons saw here a complex collection of holographic status boards and displays sweeping out in a great arch in Augmented Reality. It was all for show anyway, so that the Human crew could feel up to date on the ship's status. The ship's AI ran everything.

Bacalhaus was the first to speak. He said, "Where do we begin?"

Mún was interested to see the silent veteran find his voice and he could tell that his partner, Zallo, was left mildly bothered by the question.

Fawn Virgilis replied, "We'll follow the path taken by Hünde Rafæl's group."

"Is that the decision of our ... leader?" Zallo asked, frowning at Mún.

The avatar of Mún did not take his eyes from the pulsating, cometary lights. He said, "It is."

Fawn stepped towards a collection of AR displays and examined what she found there. She said to the ceiling, "*Mare Hypatia*? I want you to follow this path into the Object." She pointed to a trajectory recorded by the probe from the fifth planet. "As you can see there are many thousands of openings along the superstructure. I think it significant that Hünde took this specific route."

The avatar of Mún turned without moving, surprising himself as much as the crew. "Do you believe he was already in contact with the Bœzch?" he asked. "Even before he arrived?"

"Yes, I do."

Mún's mouth opened, but he said nothing for several seconds. "Why would you think that?"

Fawn explained, "Hünde's evidence for the discovery of the Object was nonsensical. How could he find a cold black ring against a black sky nearly four thousand AU away? It seems far more likely that he knew it was here, that someone or something told him where to find it."

The weight of her words struck them, and they each turned to their nearest companion. Zallo alone looked to Mún's avatar.

Fawn Virgilis continued speaking to the ceiling. "So ... *Mare Hypatia*," she said, "I want you to bring us to the iris door you see marked at these coordinates."

The ship's AI calmly intoned, "Mún Rafæl, please confirm order."

"Confirmed," Mún said. "And *Mare Hypatia*, in the event that I am incapacitated or killed, I want you to accept commands from the Humans in this room — after a command structure is decided upon by Fawn Virgilis. This order is rescinded if they compete with or counter the mission of Manticore Project."

"Acknowledged, Mún Rafæl. Now moving vessel under velocity drive towards the destination described by Gylfinîr Fawn Virgilis. Two hours, thirteen minutes to arrival."

"Onward," Mún said. He stared ahead into the sepia-white pulses of light that circled around the black eyes of the serpent.

Fel's sense of object permanence was little to none, and many events passed before him that day with so little understanding that, as he stood now in the blue black desert with the woman in the headscarf, he pined for smells and senses he could not place. He could smell nothing at all in his current state. The biomechanics of his transnatural body sealed every orifice. His eyes looked out behind a second set of transparent metal lids, his fur shifted into a different armored state than usual, the picoscale matter contained within the follicles coming together to make a completely sealed system, in every way like an environment suit over his semi-organic flesh. In this state, he did not need to breathe, and though his mouth hung open, he shook his head from time to time, trying to rid his throat of the bizarre feeling, the sensation of something stuck in his esophagus. He understood none of this, but his incomprehension did not alter the fact that he had life support for ninety hours in this state.

There was gravity in this desert, barely less than one G, but there was very little heat. Twelve mini suns — called Charon lamps — robotic balls of plasma — followed the group ahead and behind, bringing the temperature up by two hundred and fifty degrees Kelvin and lighting their path under the ribbed roof of the chasm. This was a desert in a black cathedral. How had they gotten here?

The young man who was always silent when the lion walked remembered what happened, and though he tried to share it with his feline counterpart, the lion dismissed the memory as dispassionate noise.

The young man recalled the scene alone: the *Mare Hypatia* found the entry point of Hünde's crew and they slinked along, under and over glowing veins of sepia-blue lights stretching around them like an illuminated ribcage. The iris valve door was easily twice the size of the *Mare Hypatia*'s length. It was only fully visible in the dim cavern due to the patrol cruiser's spotlights. The journey into the Ouroboros Object had been a quiet one, and no one opened their mouths for the entire two hours as the ship slipped though the alien structure. In the wheelhouse of the *Mare Hypatia*, only Fawn Virgilis spoke.

The sound that issued from the Gylfinîr Engineer was not a language easily imitated by the Human tongue.

It started off as a sweet, whistling sigh that issued from somewhere far within her diaphragm. It soon became a language of bells and winds, the divine Æincode of the Ægeleif spoken as only they could. It was a white luminescent language, a language with a brightness like a light of dawn on high tide, like the reflection on a child's eyes under holiday bulbs. Mún could call upon small scraps of this language whenever he wrote his pásscodes, but pásscoding, like magic words were to magic, was merely a means to activate patches of Æincode; it was not a modeling device. Mún could only rearrange commands, order code around according to the passwords he wrote. Fawn Virgilis could speak the code itself:

"A tha thu: ::: :: ::.::...: : ::: !"

She sang on, and the words were a celestial modem buzz spoken as if an electric choir moved together through a clear acoustical valley. No Human mouth unaided by an oracular symphony of science could vocalize this hymn that was as complex as waveforms and particles, as open and clear as photons. She sang on:

"A tha thu brüne: ::.::..: ::-.::: !
Thu soth a tha lu to bridden -------- !"

Fawn Virgilis stood upon the deck of the wheelhouse, her metal staff extended, her arms outstretched and the angelic words whirling from her open mouth. All the Humans and the avatar of the young man were left weak and tearful from the display, their minds ringing down to the core of their cognitive processes; Ascended or Moartale, to hear the lilt of an Ægeleif Advocate was to see the Æthereal numeracy behind the equations of life, was to understand the reason and clarity of the natural sciences, was to feel an ascension towards some unseen Heaven. This was the mark of the Ægeleif on the Human psyche: they were Mankind's creations, but Man himself was a servant to their blessings. All they asked in return was that Mankind use their Gripper Gates to move out into the universe and propagate, to explore, to discover, but most of all to find the cure for the Telic Death — the inevitable extermination of the universe itself, an inherent doom "planned" into its very fabric since its birth. And Mankind fell prostrate and giddy before their angelic creations, their beatific masters. What could this holy priestess be saying to the door beyond the window? How could she possibly think her Words would carry over the vacuum? But the Words extended out like particle bursts, and the iris door gave a shutter.

Slowly, and over the course of two hours, the petals of the iris unfurled, sliding open to reveal the dreaded blackness within.

Vígdís and Védís were the first to touch down with the ship's ten-meter-long utilitarian wayboat. Once on the other side of the vast portal, they reported within minutes, saying, "Artificial gravity field equal to ninety-two percent of one G. No movement. No life. No atmosphere. Frozen. The local area is safe for our Gylfinîr."

Their Gylfinîr replied, "Safe, unsafe, no difference here. Return to the *Mare Hypatia* and prepare yourselves for a long journey."

For supplies, they packed matter fabricators and Charon lamps, extra campsuits, a collapsible G shelter, various firearms, and two armored beetle suits operated by Zallo and Bacalhaus. Mún would have preferred that they all wore beetle suits, but with the bulk of the lion, there would be no extra room aboard the wayboat.

"Why don't we take the other skiff instead of the wayboat? It's bigger," Montefeltro asked as he loaded sensing equipment into the wayboat's storage bins.

Mún's avatar replied, "Fawn and I believe its fusion wake will draw too much attention."

"Fawn? Not, Madam Virgilis?"

"Ghosts are always on a first name basis with priests."

"So are masters with their slaves."

Mún stepped though the nearest bulkhead wall and ignored Montefeltro's last comment.

When they were packed and the wayboat was brimming with occupants and objects, they departed the underside of the *Mare Hypatia*, leaving dead Alon in the medical crèche as the only Human aboard.

Mún instructed the pilot, Vígdís, "Fly ten kilometers past the threshold and then get Fel down on the ground."

"What's that?" said Zallo from the back of the craft.

"Land and open his blackout box," Mún continued. "The *Mare Hypatia* has administered new pásscoding through his ticks. He won't attack any of you and he is spaceworthy. You didn't think we would design his biomechanics for combat on a space colony and not make them vacuum-capable, did you?"

Zallo swore out of disbelief.

Mún continued, saying, "No one ever seems to realize that I think of everyth — " He stopped. The young man's temperament changed then. He seemed to be reflecting on something distant and melancholy, losing his brief show of bravado in mid-sentence. Just before fading away, he watched his hands and said, "I don't understand why, but Fel can sense the Bœzch. It doesn't matter if he's on a colony all alone, if there's a Bœzch an AU away he'll be looking up at the sky, wondering how to get to them. So let his bloodlust be your guide."

They landed in a sea of blue-black sand and followed the lion into the frozen, airless night.

Montefeltro stayed in the wayboat and piloted the pressurized sow-bug-shaped craft at a languid pace behind the party, a mere meter above the ground. Zallo and Bacalhaus, cradled in the chest cavities of their armored beetle suits, lumbered alongside the hovering wayboat, constantly scanning the empty fields surrounding them. Next came Fawn Virgilis sealed up tight in her Gylfinîr armor and flanked on either side by Vígdís and Védís, her Gird of Gyl bodyguards. So they went, spearheaded by the lion, Fel, who walked and paused, walked and paused. Stopping now and then, he looked to the ebon sky or peered ahead into the glittering sand that vanished into blackness only a few meters beyond their Charon lamps, but always he continued, always he moved on with determination. The ground was their only point of orientation, and with no horizon visible from any single point, they could only rely on their instruments to tell them how far they had come or whether they had turned.

And yet there was another sense that Fel alone resonated with — music, musical notes used as pásscodes, designed and forgotten by Mún long before his transformation, pásscodes that called up the Æincode to wall off his mind with ever-changing neurological, chemical barriers against intruders.

Also unknown to dormant Mún or the party of Ascended Humans — Fel's ticks felt something ahead in the darkness: just a flicker, it was as subtle as background radiation, something probing and blind. As a precaution, the ticks fed a lone pásscoded aria, sung in countertenor, into the Lion's wakeful mind. The aria was known as the *Cold Song*, a melody from the long deceased composer Henry Purcell's seventeenth-century opera *King Arthur*. In some part of the lion, Mún remembered the opera — where Cupid raised the spirit of frost up from sleep. This frost spirit, *the Cold Genius*, was confronted by the overwhelming presence of love. Thus he sang in a deathly, halting manner, one word, one broken syllable, one breath at a time. He was accompanied by violins composed in a similar manner as the halting countertenor, and he sang:

> *Wha-at pow-ow-wer art thou-ou-ou*
> *Who fro-o-om be-lo-o-ow*
> *Hast ma-a-ade me ri-i-ise*
> *Un-wil-ling-ly and slo-o-ow*
> *Fro-om be-e-eds of e-ev-er-la-a-a-a-a-as-ting sno-*
> *o-o-ow*

But like the melancholic aria *Una Furtiva Lagrima*, the *Cold Song* did not complete its cycle or even go on to the next verse. Instead, the words faded and returned to the long rise of the strings at the beginning of the aria, returning again to the words, "Wha-at pow-ow-wer art thou-ou-ou ... Who fro-o-om be-lo-oow ..." The lion did not mind the repetition. It was comforting to hear something in this soundless vacuum, even if it was only data passing by his cerebellum. Meanwhile the part of him that was still Mún rested without knowledge of anything but his complicated dreaming; he wondered alone how he found such a high cloud to watch himself stride through the dark.

After twenty-six hours of travel, Fawn Virgilis ordered that they should make camp and rest for four hours. The Brummagarti could have continued for at least another six hours before needing a respite, but the lion and the Gylfinîr were semi-organic, and weakened hours sooner than their android friends. Or so that was how Fawn related her concerns to her party. In truth, she didn't know the limits of the Lion and thought he probably could have continued to the end of his life support before collapsing. Rage and combat seemed to be the only elements that wore him down.

They landed and parked the wayboat and fixed the collapsible G shelter around the midsection of the craft, extending the room for comfort at least five more meters beyond the side cargo doors. The *Mare Hypatia* signaled for the lion to follow the Humans through the temporary airlock and into the pressurized tent, and he followed his instructions admirably, feeling excitement for the pássloaded images of himself breathing freely. Bacalhaus and Zallo remained outside the wayboat in their beetle suits, keeping watch while the others sat in chairs and raised their feet. They made a circle around Fel. His fur remained fixed as a sheen of protective fibers for now. Only his mouth and esophagus were returned to normal, and he chuffed in delight as he rested on the covered floor of the tent, feeling the bumps of the sand below the shelter's fabric.

None of them opened their helmets. They didn't need to to relax. Montefeltro sat away from the group, analyzing a sample of the desert soil, while all the women present took turns either meditating or refilling their suits' food and water fabricators. The lion was given meat grown in the wayboat's fabricator, and it appeared to satisfy him well enough, though its flavor was unremarkable. His internal transnatural engines burned away the waste, sparing him from a bevy of litter box humor planned by Zallo.

There, their bodies rested in sullen states of rejuvenation, either confined, like Zallo and Bacalhaus, in the bellies of four-meter-tall robots, or like Fawn Virgilis and the rest, lounging as best they could in the bright white shelter — but their minds they set down elsewhere. Though they were each aware of their real surroundings, their minds strayed away for the sake of sanity. Bacalhaus, in his Quiet Place, reclined among whirling galaxies like a fish in a stream of stars; Montefeltro studied in his library rabbit hole as deftly as he studied in reality; Vígdís and Védís walked under colossal ceilings of giant Sequoia arches and listened to thrush and stellar jays up in the high branches; Zallo and a group of children rode wooly Icelandic horses over the winter lawn of his virtual estate — but Fawn, who had no inner Quiet Place, connected a part of herself to the group's Tacit Reality pub and dined with other versions of her party there.

Their real selves could contend with the tasteless vegan packets served to them by their campsuits in the real world, for here in the Cutlip Nomad they feasted well on roast potatoes, shredded pork, and boiled garlic cabbages, sharing between themselves glasses of red wine and pints of amber ale at the table near the hearth of the roaring fire. It made for a festive mood and did well to raise their morale, shining a glorious ray of light within their minds to push out the infinite night outside their camp. During the meal together they settled into a true regenerative spirit and among the sounds of cutlery scraping plates and drinks being poured there arose a steady easiness that was supported by their mutual fellowship as travelers through grim, unrelenting darkness.

Their happiness only lessened when either Vígdís or Védís Vongallo said to Fawn Virgilis, "Madam Gylfinîr, I am bothered by our manner of entry into this place."

"How so, my love?" asked Fawn.

The other Vongallo woman continued for her twin, saying, "You used the Æincode of the Ægeleif to open the portal. Why did it work?"

"I don't know ... and I am troubled and bemused by it ..." and Fawn Virgilis lowered her head to ponder alone what was said aloud.

The once merry conversation drifted on into awkwardness.

After four hours they broke camp and again set forth on their trek into nothingness, following the psychic nose of a blighted man-beast. Reports from the *Mare Hypatia* said they covered over a hundred kilometers in their first thirty hours, that they were traveling in a straight line towards no structures that the ship could find, and that now, at the end of their second thirty hours, they had traveled two hundred kilometers total. At one point, halfway through their journey, Fel stopped and crouched as if he were stalking prey; he looked to the blackness above several times, causing Zallo and Bacalhaus to aim their weapons skyward and scan the area for foes. The Humans sensed nothing, and soon the lion grew sullen, gave up, and marched on ahead as before, looking for all the world like he had lost a prize.

It was in that brief moment when the feeling of the distant probe, the subtle background impulse, suddenly broke down the wall of the countertenor aria, *The Cold Song*:

> *Wha-at pow-ow-wer art thou-ou-ou*
> *Who fro-o-om be-lo-o-ow –*

As Fel crouched towards the blackness, his ticks implemented the next five lines of the halting music:

> *Se-e-e'st thou no-o-ot*
> *How sti-i-iff, how sti-i-iff*
> *And wo-o-on-drous o-o-old*
> *Far far far far un-un-fit*
> *To bear-ear-ear the bi-i-it-ter co-o-o-old*

And the unsettling sensation was gone with this raising of the next part of the aria. The lion moved on, the Humans lowered their weapons, and the fragment of music played over and over, heard only by Fel for the next sixteen hours. The blackness continued to swallow them up.

At their next rest point, Fel ate the conjured bland meat and napped on his side under the safety of the pressurized shelter. Fawn Virgilis used this opportunity to contact Mún and ask him what it was the lion saw that made him stalk shades of empty vacuum.

Mún looked perplexed when his avatar appeared in the AR network at the foot of the slumbering lion. He said, "Fel thought he saw the leopard again ... though it was trapped in his peripheral vision."

"What leopard?" asked Fawn Virgilis. "What do you mean?"

Mún watched the eyes of the people present in the shelter. He tried to block out everyone but Fawn when he said, "Fel and I saved you from the Bœzch on Serengeti Six by chance. You were at the end of a quick dash of a hunt, and he only found you because he was chasing a leopard. He never caught it. The leopard vanished just after it led us to you."

Fawn Virgilis was slow and careful to reply. Though her eyes were hidden behind the headscarf, he could sense the consternation upon her brow. She said, "There were no leopards on Serengeti Six."

Mún faded away, and the lion growled in his sleep.

When next they shared their meal in the Tacit Reality of the Cutlip Nomad, Zallo voiced his concern for the lion's sanity: "Do we follow a mad cat into oblivion, or follow him into madness? Neither will do!"

Fawn was quick to reply: "The Will of Æsirisæ says we follow him no matter where he leads us."

Silence fell upon the table as they were reminded of their slavery, but Montefeltro broke the quiet with a polite cough. He said, "I have news about the structure of the sand we are camped upon."

Zallo sighed, deep and lugubrious. "Tell us Librarian, why is sand so interesting?"

Montefeltro folded his hands upon the table in front of him and said, "Because these are diamonds from the carbon of cremated life forms."

They were lost for words, each of them looking from one to another over their table of peppered steak and asparagus greens. The warmth and delight of the room and meal were suddenly driven from them. Only Bacalhaus broke the silence, saying, "So this is a tomb after all."

Another thirty hours and another hundred kilometers passed beneath their feet, but this time when they came to rest and set up their shelter, there was room for revelry once again, as news came from the *Mare Hypatia* that Alon Elbett was successfully resurrected and waited to join them for the night's meal and conversation. Zallo was especially thrilled, and though his real body remained outside in the beetle armor besieged by the emptiness all around, his mind was now free to sit and lark with his best friend, and this itself was a kind of golden beacon for wanderers lost in the dark.

They waited for Alon in the Cutlip Nomad and raised their glasses when he appeared by the bar. His avatar looked well, though they knew it was no sign as to the condition of his real body. But they knew he was safe — well, safer than they were — and resting in the *Mare Hypatia*. He was dressed in a crushed velvet suit, appearing ever so much like the antiquated fop, and he rushed to each of them, embracing his oldest friend and receiving slaps upon the back by the others.

"How's your real body, Alon? Still much damage?" Vígdís and Védís asked.

Alon took a glass of sherry from the bar and made a great show of his tragedy, walking in broad steps towards the fireplace like the strut of a preening waterfowl. He replied, "Oh, yes! Most of the bones are back in order and whatever got squashed flat on the inside has been fairly reassembled, but it's that damn leg the lion took that's the real trouble. I'm still in the medical crèche, and the fractals are doing their best, but regrowing a whole high grade android limb will take a month at least."

Zallo shook his head and swore, shouting, "That damn cat!"

Alon tut-tutted at his friend. "I warned you. I said it wasn't possible to kill a thing like that, sleeping or not."

"You never did!" gasped Zallo.

"Well, I meant to!"

"Then why did you stand there so long shooting your fool way through the damned monster?"

"Because you asked me to!"

"Dunce of a soft shoe, as always!"

Alon threw his drink into the fire, glass and all. "A bully, that's you by design!"

Zallo stepped towards him, rushing up to the scruffy poet like a gorilla in a gentleman's frock, raising his hand.

Fawn Virgilis shouted at them when they came to within striking range of each other. "Gentlemen!"

They stepped aside and looked to the lone figure who now stood near the Gylfinîr Engineer.

The young man, Mún Rafæl said, "Hello, Alon. Sorry I ate your leg."

Everyone separated, leaving a meter between each of them and filling up the awkward silence with the crackle of the hearth and the shuffling of feet. Though he spoke directly to Alon, all eyes, including the poet's, were on

Zallo. The tension was only broken by the sound of a chortle, genuine and robust, it was the sound of a man who was used to remaining silent about everything. Bacalhaus' laugh was deep and disquieting.

Alon protested, slapping his arms down against his sides and saying again and again, "Why is that funny? Why is that funny? It's not! It's not!"

Bacalhaus continued to laugh, now mostly to himself, and gently guided Alon to the bar, where the publican AI poured them both a dark ale. The blue man said, "Have a drink, poet."

Alon refused the drink and slinked off to a corner booth to sulk on his own. Bacalhaus did not react, but instead held the ale up to Mún without a beat, saying without pretension, "Mún Rafæl, I ask that you join us."

Mún accepted the drink and held it with both his hands, looking down into the foamy head as if he were reading tea leaves for a barfly's fortune. "Thank you," he said.

Fawn Virgilis carefully studied the young man's expression and mannerisms, but she commented on nothing.

Mún could feel her eyes behind the headscarf. He said, somewhat without courage, "Just ... do as you usually do. I can make myself invisible to you if you like."

Zallo rudely snorted, seating himself down into the booth with Alon. "We don't like. Stay where we can see you."

Mún's mood shifted instantly. His eyes tightened against the dim light of the pub, and the line of his eyes darkened. He walked over to the bar, passing Bacalhaus without seeing him, always keeping his eyes on the broad-chested Mitteleuropan, and set his ale down with a sound like the cracking of balsa wood.

From the bar, Mún addressed the men in the booth. His words held a kind of physical weight now, for he used the Will on them. Zallo moaned and gripped the side of the table. Montefeltro rushed up to him, but then stopped short, coming to an invisible barrier. Mún said to Zallo, "I still don't think you understand exactly who is in command here."

Zallo shook, changing his tone, "Please ... stay visible."

Mún released him, but only after he watched his indentured foe shake with the chills and headache that comes from defying the Will of Æsirisæ. The room once again moved into uncomfortable quietude as Fawn Virgilis decided which version of Mún this was before them.

She glided away from the young man and turned her gaze upon Zallo. She said, forcing a change in atmosphere as well as subject, "How are your children, Zallo?"

The big man nodded into his folded hands, exhaling, "All right, I think. I take them riding to keep them occupied. They miss Fjorn. I tell them he'll be with us soon, that he's just hiding from the Bœzch."

He felt the group's mutual skepticism. Zallo added weakly, "He could be."

Mún, in a sudden turn of sadism, once again turned the power of Æsirisæ's Will on the Mitteleuropan hunter, boring the question into him: "How many children are living inside you?"

Zallo was compelled to answer. Shakily, he said through chattering teeth — teeth that chattered in his Quiet Place, and in his real body outside in the beetle armor suit.

"Three," he said. "Saldai, my oldest girl, she's eleven, and her two younger brothers, Ignatz and Ingrim."

"You're a Paternæ?" The question radiated out from Mún, affecting all those Brummagarti within the virtual pub, and they felt heat from his gaze, as if they boiled in a humid summer.

Zallo gripped the sides of the table and answered, "Yes. Fjorn is my oldest boy, he gained a Moartale body only a month before the invasion ... would you ... please ... stop using the Will of Æsirisæ when you ask me questions? I'll answer whatever you want, but the Will ... it's too much!"

He did not stop. The pain worsened. "What are they doing right now?"

"Who?" Zallo shouted.

Mún burned: "Saldai, Ignatz, and Ingrim."

Zallo's head rolled back and forth, and Alon sat rapt with fear for his friend. "We're ... we're having a birthday party!"

"Whose?"

Fawn tapped her metal staff into the wooden floor, and though she was unable to attack Mún, she issued all her strength to show a bit of force, a tantrum of a servant of the Ægeleif. White light flashed forward from her staff, and it was enough to draw away the young man's attention. She pleaded with him, saying, "Mún! please! Remember your Human quality and let this man be!"

Mún's hand gnarled up into claws and his scream went to the ceiling. It was not the scream of a confident man, but that of a panicked animal: "Let him be? Let him be with his little army inside him? To plot and murder me in my sleep? None of you is my friend! I am alone!"

Just then, a second avatar of Mún Ræfæl appeared behind the first and took his hysterical doppelganger by the shoulders, scolding him, "Listen to Fawn Virgilis! Come away from them!"

Melancholy Mún lowered his eyes and replied to confident Mún, "They were plotting ..."

He put his arm around his other self. "No. Just go and sleep. You're tired."

"Always so tired ..." Sad Mún faded away, muttering low, "So tired ..."

This fitter version of the young man released Zallo from the interrogating powers of the Will. The minds of everyone present swam in excitations of violation and disgust from the attack on Zallo, though they only experienced the effects secondhand. Zallo wept, unable to help himself.

Mún outstretched his hands and said to the room, "Pardon my melancholy half. I would erase him if I could."

He put his hand on Zallo's shoulder and saw that he was feverish. "Are you all right?"

Zallo pushed the hand away and laid his head down on the table. "Just leave us alone," he moaned. Somewhere deep within his spine, three children asked their father why he looked so ill as he shared their birthday cake. "Turbulence," he told them.

The young man stepped away from them all, his conscious filled with conflicting emotions that steadied the lion's rise to wakefulness. He was disgusted with himself, embarrassed that his weaker half continued to show itself and make a theater out of his innermost fears, but he was also angry at them for giving him the opportunity to play out the worst aspects of the Will.

"Fawn," he said to the woman in the headscarf. "Fel is waking. He'll be hungry, but he's tired of that vat-grown stuff. Please feed him some of the Bœzch meat we brought along. It will keep him out of mischief."

He left them.

Fel was awake, lying on his stomach, and staring at the people around him with very little interest — until they began to feed him once again. Montefeltro and the Vongallo women helped the lion content himself with some of the remains of the demon, Sayre, which the group brought with them in a blackout box. Five lines of Purcell's *Cold Song* accompanied him yet again.

> *Se-e-e'st thou no-o-ot*
> *How sti-i-iff, how sti-i-iff*
> *And wo-o-on-drous o-o-old*
> *Far far far far un-un-fit*
> *To bear-ear-ear the bi-i-it-ter co-o-o-old*

The glistening raw chunks of bone and flesh were laid upon a tray in front of Fel, and the Brummagarti backed away, seeing that he did not like company with his meal. He lapped and tore at the muscle and fat.

Suddenly he was drawn to his feet.

The aria in his head had again been stopped, but this time the breakage was more forceful, more willful.

Fel paced around in a circle, becoming more and more agitated, stopping now and then to look to the ceiling, always facing one direction. He began to push his head against the side of the shelter.

"What's the matter with him?" Montefeltro asked.

142

Fawn Virgilis ran to the porthole nearest to where the lion paced and squinted into the blackness. The lion growled at nothing, but his fur turned to armor then sealed itself up and once again became an environment suit.

"Helmets up!" Fawn shouted, now behind her own picoscale mask. "I'm going to depressurize the shelter!"

"There's something moving in the dark!" It was Zallo's voice, coming to them over the local Outhernet from his post outside. He showed them a view from his eyes and they all shuddered at the faintly glowing wraith-like figures that rose from the diamond-dead ground. Fifty, then a hundred, then a thousand and on and on, they shimmered up, faint blue-gray centaur phantoms with no distinguishable features, just unfocused silhouettes like starlight blobs in ancient telescopes.

The moment Fawn retracted the shelter and they stepped out among the ghosts, a terrible disembodied voice clamored through their minds, saying, "Envy the Emptiness that Follows Your Doom! Who dares violate the flesh of Tautolo the Hermit's brother? You fight like nebulous cats, hissing gas in cold mouse holes, yet my hounds will find you, have you, and rend you!"

Montefeltro said to his friends over the Outhernet, "The *Mare Hypatia* has a lock on that message. Its being sent via modulated radio waves from the direction we're heading."

"From how far away?" asked Fawn Virgilis.

"She doesn't know."

"How can she not?"

"She says she doesn't."

"*Which* direction?"

Her answer was prepared for her in the form of a distant light, all at once turned on, terrible and alluring in this alien tomb. It was not a welcoming thing. It was a light, but it was a green and bilious beacon that shined far behind a field where a million phantoms pushed themselves up from their mounds of precious sands.

With a silent roar, Fel abandoned his fellow travelers and charged ahead.

Chapter Seven
Ship of Bones

Like the spindle-limbed horse from Dali's *Temptation of Saint Anthony*, the phantoms reared up on their hind stilt legs as the lion bound passed them. Lighted and warmed as he was by two pursuing Charon lamps, he dashed on ahead, a mere firefly through an ocean of suffering blue spirits. But the ghosts did not bar his passage. They did nothing more than silently rattle and gesticulate. They were wholly insubstantial things.

"The light is twelve kilometers away," said Bacalhaus from within his beetle suit. He shared the information from his imaging sensors. "Here is our visual."

All of them saw within their minds a picture of a radiant green cyclopean ship, many kilometers distant, with a single bronze tree for a mast. Sluggishly it pushed itself over the black diamond desert, through and around the centaur ghosts, and onward toward the rushing lion and his twin suns.

"Zallo and Bacalhaus, send it a fire!" commanded Fawn Virgilis. She stood with them at the front of the wayboat, protected on either side by Vígdís and Védís, staff in hand, sword raised to the enemy.

The men said nothing more to the group. They coordinated their target, and together Zallo and the great blue man leveled their two-meter-long fractal-rail riffles towards the base of the ship. They fired, accelerating the charged Mandelbrot geometries of their bullets over the heads of the spirits and into their foe. Red flash after red flash moved out from the muzzles of the weapons and yet none, it seemed, had any effect. The ship and the tree still approached. A new message boomed out to their unprotected brains. The demon, Tautolo, bellowed, "Stretch marks like tribal tattoos! I come to stretch you out over the doom of night and make your spirits thin as copper wire! Deliver up! Surrender! **Give** into temptation! Die and sleep forever! Doom is salvation! Come seek redemption for the murder of my brother! Find forgiveness in oblivion!"

The ground moved, then heaved. Where once stood centaur phantoms there now clawed up from the diamond depths the Bœzch Serfs, each lit by the single blue screaming face at the tip of every horn. The crew watched the face lights come on and on like battalions of grounded lightning bugs, row after row descending into the gloom — their Brummagarti minds calculated them in the thousands. These transparent faces that convulsed at the tips of their black spears were not Human, but were faces like sightless horses, equal parts equine and reptilian. The Serfs' knuckle-dragging arms reached up now, and grasping at the vacuum around them, they peeled off in the direction of the wayboat, heads down, silent screaming horns like lances to the charge.

Fel's connection with Fawn Virgilis' party was lost then. The static cacophony he heard within his consciousness was building in intensity the closer he got to the radiant green ship. An orchestra of violins rose up. Rumbling cellos and hesitant harps moved on. Fel's ticks blocked out the probing static with two more lines of Purcell's aria:

I can sca-a-arce-ly mo-o-ve

Or dra-a-aw my brea-ea-eath

He could see the leopard clearly now. She was faster than him and looked to be unaffected by the two-hundred-degree drop in temperature outside the range of Fel's Charon lamps, but the lion was undaunted in his pursuit. He would catch up with his traditional foe. He would run her down and bear his weight down on her neck and then ... and then what would he do? Did he want to kill her? What was this hunt for? He didn't know. He could not understand anything deeper than the sleepwalker's desire to move his legs and catch his dream, and so catch her he must.

Blurred centaur spirits flowed around him like canyon walls made of labyrinthine waterfalls, and his vision tunneled. The leopard became a golden point of light haloed by the green aura of the approaching ship and tree. Fel felt his body begin to glide. A trance state took him, and meters flew beneath his feet as he charged as effortlessly as wind through dry grass. The lack of sound, the lack of any friction other than gravity or his weight against the diamond desert, everything bobbed before him in somniferous clarity, the leopard leading him on through a lullaby of light.

The ship loomed larger now. He could see it was woven of Bœzch-like bodies, its keel knotted around horns and hands and what passed for bones of every sort. This was a towering death cart thirteen stories in height lit up by an external force field that shimmered down from spore-like sparks released at the top of the gargantuan metal tree. But he did not look at the ship; he only saw the leopard sailing before him — and sail she did, through the green radiant field, tearing open a weak spot that sealed behind her, only coming to full strength again when the lion, too, was passed through. And the leopard was gone.

Fel slid to a stop, crashing against the side of the ship and spinning away upon contact. The thing moved at a halting pace, and there accompanying its motion was a terrible scraping sound, the shifting resonance of heavy metal dragged over glass. There was sound here. There was air and earthly pressure on this side of the green energy dome. And there was still sound within Fel's mind as the static probe cut through his aria again. But his ticks rebounded with the next two lines, a repeat of the last two, with the breath of the countertenor drawn out longer, and his mental firewall was back up, defending the more cognitive areas of the feline's rudimentary brain:

> *I can sca-a-arce-ly mo-o-ve*
> *Or dra-a-aw my brea-ea-ea-eath*

Fel's armor relaxed. He coughed and chuffed the stale air as his esophagus opened, his mouth took in oxygen to fill his lungs, and his life support recharged, ready to seal him off from vacuum when his business was finished here. The Charon lamps did not make it through the barrier. They hovered just outside in the black vacuum, their limited intelligence telling them to stay near the lion as best they could.

This place stank of death. He shook his head to expunge the stench of rot and gathered his sense of direction. No orders or communication came to him from any distant source. He was alone. He relied on his local databanks, and they told him thus: kill the Bœzch. Images flashed in his mind, delivered from his robotic ticks, images of the recorded deaths of Bœzch, killed by him, accompanied by an urge to repeat. But the leopard, where was she in his catalogue of violent recordings? The ticks tried to push her image away. He looked for her despite his programming.

The carnal ship of bone and fossilized flesh scraped along the diamond dirt only as fast as a man could jog — and for Fel this was slow enough to find a foothold on the backs of the dead and climb them as easily as he would stairs. The ship was shaped like a ziggurat: fat at the bottom, smaller at the top. The leopard was somewhere near the top of this thing, he somehow knew; it was like a Pied Piper call, this feeling for the leopard, and he sensed her now as easily as he sensed the Bœzch. So up he went.

The dead embedded in the stairway remained inert; the lion reached the top. Green lights burned from many lanterns set high and hanging upon the limbs of dead Bœzch Generals. There was a large center court and a throne at the base of the metal tree. The throne, too, was made of flesh, marrow, and the osseous matter of aeons-deceased Bœzch. Tautolo, the ten-meter-tall demon, was alone on his seat of death, alone but for his man-sized draughts of red liquid, which surrounded him in hundreds of metal goblets. Fel smelled alcohol, fermentation of something bitter and metallic. Hoses fashioned from petrified intestines unraveled from the sepulchral deck and propped up on enormous wishbones; they dripped a dark clotted liquid into the goblets. The demon did not look at Fel. It drank greedily from the goblet nearest and wiped its tumescent lips on the back of its needle arms. It was the Bœzch horror known as the Hermit, the one other brother to dead Sayre, the Tweedledum to its sibling's Tweedledee. Its bulbous round body was striped in blue and white. Its head was weighted down by the single blue sapphire horn on the back of its skull.

It regarded Fel now with eyes so small that they seemed meant for a normal-sized man, like mere dimples on its face.

"Oh. It's you again," said foul Tautolo in blubbering gasps that imitated the sound of meat crushed underfoot. "You're here for me now, you're here for *me*? Me!" The horror stood upright upon its throne, wobbling drunken on elephantine legs and tiny arrowhead feet. "So you found my black fortress, little cat, my refuge away from temptation. You couldn't leave me out here to settle. You couldn't let me wallow in the dark and let me drink. So be it! I will ferment your blood, and in your doom you will be forgiven! COME!"

The firewall aria exploded within his frontal lobe and the probing fingers of modulated static waves lunged for all that he was inside. Fel's ticks fought back with another two lines, slamming the invisible gate shut with the slow, arrested rumble of cellos:

> *Let me let me let me*
> *Free-ee-eeze ag-ai-ai-ain*

Fel made ready to pounce, but the demon was ever so fast. To the lion's astonishment, he was suddenly plucked into the air by nothing whatsoever. This horror had the spell of transformation, just like his Bœzch Generals, and Fel began to feel the familiar spin.

"Not so easy to kill a foe who does not make a hole in the ground to hide himself away, eh, little cat?" The horror sensed an air about the lion just then, and peered closer, wondering what was so remarkable about this predator, that he should be able to track his prey through the dead vacuum of space. "What have you in here?"

It had been many months since Fel first felt the cold fingertips of the Bœzch penetrating his psyche, and though he could not think in the abstract, the experience impressed him with a near hereditary fear. The aria fought on:

Let me let me let me
Free-ee-eeze ag-ai-ai-ain

His two hearts leapt in his chest. Picoscale repair fractals reacted to the alarm like antibodies react to allergens, and the lion heaved and itched all over. The invisible worm of a Bœzch probe settled into his brain, seeking out the peculiarities there. Like a detective finding a secret room behind a bookcase, the horror responded to a discovery therein: "Aha! You're one of the family!"

The lion was tossed away, bouncing and sliding through the maze of goblets, nearly flying off the side of the ship and out into vacuum. His claws caught onto the chest cavities of several dead Bœzch used as deck wood and he righted himself, growling and staring down his enemy. He leapt at the thing called Tautolo once again, and again he was bounced away by an invisible barrier.

"Hünde's little brother!" laughed the horror, its arms held high. "Little Mún, don't you see my face and find a memory there? I am your brother's dear old friend, Taum. So this is why you've come? To finally be a part of our gang? Well, Hünde is much the same as before. As Wülvogarti he is even more than before, more brutal and narcissistic — and for that we love him, for that we hate him. He might keep you as a pet, after he robs you of your spirit. Would you like that? Would I care if you did? Let's have you again, o' Fel-moon cat."

Fel flew into the demon's arms once again, and each time this happened he felt as if his mind itself that was lifted. The invisible fingers slid in again. Tautolo said, "I should repair you before I take you to Hünde. You have something trapped in there that should be rung out."

No! Whether it was the ticks protesting or Mún himself, the aria tried one last revolution, delivering the final line, and a complex waveform of musical pásscodes knocked the probing fingers away:

Let me let me
Free-ee-eeze ag-ai-ai-ain to dea-eath
Let me let me let me
Freeze agaaaiiin to deeeaaaaath

But it was not enough. The aria was out of tricks, and the gates to Felmún's shared cognizance were wide open.

A scene drifted into view. Two children, Mún Rafæl and Luti Casanova, sat in black attire at the foot of long brick steps leading to a dry stone temple. It was a dour, single story temple of the Ærdent sect, whose members believed in the literal divinity of Ægeleif. They refused to acknowledge that the Ægeleif themselves were Human creations and insisted that they must be angels from outside our universe.

To the Ærdents, technology greater than that of agrarian society was an affront to the angels, and machines infused a devilish pride into people that led them to lie about the Ægeleif, pretending their angelic masters were actually products of Human ingenuity. This belief kindled a kind of convenient cognitive dissonance at its core: their standards did not stop them from using Gripperships to colonize other worlds in the universe. They spread out among the far places of the Milky Way. So here they were now, having traveled all the many hundreds of lightyears through the Ægeleif Gripper Gates only to be nearly wiped out on a verdant satellite-planet circling too close to a giant world that was twenty times the mass of earth.

Tenniel's Garden was at first a very pleasant place. A satellite to the larger, molten Alice, Tenniel's Garden was a Mars-sized green and blue garden, abundant with rolling hills, sweet-water rivers, and storybook fruit trees big enough for shade and climbing, small enough to provide a clear view to this world of green pastures. The calamity came just days after Mún's ninth birthday. Alice, it turned out, had a temper, and when she saw fit to show her true colors, she raged and exploded in the largest eruption of a single volcano ever recorded in the nine thousand worlds of Windsor Temporality. But this event was not natural to Alice for, stranger still, the reason for her foul mood was due to a birth; when an Ægeleif entity settles within a system's gas giant, they impregnate the next most massive object in system with their offspring. There were three gas giants in Tenniel's system, but for reasons unknown, it was rocky, volcanic Alice that had taken the ethereal seed of the Ægeleif. This was a rare event, what was known as a blind birth. Thus, when the nativity of the new entity on Alice burst into being, shimmering Æthereal ejecta from her birth fired from the surface of Alice and flew so high and so fast that it drew up past her atmosphere and, like a spotlight of doom, enveloped the exact spot on Tenniel's Garden where the Ærdents made their home.

Once the explosion was sighted, it was already too late. Few of the Ærdent colonists had any understanding of what they were looking at. Regardless, what could they do? The fastest anyone could travel was only as fast as their beasts of burden; they had no shelters capable of shielding out radiation, let alone the strange matter of an Ægeleif birth. Their only outside communication with the rest of Humanity beyond their little star system was with their system's resident Ægeleif Entity, Uedolpha, who lived four AU away. She only came down from her gas giant perch every three years, during the Harvest of Gylfinæ.

As young Mún sat hand in hand with little Luti on the steps leading to the temple, he wondered how many more of his friends and family would die before Harvest in two months. Their meager colony of thirty thousand Ærdents had fallen in half in just the last two weeks. This funeral was for his brother, Paölo.

No one blamed Mún for Paölo's murder — children were innocent, and their mother was too destroyed by guilt and grief to speak out. Yet there could be no forgiveness from Hünde. He cared little for Paölo when he was alive, but that was not the point. Forever seeking reasons to act out his brutality, to feel free from restraint of any kind, Hünde cherished Mún's culpability in their brother's death.

Mún was not allowed at the funeral. Luti came down from the temple and sat with him for a time. Now she took his hand and led him away, back to the ruined rooftops and blackened sett stones of their once beautiful village. Together they went into the basement of the Casanova family's home and fit a preserved reel into a replica of an ancient film projector. They chose the film from a collection of favorite nature documentaries, a ten-year-old copy of a nine-thousand-year-old recording;

holding their hands over their eyes, by chance they touched the canister marked *LEOPARD: AGENT OF DARKNESS* together. They sat upon wooden benches, and Mún aimed the projector at the white painted wall while Luti took the batteries and the solar cells down from the little window on high. They closed the door and shuttered the window just as the beginning of the movie commenced. Light from the projector flickered through film, casting the moving images against painted whiteboards while the soundtrack played separately on a tape and reel machine.

It began in darkness to the sound of crickets and tribal drums. Slowly, a violet-gray image of a great spotted cat appeared through the grass. Two voices spoke: one in an Olde Sol African tongue, the other in an ancient form of Windsor Ing'Lesh:

> *Gentle hunter*
> *His tail plays on the ground*
> *While he crushes the skull.*

> *Beautiful death*
> *Who puts on a spotted robe*
> *When he goes to his victim.*

> *Playful killer*
> *Whose loving embrace*
> *Splits the antelope's heart.*

An old white man sat amongst the trees in the night and told the story of the Leopard. Luti and Mún watched this with shoulders and heads touching, forgetting for a moment the calamity of living, wondering what it would be like to just move through every somniferous eventide hereafter prowling like animals, bereft of any concerns outside immediate comfort or fleeting rudimentary desire. This wish Mún kept secret within him, and he was amused and delighted years later when Luti admitted that she, too, wanted nothing more than to cease cognition and go into a forest as a lazy freeborn monarch.

The cellar door came open with a bang. Hünde marched into the basement followed by two of his gang, Taum and Saum Pasquale, the fat brothers of the local brewer. Mún recoiled this time, stricken as he was by the death of Paölo — he wanted only to be left in peace. His screams were shrill, and they overpowered the sounds of Luti's protests and the taunts from the gang. They called him a murderer, a betrayer of family. They kicked him and dragged him to the floor, trying to put a rope around his neck, but all Mún did was weep and scream, "None of you was ever my friend!" It was Luti who savaged Hünde this time, slashing his right eyelid with her nails. The gang of three ran off then, shouting that Luti had gone mad. She *had* gone mad, and she was more glad for it than she had ever been of anything in her life. But Mún was finally broken. He had no spirit left in him. He huddled under the projector table and wept and wept.

Cold fingers reached around him then. This was not Luti, for the memory of the scene was fading into nebulous haze, and now the fingers belonged to the arm of Tautolo the demon horror. "There he is. There is poor sad, Mún. What a shame to leave him wallowing like a pig when all he ever wanted was to be a lion. Come to me, little piglet. Weep into me!"

Sad Mún looked up once, with two glistening rivers of remorse down his cheeks, his lips quivering in fear and disgust for himself — and then he twisted into colors, and then he was stardust, and then he was gone. The lion gasped between the fingers of the horror, and he felt a great weight lift from within him. A chorus of levity sang out from his lighted spirit. No more did he feel the burden of too many shadows within himself. He chuffed and then roared in delight. This startled Tautolo, who expected the lion to fall into a passive state. He threw Fel to the floor, unsure of what had gone awry. But Fel was in the air again only a second later, this time propelled by his animal cunning. He reached the throat of the ten-meter Tweedledum thing and toppled it with the force of his total weight and inertia. The floor of bones and flesh bounced with the fall. Goblets of dark liquid spilled, and the many liters of fermented blood flowed over the sides of the necropolis in an ichorous downpour. Tautolo thrashed and screamed for mercy upon the blighted deck, but Fel held on, crushing and mulching the demon's throat with his machine jaws until it screamed no more, until it thrashed no more.

At that moment the connection between the mind of the lion and his enemy was severed. As the final spark of cognition left the demon, a history in images — not the demon's own history, but one that he himself had learned — snapped between Tautolo and Fel. Fel saw sightless horse-headed centaurs congregating in the millions around the interior of a cavernous cathedral — the interior of the Ouroboros Object. They worked to construct the ceiling of this place in a fevered trance. Fel saw a dark planet move through the Ouroboros ring and vanish. He saw the centaur men fall into stardust — their payment for plotting and scheming and murdering for their masters — while their masters, the Bœzch, saw their planet freeze in the sunless space of their new domain, here in the Hæl System. This meant nothing to Fel the lion. He was giddy without Human sadness to weigh him down. He was remorseless and heartless and merry, even at the sight of genocide.

When Tautolo was dead and his blood flowed along with the intoxicating current of the toppled goblets, Fel stood upon the body and listened to the strange creaking murmurs that now grew louder and louder. As the sound rose in volume it also rose in urgency, becoming a sound like water dropped in a well. More fascinated than frightened, Fel looked for the source of the racket. His eyes brought him to the great metal tree that loomed high over the ship, and for the first time he saw that beneath its leafless branches, upon the great trunk of the tree, the figure of a woman was imbedded therein. Like a maiden of a ship's foremast, her arms were stretched behind her, her bosom thrust forward, her legs wrapping into the Insular metalwork of the surrounding structure. A giantess, she was five meters in length. Her face and body were of the same vivid verdigris coloration and texture of the tree, and though she was fine and lovely beyond simple Human beauty, her expression was both enigmatic and frightful. When the white light began to grow around her brow and cheeks, that was when the lion noticed the sound of swift water was coming directly from her.

The lion stepped back a pace just as the giantess started to shimmer from head to foot, her radiance blinding in the sullen green pitch of the ship, and soon she was a beacon, a white bipedal sun now capable of independent motion. The sound diminished in an instant when the atmosphere left the ship. In the silence of the moment, Fel did not notice the explosive decompression or that his fur had once again became an environment suit. He was not blown from the crumbling ship of bones but was left fixed in place by whatever power the giantess held over him. She stared down at him with eyes full of warmth, though he was quickly freezing to death without his Charon lamps. They were the eyes of the universe, awash with the stars of a billion galaxies, every flutter of her sad lids like the setting of an aeon. Her gaze penetrated not only his own eyes but his poor abused mind, that gray bit of matter that was again and again remade, divided and undivided, dashed and lost and found again. Here she said to his mind in a voice as commanding as an orchestra, as slow and precise as a watchmaker, as frolicsome as a toy piano, "Your footfalls are poetry enough for me, little lion. Bend through my Gripper Gate now, lest you die discharged too soon of your duty." It was a voice that he clearly recognized from out of time. It had come to him as a tiny light once before, far back when he was a boy, frightened and paralyzed in darkness. How was it here now?

She stepped down from the tree. All was black but for her, the only radiant object in every stretch of place or time. Fel stood before her, in love, suspended in blackness, warmed by her universal brightness. She held her hands before her white, naked belly, and where she would have had a navel had she been truly Human, a vortex grew instead. She moved her hands around the edges of the whirlpool of light, as if turning a great wheel. The vortex grew wider and brighter still until it was a perfect circle of brilliance from her throat to her ankles.

"Follow her, Felmún."

The leopard appeared now, a tiny yellow dot in the center of the wheel of light, running away, always running into an infinite horizon. This time he caught a brief glimpse of her eyes, wet peridot stones reflecting the will of this gentle hunter: the will to follow the beautiful death to the garden of playful killers. He was in love for a second time that day.

Fel charged in after her, and the white gate closed behind him.

Chapter Eight
The Garden of Hearths and Lights

The grass was cool and pleasant to touch.

The light through the tunnel prepared his eyes for the glory of dawn. His robot ticks knew he now walked under a false daylight. They looked to the ceiling where cumulus clouds swirled and recorded the distance between the ground and the colony-grade Charon lamps as two kilometers. They did not know which colony it was that they had been sent to, and their transponders bleated silently in simple radio wavelengths while they simultaneously searched for this world's Etherealon Core spirit. All was quiet. Only the world of wind and forests and animals opened their hearts to them and sang aloud.

At night, the gentle balls of light dimmed and illuminated the forest like a succession of moons lined up one after the other until they formed parallel stripes of radiant lines. The shape and smell of this place brought to his mind brief remembrances of his home in the Long Savanna, but these distant phantoms were fleeting and intelligible; his eyes were transfixed on the light and how it played through the leaves of unrecognizable trees.

On most days, the lion walked alone and happy through the misted colors of red and green. He made his home between trees as wide as houses, around the colossal roots of the red giant sequoias whose top branches reached sixty meters towards the vaulted cloudscape. He sunned himself on rocky outcrops in emerald prairies where the trees were thinnest and hunted elk in dense burrows of river ferns, orange and black-spotted tiger lilies, and wide-leaf trilliums. He found a beach by a river that was as wide as a sea, drank the fresh water, saw the seals who reclined on the powdery sand and frightened them by charging and breaking away, chuff-laughing to himself as he trot off, up the slope and back to the woods.

Only a month had passed since Fel transported to this land, and in that short time he easily established himself as king of this forest, for there was none who could challenge him. There was no sign of the Bœzch. He may not have fully understood it, but Fel knew the sensation of freedom that came with power, and this was enough for a lion to contemplate on. For him, contemplation was not a rumination on abstract concepts like worry for the future or wistful longing. His concerns were only for his immediate surroundings, for the cool prairie grass he crouched in when he stalked black-tailed deer, for the strength of his voice when he roared to bald eagles high over gray shale cliffs, for his conquests when he warned away grizzly bears from his places of rest. Only his robotic ticks analyzed his environments or tried to discern location or probability of future dangers.

Fel's ticks moved with him, but they examined everything with caution while the lion padded freely and without care. Their halting aria, *The Cold Song*, had been defeated, line-by-line, along with their melancholy *Una Furtiva Lagrima*. Thus Fel's ticks collected their resources and judged the probability of their next defeat. They decided more repetitiveness with greater complexity over time was required to fully construct a new and better wall around the lion's mind, and so they settled on the bassoons, piccolos, flutes, and oboes of Maurice Ravel's seminal work of dementia: the thirteen-and-a-half-minute and three-hundred-and-forty-bar *Boléro*. The snare drum started up, ever so quietly, and the lion went about his play.

On the first night of *Boléro*, Fel slept in an open grove, where the dim blue-white Charon lamps shown down like queues of full and gibbous moons. Their pearl-strung lights soothed him as the music tiptoed up its unrelenting tempo, pushing him into dreams of other moons, of other lights. "Full moon, full moon," the words draped past his inner ear, becoming "Felmún" and spoken through vice and hate; it came to him like an echo of another night. On and on, in darkness he plunged. He saw himself running through the dark of the Ouroboros Object, the leopard shepherding him through the rising centaur specters. But this time he did not follow himself all the way to the sickly radiant ship at the end of the trail. This time, his eyes lingered back, disembodied from himself or reality, where they flowed to the crew he abandoned.

He saw them fall back upon their vehicle, at first slowly, as if in disbelief. The bright G Shelter was fully retracted, and with Montefeltro at the helm of the wayboat, they lifted in silence, Zallo and Bacalhaus each leaning their beetle suits out the open bay doors on both the port and starboard sides while Fawn and her Gird guard peered from behind them.

"What do we do? There're too many!" one of the Vongallo sisters shouted.

Zallo replied, "Let the lion go! We should fall back to the *Mare Hypatia*!"

Below them, they saw the great wave of horns crash together and circle beneath their wayboat, merging in step, becoming a churning tide of malice and collecting like a whirlpool beneath their craft. In the transparent cockpit at the fore of the craft, Montefeltro peered through his campsuit's oblate spheroid helmet with visible fright at the scene underneath, and yet he gave into an inner compulsion to pursue the great cat that vanished with his warming lights into the unknown black. He pushed the controls forward, a radiant network of avionics visible only in augmented reality, and as he did so the small dizzy feeling that crept along his temples lessened.

Zallo shouted again, "Monte, it's no good following him! He's gone! Take us back to the ship!"

He had to admit, the old mercenary made sense. Why should he press on and follow the lion into doom? He told himself that it was the pain of the Will of Æsirisæ that drove him to the lion — but there was no wisdom in trailing one's master into death. Surely, the enslaving pásscode would understand the logic of turning away. He would give into Zallo's bluster, and he told himself out loud that this was best for Manticore Project, as if audibly saying it would convince the program within his brain, just as one prays to their God to convince Him that sin is not what it is. But the Will of Æsirisæ was not a stupid god. The programming was specific in its mission to hold the enslaved true to their master. The dizziness in Montefeltro's temples began the moment he turned the wayboat slightly to starboard.

He was alone in the pressurized cockpit, separated from the rest of his group by a meter of bulkhead, and yet Fawn Virgilis sensed his distress even before the craft began to lurch. "Monte!" she screamed in his mind. "Don't listen to Zallo! Follow Fel or the Will of Æsirisæ will shut you —"

The wayboat's limited AI tried to correct Montefeltro's course, engaging safety systems that would redirect the craft from the ground, but in his delirious state of mind, the Librarian took this to believe that the vehicle was out of control. He fought the Augmented Reality status boards, plunging the wayboat again to the starboard just as it had corrected itself, but now diving the ship in such a fashion that, at this close proximity to the ground, the ship's AI could no longer compensate. Down the ship plunged, striking the gathered Bœzch Serfs below and flinging them from their feet like a steel dart into a field of toy soldiers. The Charon lamps followed the wayboat down, providing the only illumination to the disaster while the ship rolled and crumpled until sleeping Fel pushed back from the dream and into a black abyss. He woke with a roar and a whimper.

Fel was up early the next day, forgetting his dream, living through the pang of a doubt he could not comprehend. He sought to alleviate his distress without understanding why. He left the glade and hunted in the golden morning air. He moved with no clear purpose or direction. He slept in daylight, in caves or under rocky overhangs when the rains came, or when he had fed himself to bursting. After the dream of the wayboat crash, he dreamed of nothing. He sprang alert at hours before dawn to the sounds of the spotted owls waking up to take flight with him. His meandering path moved in circles between forest, prairie, and riverside sands. River otters gave him great joy as he watched them play in mirthful acrobatic patterns. Mountain lions gave him a wide berth upon the open prairie lanes, and to this his chest swelled with a tremendous pride. Bats and flying squirrels ran his attention span in circles, causing him to play at ghosts in the heavy woodland, leaping from under the towering branches, chuffing and roaring in anticipation for little things thrillingly out of reach.

Bassoons and oboes rose into cymbals and trombones. He was at home.

In the fourth month of his wanderings, and nine-thousandth repeat of *Boléro*, he found himself at the foot of a tall mountain that stretched up through the ever-present clouds, cresting at only a quarter of a kilometer away from the nearest Charon lamp. The lamp directed its heat away from the mountaintop, and so the misted peak was snowcapped from as far as halfway down the precipice. Fel followed a rabbit to a summit just below the snow, and from there he stopped at the edge of a flat bluff. It was early morning. Sparrows moved together through the web-work of mists, darting and vanishing under cover, only to rise together in undulating formations. A cumulous wall of fog drifted past him, at once blocking the view to the forest below and enveloping him at the edge of the cliff. He sat on his haunches and waited in the world of white, his breaths curling out from his dark lips in twirling exhalations of calm. He dozed briefly, rocking slightly on his feet, only to be perturbed awake by a sudden clearing in the clouds. All at once he could see everything. To his left was the grand green prairie with its herds of buffalo and the wall at the end of this colony, but to his right, beyond the great forests and river, there was a sea with a network of islands and bays, another river and another prairie, then a gray wetland and black marshland and on and on, disappearing in a worming brume like the haze of a grasping blue sky made of nebulous fingertips.

Like Long Savanna, this was a toroidal colony. The ceiling of Charon lamps and transparent metal curved up and away in an inverted horizon. Fel's ticks could tell this colony held the same circumference as Long Savanna: nineteen hundred kilometers. It was much, much wider than Long Savanna, however. While Fel's original colony of kopjes and African plains spread a width of a hundred impressive kilometers, creating an area of one hundred and ninety thousand square kilometers, his ticks understood this new colony as being ninety colonies connected at every hub, end-to-end, their port and starboard walls opened to their neighbors. This was a small continent: a super colony, a spinning wheel of life nineteen hundred kilometers in circumference and nine hundred kilometers in width. Fel's ticks identified it as Super Series Colony Barbary Combine.

As he watched the sights unfurl below him, the great curtains of mist drew back so that he may see all of his kingdom. He sat neither impressed nor ambivalent, but neutral to his senses. Only the darting birds over the forest and specks of moving animals down on the prairie floor were of interest to him. When smoke was visible from the next prairie over, Fel's robotic ticks zoomed in using the lion's eyes as their lens. Fel immediately shook his head to reclaim his eyesight. The ticks analyzed the particles of the smoke and decided it was wood burning — a controlled blaze, possibly from a stove, fireplace, or campfire, considering the limited size of the plume. Fel decided he would roll in a sunbeam. This was followed by a nap on the side of the cliff while his ticks plotted to steer him toward the direction of the fire. They were unsuccessful, and he loped off downhill after he lost a raccoon up a tree. With frustration mounting amongst his ticks, their chatter whirled between themselves, forming a singular point, a singular suggestion that gained order amongst them in the same way disparate weather forms into a tornado. Their complaint whirring around them, the ticks cried out how they wished the lion would obey, and with no answer present, their call drifted, pricking up the ears of another nearby. Black spots ripped over golden muscles. She walked down from the heavens to meet him again.

That night he dreamed for the first time in many months. In his dreamscape he moved under so many stars his heart leapt with fear when he realized he trod upon the backbone of the heavens. Like old Bacalhaus, he swam the ocean of galaxies and nebulae, spinning in place under and over the cosmos, a silent spectator in a theater of color, fires near and far, pin lights and pinwheels of ethereal matter, all whirling about him on a stage that orbited its audience of one. A star approached him, burning yellow and bright — it leapt from galaxy to galaxy, hiding in clouds of cometary objects and lighting them up like ripples of light over pools of sequin dresses. The star approached, taking the form of a cat then bristling with spots, and so the leopard was at his feet again.

Fel did not give chase this time. The two of them came close, almost touching noses, and he looked into her clear green eyes and saw himself sitting by her side. Together they floated down onto the backs of the elephant clouds. Together they rested arm in arm like old friends and put their heads down to look out over the world. Below them they saw a house at the edge of a prairie. It was a twisted craftsman-style house, green wood and dark gray gables, four rock corners topped with columns painted red, everything sloped and bent in a cartoonish manner. It remained pleasant, despite its malformed outline, because of the cheery rock fireplace from which there poured curls of white smoke into the mint blue sky. Fel looked at this and felt a strange compulsion rise. He turned to the leopard, as if to ask what it all meant, but she was gone. He stood up, turning about in circles in quiet panic, whimpering in a manner uncommon to his species. He looked down again at the little house. She was there, standing on the steps to the front porch. He could not reach her from his elephant cloud, and so he roared in frustration.

It was then that he noticed that he was listening to *Boléro*. This was in part due to the sight of the leopard matching up with the climax of the musical composition. As the famous three-hundred-and-twenty-sixth bar was reached and the melody whirled past the escalating trumpets and snare drums into a sudden frenzy of trombones and cymbals, that was when she appeared to him. Daunting *Boléro*: it was an obsessive piece, written by Ravel after he suffered a blow to the head and eventually succumbed to the horrendous maladies associated with aphasia and frontotemporal dementia. Repetitiveness was the lion's curse as well, repetitiveness in daily action, repetitiveness in nightly dreaming, repetitiveness in loss of cognition, a sudden rise again into intelligence, and a just as sudden loss of mental facilities. Like a sufferer of dementia, he, too, continuously lost some part of himself here and there as time wore on, little bits of him ripping away as horrors and dreamers and programming hacked away at all that once was Mún Rafæl. Thus, as he noticed that he was listening to *Boléro*, so, too, did he forget it. Like an old woman who is honestly surprised to see you, though you've been there in the room with her the whole time, she turns around, and is surprised to see you again; every minute was a dream that astonished the lion and every dream was a collection of blossoming astonishments held up and heaped upon his shoulders until he forgot the weight of the world and went looking for another burden.

When Fel was awake, he found *Boléro* had abandoned him. All was quiet. He finished eating the stag killed the day prior and then he left the great redwood hollow he used as a den. He trotted upon pine needles and sniffed the air under the blanket of cathedral branches. His ticks helped him by stimulating his sense organs, feeding him the image of the smoke as seen from a distance and combining it with the very faint smell of burning wood that drifted in the afternoon air. This, too, was an illusion projected by his ticks, but their programmed desire to make the lion follow any lead that could bring defeat to his enemies was real enough. The simple logic of the ticks stated that smoke equalled Human-made fire, since Bœzch had no use for hearths or warm lights, and Humans should either be rescued or protected from Bœzch — also, Bœzch would detect Humans who make fire and eventually appear to devour them. It was reasonable, then, that the lion should move towards the direction of the fire. Fel was unaware of any puzzles that needed solving. Real smoke or not, he followed his nose.

When he set out from the great redwoods it was noon, but by the time he walked to the end of the river and out to the sea, the Charon lamps overhead were dimming into evening, and Fel found himself pacing the shore, desperate to cross a hundred kilometers of water. Frustrated, he rested a while. There he saw a pod of blue dolphins leaping out of reach in a nearby cove. They were many ages and sizes, and he lost track of their numbers, for often one vanished beneath the water and was replaced by two others. He watched them and felt giddy at their joy. They did not avoid or attack him; instead they seemed to sense something unusual about him, and forming a playful circle under the reef where Fel watched. One after the other, they swam away from him and returned again, until he followed their path with his eyes. After several turns at this, Fel finally noticed a thin sliver of white that glinted on the surface about two hundred meters down the shore. He roared to the distant dolphins, intuitively releasing a sensor package upon the waves. When the sound returned, he stood suddenly, surprised at the image that was delivered back to him: he detected a bridge of land at the end point of the dolphins' circle. Fel, completely against his animal nature, for a very brief moment, seemed to feel something like gratitude swell within his breast.

The lion stepped from the top of the rocky cove and down onto the wet sand. After trotting over the pebble-and-shell-littered beach to the bridge, he found it to be a thin shoal where dead seaweed and tiny crabs commingled in a miniature ecosystem. The waters on either side kept a low tide as mitigated by the spin of the colony. He did not linger here but quickly crossed by breaking into a jog.

Twelve hours later it was morning again, and he was now in the high grass of the brackish estuary on the other side of the sea. He found a dry spot in the high riparian grass and rolled back and forth for a bit, listening to the sound of the seagulls fighting over fallen fish, the blue electric lines that coursed along his biomechanical hide reverberating to their squalled chirps. He was tired. He was hungry, too, though he was just too satisfied in the spongy grass to do anything about it. On his back, belly to the sky and paws dangling limply over his head, he dozed and snored so loudly that the gulls scattered, continuing their argument over the water and far out of reach of the sleeping monster on the shore.

Up, commanded his ticks. *Time is wasting. Get up and continue the journey.* He defied them, pleasing himself with his immobility, laughing at whatever tried to turn him over. As before, the ticks' frustration grew, reached out to the world around them, complaining to anyone who would listen. As before, golden ears somewhere nearby pricked up and answered the call.

When yellow feet trotted up to his side, he blinked into wakefulness and stared into the amber ale eyes that scrutinized him. He flipped over onto his feet slowly, confused but for a moment, though some part of him realizing he exposed his soft underside to this wild world of claws and beaks and teeth. Stepping back from the leopard, he stopped and peered around her, seeking the understanding he could not have: the question a sapient being would speak aloud about dreams and wondering if one were awake. She did not run from him this time, but turned slowly, always watching him, and walked on at a leisurely pace through the misted grass towards the prairie beyond the marshlands.

He remained cautious, moving always behind her through the saltmarsh, never treading near enough to come up alongside. The cordgrass was high and grew in reedy clumps upon irregular tufts of land and brackish pools of water. He had some difficulty following. She did not always move through open spaces, but often glided like a phantom through the greenery as if she were more a ghost of his mind than of the world. As she led him by the reins of his animal curiosity, the Charon lamps overhead hung like brightening Christmas lights, moving morning into the six O'clock hour, saturating the cool gray false dawn until a perfect Maya blue haze was woven into a playground for thrush, robins, and stellar jays. Fel was startled once. The leopard, having raised her head to eclipse the many lights, grew faint all along her body, and for a moment it was as if the dragonflies that followed them now rushed through her, and soon he was following a cloud of little yellow eyes, and their little black wings were the spots of the leopard's coat, and then she was alight with a hundred beating wings. She did not dissipate with the leaving of the dragonflies, but Fel had grown so distracted by the sight that he fell into the water twice, disturbing tadpoles and turtles.

He did not notice they were moving higher, away from the yellow-green cordgrass and onto the long emerald waves of the prairie. When they reached the property line of the strange crooked house, the smell of logs burning and potatoes boiling roused only part of his senses, but he was still mostly oblivious to the world. He only saw that she had left him once again. Fel sounded out in exasperation. He had little capacity to cry out in frustration like a Human or use the words his Human half would have if a man still lingered inside him. Frustration needed no words to be expressed. It only needed a voice. So he roared to the sky until the sound of his voice became a clear and desperate shout, until he sighed and chomped down on nothing.

Footsteps then: from within the house a scurrying of little feet on wood planks could be heard. The red oak door above the steps to the porch opened with a torpid creaking. Fel inclined his head to the right in a quizzical manner, and he was soon staring at a face of a little man, then two faces, and they were blinking at him, one standing over the other, keeping their bodies protected by the length of the heavy door.

They were not Human, but nor were they Bœzch. Slowly they stepped out, the first following the second and clinging to the coattails of his friend until the other gently shoved him off. They stood barely taller than a meter each in identical suits of black brocade cape jackets. Their figures were petite, their necks as tiny as bamboo sticks, but their blue-white heads were ovoid and elfish, inclining their features towards the innocent, childish, and beautiful. They had no visible ears. Their eyes were large and white with small violet dots for pupils. They wriggled their pinkish nostrils like rabbits and grimaced towards the lion with small mouths in complex but awkward expressions. In unison, they scratched the wiry shocks of ice blue hair at the tops of their wizened heads, looked at one another, looked at Fel, and then finally nodded to one another as if confirming some subvocal suggestion between them. The first one out the door touched a button on his sleeve, a warning bell sounded somewhere in the house, and Fel was surprised to find himself contained under the semi-opaque barrier of an anti-Casimir field. He paced within the field, occasionally swatting at the barrier, testing its strength, growling to himself, though the two little men did not react to his anger this time.

They stepped down from the porch, and the shorter of the two said to his friend, "Well would you look at that, Hvitt?"

"I'm looking at it, Rost," replied the taller companion.

The nearer they came to the grass where the lion protested his confinement, the calmer the great black cat became. There was something about them, a detached sense of friendship. They shared his feelings, but they were able to articulate themselves where he could only grumble.

The one called Hvitt raised his arms and cheered then, startling Fel into a more unpleasant mood. Hvitt shouted, "He actually made it!"

"In the actual!" Rost exclaimed.

Fel roared again, this time much louder, more admonishing and territorial. The two little men backed up a pace.

"Careful!" said Rost. "Not so close now. He'll still eat us up."

Hvitt nodded and swallowed. "Right."

Rost then pressed another button above his long shirtsleeve and another anti-Casimir force field sprang up around the two of them. "How's that?" he asked.

"Much the better, thank you."

Hvitt stepped up to the place where their barriers almost touched and tried to peer into the whites of the lion's eyes. He cupped his hands over his mouth and yelled, "Mister Rafæl, are you in there? You found us! It's Hvitt and Rost. Remember? Hello? Hello?"

Hvitt looked to Rost, who was now holding up a small device in front of the lion. Holographic images and symbols hovered above the dumbbell-shaped machine. Rost shook his head as he watched the data flow. "Nothing?" inquired Hvitt, squinting over his friend's shoulder.

Rost tsk-tsked and said, "Not even a speck in his AR Outhernet."

"Then how did he get here?"

"Well, he pásscoded a program for that."

"Certainly," said Hvitt, "but he didn't come by the *Mare Hypatia*. We would have got a warning from one of the spaceports."

Rost held up a pale blue finger, saying, "Here we go. Located his ticks. They're still working perfectly. I'll pàssload his journey."

Hvitt dug in his front pockets until he found what looked like a bottle cap. He placed the device upon his own forehead where it stuck and began to issue small points of light moving counterclockwise around the circumference of the "cap." "You want to replay it in Tacit?" he asked.

Rost bared his teeth, making a sour expression exactly as if he had bitten a lime. "Ooooo ... I suppose that's the fastest method."

Hvitt talked mostly to the air and rarely addressed his friend by looking him in the face. He scratched his elven cheeks now and watched a cloud unravel, "Do we have time for something slower and less ... feely?"

Rost, too, had an odd way of conducting himself. He often stood with his arms apart, as if he were afraid to touch himself. As he mused aloud this time, his arms slowly extended farther until he looked to be hugging an invisible globe. With trepidation he coughed, saying, "Dunno. What if he's trailing a googolplex of Bœzch behind him?"

"Are there that many?"

"Dear, oh dear, I should hope not!" Rost croaked.

"But they don't seem to care about Tishbyts."

"They adapt. Remember the Brummagarti."

"Right," said Hvitt. "Let's have it."

Rost placed his own bottle-cap-like object upon his forehead and pressed a holographic button upon the dumbbell-shaped device in his hands. They shrieked together as Tacit Reality waveforms dumped millions of Outherbits of sensory information into their brains. These two were not accustomed to interacting with the virtual. It was in their nature to despise closeness with other sentients, and the Tacit experience was a social misfit's nightmare. Though they were touched for only a moment by the sights and sounds and emotions experienced by the lion through the many, many months since last his comrades saw him, it was enough to send Rost to his knees heaving and wrenching and Hvitt clawing at the bottle cap input device. Like a cat watching a bird from a window, Fel stopped growling and roaring long enough to be fascinated by the spasms of the strange little men.

"Oh, my, my, my. That's quite the drama," gasped Rost, wiping his mouth and returning to his feet.

Hvitt wiped the tears from his eyes. He muttered, "Quite a tragedy." Then he finally brought his eyes down from the sky and looked at his friend, saying, "Who do you suppose the giant woman was at the end there?"

Rost shrugged. "Looked for all the world like an Ægeleif to me."

"Certainly, but which one?" asked Hvitt. "Didn't look like Jeüdora. But familiar."

"You can tell them apart?" replied Rost.

"Am I supposed to?"

"Yes!"

"Then it's not Jeüdora!"

Rost then puffed out his gut and spoke as if he were delivering a great wisdom to no one in particular. He said, "If it's not an electron or a waveform, what's one thing like from another, I always say."

Hvitt groaned, "That's just ... that's just nonsensical."

"Not as nonsensical as the leopard," said Rost.

Hvitt waved his fingers in a gesture of agreement. "Now there's a truism. What do you suppose that's about?"

Rost offered, "Maybe he's hallucinating."

Hvitt considered this until a new spasm of anger from the lion hurried him along. "But it led him to the Gylfinîr and to that Hermit demon!"

"And to us!"

"Exactly!"

They both stared together at the lion, which, for the moment, caused his temper to fade in an awkward reprieve. "Here's a queer thing," Rost mused. "Maybe his navigation systems are one loaf short of a dozen. This leopard, it appears approximately ten seconds after his ticks send his pilotcode as an airburst. They do it whenever he disobeys their orders. Like a meson-beamed tantrum, I think."

"But where does the leopard come from?" queried Hvitt.

"And why hasn't he detected the Bœzch here?"

Hvitt shrugged. "Why was he able to detect them before?"

Rost looked as if he were about to answer, but then Hvitt frowned, rechecked the instrument in his hand, and dialed a holographic knob. A blue grid of light sprang up from the grass around Fel. The grid moved along his body starting at his tail, causing his fur to rise along with his panic. He circled the interior of his anti-Casimir cage, roaring louder than ever and striking the semi-opaque field over and over until his consternation ebbed.

Rost shrieked in terror, "Oh! He's acting up! What did you do to him?"

"Remapped his systems!" Hvitt screamed in reply.

"Ah! Clever! That'll speed Manticore along then!"

The lion's roars grew and grew in intensity until both the little men were backing away and holding their hands over the areas of their heads where most people had ears.

Hvitt tried to hold the instrument up to the raging lion, but he doubled over instead and looked to his friend, asking, "Can he break through that field?"

"Of course he can!"

"What shall we do now?"

"I have a thought!"

"Just the one?"

"One's enough!" Rost shouted. "Here's what I say: Send him off to *her*! Let him cleanse this colony!" Rost paused for a moment, collecting his thoughts over the din of the beast and continued, "What was the last message she transmitted?"

Hvitt peered into his instrument again and read aloud, "She said, 'Your flicker-flame snuffed in sheets! Suffer not a mind to live!' Whatever that means, she's a murdering atrocity, and our cat here is the perfect doer of the deed that needs to be done!"

"How many children is it now ...?" Rost stopped himself.

"Too many," continued Hvitt. "The others won't be online for at least a month. It has to be Mister Rafæl," Hvitt said in a normal volume, not realizing yet that the lion had calmed himself by looking at a cloud.

"Seems only right. It's what we prepped him for."

Once again, Hvitt stepped closer to the shielded lion. Fel rose to his feet and snarled at the approaching humanoid, but Hvitt held his place, fighting the instinct to flee like a rabbit. "Mister Rafæl ..." began Hvitt. "If you can understand me, I hope you'll be a good biomechanical fellow and follow the ping we're sending into your pilotcode via your ticks. We would very much like for you not to eat us when we release you from containment." Fel's growls turned to deafening roars again, for the sense of confinement was weighing on him, and he did not respond well to frustration. Hvitt cupped his hands over his mouth and tried to shout over the lion, saying, "You need to head only in the direction we've pássloaded to you! It should take you about five or six hours by foot!" Rost took his friend by the collar and dragged him away from the place where the shield walls met, but Hvitt insisted on finishing his instructions. "You'll know you're in the right place because everything looks wrong! It's a part of Barbary Four, a place with hills where fractal-theory went rudimentary! Dianthus the Head has set up camp there! You should make a fine mess of her, for she is more terrible, more evil than any you have faced thus far! And remember, when in doubt on your travels, listen to your broken music. The many fragmented musical scores saved in your ticks contain domain ontological pásscoding!"

"Which you designed!"

"Yes, and they are pásscodes that will protect you when all other psychological firewalls fail!"

Rost ran to the door of the house, motioning in exaggerated gestures for Hvitt to follow. "That seems about right!"

Hvitt followed his friend with a small leap. "Yes, I think so!"

"Let's hide under the house like terrible cowards!"

"Yes, let's! To the lab!"

"To the lab with the meter-thick doors!"

"Away, away!"

And they did.

They slammed the door shut behind them, releasing Fel, who sprang from his semi-opaque cage. He ran up the steps, only to bounce off another anti-Casimir screen surrounding the entrance. He shook his great black mane and chuffed, almost in laughter. Fel was left alone in the matted prairie of gold and blue grama grass, and soon his passion subsided. He sat and waited outside the crooked house, pining for company, but wary if he should be caged again. Behind him, clouds rose like mountains far up into the false sky, hurrying past in time-lapse fashion. He chewed on the yellow and orange blossoms of milkweed plants. He rolled in purple coneflowers. The pássloaded programming struck his senses then. Bœzch. One hundred and eighty-nine kilometers away. He chuffed a real laugh and bounded off in the direction of his prey as *Boléro* struck up the first rat-a-tat of its snare drum.

Chapter Nine
Head of the Woman

Fel watched the path ahead pass under his feet while his ticks analyzed a recording of the last words of the little men: "A place with hills where fractal-theory went rudimentary." In this place the valleys and hillocks twisted over one another in geologically unnatural, self-similar geometric forms of a true Mandelbrot set of fractals. Rocky hubs of polynomial knolls of green topography reached out over complex curves of green grass, breaking apart into branches of land and vegetation like earthen Rorschach tests. The tufts of white primrose flowers, moss tapestries, and fuchsia melancholy thistles grew in clotted patterns: patterns of silk paintings blotted with alcohol, carpets of fungus viewed under a microscope. Barbary Combine, though named after a part of the Neo Afrikahnen continent of Earth, was like its namesake only in title, for its ecology was based on more temperate climates. Barbary One, Two and Three were similar to the kind of coastal forests found along the Pacific shoreline of the North American Continent, but Barbary Four was meant to be a kind of Celtic Highland. This was a broken concept now. For some reason its growth systems had gone berserk. Fractal-theory evolution pushed hills into the shape of tidal waves, grew trees hanging upside down under emerald arches that should have been the tops of hillocks, lochs pooled into newly formed chasms between fragmented and inverted mountain pastures. It was a mad, beautiful landscape and Fel had wandered into the heart of it, his nose in the air, his ears turning all about, his mind set on hunting.

He was seeing the leopard more frequently now. Every thirteen minutes, every strike of the trombones and cymbals of the three-hundred-and-twenty-sixth bar of *Boléro*, she flashed at the edge of Fel's vision. She was following him. This was his sensation by sight, but his ears detected her ahead of him, and to his consternation, it was always the same. Yet, like all repetition, he soon grew used to the pattern and accepted her along with the sound of the ever-increasing tempo of *Boléro*, its triumphant ending, and its reticent beginning.

Twice he had moved past upended Human structures as the leopard blinked away. Both had been, at one time, single-room ranger stations, but their mesh-metal foundations could not withstand the transformation all around them, and what was left was shattered bits entwined in roots and branches, broken glass littering limestones, various technical equipment, and fragments of bedding scattered like flowers among gravestones. The shadows dimmed all around him. It would be night again soon. Fel did not find the overgrown structures or the labyrinth flora all around him disturbing. The goal at the end of his journey was now a constant pressure fixed on a single point somewhere so close that the fur on the back of his mane passed electrostatic charges from his spine. Ambient energy flexed across his frame. He moved as a kind of quadrupedal electric eel, shimmering a dark blue path through a coral dreamland.

The Charon lamps dimmed until they became a range of moons set so close together they appeared as a single radiant line fading into the cloudscape of the false dusk. Much of the shape of the valleys and avenues Fel traveled through was identical in structure from hill-to-hill. The line of moons and the constant repetition of the geometric landscape cast Fel as a lone king in a world-wide chessboard. He moved on as night fell, and he flickered from white square to black square, seemingly teleporting through the shadows.

The rain began three hours after nightfall. It swept down in torrential sheets, dousing the lion, who at first didn't recognize the sensation. All during his hunt on the Long Savanna, Fel had wandered during the dry season, and from there he had walked through blighted Serengeti Six and the deep dark of the Ouroboros Object. He could feel his target very close now. The rain served as only an irritant, never swaying him from the kill at the end of his present journey. When he first arrived in Barbary Combine, he could still feel the Bœzch, somewhere beyond the picoscale steel of the colony's hull, and there was an ethereal glimmer of a sensation here as well — but it had been so faint he had mistaken it for the general feeling of Bœzch somewhere far, far away. The pilotcode set by the two little men had corrected his senses. His awareness of the Bœzch within this colony was like a long exhalation of wind from over a valley, a strident work of telepresence administered to him by his biomechanized systems like a whiff of honey recast into a marker on a map.

Half-moon ribcages of fractal arches twisted up around him. Through the gray and black streaks of rain he could see that he was in a narrow passage of rock and grass at the base of the mad escarpment. The pilotcode told him, not so much in words as instinct, that this passage would go on until it reached the heel of a broken river, and on the other side of that river ... his target? He put his head up, listening to the crashing waterfall of the storm around him.

There was something else now. He roared once, allowing his sensor packets to feel along the walls ahead. Something was coming from ahead, moving toward him at a terrible speed. Fel spun about, looking for a place to run, seeking higher ground or any passage to move out of the way of the speeding mass. It hit him then, a flood of river water from the overflowed banks up ahead. Though his environment sensors understood the emergency and sealed him up as surely as if he had stepped out into vacuum again, he could not defeat the ferocity of the tide. Fel lost his footing and was carried away, turning over and over, striking the rocky sides of the passage in blows that would have slain an ordinary lion. He went down and was jammed within a crevice in the fractal geology. He padded the floor of the passage, trying to push himself free from the wedge, but this flipped him completely upside down, spinning like a gimbal. Several objects struck him. He saw what looked like eyes, an open mouth. They hit him as hard as cannon fire and he was ejected from his wedge. The water now carried him up and up until he rolled over again and found himself crawling to a shoreline that was once the top of the passage.

Once he was free from the flood, he stood upon the rain-soaked arches, still vigorous, and shook himself free from his sealed state. Something had happened to one of his ticks. It was damaged somehow in the plunge and its self-correcting systems were waiting for aid from surrounding ticks. The damage was minor, but this tick was in charge of running the application for Fel's current musical firewall. While Boléro continued its steady march towards the climatic bar, the data began to warp. The music now lumbered along, sounding as if it were immersed under a heavy oil, dragging itself through molasses flutes and sour gum oboes with a pace as difficult to span as a peat bog. This altered the Pásscoding on which the music was based. His thoughts coalesced with the fractal landscape.

As Fel strained his mind listening to the weary melody, a waterfowl was surprised by the sudden presence of the lion and squawked in exasperation before attempting to make flight. Fel, without understanding why, struck her down before she could escape. He stared at the fresh kill through the gray mist that saturated the nest she had made for herself in a nook around the tip of an arch. She was a white goose. He continued to stare at the sad broken thing, her neck turned under left wing; there was not a mark nor a spot of blood upon her coat. She looked as if she were being coy, hiding her face in a way that brought a sudden memory to Fel: an amber-eyed young lady playing beneath a sheet, the morning light dusting the soft perspiration of her skin. Sadness suffused his senses for a moment, and then a haunted feeling that made him uncomfortable; was it guilt? He sighed and moved away from the goose. Bar 326 of broken, molasses-*Boléro* slogged into bloom, and the leopard blinked to-and-fro. Trotting along the tops of the arches, Fel followed the yellow smudge towards his original destination.

The syrupy thud of *Boléro* creaked on again when Fel found the bodies along the high banks of the passage. He was twenty meters from where he killed the goose. They were all Human children, no one more than twelve years old. Their time in the water had washed their tattered school uniforms, but it did not take away the blood. More than four hundred of them lined the flooded surreal passage on either side, and the heavy rain was not enough to disguise the violence that had been done to them. Many were missing limbs. They were each crushed around the shoulders, the bones splintering out through their ribs as if they had been tortured in a vice. Surrounding him, little faces of those who still had heads curled open-mouthed in final, momentary pain, their comprehension of what had been done to them extinguished with their lives. Fel stepped over their poor bodies, exploring some animal reverence, but knowing not what to feel. There was every shape and color of babe here, the brutality that had been done to them like a last straw after their of months starvation and abuse. Little skeletal hands grasping empty stomachs, what was once full of fresh purpose now bloated in death. Fel's hearts ached in a near parental panic, but through the aqueous membranes of the storm all around him, his eyes narrowed when he found the source of the flood. The sweeping gray river twisted through a valley shaped like the back of a seahorse, and the massive colosseum building was crushed on the side opposite the river by the landscape that jutted up all around. Fel was less than twenty meters away from the structure when he emerged from the passage, and he could now see the sluice-gate-like door on the side with the river. From here the bodies flowed out into the wilderness of the fractal escarpment and carried the fresh taint of the dead through the fall of the heavy rain. Fel waded back into the water and paddled himself upstream.

The faux-brick, Mitteleuropan necropolis had originally been a building resort. The bottommost section was a spaceport that lead out to the exterior of the colony, but the spaceport was nearly five kilometers below Fel's feet. Here in the colony's interior, the enormous building that protruded from this side of the spaceport served as a hotel, colossal amphitheater, and waterway gondola park for the arcade that was built along the sides of the river. Fel's ticks recorded the words upon the great monument sign that still sat spotlit above the high gables of the hotel: Welcome to Barbary Four's Survivalist Hotel Colosseum. Spaceport 4.1 Serving the Retrograde Line of Hæl System. As Fel paddled towards the gate, he passed under fishing piers that held structures dedicated to near-Victorian-style pleasures: a Ferris wheel with glass buckets, a carousel of white horses and golden bears, little red and white shops that once sold confections, and games of chance. A scream howled up through the open gate at the bottom of the hotel, and Fel paddled faster into the den of death.

Here the little bodies pooled in heaps and mounds around the edges of a great hollow chamber. This was the dock where the old gondolas came to pick up tourists for a romantic wade between the colosseum and the arcade, but now it was a sepulcher of squalor and misery. It was easy for Fel to reach the level of the dock, for the water had risen and the chamber was so glutted with dead children that, reluctantly, Fel used them as a stairway. Cold seeped in around him the moment he stepped from the water, bits of flotsam, tattered flesh and mould sticking to his fur as he heaved himself up into the room that, with Doric columns entwined by filigree arches, looked as if a Grecian bathhouse were in the midst of being consumed by an Art Nouveau fungus. The darkness was thick with disease, a sickly old sepia radiance creeping in around the edges of the ceiling. He shook himself once, and though he could not avert his eyes from the violated cadavers that lay in oily piles upon the stone staircase before him, he strode ahead without trepidation. Fear did not take him; instead, he felt something new rise within him, though he had not the words to understand his own mind. In any language, rudimentary or cognitive, it was a thing like vengeance.

The dock connected to a stone and metal facade that curved to the left, lit in filigree fragments of light from the broken skylights overhead, and widened to an open archway. Beyond this, eventide glimmers of distant Charon lamps illuminated raindrops and floodwater overflowing the passage. He trod forward carefully, bouncing along on silent footfalls, crouching lower as he went, until he was the very figure of an ordinary house cat slinking around a garden wall. He passed under the many arches, curvilinear in the way they embraced the structure of the massive building, and he vanished completely whenever he passed into the deep shadows along the base of the facade walls. He froze at the sound of rising screams. The screams of children, in panic, in anger, at war. Fel steadied ahead and increased his pace without increasing his profile. At the end of the tunnel he broke into the full "moonlight" of the evening Charon lamps just as the rain began to clear. He stepped into chaos.

Hundreds of children lie dead, but scores more raised swords and hatchets, slings, and fractal rifles against a common foe that stood its ground. It was the one like Odin's Fenrir. Fel's ticks recognized the six-meter-tall flayed mongrel. Holographic words splayed out in red above its snarling, chirping mouth read: Ambros the Wayfarer, HOUND Of RESURRECTION, Your Flesh, Your Flesh, Take and Take, I Take and Take and Make Amends to the Blood of Giants. The horror hyena took its place in the center of the wide, flooded colosseum, standing upon a dais that glistened with its bile while all around it Moartale Human children rushed the platform, weapons swinging, war cries shouted, and the demon snapped them up one by one, shook them about and spit them out dead upon the wet ground. Watching over this scene was a second horror, the only female Bœzch demon, Dianthus the Head. She stood within a section of the stands of the colosseum that was void of seating. The nine-meter metal bride looked down upon the events in the theater with no earthly expression. Her eyes burned like the drifting cinders of campfire lights, but she was a thing void of all passion. The radiance within her was the energy of a machine built to perform a task, her eyes just the headlamps of two impassive locomotives parked side-by-side, waiting for some absent engineer to give them purpose.

Fel did not wait for the scene to crystalize. He shot ahead, maneuvering through the crowd of warring children, charging straight on towards the mongrel that took the form of his natural enemy. At that moment the rain stopped, and the arena was open with no place for a four-meter-long feline to hide — and yet the Bœzch demon dog did not turn its attention towards the charging lion. As with all the Bœzch before, Fel, as a non-sapient animal, was invisible to Ambros until he drew near enough to attack.

And attack he did.

Though he was himself huge for a lion, Fel was, in comparison to Ambros, but a small cat leaping to the throat of an oversized dog. The children backed away, startled by the sudden appearance of the black feline hanging onto the flesh of their enemy. Ambros, too, was startled, but the demon was still more powerful than Fel, and it snapped once, peeling the cat away from its shoulder; its terrible metal teeth clinging to Fel's armor, it flung him fifty meters in the direction of Dianthus. He struck the flooded arena floor, rolling over and over but rising to his feet in the end.

He shook himself once and charged the hellhound again. At that moment the broken, muddied music of *Boléro* achieved its climactic bar in a devil's tongue of gummed harmonics, and Fel could see the leopard running alongside him. He narrowed his vision to Ambros, emboldened by the company of the golden phantom cat. Ambros steadied itself, legs apart, and received the weight and crash of the lion and his ghost companion without so much as a shift in weight. As Fel struck, Ambros became gelatinous. The red bile and bloody mass of it became translucent, as if it were a great amoebic sculpture, and Fel plunged into it. His systems sealed, he found himself floating in a mire of red with the only opaque object within the structure being a single jewel-like eye, as big as Human a head. The eye blinked once, without lids — a strange horizontal dilation — and Fel was ejected with immense force.

He blasted into the stands and broke his picoscale-carbon back upon a colony-grade support column, tumbling over in upended seats, flopping over in pathetic rag doll fashion before the great iron wedding gown of Dianthus. Alarms sounded from his ticks, only audible to Fel. His hearts were aching, both going into cardiac arrest. His repair systems fumbled to compensate for the trauma, but some agent was working through his biomechanics, some poison from the hellhound was shutting down his machinery. Gasping and in shock, all feeling below his shoulders gone, Fel strained to look up at the face of the horror, Dianthus. Her cold, dead expression remained as she trained her Medusa eyes upon the dying cat. Without a word, she took a metal head that was chained to her apron and pushed the head through the space where her impassive face sat framed in a bonnet. Her original face fell away into her neck, while her new head, with sinister cheekbones pitted under charcoal eyes, roared deathless mirth down at the lion. Her new head called out to Ambros, her arms raised high in triumph. "Ambros, Hound of Resurrection, restart the flesh and show us where it belongs!"

Ambros howled a howl of a great Norse horn, and with his lamentation he turned to red gelatin again. From the single eye deep within the glutinous mist, a shockwave of lightning and ichorous copper bile reached out like ripples in a pond. Everywhere the sickly electric ripples spread, the dead twitched, then rose, then stood upright, their wounds sealing, their bones mending, their limbs returning, their lungs gasping for life. Fel, too, gasped. The poison left him then. His hearts both restarted, his spine was rebuilt with a speed unattainable even by his picoscale repair fractals, and he found himself standing with great vigor - and yet, whatever had been done to him, he found himself mollified. He could not attack. He could only stare up in frustration and wonder at the metal woman. He forced his eyes away from her terrible sneer. There in the open amphitheater below, the resurrected children dropped their weapons and shuffled off en masse towards the outer rim of the colosseum grounds. A great line of youth moved in from the flooded hall where Fel entered, and seemingly all the children he had passed on the hills beyond and in the dock below were returning as well. Ambros was disinterested. The hellhound, now set again in his original state, turned away from them and watched his master watch the lion at her feet.

Boléro stopped. Fel's mind was open to them again. Dianthus said to him, "WHERE. ARE. YOU."

Another child stepped between the lion and the woman now, a distant but familiar gray boy with crystal blue eyes, whose nose was prominent and handsome and whose body was a phantom of photons visible only in Augmented Reality. The avatar of child Mún Rafæl was maybe ten years old at the most. He wore the school uniform of a Ærdent child of Tenniel's Garden. He held the mannerisms of a frightened and confused youth — but there was still something wild about the totality of his features. It was the face of a boy who would only remain frightened as long as he did not understand his surroundings, but his great intellect made his surroundings a temporary unknown, so that his trepidation stuttered ahead, his confidence deposited in his wake.

The boy spoke first in an uncharacteristic stammer. He said to the horror, "Where ... w-where is Luti?"

The horror laughed, took a bronze head from her apron, and held it up as if she were ready to recite Hamlet. She turned the metal face towards the avatar of young Mún. He drew back at the sight of the adult face.

"Hünde?" said Mún.

The metal eyes opened, and the head of Hünde replied to the boy, "Well then, it's the property ... that *was* you on Serengeti. I knew there was something particular to that lion's gait. It was a feminine walk, wasn't it? Tiptoe, tiptoe, little kitty feet creeping to the saucer and milk. How long did it take before you realized Wülvogarti was a dear lost relation to you, Mún? Did you see my eyes burning as I puzzled you out? Did that set recognition in your barren imagination? Or did some underling have to squirt the idea into you?"

The lion, fully awake, stepped up to the side of the avatar of the child, as if offering support. Child Mún felt emboldened by the presence of his physical self. His avatar flashed once, and grew into the full figure of his adult self, and yet, though his adult form was restored, his diction was not. He stammered, "M-oove away fff-ff-rom me! I w-w-will kill you when I f-f-find you but ... t-t-taunt me now aa-and pro-prolong the ag-agony you will suffer!"

The head rolled its eyes. "Death comes so easy to you now, hmm? You've come a long way since murdering Paölo."

"And h-how many people have you killed?" said Mún.

Dianthus acted as a vessel for the head in her hands, walking it around the AR young man and his lion self. She moved the head in an almost comical fashion, treating it as if she were a puppeteer, shaking it when it laughed, nodding it when it said something it was proud of. The head of Hünde talked on, saying, "Hear our wisdom, brother: do you see the work my kin do here? The Hound of Resurrection brought you back for me. Just as he killed you for me. The children are for testing, but unlike them, you were given a chance to serve the cause of Œlexasperon and his Bœzch Pantheon. Because you are a murderer, you were already one of us."

"I didn't kill Paölo!"

"Shut up! Oh, Mún ... lie down and surrender. It would be so easy to remove the idea of you. The universe says to itself, 'I have a theory that I sometimes see through the eyes of a man with an animal fetish and a knack for puzzles.' Watch us disprove you! You were meant to be a horror! To aid me as I serve the new script of the universe as it will be Ünderwritten by the Bœzch!"

The disembodied face pushed close to Mún's own. "The universe should only function as a theory engine, Mún. Through the minds of thinking beings, it should exist to make lists of hypotheses and assumptions about itself to sustain the Bœzch hunger. How do you rank on that list,

Mún? Will you eat with us, or, like Luti, will you be eaten?"

Perhaps it was *her* name, or perhaps it was only the sterile fashion in which the disembodied head ground out the words; perhaps she had always been there; for in his vexation, Mún felt his periphery fill up with the *idea* of his beloved, as if a signal had been sent out from within him, when his distress could go nowhere else, and he felt himself beg for her presence. *Help me, please,* he heard his inner voice say. *I can't do this alone.* As he prepared to answer the puppet head of his brother, a yellow light eclipsed all of Mún's vision — a light like a gentle hunter throwing on a spotted robe, creeping up on his field of vision as easily as if it were a field of grass. Mún looked to his lion self, now fully a separate being from his avatar, it seemed. The lion, too, felt the approach of the golden presence, and this time they were both certain it was Luti.

Despite the feeling that drew his attention away, Mún shook his head and replied to his brother, saying, "Y-you're doing that nn-now? The c-c-cliché villain's offer to the h-hero? Will you ever be anything more than an a-actor?"

The head of Hünde shouted, "Look at my work, Mún! Each man, woman, and child killed in this system is a sacrifice to the memory of our brother! You snuffed him from your thoughts for your terrible guilt, but this is how you will pay: you will serve me like an animal and watch as we devour the foundations of the cosmos!"

Mún said nothing, but let Hünde rant on as he watched where golden Luti's phantom moved. Down the stands and over the rail and into the flooded arena, she crept on towards Ambros, who did not notice the ghostly stalker; through lines of weary children hugging the walls, some in shock, others weeping, none saw the leopard among them.

Hünde's shouting was thespian in its absurdity. He ranted on, his eyes wound up into his iron lids, his teeth full and bright, "Mother opened your eyes to the world, Mún, but I've always sworn I would slam them closed! So many times I thought of life without you! So that was our bargain! That is why I let the Bœzch command me. That I should one day use my power to humiliate you before crushing the breath from your lungs. I asked my masters to change you, to deform you in some fashion that is easy for me to ridicule. You were meant to be the demon horror of Long Savanna. But look at you. Alone and without your precious Luti. The great revolutionary, the wonderful thinker, stuck in the body of an oversized house cat!"

Mún turned back to face the nonsensical head in the demon's hands. He concentrated for a second before shouting, but the stammer would not leave him. "W-we never d-d-did anything to yy-you! Yy-you hated u-uuhh-uss from b-birth! You d-d-don't need Pa-Paölo's death a-as an excuse for murder! You were always r-r-raging under the skin and w-w-waiting to act!"

"And what were you?" The head screamed, "I was the artist! I was the great creator!"

"H-how ww-will we end this, then?"

"I repeat the offer: eat with us, or be eaten by us."

Mún said nothing. He watched the phantom leopard as she coiled herself behind Ambros. No one else saw her but Mún.

The head of Hünde said, "No answer? Very well. You've taken three of my friends thus far. I will find revenge for them in three hundred children. Dianthus! In the name of great Œlexasperon, torture this stray to ashes!"

196

Time seemed to slow then, curving like the curl and crook of *Boléro*, a grotesque distortion and bending between the pitches. Mún saw the lion leap to his feet, his eyes already flashing bright from the heat that built up within him. He roared half a cry before the sound was choked off by a fireball that passed from between his teeth. Mún watched as the fireball pass by him in the slow, sliding portamento of ruined time. He looked on with lethargic surprise as the head of the woman was struck center on, exploding from the sudden change in temperature. The lion took another step forward, as if daring the smoldering fragments of the head to fight back. Satisfied, Fel chuffed once and his mouth and eyes cooled, the blue electric lines upon his back fading. The head of Hünde fell at Dianthus' hem, facedown upon the metal stands, its eyes closed and all animation gone from the puppet-thing.

The Norse horn cry of the Hound of Resurrection broke the languid silence. Ambros was translucent again, and from his red gelatinous form the arcane tendrils of burgundy fire rolled on and over the still-standing remains of Dianthus the Head. Children down in the flooded arena hid their faces in their hands or turned their backs and hid. Dianthus snapped back into life, a new head hissing up from her metal collar, whirling into place, a grin rising mechanically at the corners of her mouth as if assisted by industrial pistons. Such an enormous creature she was, and yet she flew back from the lion and his phantom master as easily as a hummingbird, landing upon the tops of the stands, collapsing the weakest parts of the structure around her. She took a heavy support column of the Doric Nouveau variety and, pulling it up from its moorings, wielded it like a bat, sending it crashing upon the stands, striking where once the lion stood, the cacophony reverberating all around Mún's avatar like a wall of synthesized guitar sound. Fel bounded around the perimeter of the fallen column and tackled the gigantic metal woman. Again she toppled, the great black feline pummeling her over and over with his radiant claws as he fell back upon the stands. "Ambros! Where are you! Ambros!" she cried out until Fel extracted her jaw.

But her protective hellhound did not come to her aid. Mún watched as the great red monster dog writhed on its own in the center of the arena. It convulsed and howled up in pain, turning and shaking its neck, becoming translucent several times. Mún finally understood its calamity. There, as the thing blinked again and again into the gelatinous state, Mún could make out the shape of a golden feline struggling with the hellhound's core. A final scream like seagulls dying in a great bloody collective, and the leopard popped away from Ambros with something fixed between her teeth.

Ambros collapsed.

Dianthus drooped into her shattered frame.

There would be no resurrection.

When all was quiet, Mún peered down over the rail of the stands and into the faces of the shivering children. Fel's ticks estimated there were over sixteen hundred of them, and none of them could see the phantom that accompanied the lion. They saw only Fel, and they all watched him now, pooling at the far end of the arena away from this majestic predator, uncertain as to his purpose here among them. The leopard was gone from Mún's sight again, but not from his mind. He knew she was close — closer than she had ever been: it was a feeling of two worlds inching together on an invisible trajectory, and he hoped they would collide soon.

Fel, though weak and hungry, moved over towards Mún, now accepting this faint avatar as a companion of a sort. Mún reached over and patted the lion upon the head. Fel's telepresence allowed him to believe the touch was firm and congratulatory, and for once the lion did not mind the company of his bothersome ghost. Together, the two of them sat and watched Dianthus' heads burn at the apex of noon. The avatar turned to his lion body, took his great black mane in both his phantom hands and brought their eyes together, saying with absolute resolution, though the stammer remained, "W-w-when we f-find Hünde, we will eat h-him alive. Do you under-understand? For w-w-what he did to the children hh-here, we ww-w-will consume him for days b-before his last cry ends."

The lion chuffed in deep exhalations.

Chapter Ten
Adoration of the Child

Since his resurrection, Fel's biomechanical ticks appeared to be malfunctioning. They sensed nothing about his environment except what was within the grasp of his enhanced senses. Birds still swooped and sang above, the ground was firm and dry, places of shade and cover were plentiful, and game was easy to come by; this was all Fel needed to pass his time as he tended to the children of the colosseum. With the silent phantom, Mún, walking at his side, he would hunt for food for the children, bringing deer and rabbits to the refuge, the arcade storefronts. The shellshocked youths seemed grateful for the lion's aid, though they kept a fair distance, unsure of why he was helping them.

So Fel was alone but for his other self, and Mún walked in silence, his head down most of the time. The young man disappeared now and then when the lion moved in rapid bursts through the fractal gardens, but he returned when the hunt was done, only to stare for long hours into his animal self's eyes, as if he was searching a carnival mirror for some sign of a normal reflection.

At night, the phantom Mún laid his head back upon Fel's sleeping stomach and drank in the images from the lion's dreaming. Mún could not sleep in any real sense. He could only watch as a spectator in the dreaming of his lion brain. Perhaps it was his time feeding and protecting the children here near the arcade that caused the lion to dream. Perhaps Mún was just curious about his own lost childhood. Regardless, the dreams were always about Mún's, and thus Fel's, time on Tenniel's Garden.

When Mún was nine years old he still played games of hide and seek with his friends, because Tenniel's Garden, despite its beauty, was often a boring place for children.

On a blue spring day children gathered and waited for Mún to show. There were Luti and Paölo, of course, and the fraternal twins, Cliovanni and Cálo, but new to the group was the older Mitteleuropan girl, Dyana, who went everywhere with her mongrel dog, Amberson. They liked to play their games near an abandoned section of the long and narrow village. Here, the adults and elders of the village left them alone to wander and explore. In a population of less than thirty thousand, it was rare to find parts of the new infrastructure that were suitable for the openness and depth of childhood exploration. But a shake-up in the cult-like population had recently left parts of the village unoccupied as four thousand neophyte colonists, unused to the severity of a near-Luddite existence, gave up and returned to Windsor space. This included Mún's father, who abandoned his family the year prior.

Standing beneath an imported elm that grew leafless and dour in the small square between abandoned Tudor-like houses, Dyana towered over the other children with hands on hips, feet apart, and mongrel Amberson panting low at her side. She demanded, "Why can't I play?"

It was Luti who was first to reply. She leaned against a far wall, folding her arms over the red plaid of her school uniform. Her amber ale eyes furrowed and her jaw upturned in mistrust, she said to Dyana, "Because you're friends with Hünde, that's why."

Dyana, a head taller than Luti, dismissed her with a shrug and patted her dog. "So? Mún's related to Hünde."

Cliovanni stomped her foot and shouted, "That's different!"

It was a clear day, and the yellow caterpillar birds nesting on high branches purred down from their ten-legged suckers and startled the children into lowering their voices. Little Cálo cupped his hands and offered, "He can't help his family life."

"We can't choose our brother," tiny Paölo concluded.

"You can, too," said Dyana. "They do it all the time in Tacit R."

Luti still leaned against the wall farthest from Dyana, and from a distance the two girls could be mistaken for sisters. Luti insisted, "You don't know. None of us ever tried it."

"We can't try it," said Cálo.

"So you don't know," Cliovanni reasoned.

Balling her fists, Dyana stomped her foot and snorted in the fashion of a bull. She whined, "I just want to play!"

Dyana's high whine was followed by an atonal whistle. They all turned their heads to see. Mún approached from the south side of the abandoned quarter, whistling a series of single notes, incongruous to any harmony, one hand at his mouth. Between two fingers he held a small hard candy to his lips, through which he blew and whistled on his merry way, head down, clutching a cloth bag of circular candy mints with his other hand.

"There's Mún," said Paölo. "Ask him."

"Mún! I want to play with everyone! Tell them you'll let me!"

Mún stuffed the bag of mints into his coat pocket and shrunk back at the sight of Dyana. There was no bad history between them, and yet it was enough that he knew she associated with Hünde's gang, with Taum and Saum, Marcél and Emméte. Mún couldn't tell yet if he mistrusted her beyond her terrible choice in friends. She was new to the colony, her parents having joined the Ærdents only six months prior. It was possible she hadn't yet realized just how awful his brother was.

Mún looked behind her. "Where's Hünde?"

"He's not my leader."

She was a year older than Mún and Luti, three years older than Paölo and the rest, and yet she drew back a pace from them: tiny upturned jaws and little toe-taps of aggressive footing, they surrounded her as if they meant to stone her.

"Hünde's being mean to me," said Dyana, her eyes downcast, her lip trembling.

Mún sighed and muttered, "All right." Then he said, "But Amberson can't come."

"Why not?" Dyana cried.

Luti stepped away from the wall and shouted, "Because those are the rules!"

"It's not fair!"

Mún pointed to a rope near one of the abandoned patios of the surrounding homes. "Just tie him up at that tree. He'll be fine."

"I can't tie a knot."

"I'll do it," said Paölo as he skipped off towards the stone patio. He trod back with the heavy rope that, when gathered in a heap, was nearly the width of his upper torso. Little Paölo wrapped one end of the rope around the base of the great leafless elm and then set about making a knot. By his third attempt it was obvious he didn't know how. He stood in frustration, looking at the tree, the rope, the panting dog, and then to Mún.

The older Ræl brother took the rope and tied an adequate knot around the base of the tree. Gray and black-spotted Amberson stood up and faced Mún when he approached with the rope. The mongrel did not growl, but there was a strange presence about the dog. Their eyes connected, and within those yellow pools Mún felt a wave of déjà vu overtake him. The dog did not wag its tail or react in any fashion other than this, the infliction of presence. Mún stepped back and said to Dyana, "Is he going to bite me?"

"Not as long as he knows where you are," Dyana replied.

With her face buried in her arms, Luti leaned against a half-built cyclopean wall and counted up from one to one hundred. The children scattered at the start of one, but before Mún could make off on his own, Dyana grabbed him by the hand and guided him to an empty home some seven houses distant. She put her fingers to her lips whenever Mún tried to ask where she was taking him, and soon they were standing by an open hole on the side of the empty house. It was a half-finished basement window, with bricks and carpenter tools still lying in disuse near the hole. Far away, they could hear Luti as she reached eighty out of a hundred count.

"In here," Dyana said, going on her hands and knees at the window opening. She was through the entrance, on the other side and waiting, before Mún could ask what she was doing.

The basement smelled of the high iron dirt of Tenniel's Garden, the smell every Human structure acquires upon abandonment, a cavernous smell of depopulation. Through the darkness Mún followed a beam of light from the window and saw that the concrete floor was covered in broken jam jars and straw that was wet from seeping ground water.

Dyana tugged at Mún's arm, pulled him close to her and whispered, "Here, look at this."

She held up a small, white egg-shaped device. It looked to be made of hard plastic. One end was black and semi-opaque. The other was featureless but for a single red button that only appeared when her hands were close.

"What is it?" asked Mún.

"You don't know?"

Mún shook his head.

"It's a conker." She offered it for him to see.

Mún took it into his own hands and turned it over. He handed it back. "Is it ... Society technology?"

Dyana laughed once quietly and said, "Of course. Look at it. It's smooth and durable."

"Where did you get it?" Mún asked.

"Same place your father got that flat-film projector."

Mún shook his head. "He built that."

"Where did he get the flat-films?"

"Those were recordings — transferred from pásslogs."

"Onto film," insisted Dyana.

"Yes," said Mún, nodding.

"And where did he get the film and recordings?"

"From ... from a friend. His friend used to visit with the winter ships."

Dyana held up the conker like a trophy prize, excitement growing upon her face. She said, "And that's where I got this."

Mún shrugged and walked over to a far wall, trying to stay out of sight of the open window above their heads. "All right."

Dyana followed him. "Aren't you going to ask me what it's for?"

"We shouldn't talk. We'll be found."

"Aren't you going to ask me what it's for?"

Mún shook his head no, his eyes never leaving the window.

"You don't care?" Dyana teased.

He didn't answer her.

"That's too bad, because it's for you."

"What does it do?" He looked up in time to see that she was pointing the thing at him.

There was a low "PIP" sound, and Mún's skull thudded against the wet stone floor.

It was quiet and he was alone. Everything was dark, and yet he knew his eyes were open. He tried to call out, but his mouth would not move — or rather, it was open, but he could make no sound from it. He could not feel his limbs, his torso or his head. But for his heart and lungs and other vital organs, he was paralyzed. Still, he was cold and damp, and there was pain enough to remind him he was alive. The pain in his back ebbed and vanished in a spiral pattern, starting at his shoulders and curling up into his spine. Along with the aches and cold there was a sensation of needles running up and down his limbs like waves of centipede feet. The effort to scream was beyond him.

He was only able to move his eyes. There was something above him in the blackness. Tiny pin-lights like distant stars glittered far above his head. He stared at those points for what he thought must have been hours before he realized they traced the outline of a faint shape, a box or a doorway frame. A window. It must have been the basement window through which he and Dyana entered. But these were not stars passing their light through the opening. These were pin pricks of luminescence from holes in whatever had been laid over the window. Mún had been boarded up.

Through the panic that churned in his chest, Mún reasoned with himself. Dyana couldn't possibly have sealed him in with any means of permanent construction. His friends and his brother were only seven houses away, they would have heard or even seen her hammering up a wall or laying down bricks. There must be something portable covering the window from the other side.

But his reasoning made no difference.

He could not move.

He could not shout for help.

He trembled in the dark.

Mún was damp, and he was sure he had wet himself. He was very hungry when the tiny specks of light disappeared. His thirst was terrible, too. He wondered if his bag of mints were still in his coat pocket. It would be exactly like a conspirator of Hünde's to finish off a cruel trick with a robbery. And that, Mún was certain, was what Dyana was: a member of his brother's conspiracy. She hadn't been on Tenniel's Garden long enough to rank high in Hünde's gang. This cruel prank she played on Mún must be part of her initiation into the group. *I should have heeded that look on Luti's face,* thought Mún. She always sensed when Hünde was plotting, and she understood the value of constant paranoia.

Night must have fallen. He weighed the idea of whether his friends and town Elders would search for him beyond dusk. Ærdents did not trust the night, and Mún was sure that if no one found him within an hour of the first loss of daylight, no search would commence until morning.

He tried to sleep. His eyes would not close.

Mún was awoken not by the return of the tiny specks of light, but by the sound of his own name called out over the empty square outside, filling the darkness around him. Like an anesthetized patient, he slept without dreaming, and when the voices filled his head at dawn he thought his dreams had begun and wondered what it would be like to be awake and trapped in his own body. It was when he heard Dyana's voice among the others, mixed in with Luti's and Paölo's and even Hünde's, as well as their mother's, that he felt his frustration would kill him. *Dyana knows where I am!* he wanted to shout out. Mún's desperation doubled when he heard their footfalls at the place outside the specks of light.

"Mún! Where are you?" sad Luti called.

"Mún! Where are you?" clever Dyana sang.

"Mún! Where are you?" evil Hünde repeated flatly.

"Have you searched all of these houses?" he heard his mother ask, her voice strained with worry.

"Yes, Sister Rafæl, every one." It was Dyana again.

He heard them move on, soon calling his name in the distance.

"Where are you? Where are you? Where are you?"

Silence followed.

He was too thirsty to cry.

He thought perhaps that it was later that night when he heard footsteps at the basement window. It could have been another day. It could have been early morning. He had fallen asleep in the gloom and woke with terror, trapped in a sleep paralysis he could not wake from. But he was awake now, and so very distraught for it. His heart skipped. There was a scratching at the blocked up window.

"Mún ... Mún, can you hear me? It's me, Emméte."

Mún could have groaned. Fat Emméte was another one of Hünde's gang. *Not the most violent of the lot, but ...* thought Mún as he trailed off into a sour memory.

Emméte's pink lips smacked, and he paused as if in consternation before he said, "It's true, isn't it? Dyana told us what she did. You can't move, can you?"

He was silent again, except for the smacking. Was he eating something? Was this Mún's new torment, like the grade school game of showing your friend the contents of your mouth?

"I'm sorry, I'm so sorry, Mún ... I want to help you. But Hünde can't find out. Oh, he can't."

Mún waited. Nothing happened. The smacking subsided, becoming little ticks of the tongue as Emméte attempted to gather up courage. It would be a fruitless search, Mún knew. Courage for Emméte was a far-off country, an imaginary land he only knew in legend. Years ago he was friends with Mún, but even then, he was so weak, so constricted and lackadaisical. Both Mún and Emméte had been targets of Hünde's violence, but Emméte couldn't stand by his friend. His mind wasn't built for it. One night, the two boys had played by the stream that ran by the music shop, catching amphibious worms in a jar, happy as boys should be, when Hünde and the twins, Taum and Saum, sneaked up on then both, held them down in the muddy stream and tried to twist the worms under their eyelids. Mún fought them off, but little fat Emméte only cried and cried until he polluted the stream with his own vomit. The next morning, Mún saw his friend by the stream again, but when he opened his mouth to say hello, Emméte spit down his throat and thudded off to join Hünde's gang. They never tormented Emméte again. Mün could still feel the saliva that was not his own strike the back if his throat and slide down, down, down into his stomach: Emméte's nesting betrayal.

"I want to help ... I want to help. But Hünde .... Maybe if I come back in the morning ... he'll be going off to study his part for the play then, and ... no ... I have to hold the props."

More silence, followed by more smacking. Mún wanted to scream: Stop smacking! You're in my ear! Just sitting there on my eardrum, chewing away!

"All right. I know. I'll tell your mother where you are when ..."

"Emméte! What the hell are you doing?" It was Marcél, one of Hünde's more calculating narcissists. He had taken Mün's place as Emméte's friend when Emméte joined the gang, but the boys were not equals.

"I'm just teasing him, Marcél! Just making fun of him, you know? I ... stop!" Emméte's voice was lost in his own piggy squeals, and Mún heard the distinct sounds of heavy slaps and boot-kicks. Marcél was friend and chief abuser all in one.

"Please, Marcél, please, Marcél, please!"

"You idiot! You stupid, stupid shithead! You're lucky it's me who caught you and not Taum!"

"Yes, yes, yes! I know, I know! I hope you die, Mún! See? That's all that I was doing, Marcél!"

"Just leave, you little bitch!"

Slaps and punches faded into the distance.

Hours later, Mún was surprised, even impressed to hear the lip smacking return to his barricaded window. It was a long time before Emméte would speak again, and when he did, it was in the smallest voice possible, a strained whisper that sat along with the lippy smacks on Mún's eardrum, paradoxically attempting to give information by saying nothing at all. Finally, the frightened boy said, "I'll come back to help you out tomorrow, Mún. They won't know it was me. I promise. I'll come back."

Footsteps and lips plunged away from the window then, and Mún never heard either again.

Days passed. Mún counted them by the movement of the specks of light, but his counting was in reverse, for his delirium was crippling, and time seemed not to move, but to slide around him like black amber. *Black amber*, he said to himself over and over, forgetting his name in the darkness; he thought of himself as a small mammal in a hole, waiting for winter to end, waiting for the black amber to lift its fluid curtains from his eyes, waiting for the predators to drift by. Though he was not predisposed to do so normally, his mind formed a poem in the dark:

> *A boy on his back*
> *At the bottom of his well*
> *A boy on his back*
>
> *In black amber, black amber, black amber*
> *Hither, where am I, that I follow*

Hitherto blood flown blackened vessels
In black amber, black amber, black amber
Hitherto I lie in black amber
In black where or where am I where am I

"You don't know?"

The voice appeared somewhere above his head and was accompanied by a drifting light, a shining marble of radiance that drifted against the stagnant air and settled near his unmoving face. He studied it for what seemed like days to him, and in truth it was several long hours before he understood the voice and the light were the same. It was like staring into a snowflake, magnified, backlit and set aflame, a churning geometric plane in perfect symmetry to all of its sides and shapes. The light became a vortex in his eyes, twisting, scintillating, only the size of a marble, and soon he was asking himself questions, and soon he was interrogating the light with his innermost thoughts.

Who ....

The voice replied with a question: "Why don't you know where you are?"

It's dark.

"Are you being born? It is dark just before birth."

Yes. No! I've been tricked! I can't move, and I'm trapped! You have to help me! Please!

"We are all tricked at birth, you see. We are all told it is glorious on the outside, but I suspect that is a lie."

Where are you?

"In the unborn place. Like you."

No. I have a body. I'm alive.

"Really? But you are in black amber. You said so."

I don't know what I'm thinking. I'm thirsty. I'm hungry. I can't feel anything.

"Such is the unbirth."

No! I'm not unborn! I'm alive! I was tricked by a girl. She had a weapon and a dog!

"That is frightening. I want to be born soon but I don't want to be abused. Tell me what it is like, if it is true that you are alive. Tell me, is it happy to be outside of birth?"

It can be very nice. There's music and candy and good food. I like to play music but I'm not very good. But I still like to try. My father gave me a projector before he left and sometimes I watch musicians play. So ... yes, it can be very nice ... except for the bullies.

"What do they do?"

My brother Hünde. He has a gang. They're always attacking my friends. But Hünde attacks me personally.

"Why?"

I don't know. He hates me. He's an actor. He's only a year older than me but he's always in plays. He says he's a genius and that no one should pay attention to me. I was a mistake. I shouldn't have been born. And because I was a mistake, I'm his property and he owns me and he can do whatever he wants with me.

"Birth can be a mistake?"

I don't know. That's what Hünde says. Luti tells me it's not true.

"What does Luti do?"

Luti is my best friend. But she's a girl. Hünde doesn't know what to do when she fights back. When I try to fight back, he just beats me even harder, but Luti seems to know how to put him down.

"Put him down?"

Yeah. Right in the ground. Last week, I was practicing with my guitar on the little hill near Blue

Mountain, and Hünde found me. He was walking between towns and was still in his costume from his Harlequin play. When he found me sitting near the rocks, he took my guitar away and smashed it. I fought back but he beat me. I got up three times but he beat me every time. He's just stronger. But then Luti showed up and she kicked him in the stomach. He didn't know what to do. So he just screamed until the village elders found him.

"What do the ... elders do?"

Nothing. The law says Ærdent children are innocent and incapable of being bad. So they just let us do whatever we like. We could kill each other and no one would punish us.

"That does not make sense."

I know.

"Why don't you correct them?"

I don't have the power.

"But you are alive and outside of birth."

That doesn't mean anything. I'm just a boy, and not everyone can be stopped.

"Would you agree that some of your kind are not limited enough?"

How do you mean? Like ... restricting people?

"Yes."

We're restricted from using technology from the Engineered Years.

"And yet you still inflict great harm upon each other. You should be restricted."

What's your name?

"Ah! Names. I like names! What is your name?"

I'm Mún Rafæl.

"Mún Rafæl, that is good. I think I will like to be called Æsirisæ when I am outside of unbirth."

Æsiriæ? Like an Ægeleif name?

"That is me, yes."

What?

"I should go soon. Birth will happen."

Wait! Can't you help me?

"I can."

Please?

"You have mints."

I ....

"I want them."

Take them! But I can't move!

"Thank you. I will like mints. Here are your legs."

A river of needles flooded his limbs, becoming herds of swimming stallions, kicking and thrashing under his skin. Feeling and mobility returned to his body, and the first sensations were of pain and nausea. His head throbbed with the hammers of little men behind both his eyes. He turned to his side to retch and gasp.

"I'm in here!" Mún tried to yell but found he could only whisper and croak.

Again he opened his mouth, but this time taking in as much air as his lungs would hold, and then pausing as he wondered if his lungs had broken, he screamed out over and over again, "I'm in here! I'm in here! I'm in here! I'm in heeerrrreeee!"

Time was yet a dead thing to him. He had no method for knowing just how long he repeated that single line, but he was determined to continue until his voice stopped dead or he himself expired from the effort.

Yet, he lived.

When the elders followed the voice that haunted the empty sector of the village and found the starving and dehydrated boy, they did not ply him with questions. They returned him to his mother, to his nightshirt and to his bed, and called the village doctor and nurse. Though Mún hated needles, he did not protest when they placed a plunger as big as a golf tee into his arm and fed liquid into him from a hanging glass bottle. His mother moved around the doctor and nurse, arguing with them whenever they demanded she wait to feed him. Mún could not make himself eat the broth from the soup, but it was satisfying enough that he smelled the mix of fish and vegetables whenever his mother held the bowl under his nose.

   Over the next few days of resting he was interviewed once by an elder, and many times by his own mother. Mún knew they would confiscate and destroy Dyana's conker, but he also knew that that would be the end of any repercussions for her. Children were the true tyrants of Tenniel's Garden. Innocent of any evil, children could not be asked to behave better, for they were already perfect. Like every Ærdent child, Mún, too, took advantage of the helplessness of the adults around him. He had stolen the bag of mints from the confectionary across from the village square, and the shopkeeper had done nothing to stop him. Thinking of his near-death experience now, he regretted his spoilt routine. He didn't want to be a typical Ærdent child, immune to any and all reprimanding, only to grow up to be an adult who is helpless before a rabble of perfectly awful children. He had studied animal life with Luti. He knew that even unthinking mammals lived within social boundaries around each other. Animals, he decided, had a dignity and nobility about them that was apart from his Human kin — and though he knew deep down that this was a kind of intellectual dishonesty, he no longer cared enough about Humanity to think on it further. The cognitive dissonance would live on in him, and like a new religion, he would follow and obey. From now on, he wouldn't behave like a typical Ærdent brat. From now on, he would be like one of those cubs from the documentaries. He would know his place and better himself like an animal would.

While he rested over the next two weeks, Mún thought of the mysterious light that saved his life for the price of a few sweets. It wasn't a dream. He was certain. Had he been hallucinating? No. There was a clarity and weight to the light. Was he contacted by a spirit, an unborn Ægeleif feeling out her world before her birth? He told no one, not because he feared ridicule, not because he doubted his senses, but because he had not the strength to speak for long. As he watched his mother work outside his bedroom window, he wondered when he should confide in her. But he was so very tired.

Tiny winged caterpillar-like bees, called katees, hovered outside his window. Mún's mother, a katee keeper and the village's sole supplier of honey, labored outside in the front garden. Katees were without stingers, but their tiny feet contained a substance that slightly burned, and so his mother wore a mesh over her black Ærdent Sister dress and bonnet. She did not look comical to him. On the contrary, he always thought the mesh, which blacked out all of her features, added to the languid feeling of distance he felt between them. He knew almost nothing about her, except that she cried often, even before their father abandoned them. He remembered that when his father ran his music shop, she worked apart, with her insects, closing her features off to even her husband, preferring the company of the katee hives with their tiny wings altogether making a sound like a toy piano. She was a dark marionette to all her family, and Mún had grown used to her as a mere extension of his own shadow, as if the sun were always setting at his face whenever the mournful figure sulked somewhere behind him.

Mún was standing in his nightshirt at the foot of his iron bed, the floorboards cold and splendid at his feet. He was stepping back and forth over the lacquered wood when he saw Luti approach. He could see her standing outside, near his mother as she collected the trays of katee honey. His mother was a blotted-out thing risen up in space before little Luti, and the overwhelming gloom of the maternal Rafæl in the presence of the bright young girl served as a mirror to Mún's thoughts, a well of black amber where a single bulb of light whirled nebulous and clear. He watched his own feet now, marveling at their mobility, so very pleased that they were his to command once again. Small steps he took, still mostly in pain around his ankles, but it was a dull pain now, more an irritant than a calamity. Forward he stepped, making a circle around his bed in the sunbeam that drew a line down the center of the room. Into the beam he stepped and out again, humming atonally to himself, stepping lightly until his feet found something that was not there a moment ago: a small cloth bag.

Mún starred down at his feet. The sunbeam blocked his vision from the contours of the bag, and so he went to his knees to examine the object.

He held it up by two fingers.

It was his candy bag, the one he surrendered to the dream sprite named Æsirisæ.

He drew open the string on the small bag, and the smell of mints completed the mystery. It was empty.

The sound of a fog horn blared over the heavens. Not an audible sound, but a sound within his inner ear, a turgid thing that held a long note at the back of his young mind. Mún jumped to his feet, dropping the bag, and padded over to the window. Outside, Luti was staring into the sky while his mother was prostrate upon her belly, holding her hands over her head. Her katees whipped around them in an insect vortex, while every manner of flying creature scattered in the immediate sky above the village, forming strange patterns as species intermingled in ways that were unnatural to them. Mún followed Luti's eyes to the distant patch in the sky, where the massive planet Alice dominated the horizon. There on the surface of the orange and red behemoth, a white speck grew brighter and brighter, until it was a star on the surface of a great quilt of burgundies and magentas, a swirling white hole perfectly reflecting all light and yet not blinding to the eye. If it were not the kind of sight to terrorize, it would have been pleasant, hypnotically so, for with the sub-auditory illusion of the foghorn there came a feeling of lightheadedness, of being ever so lightly tickled by a remotely projected sense of relief.

Mún steadied himself and came closer to the window, undoing the latch and pushing the double panes open as wide as they would go. He wanted to call out to his mother, to ask Luti if they were both all right, but he was too transfixed on the light in the sky. The sub-auditory foghorn flattened out, soon becoming a thin tin whistle, undulating along with the shimmering waves at the heart of the spiral star. It was a Pied Piper call, a somewhat merry tune just above a fugue, sonorous enough to bring joy and giddiness, conservative in that it did not overextend itself. It was the sound of when one is grateful to find their expectations met, their comfort secured, and their faith in beauty confirmed.

The sky stood still. The silence that followed the quaint joyfulness was like a sudden weight upon the bridge of the nose. Mún felt thirty kilos heavier, and he slumped into the frame of the open window. The silence was momentary, soon replaced by the panic of the birds, the unsettled hum of the katees, and the irrepressible weeping from the dark heap that was his mother prostrate upon the flagstones. Luti, too, came back to her senses and, like Mún, was left crestfallen by it. She helped the dark figure to her feet, and Mún saw his mother tear off her hood and screen and dab her eyes with the cloth. She said over and over, "Oh, no, no, no no nooo ..."

Within a week, people began dying. The malady appeared to target random victims, beginning as a kind of aphasia. The old and the young alike would wake up and say to their parents, spouses, siblings, or friends, "I feel like I've walked into a dream ..." and then they would stare into nothingness and refuse to define what they meant. Soon, the stuttering would begin, followed by an inability to remember how to use common objects, and soon they could not comprehend what the object was at all. These were simple items, like keys and tools and furniture. Later, they would cease to remember their own faces or those of their friends and family. They would crash into depression, then euphoria, laughing through the night and into dawn. By the third day, their sexual libido increased, then failed altogether after they woke in their neighbors' beds. They became violent and moody, slapping and kicking at their surroundings, then exhausted and melancholic. They would lose their ability to dress themselves, forget hygiene, forget how to feed themselves, forget what food is for, and they would stand there swaying in door frames, clutching the brass handles, their mouths agape, their eyes dead, and they would gasp and gasp, making a great and terrible O of their mouths like dying fish in a drained lagoon.

Everywhere Mún went now, the great gaping O's were there before him. He was one of the few unaffected by the malady, but it was not so great a relief when he was surrounded by the dead and dying. Luti was a great help to him, and so was his mother when she finally accepted her surroundings. Hünde was ever spiteful in his excellent health, spending all his time with his gang of bullies in the abandoned section of town, away from the moaning O's and soiled adults.

Mostly it was adults who suffered — but it was during the seventh week of the affliction when Mún's brother Paölo walked into the family study, looked into the faces of all those present — Mún, their mother, and Luti — and said just above a whisper, staring at the mantle above the fireplace as if he addressed an insect there, "I feel like I've walked into a dream ..."

His decline was more rapid than many of the others in the village, and towards the final stage of the disease his suffering was far more terrible than any Mún had witnessed. It had been a full month of spitting and moaning for Paölo, and where once there was a bright young boy just learning to tie his shoes and count on a conventional clock, there was now a shrieking old man, a black-eyed zombie with a gaping mouth and a packed diaper. They kept him in the courtyard, near the woodpile and katee hives, because it was outside Mún's window and the easiest way to keep an eye on him. They fixed a tent and tethered him with a long scarf to a spike in a gap between two sett stones.

Hünde only visited once, and only appeared to express his disgust with both Paölo and the family's treatment of him. As Luti and Mún both took turns washing the young boy in an outdoor tub made of tin, Hünde stood with hands on hips condemning the all those afflicted, and marking as fools all those who stayed to help. He was chased away by Luti again, and his words were never important to anyone, but this time he had struck a chord with Mún when he exclaimed, "So this is it then? You're just going to spend the last remaining days of your stupid lives wringing the shit out of these walking ghosts? I bet you already have it. I bet you caught it from everyone you helped. Not me, I'm out where it's safe. Not a diseased tit within a thousand meters of my gang. You two don't have the guts to kill yourselves when you get it! Look at you! You're already dead, but you just keep on cleaning!"

Of course, they worried about the infectious nature of the malady, but Mún's mother assured them that this was a disease of the mind that afflicted them only because of their proximity to the birth of an Ægeleif. Only those beneath a certain mental constitution would be stricken, and if they hadn't caught the malady yet, they most likely would not at all.

But this did not settle the problem of the idea presented by Hünde, the arrogant inkling of a quick death for all. In truth they both wondered about the moral and ethical dilemma of tending to the dying, knowing they were prolonging their suffering as well as providing relief. How much longer could they tend to these victims before help would arrive from Windsor Temporality?

The dilemma was also on Mún's mother's mind. Every evening she would cut the wood in the yard with her small hatchet and then cry herself to sleep by the side of the burning hearth, collapsing in her plaid armchair, clutching photographs of Paölo when he was healthy and clean.

One evening, Mún fell asleep beside her chair as he stared into the fireplace; the heat of the embers and the exhaustion of tending to the sick fell over him in the manner of a silent lullaby. He woke after an hour, surprised to find his mother gone but supposing she finally went to bed. Smothering the fire, he retired to his own room, intending to wash up at his nightstand and hit his pillow with his face until one of them was the victor. But out his window he saw a figure move under the light of full bright Alice. His mother stood with her little hatchet, there by Paölo's tent, and she stared down at her youngest child with all the regret of the world.

She raised the hatchet.

"No!" Mún screamed.

But the axe was down and in Paölo's head before Mún could lift himself from the window. His mother walked off then, the dark specter of a woman receding into the night as a broken marionette's shadow, leaving Mún to cradle his brother's filthy corpse.

There was no dignity to the scene, just the calamity of life seeping out of the three of them, though two remained alive — but Mún's mind was already working, pulling itself out of the minutes-old tragedy. He would have to save his mother from the town Elders now. He would test the law, and see if the innocence of Ærdent children extended to them getting away with murder.

Chapter Eleven
The Wayfarer

It had been two weeks since the slaying of Dianthus and Ambros, and now the children were hungry again. Fel was out in the maze of the fractal landscape, hunting deer for himself and his orphans. He found himself in a familiar terrain, a narrow gully that showed signs of recent flooding. The air here felt out of sorts with time, as if mists flooded into raindrops in reverse, and dandelion seeds blew together instead of apart. The lion watched his phantom companion wade in the ankle-deep water down below. He appeared to be searching for something, and Fel sensed he could not help him. The young man vanished and reappeared at Fel's side, then mused aloud, "S-oo w-what happened h-here?"

Mún should have had no memory at all of this land. From the time on the Ouroboros Object, when his melancholy self was erased, to the time of their fight with Dianthus, he was an inert part of the lion's brain, but he too felt some awareness of something larger than himself. The sense of déjà vu was somewhat frightening to Mún, though he did not understand why. As the ghost of the young man drifted near the gently panting lion, he looked about the landscape and convinced himself that everything was going to be all right.

"It's fine. Everything's fine," Mún repeated to the midday sky.

They were sitting at the top of the gully together. Fel had chased and lost a deer somewhere along the geometric ridges of the grassy hillocks, and now they rested and studied the swift lavender clouds gathering under the faint blue sky. They saw the Charon lamps disappear into the inverted horizon. They found the remains of a goose, struck down only two weeks prior. Though she was half-eaten by worms, she still lay as if she were being coy, hiding her face in a way that brought a sudden memory to Fel of an amber-eyed young lady playing beneath a sheet, the morning light dusting the soft perspiration of her skin. Mún saw the image pass between them, and together they sighed.

But the lion was not finished with the corpse. Mún watched Fel as he leaned in close to the dead bird, coming down on his forepaws and inching his nose up to it.

Mún said, "Don't e-eat that. I-it's been d-d-dead f-for who kn-knows how long."

The lion chuffed to the corpse, and then with a sudden shift in the momentum of time, slowly, as if in languid repose, Fel turned white-translucent, radiant and pure. Mún cried out against the glare. In his translucent state, the lion took the appearance of carved ice, and all his defining textures were gone. There was a thing lodged deep within his shell. Mún squinted to see that it was actually watching him back. A single lidless eye turned within Fel's semi-opaque body. It looked past Mún to the surrounding ground, flashed once, and shafts of lightning struck the dead goose. Time again slowed down, then reversed itself locally, just around the area of the bird. Meal worms moved back into their larval state, grasses grew into seeds, were scattered by reticent winds, were wetted by absent rains, flesh returned to the bones of the bird, and the sound of life issued up from the beak of the newly living creature. In shock, the goose did not hesitate to flee. When Fel returned to normal, he caught a glimpse of the bird in passing, and seemed equal parts dismayed and relieved at its restored beauty.

Mún had not the time to ask himself what had happened, for he was already on to the next mystery. Time continued its cumbersome momentum to nowhere. Clouds slowed their pace, wind dissipated, and two quiet figures appeared side-by-side, in the same positions as Mún and Fel, but only a meter apart from them: a phantom young woman and yellow leopard.

Mún Rafæl and Luti Casanova said nothing for a time. Then, as if waking to an inaudible alarm, the two ghosts embraced without thinking as their cats looked on.

"H-how are y-you here?" asked Mún, weeping into her kisses.

"How am I? What about you?" she thumped at his chest with her small fists, burying her face in his tears.

Mún replied, his phantom arms around her ethereal shoulders, "I-I'm n-n-oot certain ho-ww I came to th-this colony, but I-I've been on a l-long journey. After you died I f-f-followed on with th-the mission."

Luti pulled away slightly, looking up into his face, saying, "After I died?"

"Y-yes," said Mún. "When the Bœzch atta-attacked and k-killed our pride on Lllong Savanna."

"I didn't die."

"But ... y-you did. And I've be-been following your l-leopard wherever it appears."

Luti held both his hands in hers and frowned in frustration. She said, "I ... Mún, *I've* been following *your* leopard."

"I d-don't have a ..."

She walked closer to her feline body and said, "Tell me. Is my cat body standing next to me right now?"

"Yes," said Mún.

Luti continued, "What kind of cat?"

"A-a leopard."

"And what kind of cat do you have?"

"A l-lion ... of course," Mún slowly replied. He held his tongue for a minute, then he said the obvious, for he knew not what else to say: "So-something's n-not right."

"Tell me," he said, looking back and forth between the two predators. "What ... do you see?"

She put her hand on the back of Fel and said, "This is a leopard." She then stepped close to her own cat and pointed, saying, "This is a lion." Both cats chuffed.

Mún shook his head. "No .... In your mm-memory, d-did I die on Long Sss-savanna?" Despite his stammer, Mún said the words so clinically, Luti drew back at first, then raised her eyes to his, virtual tears welling up under semi-transparent eyes.

Luti said, "Yes. I was the only survivor of the pride. Then I came to Serengeti Six and killed the demon, Sayre and then his brother Tautolo on the Ouroboros Object. Each time, my lion chased a leopard. Your leopard."

Mún nodded. "It w-was the same for mm-ee. B-but put me in y-your place in every scene."

Luti sat upon the grass, near where the goose had been resurrected. Mún noticed for the first time that he and his fiancée were dressed exactly alike. He couldn't remember if her avatar's appearance had been programmed with his own ban collar grey suit, but he was growing tired of comparisons. He sat next to her in silence, slumping into her shoulders. They both watched their cats for several minutes of quiet.

227

"What is happening to us?" Luti asked the sky above them.

Mún answered, "Wh-what did H-hünde say to you when you con-confronted his hh-head in the colosseum? Di-did he offer y-you to join his d-demons?"

"No," she replied. "He only mocked your death. He said this whole charade, waking the Bœzch, the attack on the colonies, was simply to see you made into a lower demon that he could abuse forever. Then your leopard attacked Ambros and gave my lion, Nova, that resurrecting eye. Nova swallowed it before I could stop her."

"W-we aren't sharing the same reality," Mún said with an air of confirmation. "And yet we're entangled. Fel didn't swallow the eye, and yet he has it, too."

Luti took his hand again and this time held it to her breast. "That's not possible ... is it?"

Mún gripped her fingers tight and said, "I s-saw you die. You saw me die. W-we each hh-have been ff-following each other's ca-cats but each of us ss-ees the other's cat as a l-leopard that mo-moves out of synch with our worlds. It's a bridge between us. It ha-has to be. But, how?"

A gentle horn sounded, a sound like a bass guitar strummed through a conch shell. It was all around them, and they leapt to their feet. The lions seemed unaware of the sensation, though Mún felt lightheaded. The sound continued, and as it changed pitch, growing lower, the ground and sky began to speed up, slowly yawning forward towards normal momentum. Mún saw Luti and her cat begin to fade.

Luti cried out, "What's happening now?"

"W-we're moving apart," said Mún.

Luti held onto him, pushing her face hard against his chest. "Mún, no! Not when I just found you!"

"We'll s-see each other again!" he shouted over the sound of the horn. "We hh-have to! Follow my l-leopard and I'll f-follow yours!"

"I will!" she wept into him, holding his shoulders. "We'll b-be together again!"

"I know!"

"I lo —"

The young man and his lion were alone again.

The two of them rested at night under the line of false moons, their backs on the soft grass of the distorted landscape, Fel seemingly transfixed at the sight of the gently glowing Charon lamps, Mún lost to the night. Through the haze of a night fog that crept upon them, the Charon moon-lamps smeared together as tears gliding up the inverted horizon like glittering avenues traversed by faceless nocturnal life. The face of his beloved drifted over his imagination, and he wondered at his sanity. What was happening to his reality, to his senses, to his ability to speak without stammering? Was he falling apart, finally? Would he end up like the original EtherCore of Long Savanna, just a lingering, lifeless ghost at the side of the lion? He reached into Fel's mane, forgetting just how much of the great cat's feelings were his own.

Fel remained on his back, his paws curled to the evening sky. He was relaxed and calm while the phantom young man was troubled and searching.

"It's g-going to be all-all right," Mún whispered aloud.

The night whispered nothing in return, but hearing himself say the words made him feel better. He found this strange, though he didn't fight the feeling. Instead, he decided to make a catalogue of his own mind. This was the only way to be certain he wasn't losing what was left of himself. But how to do it?

He would begin, as always, with a song. The Bœzch defeated each of his musical firewalls, and each of the scores that he embedded with domain pásscoding were seminal works from antiquity. He thought on this and frowned, saying to his lion self, "I'm a m-music lover, but n-nnot a mu-musician." He could appreciate the bars of music, even understand the octaves high or low, feel the frequency as it changed, sometimes see the notes in his mind as the harmonies sailed past his ear, but construction of a modern melody that he could weave his pásscoding into from inception was a feat he had never attempted.

Mún sat up, fleeting thoughts burning away with the feathered dimness of the night. He felt ideas pass through his mind as if the surface of his brain were fingertips in running water. A thought. Any random thought. What did one call the first meal of the day? The concept eluded him. The word hid from him. One word or two? "Morning foods?" He scratched that out, caught another thought and held it to him like a wrestler. It squirmed, but he stuck it faster to him. Mún gasped with the elation of a rescued concept. "Breakfast!" For the moment, he cleared his mind.

The lion, with one eye half open, watched his ghost companion as he called forth data from the robotic ticks in the lion's mane. The young man sat cross-legged on the hill. He accessed a holographic window seen only in Augmented Reality and activated an application therein. He began to create, to mash together disparate sounds and alter their harmonies, apply feedback, distort their tempo, and layer and remix loops and tracks of music into something more complex than anything he had yet embedded.

Fel carried a dead deer by the throat all the way to the arcade pier. He was going to deposit it in his usual spot near the carousel with the white horses and golden bears, but today the children had learned how to switch it on, and it was turning at a mild pace, electronic harmonies issuing from the mouths of the semi-intelligent robot horses. The children on the backs of the carousel animals waved to Fel, though they didn't approach him. Mún appeared at his side and pointed to the doorway of the largest candy-striped shop. There, several of the older kids shaded themselves under the gables of a hat shop, standing outside, trying on bowlers and caps. One of the girls looked up and saw Fel. She and the rest of the children were cleaner now, less tattered. They had worked out how to re-power the arcade, how to make the clothing fabricators churn out outfits to replace their spoiled school clothes. But they still couldn't fully operate the food fabricators. The most they could get the machines to do was copy whatever Fel brought them by a random factor of two to ten.

More than half of the sixteen hundred children Fel rescued were now deranged, their spirits broken by the constant pattern of death and rebirth at the jaws of Ambros. The spaceport hotel was turned into a makeshift sanitarium by those children who remained mentally competent. Fel and Mún knew the leader of the sane. He was a tall blond Mitteleuropan boy with a wide brow and narrow eyes. A Moartale Human like the rest, he could not see Mún, and it never occurred to this haunted-looking boy that their hulking feline protector might have a ghost of his own.

The girl by the hat shop was wrapped in a costume that she pillaged from the abandoned storefront along the arcade. In her tailed, stylish brown coat, white blouse and billowing trousers, she stepped forward, still keeping a runner's pace between herself and the lion. Upon seeing Fel and the deer, she cupped a small brown top hat to her mouth like a conch shell and called to a figure three stories up. The blond boy stood in front of the hotel monument sign, where he stretched to adjust the letters there. The afternoon waned and the screaming patients in the sanitarium needed tending, but the boy was lost in his thoughts, using a light pen to alter the pásscoding of the signage. The plasma letters of the sign, if translated from Ing'lesh to their Old Earth English equivalent, would have appeared changed to spell out: Welcome to Barbary Four's Survivors. Serving the Lion of HeLl.

The girl called up to the boy, shouting, "Fjorn! Your friend's back!"

The boy named Fjorn returned a shout, "You need him just as much as I do!"

"He brought dinner! I'm not popping the butthole out of this one!"

"You didn't gut the last one, either!"

"I watched you do it!"

"That's not the same, Besha!"

"I don't like it!"

"And I do?"

"Be a gentleman, Fjorn!"

Fel grew impatient and dropped the deer at a bronze fountain near the hat shop. He sensed something out of sorts with his other self, and the squabbling of the children was a distraction he sometimes needed. He roared once, and though his manner wasn't aggressive, the children jumped and fell silent. They all looked after the lion as he moved away. He seemed lugubrious. They were curious as to why he watched some part of the air before him, bobbing his head as if he tracked an invisible butterfly, but he was moving away from them and they were relieved. They would feel relief again when he returned.

Invisible to them though he was, Mún was no butterfly, and yet he had a kind of meandering pattern to his progress, as if he were carried along via the air currents, drifting from leaf to flower on a week's worth of life. He was struck by an idea that would not leave him, a inkling that he pinned to his mind like a moth to a cork board — and yet, despite the presence of his notion, he doubted his direction. Troubled, he wandered from the lion's side, toward the colosseum entrance near the water, that place that once was clogged with so many dead children that Fel had to use them as stairs.

He wanted Fel to follow him. He would stray far from the side of the great cat, then return, only to wander away towards the colosseum again. He repeated this process over and over until, after several minutes of this, Fel followed out of annoyance. The pier-side entrance was located many meters away from where the children had made their camp in the arcade. It seemed clear to Mún that none of them had returned to the colosseum since the day of their rescue. At least it seemed that way in the beginning. The ghost and the lion found it easier to enter the galley where the little white gondolas now rested in their berths, bobbing gently at the safety mark of a river restored to its normal hight.

The colosseum floor was a bright gray picoscale metal surface. It was dry. Here once was calamity, the signs of distress still fresh everywhere. Heaps of clothing, dark patches of dried blood, knives and swords and pistols lying in piles, and there in the center lay dead Ambros, his remains burned to charcoal by Fel — the lion's last action before abandoning this place two weeks prior.

Light glinted off something in the stands. Mún walked towards it and Fel reluctantly followed, asserting his disapproval in small aggravated chuffs. Mún projected himself to the top of the stands, but Fel had to trot back several meters, then run and leap to the top of the single-story wall. The ghost of the young man pointed and Fel saw a small, picoweave sword protruding from the charred breast of Dianthus. The footprints in the blackened stands were a child's shoe size. Mún walked past the demon's torso. He was more interested in a large metal ball that lay lodged between two rows of seats farther up the stands. When Mún gestured for Fel to follow him to the object, they both saw that it was one of the heads that used to hang from Dianthus' apron. Though it was the head of a metal giant as big as a sitting man, Mún recognized its face immediately.

"Give it a b-b-blast," said Mún to his cat. "Bring it to l-life."

Fel stared uncomprehending.

Mún put his hands together and pantomimed the wings of a bird flapping away. He pointed at the head again and repeated the pantomime, saying, "J-just a little bit, Fel. Make this head move."

The lion backed away, either refusing or still unsure of the instruction. Whatever his ghost asked of him now, it filled him with unease. Mún frowned and said, "Then I'm s-sorry f-for this."

An intrusion took place somewhere on the lion's side of their shared cerebral property line. He felt fingers sliding into his face. Not the sickening, penetrating tendrils of the Bœzch, but a more familiar, comforting presence. The sound of wings rising in a gale: a pásscode was activated, similar in structure to an old fugue melody, but many octaves too high — a password that set in motion a kind of Pavlovian program that compelled him to ... to what?

White lightning consumed the ebon cat, softening his hide into translucence, turning him transparent so that for the moment he was a stained glass pictorial set against an ethereal light. Inside his torso, and looking out into the world, the hidden eye turned within the space that Fel would otherwise occupy. It blinked once without lids, and the lightning flashed out over Dianthus' great metal disembodied head.

The demon's mouth creaked open with a sound that psionically ran against the contours of the mind, so that even the children far from here, running about the arcade pier, heard pipe organs undergoing a raucous tuning. The head screamed into wakefulness, demanding, "Where am I? Where am I? Where am I?"

Fel returned to his solid state and slumped into his belly. When he saw that the jaw and eyes of the head were moving, he rushed forward and roared, but Mún calmed him with touch of his fingers. The young man sat down cross-legged before the head. He turned sideways in order to set his eyes parallel with the canted face of the demon. He said, smiling, "Hello, Dyana. C-can you ss-still see me?"

Her iron eyes rattled and turned towards Mún. "Where is my dog?"

"Dead." Mún shrugged. "B-blown to cinders."
She hissed.

Mún leaned forward and said, "Tell m-me a-a-about this resur-resurrecting eye. D-did you t-take it from an Ægeleif?"

"I want my dog," clanked the hinged mouth.

"Why w-were you killing a-and resurrecting the ch-children over and over?"

A momentary pause fell between them. The head seemed to be staring far off, somewhere past its Human guilt. "We have trouble with young minds. We needed to test their elasticity."

Mún shook his head, asking, "Is it J-Jeüdora's eye? Is tha-that why the Gylfinîr c-couldn't c-contact her on Bram?"

Her face closed up and she took on an expression of stifled outrage.

"Ah," Mún replied.

Dyana's metal head rasped, "Hünde didn't like the way she was looking through him. Her right eye tapping and ticking in his bloodstream, threatening to reboot his Bœzch frame ... it could not be tolerated!"

"How d-did he over-overpower an Ægeleif?" Mún demanded.

The sound of gears grinding, and the face formed a mockery of a half smile, heating the air between them. The lion shifted at Mún's side and growled. The bronze lips of Dyana said, "Their minds are very open and vulnerable when they are alone and away from their Gylfinîr Engine Priests. Devour the Gylfinîr and take their minds into your body, and the Ægeleif will fall before the Bœzch after confusing my masters with the Æthereal powers of their protectors."

"It c-c-caan't be th-that simple," said Mún. "They aren't b-blind."

"B-b-b-b!" she mocked.

Mún shouted, "They c-can see you aren't a Gylfinîr!"

The head said nothing.

Mún continued. "Ah ... that's r-right ... the Conjurer. W-well, he's finished c-casting illusions."

The head remained silent, showing no emotion.

"S-so you t-took Jeüdora's eye. Hhh-how is it absorbed into the b-body of a host?"

"Entangled!" the head of Dyana shouted. "Dislodge them from the theory of their own existence, then wrap them up with some other vegetable, mineral ... or animal, and they entangle their new home as if it were a pocket universe. If entangled with a living being, the host becomes a Wayfarer, a great traveler of the road of whatever power is the Ægeleif's specialty — Jeüdora is the Resurrection Queen."

"Is Jeüdora a-alive?"

"Am I?"

"I d-don't know."

"It is the same with her."

Mún was growing impatient. By appearance, he was unflappable, but his agitation began to show on Fel's face, the lion's lips slowly snarling up over metallic fangs. Mún said, "Is she on B-bram or has she b-been moved to Bosh Übor?"

"She was in my dog. She is in your cat. She is in you, Wayfarer."

"Th-that's an eye. Where is the r-r-rest of her?"

The metal face contorted. For a moment she seemed exactly like that wry young girl who once paralyzed Mún and left him to die in darkness. But the familiar moment faded as she lowered her eyes. Except for hints of disgust where her steel lips curled down, she was unreadable. She appeared to be nothing more than a toppled statue, and had she been abandoned for a millennia, her Mona Lisa face would seem just as mysterious to future explorers as it was to Mún now. "When my masters transformed you on the Long Savanna," she began, "they had among them a Seerer General. He carried with him the eye and attempted to insert it into you. Through him we saw you vanish, and for the briefest moment there was a glimpse of a leopard, but it, too, disappeared. We assumed this meant your pitiful frame was unworthy of the Bœzch gift, and that the theory of you was lost even to the Bœzch appetites. The Seerer departed Long Savanna then and brought the eye to my dog, here on Barbary Combine. Ambros tested his powers on the Seerer, of course. Eating and resurrecting it again and again until the very idea of a Seerer collapsed from reality. That was a mistake. There are no more Seerers now. We didn't know that the *theory of you* returned as a lion. We should have always known where you were."

"Where i-is Jeüdora, Dyana?"

Mún could feel her revving up as she said, "Where are any of us? Where are we that we settle on fits? Where are we who work in shifts? Where are you who ..."

"Stop!"

She sang on, a tongue like cold fingers, weaving the spell with her words that would allow access to Mún's mind, "Where are you who suffers not a mind to live?"

Mún resisted.

It began with the end of *Boléro* compressed with an echoing, whispery wah. Its punched-up bass was ushered along with a repeating one-second loop of a crushed sample of the violins from Purcell's *Cold Song*.

"What are you ...?" the demon head of Dyana began.

Six seconds in, *Boléro* was overtaken by the first verse of the *Cold Genius*, the words of the halting vocals compressed through a sweeping flanger as the counter tenor sang, "*Wha-at pow-ow-wer ...*" The demon tried to push harder, but two more repetitions of, "*Pow-ow-wer ...*" seconds apart were cut off by a sudden interjection of the beginning of *Una Furtiva Lagrima* with bassoon and strings ripped into static until they took on a semblance of fuzzed-out electric guitars. The demon's eyes rolled about, confused by the layered synths, until her eyes refocused and she shouted over the radioed harmonies, "Play your fiddle, little Mún! Play on and on, but we have the final doom! I've called the hounds down from the mountain! They've heard my cry! They'll stampede down upon you and —" She was cut off under a cascade of white noise. "*Wha-at pow-ow-wer art thou-ou-ou ...*" the celestial reverberating lyrics swept and hissed through an explosion of distortion that was again the warped end of *Boléro*. The demon found no foothold into the mind of the young man or his lion. The firewall of sound was in place, the head of the demon locked out and screaming from the injustice. Mún nodded to the lion, saying, "Here we are ..." and with a sound like snapping steel bars, Fel tore her mind from her metal cranium.

As they exited the colosseum, Mún was unsure if the information he extracted was worth resurrecting the demon. Although the fifty seconds of his musical firewall was a success, he didn't know how Dianthus/Dyana's power compared to Hünde's or his remaining gang of beasts. But it felt stronger. It had to be stronger.

He named the mix *A Furtive Cold* and again told himself that everything would be all right. He felt that he had a better defense now, one that could possibly turn away all of the Bœzch — so dared he to dream, to dream and discover a path back to Luti. If it was true that the leopard was a walking pocket dimension, built on some impression of the theory of him and his beloved, could he meet her there? Could they populate the yellow stars together, safe and alone in an Eden outside of space?

He would dream.

Chapter Twelve
Down to Limbo

Mún spent the next few nights working on his opus while Fel sought out the world around him, caring little for the work of his phantom friend, and ignoring all else but his quiet joy in the freedom of the surrounding woodland mazes. The young man worked slowly while the lion played, building and layering the parts of the harmony along the loose structure of a mash of tempos. It was not an easy task. Whenever Mún paused, he took note of the fact that both he and his lion self appeared stuck in patterns of repetition. But the recognition was brief, and whenever it seemed certain that he was about to fully expose the crux of his repetitiveness, he would forget the pattern until the next lull in his work.

The lion began every morning the same way. He rose to the sound of raccoons as they were chased from the nests of black grackles at the tops of evergreens. He watched as the scene played out under trees that grew in canted geometries on the sides of the fractal-distorted ravines. He chuffed and rolled in the false sunlight, immediately setting out to explore. But his joyful excursions were a space of time encapsulated by moments of sudden anxiety. For reasons unknown even to Mún, Fel would stop and roar and chuff to himself, pacing in broad circles through the red canyons and green ravines as if he were caged and driven mad, pining for freedom.

Yet, he was free.

He would eventually snap from his stupor — usually after an hour — chase a rabbit, and then return to exploring. Towards nightfall, if he hadn't found a deer for the children or himself, he would fall into another hour of panic and delusion and then snap from this episode just as Mún took a break from his work.

Mún did not work quietly on his composition. Everything was a great cacophony of noise in the beginning, a wondrous swelling of feedback that filled the places in his memory where lurked a great vast blackness — that which haunted him since his return to cognizance; Mún was convinced that, in the time before he was brought to life again, there in the colosseum, he had seen the empty void whence the Bœzch horrors came. But unlike the blackness, the noise he now made felt directed even when it was halting, as if he stepped out of chaos to march in place, slowly inching up to some point in the inverted horizon; he wanted to fill up the abyss in his memory with the sound of angels. This noise he made was a new and better horizon, a simple flat line he could use to set his bearings and know relief from the midnight gorge of the Bœzch.

It was on the fifth day of Fel's wanderings when Mún noticed that the music was leading the lion. Mún remained confused and despondent with his stammering and his clouded concentration, but when he composed his opus, the music and intention of his will grew clearer whenever he faced a certain direction. The direction was not always the same. Only the distance was consistent. On the fifth day, right around the false sunset hour as the Charon lamps dimmed themselves into an orangish hue and the bats began to totter from their mossy nooks, the stricken young man discovered that he and his lion companion had been making a perfect circle of movement a kilometer around the perimeter of the arcade and colosseum. Now they were winding out from the circle, moving farther away from their base and closer to the ragged mountains towards Barbary Combine's port side, down the way to the next colony in the link, Barbary Five. There Mún saw it, a cloud of smoke in the distance, riding low over the grassy plains leading up to his position above the fractal canyons.

Fel saw it too, and Mún queried the lion's ticks, silently asking for an analysis of the brown and gray cloud. The lion squinted ahead, allowing the ticks to use his augmented eyes as binoculars. Mún could not directly see through his counterpart, but he felt there was something about the cloud that Fel found disturbing.

Just then, Mún turned to the sound of soft footsteps behind them while Fel kept staring to the area far off. Three of the children were approaching. One was the tall blond Mitteleuropan boy with a wide brow and narrow eyes, the one the girl called Fjorn. The girl was with him, too. She wore a wide brim hat and, Mún remembered the boy called her Besha. They were accompanied by another teenage boy, a long and lean ginger lad who stood with his hands on his hips while Besha strained towards the distant cloud with her own pair of binoculars.

They cautiously strode up to Fel, taking no interest in the spot where Mún's avatar stood. Instead, they followed the big cat's gaze, and Fjorn and Besha fiddled with the binoculars while the other boy kept a wide space between himself and the lion.

The binoculars were small, appearing to be only thin goggles without any sort of strap or earpiece. Besha held them up to her nose where they stayed on their own, hovering upon the bridge there. She said, "I still just see a cloud, but it's not magnifying."

"How far off is it?" Fjorn asked, frowning.

Besha replied, "A few kilometers at least. But I can't tell what it is."

"The zoom's on the side, next to that little red dot," the other boy said, pacing anxiously away from them.

"I don't see any — oh!" But she did not find the controls for magnification. A holistic message sent both a signal in telepresence to her simple cybernetic implants, while at the same time displaying the words "AUGMENTATION UP" in the corner of her retina.

Besha shrunk back in shock, for here now was a young man standing between the lion and her group. His features were dark and Hiichiim, a gray ban collar about his neck, a hawkish nose, and hair as gray as static. "Who the —" she began.

Fjorn watched her face and interrupted, "What is it? What are you looking at?"

"There's a man here!"

Fjorn took the binoculars from her nose and looked at them. Frustrated he brought them up to his face, saying, "You've turned on the AR detector." Then he saw Mún and stepped back with as much shock as Besha. "Have you been here the whole time?"

But before Mún could answer, he and the group of children stooped in surprise as Fel suddenly craned his neck to the sky and let out a booming war cry of a roar. Mún understood this sound; the robotic ticks delivered their cache of images then. Mún could see them now. There under the cloud of dust and turmoil stampeded a super pack, hundreds of wild dogs running with a crazed intention. The image from the ticks rendered in Mún's mind magnified the faces of the lead canines, and what he saw there chilled him. These were not living things. Their limbs and torsos appeared whole, but around their tumescent necks Mún could see a kind of biomechanical stitching, and all above the neck was rotting and dead. There were many with heads of bone or with hangings of rotten meat that flapped above the rattling of teeth and bare skulls. Their eyes were white and dead. The last words of Dianthus came back to him: "I've called the hounds down from the mountain! They've heard my cry!"

Mún consulted the ticks once more. At their present speed and distance, the hellhounds would be on them in twenty-tree minutes. He turned to the boy Fjorn, and he could tell by the youth's face that he, too, was gathering information on the approaching madness. He tore his binoculars away and screamed, then replaced them again and looked to Mún. Mún shouted at him, "Run!"

Fjorn stood blinking a few spare moments. He looked to the ghost, to the lion, and then to the oncoming horde, then he whirled and took Besha by the hand. Together the children followed Fjorn back towards the arcade, nearly a kilometer away. Mún was glad to watch them go. He could not yet guess the strength of the dogs, but he wanted more than anything to face them alone with Fel, and for the children to be safely behind them.

He could hear them howling now. It was a sharp, cloud-born sound, an osculating whimper echoing through a far-off valley, stifled and condemned. A long, sweeping grassland connected the bottom of the far mountain range to this topsy-turvy canyon. Mún stepped backwards and motioned for Fel to follow him. It was hard to get the lion's attention, for he was mad with bloodlust — a sudden punctuation of the repetitive madness that recently gripped them both. They were coming on like thunderclaps now, the whimpering sound dropping down onto a doom a cappella. Mún blinked away and reappeared, moving to the far side of the fractal canyon, leaving a twenty-meter drop that spanned another five meters between him and his lion self. He motioned for Fel to look at him again, and this time, finally comprehending, Fel tottered back, then ran and jumped the canyon to meet Mún on the other side. With the canted gorge between them and the hellhounds, they would at least have the advantage of this land's weird geometry.

Fel paced, mad with the intuition of what was coming. Mún used the lion's augmented eyes and the robotic ticks to pull images to the fore, and he stood now within a cloud of hovering pictures blanketing him. He marveled and stared, sick at what had been done to the dogs. How had it been done? There was no sign of a laboratory anywhere within the arcade, hotel, or colosseum complex. Was there another base of horrors up in Barbary Five's mountainous zone? Something else clouded Mún's imagery then. He was seeing overlays of gray, dusky forms transposed over the images of the running hellhounds. He stared closely, trying to make out the huge lumpish shapes. They were like clouds, with thick gray humps and long, turning trunks ... and then, he realized, they were elephants. Mún blinked and peered past the bank of images. There were no elephants anywhere on the planes ahead. Then all through him shivered a collective thud of a dire pang, shared between him and his lion self. He remembered elephants sliding into a chasm, one after another, sliding and crashing and dying. He remembered the screams, the panic, the helplessness. Mún shook himself and turned to his friend. He realized then that this was truly his only friend, and together they now suffered a resurgence of a repressed trauma. There were no elephants here before them, but the mania and panic the lion fought was little more than a sickening phantom from his past.

It had been ten minutes since the children peeled off to safety. This calmed Mún, and the sense of security was shared with his lion self, though Fel continued to pace to-and-fro on the wall of the gorge. Mún allowed himself a moment of stillness. He looked to the false sky, up to the great transparent ceiling with the dimming Charon lamps. It was a cloudless evening, and he noticed something glinting like a star just above the inverted horizon, perfectly set between the place where the distant darkness was blotted out by the Charon lamps and the exterior running lights of the super colony's inner tier. Even if this had been a single colony like the Long Savanna, there should have been no stars to see within Hæl System besides Hæl Damiano, Foss, or the outlying Étienne. Something was moving outside the colony, traveling through the central hub. A ship?

Mún tried to think of some trick to get Fel to look up at the shining dot far in the sky, so that he could use his augmented eyes to enhance the object, but his attention was drawn to a new sound. Mún gasped and moaned a long and breathless sigh. The children were returning.

There were fifty of them, and they hurried onward to Mún and Fel's side of the gorge, carrying with them picoweave machetes, hatchets, handguns and rifles. Mún noticed now that some of them wore different kinds of AR tracking instruments over their eyes. They were looking up at Mún as they approached, and what he saw in them was not youth. He saw soldiers in every one. He had forgotten that these were no longer children. Each having died a multitude of times in the maw of the Wayfarer, each had grown accustomed to fearlessness, to sacrifice, to death, and there was a fellowship among them that was untested even among the most experienced mercenaries of their time. They were broken things, each and every one. Mún felt an instant kinship with them then, for they reminded him of some other broken children, lightyears away and a decade in his past, fighting to the death over a dementia-stricken world.

Fjorn himself carried a small picoscale fractal gun, while Besha walked beside him with fractalwire rifle, the both of them looking all too familiar with the operation and care of their weapons. Fel, too, watched them. Was that pride in his expression, or was Mún anthropomorphizing his animal half?

The ghost of the young man called down to the orphan musketeers, "Just s-stay be-behind the lion!"

Besha grunted. Fjorn strode on.

As the children approached, Fel was back to his pacing, never taking his eyes from the coming horde as he turned in a circle there on the ledge of the canyon. The cackling howl of the hellhounds was deafening now. It filled every corner of the sky and cancelled out the natural gentle patter of the colony world. Whatever lunatic command had been issued by the severed head of Dianthus had pushed the zombie horde into an unstoppable run. They were dead and fearless things from the neck up, but their hindquarters were yet mortal, and many of the beasts' bodies collapsed in death from exhaustion, their still-howling undead faces screeching as their limbs fell under them and they were trampled and crushed. Yet the remaining horde plunged onward. They would leap the gorge when they arrived, Mún understood that. He wondered what of their first attack: what would the lion do?

He saw Fel begin to charge. His internal biomechanics were churning, his knuckles growing white. Fel's back arched and his stomach swelled, and at that moment Mún realized the lion's intent. He looked back to the approaching child, then to the horde, now seconds away. Mún screamed to his lion self, "No, Fel! U-use lightning, not fire!" But it was too late. A great swell of flame tumbled out from the mouth of the enraged cat, and he turned and reared up his molten face. In a flash of cinders the hellhounds leapt the gorge at the same moment the lion released his blast upon them. They rained down upon the heads of the cat and the phantom man, and engulfed the child soldiers in a firestorm that incinerated all in its path. Mún saw Fjorn shove Besha down the hill behind him. A smaller boy turned to run and rolled into Besha, tripping those around her, and they rolled with her. Fjorn and fifteen others in the front were fully engulfed in the blazing sea of light. Then the next wave of hellhounds were over the ravine, pulling at the lion's hindquarters and neck with their rotting fangs, making little purchase in Fel's armor but tripping him up in the still-burning pools of Human child and undead canine alike.

The remaining youths now recovered from their surprise and were engaging hellhounds up close, though they were outnumbered at least ten to one. Shorter boy and girls with swords and hatchets moved in front of their friends armed with projectile weapons, while those with guns and rifles fired over the heads of everyone else. This was a practiced tactic, honed in the devilish colosseum over the past several months. There was no weeping or calling out to those who had fallen. They were as inscrutable in life as they were in death, for they knew that every state was temporary. Yet, despite their courage, they were losing to the hellhounds one by one – down and down they went. Fel was pushed around the tops of the gorge as if he were upon an ice rink, but here the ice was the gore of the fallen and the strange green ichor that dripped from the bleeding hounds. This was a part of their insidious construction: that they should rend and howl as monsters in melee, but once they were truly expired, they would melt into a slippery, acidic oil.

Mún, a helpless phantom in a world of mortal danger, could only look on as chaos rained around his friends. There was nothing he could think to do. His mind, his last cognitive part of himself, shook and screamed obscenities, and all the while he was sure he heard elephants trumpeting and crashing into an invisible abyss.

And then the sky broke open above them.

It started in the empty air; thunder rolled on in reverse, a peal of lightning struck out from a single spot, far from any cloud, and it swirled and grew in a great vortex of shimmering, transcendent light. It seemed at first to fall quickly to the ground, but Mún soon understood that it was stationary, and it was the spin of the colony that came up to meet the light. Once the vortex of white touched the top of the gorge, it unfolded itself like a sack of cloth. Hellhounds and the remaining children alike moved with unsteadiness around the circumference of the thing, still vying for a chance to tear at each other, but holding their distance from this new threat. Fel used the distraction to regain his balance. He threw off two hounds and crushed a third under his sternum, using the blighted thing as leverage. Then, within the flickering spotlight of the alien light, a great wind burst forth from the vortex, knocking everyone but Mún from their feet, and five figures stepped from the light. One was a giantess: the figure in the great

iron tree, whom Fel released from captivity on the
Ouroboros Object. The others were welcome friends:
Fawn Virgilis in her armored skirt and concealing
headscarf, her Staff of Æthax and Sword of Évir raised
above her head, Bacalhaus and Zallo's beetle armors with
fractal accelerators drawn, and one of the Vongallo women
in her armored campsuit, already firing her pistols into the
hounds nearest.

Seeing them, Fel chuffed in happiness and set to
mauling his enemies with an unrestrained enthusiasm.
Mún could feel the shared giddiness between them, and
such was the intensity of their glee that the lion seemed to
understand the desire held by his phantom young man: that
the children who had fallen should rise again. The lion
turned translucent and white. Clear, joyous light flashed
out from him, and Fjorn and his friends rose up naked from
under the charred bones of hellhounds. They blistered their
feet on the still-hot ground, causing them to retreat, not
from fear, but as merely an instinct to pain. One of the
beetle suits paused a moment, looking on in the direction of
the retreating children. He stumbled at the sight of them,
ignoring the rotting canines snapping at his armor. But
then its pilot, made sober by something he saw in the faces
of the waif-like grins of the children, pushed on through his
companions and went at the still-surging hellhounds with
such a fury, it was if he had been a bent centenarian
suddenly restored to youth by a magic tonic. His fractal
accelerator rifle lashed out azure blue in every direction,
and everywhere the ordnance turned, hounds were blown to
ribbons.

They each beat back the enemy on all sides,
forming themselves into a fighting circle around the center
point where the giantess and her guard first appeared, now

with Fel at the point, Fawn Virgilis at his left cutting down what the lion missed, one of the Vongallo sisters protecting the Gylfinîr's flank with the rat-a-tat of her pistols, and the two beetle suit pilots roaring through with their rifles, turning all that approached into pinkish foam. The hellhounds finally began to shrink, their bodies now forming a wall of corpses where they fell together in writhing groups at the edge of the gorge. Finally, the white giantess had had enough. She brought her brilliant hands of light together in a single clap, and a wind that was only felt by the enemy brought the wailing dogs into the air like autumn leaves before a gale, and dropped them back over the wall of flesh, where Fel ended them all in a single arc of lightning.

Ash and dust fell like black snowflakes, and the sudden stillness was unnerving to Mún, who stepped through the wall of dead as a ghost and strode wide-eyed past the familiar company and up to the giantess at center. He kneeled before her, his palms nearly flat upon the scorched soil, and said without looking up, "Thank you, Ægeleif."

She laid her hand upon his back, and whether it was a trick of telepresence, he could not tell, but he could feel her warmth upon him as clearly as if he were physical. Her caress coaxed his eyes up to hers. She said in a tongue like a patter of tiny waterfalls, her sighs underlined in phantom pastel strokes upon the canvas of his mind, "Rise up and know me, and you will see an old friend from darkness."

Mún did as she commanded. His consciousness fell into her eyes, those great whirling galaxies under radiant white lids, half-crescent orbs, locked in a sleepy droop of understanding. He knew her.

Their attention was drawn from their circle then, as a small figure crawled up over the wall of smoking hellhounds. It was Fjorn, now clothed in a poncho thrown to him by a friend. Fel roared low up to him and the boy waved in return. The boy stopped himself, for the beetle suit closest to the lion was opening, revealing the stout, mustached figure of Zallo Frautmorgan, who unbuckled himself from his armor and ran the distance to his child. They embraced in silence with the shadow of dead hounds on the brow of the man, and the eternal radiance of the Ægeleif on the face of the boy.

The false dawn shined down from the faintly orange Charon lamps strung high overheard like dimming Christmas decorations. Fel sat with his phantom self on a wood and metal fishing platform under the arcade pier. The sloshing of a small white gondola, dipped pale sienna in the morning light, was the only sound beyond the remote calls of grackles and hidden toads. Fawn Virgilis approached Fel and Mún alone in her little boat, pushing along with practiced ease. She tied her boat to the stationary platform, which was still soiled with sand and grass from the recent flood, and stepped up to meet the ghost and the cat. She smiled under her headscarf and said, "I never tire of that. I was once a gondolier ... in another time before my Ascension ..." Then she added, becoming quiet and leaning forward, "Æsirisæ was surprised to see you still lived."

"So w-was I," Mún replied, while the lion watched him, a half-moon gaze upon his hairy brow.

The Gylfinîr paused a long moment, seemingly counting the lion's breaths between the seconds as she stood in silence. She continued, saying only, "You, your cognizant half, I mean."

"Y-yes," said Mún.

"She thought the demon had erased you before she sent Fel through the Grip Point."

The young man stared beyond her, craning his neck to the bottom of the pier, sensing something there. He said, "He d-did. I c-came b-b-back."

"How?"

"I w-was called."

"By?

"Hünde and Dyana."

"From where?"

He could feel some webbing of his mind begin to clear. There were fingers there, brushing the filigree aside, pushing into him — they were not demanding, these fingers, not like those of the Bœzch — they were the caress of a friend who lifts up the window so the breeze will cool your brow. The Ægeleif was near, Mún knew it was her: Æsirisæ. She was above them, resting her immense shoulders against the firmament of the pier, stretching in her shining arabesque garments, closing her eyes and telling him everything would be all right.

With the radiant goddess near him, Mún could feel his aphasic mind clear, and he spoke without his stammer for the first time in days. He said, "I blinked into existence again, hovering over the remains of the Bœzch's last universe. Just like the first time they tried to kill me."

Fawn Virgilis followed her own gaze with her body, lowering herself before Mún and resting on her knees. "Describe what you saw there."

"I saw a great unraveling of the Æincode," he breathed.

"What do you mean?"

Mún's face fell in restrained memory, his eyes revealing a place of deepest pitch, for he was no longer looking at anything within this world. He heard elephants and arias. He saw blackness beyond the light. After a time, Mún breathed out, "When they eat the theory of you, you see it. In bold, full sentences, you see all their concepts blast past you on their way to replace you. You see, the Ægeleif teach us that our universe is anthropic, that it functions because we observe ourselves in it. But it could just as easily work without us if the Bœzch were allowed to rewrite the Æincode to exclude the theory of our species. You understand? When you look at the Bœzch, they aren't fully in this plane. But as they remove the observation of Humanity, and the awareness that Humanity has for itself, the Bœzch replace it with a concept of themselves, solidifying their place here."

Mún buried his face in his hands and gnashed his incorporeal teeth, and as he did so the lion's lower jaw jutted over the upper lip, revealing fangs like the teeth of an icy crown. In that moment, Mún did not know if he channeled the lion's own despair or if he burdened his feline self with his many Human emotions. "The universe is too big for us. Better for us all had we never been explorers," he said and stared away, his gaze rising to the underside of the pier, watching the small fragments of Ægeleif light that pushed between the cracks like forgotten shafts of divinity drifting down to Limbo.

"Do not be so quick to dismiss the migration of our people," said the Gylfinîr. "This is the farthest we have ever been, and in truth this is the farthest any of the sapient races who have their own versions of the Ægeleif have ever been."

At that last sentence, Mún brought his gaze back down to her, but his face held no expression. Fawn Virgilis nodded, saying, "Yes. There are more versions of the Ægeleif than the Human construct. But more to the point, our being here means we are pushing father to discover the cure for the Telic Death of the Universe, farther than any of the older and wiser beings in all of Gylfinæ's many aeons of expansion — and as we step out to these reaches, we unveil more of her current anatomy, and we are able to make a chart of the universe as she is now instead of how she was. All those past astronomers ... all they could see was the past itself, for that was the Curse of Lightspeed. We are their future envy, but when we make paradise and revive the dead, they will rejoice at our shoulders."

Mún rolled his head against the torso of the lion, and the telepresence between them made both slightly react to the shift in weight. Fel half-closed his eyes and made a small sound from the side of his whiskered mouth. Mún said, matter-of-fact, "We build a future for the past to have a place again, but what about our present, Fawn? This big cat beside me doesn't give a damn for anything out of sight. And out of time is too far gone for anyone."

She laughed, though not bitterly. "You sound like the pre-Engineered."

The young man shrugged his shoulders against his lion self. "Were they so bad?"

"Yes. Of course," she said, shaking her finger in schoolmarm fashion. "Though they had the means to migrate, they did not use their resources to travel to other star systems en masse. Instead, to protect their longevity, they retreated into virtual realms. Their forms of communication grew more terse, their attention spans waned, their brain sizes evolved into smaller, platitudinous systems.

"Look there," she said as she pointed to a figure far off on the shoreline opposite — two figures, actually, for Mún saw the smaller of them step out from behind the taller. It was Zallo and his Moartale son, Fjorn. "You know our history. Look how much taller and more refined a Moartale Human child is compared to his pre-Engineered ancestors. That's not six thousand years of evolution. That happened in the span of dusk to dawn after the eve of the first speaking of the Æincode to Humanity."

Mún did not remove his head from the side of the lion. He continued to watch the other shore. How happy the maddened soldier looked as he walked with his family — and by maddened soldier, which did Mún mean, father or son? They were one and the same now. They were soon joined by a third, the girl Besha. She still carried a rifle strung over her shoulder by a thin cord. She shook the elder Frautmorgan's hand. Zallo smiled down to her. Mún took his eyes away from them and said to Fawn, "And what did the holy Code do to those it did not immediately convert?"

The Gylfinîr's silence was cold. "It was not the intention of the Ægeleif that so many should die."

"Really," said Mún.

Fawn Virgilis continued, her speech quickening to mask an old wound, "The first three Ægeleif entities, Rafæl, Eüllo, and Göthe — traveled through the collapsing remains of Proxima Fujiai's gas giant. Each stepped through their individual gates and carried the map of the known universe to each of the three systems that held Human life: Olde Sol, Alpha Centauri, and Epsilon Eridani. One by one they spoke a portion of Æincode to the people of these systems and they recoiled in horror when they discovered that the pre-Engineered Humans were not yet ready for so a powerful gift. Billions of people went mad in an instant as their eyes were opened to the naked structure of the Æincode. Telic Death, the part of the Skript that envisions the planned destruction of the universe, drove many more to agnosia. It was the end of religion, nations, and solitude of the mind. Many ..."

Mún interrupted, "Killed themselves."

Fawn pushed past his pessimism, saying, "But those who survived looked around them and wondered how they could touch that brief moment of understanding again and survive. The Ægeleif rebuilt the Human world under a new model: Gripper Gates would give Engineered Humans the ability to move instantly to the farthest shores to discover and wield the full Æincode of the Ægeleif. But for that they must first uncover and map all of the universe in real time. Only then, when the boundaries are revealed, will we be able to write the rest of the Æincode that that will in turn grant us the ability to tweak and hack mass, particles, and waves."

The phantom young man sat up, but only because the lion grew bored and turned over on his side, lying his head between his paws and closing his eyes. Mún protested the simplicity of the Gylfinîr's last statement and said, "But it wasn't the end of politics or nations." Then, growing more excited, he added, "It certainly didn't swing an axe down on religion! I was an Ærdent!"

To this she laughed, and Mún felt for the first time that she meant to sting him. "You state it as if it were a fact, as if it were your species! You were no such thing. Your *parents* were Ærdents. You *are* Hiichiim. That is your race and the race of your parents — and mine as well.

But the cult that they brought you up in was not yours until you accepted it. But did you? You could have stayed in the cult, gone on to another colony. But where did you go? Hmm?" Fawn waited for Mún to answer. He remained silent. She counted on her fingers, saying, "It has been six thousand years since the beginning of the Engineered Years. Mankind has had time to return to folly, but not in so many numbers as there were before the coming of the Ægeleif. You can count on both your hands without filling up all the digits all the cults present in the sphere of Society."

"Cults!" shouted Mún. The lion growled in his sleep.

She dismissed his outrage with a gesture, a flick of her hand and an upturning of her head. "What do you call them? A Luddite rabble who placed their people on the face of a dangerous planetary system and then recoiled in horror when the predicable happened? The Ærdents were fools complicit in their own deaths!"

Mún continued to shout. "We were seekers of the truth!" The lion turned over in his sleep.

"Then why did they start by denying the truth?" Fawn demanded. "The Ægeleif are the creations of Humankind. They are not angels sent by any god. Your people were obsessed with mystical things bigger than themselves, and that is not the true purpose of the Æincode. The language of the Æincode is much like pásscoding. Both can be wielded like notes in a symphony, yet while pásscodes are used to create computer macros, the Æincode models gravity, electromagnetism, strong and weak nuclear force. That is all. There is nothing more mystical than the illusion Humans fall under when they hear it spoken aloud, because it rings all the forces in the universe that you are a part of."

He could feel her eyes burning him under her black headscarf, and he turned away from her, preferring to stare at the tadpoles swarming like black broken lines around the lily pads that bobbed near their platform. "And what if, while you grope around in the dark for the cure for Telic Death, you find the hand of a Bœzch holding the torch?"

Fawn Virgilis paused before answering, regaining her eloquence in the interval. She turned compassionate again, her words drifting up from her sternum. "Why do you suddenly doubt the Ægeleif? Is this a return to your gloomy self? Where is the commanding Mún who enslaved his fellow man on the *Mare Hypatia*?"

He felt flushed with loneliness then, his words filling his head as if from a remote place. Was the Ægeleif leaving the pier above? "I don't ... it's just ... you ... you used the Æincode to open the portal at the Ouroboros Object. Why did that work? It was an alien Gripper Gate, built by the race the Bœzch enslaved in their prior universe. It brought them all here to begin the process of eating all over again. It didn't feel entirely in phase with our dimension, just like the Bœzch. The Æincode shouldn't have worked ... unless it's changing."

"Come with me," said Fawn, and she returned to her gondola, pushing from the platform with her long, candy-striped oar.

The lion stood up and shook his mane. He did not follow the black-clad Engine Priest onto the boat. Instead, he made his way back up the stair to the morning-lit deck of the pier and its white arcade and followed close behind the giantess, Æsirisæ, as she strode away in calm, balletic steps, keeping parallel with Fawn in her gondola. Mún vanished from the platform and reappeared that same instant in the boat, seating himself and watching the beautiful Ægeleif angel in her mythic, silken attire walk with the black lion in tow, like an illusory child strolling with her kitten.

Fawn Virgilis repeated to Mún as she rowed to shore, "As I said, the entire breadth and mass of the universe is a Skript that is Ünderwritten in the Æincode, and it was this discovery that allowed my forbears to write the Ægeleif into existence. Through them we found that the universe had a name for itself in the code. Gylfinæ is the name that our prefecture of the multiverse responds to. Thus far, only a portion of the Skript has been revealed to us, and so we pan out among the stars mapping the Skript as surely as we map the planetary systems. When we know the full breadth of Gylfinæ we will know the full purpose of the Æincode. We Gylfinîr whisper the Æincode to everything around us, and in this we often find new phrases in the Skript that were once hidden. When we made orbit around the Ouroboros Object, it was my intention to prod at its corners, but ... but when I saw the Æincode written above the portal, my hearts filled with dread, for it was partially rewritten."

Mún was still watching Æsirisæ, and she him. He blinked away from that immobilizing gaze just long enough to understand what was being explained to him. He stammered once again, feeling his aphasia creep up on him as the distance spread between him and the angel. "B-but you made it work," he said. "You o-opened the door."

"I read the portion that held the door. The rest was lost to me."

He sat lounged in the bow of the craft, blinking with lips apart, trying to mouth fawn Virgilis' words back to himself, hoping the sound of his own voice would make them more clear. He replied with astonishment apparent upon his tongue, saying, "But the Bœzch c-came here m-millions of years before us. The writing above the door must have been new. They wouldn't have been able to write the code for our universe before they entered it, would they?"

Fawn continued to row while standing, shaking her head slowly, her face pointed ahead. She said, "More to the point, if they rewrote that portion of the Æincode millions of years ago, how much more could they have rewritten by now? No, the words above the door must have been new. I would feel it if it were otherwise. "

"Th-then we still have t-time to stop them?"

"We must."

Mún mouthed the old saying, "We must go on ... we have to go on ..."

She stopped rowing, allowing the narrow boat to glide quietly toward the green shoreline. She set her stare upon the phantom young man, leaning ever so close to his face, and he felt her eyes, even through her black shroud. She said, "But I will know once you tell me what you saw when Tautolo reached into you."

Mún was so stunned by this, he did not notice that the feeling of wholeness was returning to him. They drifted closer to the place where the Ægeleif now stepped down onto the waterfront, sitting herself down there, holding the immense lion in her lap like a common house cat. He did not stop himself to wonder why, if his mind was really inside the lion, did his aphasia worsen whenever his avatar, projected as it was through a simple electronic network, was far from the Ægeleif? He didn't think of this, for his mind was locked on a memory of Hünde, standing over him with an enormous stone clutched in both his soft, artisan's hands. Mún said, after a time, "A memory of wicked children."

"I don't understand."

The young man felt his precise cruelty return to him. He was again becoming the kind of man who could enslave his crew to do his bidding, and he directed his lion's gaze to the Engine Priest as she stood over him, seeking suddenly to dominate the conversation. "No, answer me now. What happened after I was transported away with Fel? That was Alon in Bacalhaus's beetle suit. I saw him limping from the shell just before dawn. Where are Bacalhaus and the other Vongallo sister? Is Montefeltro aboard the *Mare Hypatia*? Did you move like me through the gate with Æsirisæ all the way from the Object, or is that my ship I see glinting in the central hub?"

"Ah. There's my Felmún." It was Æsirisæ who said this. With a jerking bump, the gondola ran aground against the emerald grass where the Ægeleif giantess stroked Fel's mane with one hand, while cupping his body in the other. "Oh, soul o' the great cat, would you hear our tale? I should be quick though, for our enemies bear down from blackest space, and we have little time to prepare before the end. Listen."

Chapter Thirteen
The Last Judgment

"They were in the black abyss of the Ouroboros Object. Their small band made a circle of light against a vast horde of the sickening unicorn serfs of the Bœzch lower pantheon. Up came the foe, whose red and ebony horns forever impaled the last thoughts of their centaur slaves. Up the enemy rose through the diamond-dust remains of their once corporeal servants, moving silently in the vacuum, their radio squeals lost upon untuned channels.

"But that was then — nary a month ago to you, mere moments to me. Let me take you back farther, and risk our few hours remaining to explain the Last Judgment upon my shameful brow.

"I remember you, oh sweet Felmún. You were held down in the darkness, and I was yet unborn. You called to me with your poem:

> *In black amber, black amber, black amber*
> *Hither, where am I, that I follow*
> *Hitherto blood flown blackened vessels*
> *In black amber, black amber, black amber*
> *Hitherto I lie in black amber*
> *In black where or where am I where am I*

"You gave me sweets, and I gave you riddles. We spoke of violence between you and your rivals, and I began my road to ruinous contemplation.

"When I was born, I brought down misery upon your world, and for that I am forever heartsick. I saw you once again, this time in the miserable light of your ruined township, the harm of my birth evident in every direction. I turned away from you and asked my mother, Uedolpha, to send me far away, to some undeveloped system where I could atone for my crimes in darkness. But Mother could not find me guilty, for the seed had been hers to cast. How was I to direct my own beginning, or its proximity to life? No, I was deemed worthy and sent to Odin System, a great center of three metropolitan planets. I would share this system with Holæstin, who manned the Gate to Windsor Society, while I would hold the way open to Thrundin System's new frontier.

"My gas giant was a Neptune-sized world known as Sigmundr. I spent my days and nights as all Ægeleif did: I walked the clouds of my sky-filled world with the slippers I weaved from the mists around me. I listened to the poems sung to me by the Gylfinîr Engine Priests of merchant ships, and I opened the Gate for them with pride and warmth in my ethereal breast when the poems they paid me were like Eddas of Human compassion. As I walked each week long days under azure skies above and over onyx storms below, I learned to love my place in the universe, and I grew to forgive myself the crimes of my birth.

"But like the wisps of methane that curled about my gowns and vanished into the gale winds, my happiness was fleeting. I had grown accustomed to flattery. It was not a thing for an Ægelief to desire. We are supposed to allow the travel of ships through our gates by cultured crews who express their civility in poetry — poetry of love and compassion, of insight into nature and the psychology of children. But I — I had grown fond of being worshipped. More often I turned away ships whose Priests gave me only philosophy. I wanted to be desired, for in desire, I think, I was able to better convince away the crimes of my birth.

"The pirates who eventually found me did not include in their poems their true intentions. They mentioned nothing of traveling through my Gate to abuse the Moartales of Thrundin. They didn't need to put up lies or pretend to be merchants or explorers or ministers of goodwill for me to give them passage. No. All they needed was a silver tongue and stanzas full of praise and flummery, and the silly witch of Odin would give them the way through to death and plunder. And so I gave them a pass, and three thousand deaths were added to my list of crimes.

"I buried my face and wept when the Windsor Temporality took arms against the pirates and freed the people of Thrundin. The Gylfinîr Priests in orbit around my little Gate assured me that, again, these crimes were not my own. I was a fool, certainly, but how was I to know such evil lurked in the hearts of Humanity? But I knew. I drew a memory of our talk in the dark. You spoke of the war that your brother, Hünde, waged upon you and I said then that perhaps Humanity should have restrictions placed upon it for its own good. Slavery — that is what I meant — and so I composed my corrupted pásscoding, the Will of Æsirisæ and bade my Gylfinîr Engine Priests deliver it to Rafæl herself.

"The response from the Ægeleif Body Divanté was swift in its censure of me. My powers were diminished, my post abandoned, and I went alone into the universe, moving from gas giant to gas giant, alone and weeping without hope or direction.

"That was when the Bœzch found me.

"How could they discover so small a thing as a giantess among the trillion stellar multitudes? I will tell you. And it will shock and horrify you, for it is the terrible secret of the Gates. I can see by the look that plays upon the mouth of Fawn Virgilis, she wishes that I not divulge this thing which is only shared between Gylfinîr and Ægeleif. But I must, dear Fawn. This cat and his man-spirit are one of us now. Why, this very beast is made Ascended by some of the same style of biomechanics used to remake you. By his very Engineering, you and he are siblings of the Wire. No, I must tell him.

"Mún, have you ever felt out of sorts when you travel through a Gripper Gate? When you arrive on the other side to your destination, does the universe you step back into feel unused to you? A Case of Disquiet, we call it. I understand that you have only moved through a Gate thrice in your lifetime, but I assure you the feeling that crept up your spine each time was not a phantom sensation. You did not just travel to some place lightyears away in an instant. Three times you have moved through Gripper Gates, two times you have traveled to an alternate universe, each one out of an infinite number, all of the infinite alternates called Gylfinæ. Every person who has ever used a Gate to travel farther than four lightyears has vanished from their original universe forever, to be replaced by another version of themselves whose mass takes up the space where your atoms originally thrived. So there it is. The idea of interstellar travel causing a person to vanish from their own universe, to appear in a slightly altered version of their own, without ever knowing the difference, is a horrifying scheme. The traveler doesn't detect the difference because the altered events in one universe often have nothing to do with anything in the local Human part of space. In one universe, a star eight billion lightyears from Olde Sol System shines slightly brighter, while in another universe it does not. This is completely without consequence to Human events. Thus, you have no reason to believe that you are not in your original universe — unless you are an Ægeleif.

You may well wonder now, how can we then map the entire universe and discover the breadth of the Æincode if we're are not in fact mapping the same universe. The answer is, we cannot. In almost every version of ourselves, we are mapping the Skript, and almost none of these Skripts will match. We will, instead, be left with various patchworks of maps, none of them truly connecting — none — or almost none. In a multiverse of infinite universes, there are an infinite number both designed to die and designed to live forever. Thus, an infinite number of universes, and an infinite number of your descendants, will die in the Telic Death of their universe — but also, an unending number of your descendants in an infinite span of universes will be saved by our mapping of the Code. So then, there is hope. Why keep this a secret, to be shared only among the Ægeleif and their Engine Priests? You see the reason: overwhelming despair. The order brought about by the coming of the Engineered Years will be lost as Humanity ceases to search for the cure for Telic Death and instead plays a shell game of trying to find the right universe to live in. This is already happening in a small number of universes in the Infinitum, and since it is a finite number in the endlessness of all, it as if it is not happening at all. You see? No? I think you do.

"You say you saw the dark, empty dimension whence the Bœzch came. So have I. When we move through the gates, we move to an alternate version of our

Gylfinæ universes. But there are other names, other designs, other types of universes that are disconnected from our multitude of Gylfinæ. The Bœzch are from Huennboros, a dead zone jammed between two versions of Gylfinæ with no alternates of itself, a single pocket of doom drained of all its vitality by one of its few sapient species, the Bœzch. I am wrong to say they found me, for in my wanderings it was I who found them.

"Perhaps I was hoping I would eventually stumble into a version of Gylfinæ where I made none of the mistakes of my past, perhaps I forgot this was folly, but it was my insistence on finding something new and completely different from what I recognized that opened the fatal stair down to Huennboros.

"An infinite number of myself stumbled out into black mists where I formed up into one terrified entity, non-Euclidian rune shapes of purple lightning-lit clouds of unidentifiable chemicals, where negative spaces of jellyfish shapes pushed on through, luminescent, moving broken and lugubrious, as if filmed in reverse. These were not the lighted layers of latitudinal storms of ammonia or water vapor that I was accustomed to. This was a circle of mythic Hell, though soulless, without even the company of the damned.

"Struck by the darkness of the ruined Jovian world I stepped into, blinded by the utter lack of massive worlds detectable in any direction, I searched in terror for another agent to jump to. Many parsecs distant, I found Huennboros' version of the Ouroboros Object, and without understanding what it was I steered myself to, I brought a Gripper Gate into existence and leapt through it. I arrived within more darkness that was broken only by a violet star, or a thing like a star, but altogether sinister in that I could feel its far-off glare as a thing of hatefulness, as if the Sun itself was spiteful towards the ambulatory creatures built from its very own stardust. There were other stars in the sky, but they, too, took a surreal coloring as dots of green and colors I have no name for strobed out of harmony with each other. I realized after a time that this new point of mass was both above and below me. A perfect circle was what I floated through, a ring with me at the center, and the inner walls of this ring equidistant six thousand kilometers above and below me. I did not stay long. The Object activated, and brought me back to all the infinite Gylfinæ, to the Ouroboros Object in the Hæl System. There, Tautolo the Demon found me.

"Without a Gylfinîr like Fawn Virgilis to shield my mind, I was left open to the Demon's might, and he bound me thus to his ziggurat of bones. I was his trophy. My will was weak, my strength sapped — I do not know how long I lingered — but I could feel the presence of another Ægeleif, Jeüdora, somewhere within the system. I could feel her anguish, as I do now. She is silent now, but when we were both at our most desperate, our thoughts touched across the vastness. They had taken her eye, she said. They had taken her down from her failed star, Bram, and encased her in a living circlet, like a writhing crown of thorns upon the highest peak on Bosh Übor. There Œlexasperon, the emperor of all the Bœzch, lies curled at the foot of his prize like a guarding hound.

"They have been trapped for so very long. They forced their pan-dimensional slaves into building the Ouroboros Object, so that they might travel to this universe. But they were tricked. Jeüdora tells me that the hateful Bœzch homeworld froze when they arrived in Hæl System sixty thousand years ago, and that the slaves set the

Bœzch planet on a collision course with Bram. They could not have known that one day Bram would become an interstellar gateway. Now awoken by the approaching heat of Bram's star, Étienne, Œlexasperon waits for Bram to crash into his planet, that he might move the whole of his hell through the Gripper Gate and on to Human Society, replicating his Bœzch from one version of themselves across the many alternates of Gylfinæ as if they were a cancerous cell gone malignant and unstoppable. I do not know if they have yet spread among the alternates of Gylfinæ's Hæl System, though this is more my hope than guess, for their makeup is alien to me, and my crimes of weakness drag me through muddied visions ...."

When Mún was sure the Ægeleif had finished telling her tale, there upon the grassy slope of the river's shoreline, he stood and paced with his thoughts. Fawn Virgilis and Fel stretched. Mún gauged his own mind before allowing his mouth to open. Finally, he said, "They have spread to other versions of this system. I've spoken with my fiancée. In this universe, she is dead; in her universe, I am dead. There is a point at which we meet, yet we cannot touch, and the vessel through which we sense one another — I don't understand it. Through either of our eyes, the other is seen as a leopard, though each of us knows our minds are held prisoners in the bodies of lions. Does that make sense to either of you? Is such a thing common?"

Both the Gylfinîr and her Ægeleif stared on in misery at this news, but before either could comment, the lion rose to his feet and began his crazed circling and chuffing, like he had in the time before his battle with the hellhound horde. Mún watched as Fel would circle and fret, then look back towards the direction of Barbary One. Again he wondered why the lion acted so very anxious towards a section of the colony. Then he realized: perhaps it was some place beyond the colony. Mún slapped his own forehead for being a fool. He had forgotten that the lion need not look "up" at the false sky to gaze into the heavens. After all, this was not a planet they walked upon. Mún attempted to make contact with the *Mare Hypatia*, which was still parked as a distant speck of light in the vacuum of the colony's open hub. He received no reply from the ship's AI.

"What's wrong with the *Mare Hypatia*'s personality?" asked Mún. "I can't contact her."

Fawn Virgilis stood and walked beside the lion as he paced and scratched at the ground in agitation. She placed her hands upon the great cat's spine and said to his phantom young man, "Because the mind of the ship has been supplanted by another."

"Whose?"

She replied, "When Montefeltro's body was destroyed on the Ouroboros Object, we had to find a suitable vessel to store his soul."

Mún stared blankly for a moment, at first not understanding the meaning of her words, then he said, "Montefeltro is ... dead?"

"Only his body," said Fawn. "Both his and Vígdís Vongallo's android bodies were destroyed, but we were able to save both of their minds. For Vígdís, her sister Védís has accepted her into her spine, while Montefeltro has taken over the duties of the *Mare Hypatia*'s AI after it was damaged in our escape from the Object."

The information felt remote to Mún. He wondered just how much more inaccessible, how far-flung it would feel without the Ægeleif shining over his phantom head, bringing solace to his fretting brow. He said with some consternation, "And Bacalhaus?"

Said Fawn Virgilis, "He is aboard the *Mare Hypatia*, assisting the Librarian in his settlement. He has considerable skill and understanding of transferring personalities from one body to another. We would have lost both Montefeltro and Vígdís if Bacalhaus had not acted so quickly — "

Mún interrupted, impatience returning to him as guilt crept up on his periphery. "I would like to know what happened after Fel and I were transported away from there, but first it's urgent that the *Mare Hypatia* scan the area of space in the direction beyond Barbary One. Can Montefeltro do that?"

Fawn pointed to the tiny bright dot in the blue between the clouds. "You can ask him yourself. Access the channel you used when you visited the Cutlip Nomad."

This seemed so obvious that Mún blushed at his own oversight. What was happening to his wit, his impulsiveness? He must not lose any more pieces of his personality. He must keep himself together, if only for as long as the mission lasted. He could be content to fall into complete ruin once he was successful. The thought made him smile, and he vanished from the company of the Gylfinîr and the Ægeleif, leaving them to look out over the river together, both watching where Zallo walked with the warrior children under the mists of morning.

Mún did not reappear in the Cutlip Nomad. He attempted the connection, but his link into the Tacit Reality realm flashed briefly before him as if he were looking out through the arch to an elevator lift, but then he shot away, just as his hand reached to open the gate, and was forwarded to someplace directly within the *Mare Hypatia*'s EtherCore network. Instead of his usual spot beside the rustic fireside, a great oaken door reared up before him, and he saw himself reaching for the nickel door lever in the shape of a twisting rabbit as he crept into Montefeltro's library.

"To both of us, welcome back from the dead!" quoth a voice from everywhere at once.

It was another moment before the confines of the library finished forming up around him, though he was certain it had always been there, as complete as any other Quiet Place within a Brummagarti. Mún blinked around him as the floor stuck under his feet before he could fall into blackness, and a plaid sofa rose up to meet his backside. It was the old library, now expanded and reassembled to fit Montefeltro's new body, the *Mare Hypatia*. Mún outstretched his arms across the sofa and felt the familiar motifs of laughing rabbits around the cushioned frame as Montefeltro's avatar, quite literally a ghost in a machine, climbed down from a high ladder attached to a quarter-kilometer row of books and prancing hares. Mún waited until the Librarian came down to meet him before he asked, looking up into his eyes, "Are you ... comfortable here?"

Montefeltro threw his arms up, gesturing around him to his marvelous, lapin-filled chamber. He replied, "If that's your way of asking how I'm feeling, then yes, I'm fine. I always preferred my inner life."

"I'm sorry," Mún said without thinking.

"Why? Sorry that you killed me?" The Librarian's response was without malice, though the dispassion of it stung Mún all the same. He opened his mouth in retort, closed it and looked away to the window and the green hill beyond.

Montefeltro continued, still indifferent, taking up the seat across from Mún, and saying, "Yes. It's your fault the Vongallo sister and I were struck down. It was your orders that bound us to the Will of Æsirisæ. Any deviation from your orders would shut us down. When your lion body ran off to fight alone, we attempted to pull back to the *Mare Hypatia*. This was interpreted as a violation of your order."

Mún remembered the lion's dream in the dark. It crept up on him on the platform under the dock, as he had lain there waiting for dawn, wondering where to go with his composition. "And you crashed the wayboat?"

Montefeltro clasped his hands together and smiled. He said, "You and I together, yes. You were too untrusting to allow our free will, and under your spell I was not strong enough to fight you. If Alon had been unsuccessful in convincing the *Mare Hypatia*'s AI to move into the ring, we would all be dead. Real death."

"What happened to the *Mare Hypatia*'s AI?"

Montefeltro pointed to the window, and where once stood a pleasant hill, now a terrible benighted gloom descended. Images clashed — recordings from each crew member, their Brummagarti and biomechanical eyes having recorded moments of anguish in the dark — and Mún again saw the swirling Serfs from his dream. He saw the wayboat go down. He heard Montefeltro say, "There were other things lurking within the Ouroboros Object more powerful than the Bœzch Serfs. My body was smashed and splintered in the crash, and though my head was crushed and burned, the inner protective casing of my TEA Cell pushed me into my library; from here I waited and watched

as the tumult went on. Vígdís was in the same state as I.
Her sister, Védís, though burned through her campsuit all
along her left side and exposed to vacuum, protected our
Gylfinîr all through the tumble of the wayboat. In the end,
however, it was Fawn Virgilis who saved her remaining
Vongallo guard, for she used the trick of her kind and
became insubstantial for a moment, pulling Védís along
with her before the explosion could consume the rest of her.
As for Zallo and Bacalhaus, the former sewed more
confusion by unloading the entire supply of his beetle suit's
fractal torpedoes to increase the destruction the wayboat
had carved through the Serf horde. Bacalhaus, meanwhile,
for what reason I'm still unsure, used his own beetle suit to
pry open the twisted cockpit that was my tomb and remove
what was left of my head, taking it with him. I owe as
much thanks to him for my life as I do to you for my death.

   "Zallo's display of firepower confused the surging
Serfs into thinking there were more attackers present than
in actuality — or so that's how it seemed — and by the time
they came running through the constant firing of our
remaining ammunition, Alon was sweeping in from above
with the *Mare Hypatia*'s ship scale guns lancing up the
circle of death like a lightning-born banshee, bless him.

   "As the ship came to within our reach, and we
boarded one by one through the lower airlock, we didn't
know that another Bœzch General lurked out there. But I
could feel the disturbance in my library. It was empathy —
empathy for each other began to feel like an impossible
feat, as if our very souls, if that's what we call them, were
becoming gray, colorless. We were bewildered. And then
we knew the sensation. It was the *Mare Hypatia*'s
EtherCore dying. The Bœzch thing was on the hull of the
ship! Its hideous fingers stretched out along the lower pile

of the forward cannon tower, where it soaked up all that there was of our poor ship's AI. Again, Fawn Virgilis used her insubstantiality and moved through the deck like a ghost, surprising the thing while it was drunk on the ship's cognizance. She took off its hands with her Gykfinîr sword, knowing it was helpless to drink her own mind without its ability to touch. The thing tumbled away in the darkness below, and again it was Bacalhaus who acted for me, taking what remained of my head to the ship's EtherCore deck and expertly uploading my entire TEA Cell in less than twenty minutes. And then ... I felt more alive than I had in all my few centuries. I was a ship! The universe was my library now! Another curious thing: the transfer had ended my service to you. I was free of the Will of Æsirisæ. And so I bid you farewell and moved us back out and away from the Ouroboros Object."

The memories of death and fire through the dark of the Ouroboros Object faded from the window, the light of the splendid hill raising like a Vaudeville curtain. He said nothing, waiting for Montefeltro to speak, and the Librarian, smiling whole and true, laughed with a gusty earthiness that seemed new, almost unflattering to his character. He held a face like those mirthful rabbits of which he was now surely a king, and said, "But do not cry for me, my dear Mún." "As a matter of appreciation, I would like to thank you. It's as I've always believed: sometimes from the worst of things come the best of things. I was always meant to inhabit a ship. And I have your stubbornness to thank for it."

Mún heard himself say, "Well, you're welcome."

Montefeltro smiled in silence now, filling a briar pipe with apple-scented tobacco.

"What of the Ægeleif?" asked Mún. "How did you rescue her?"

"She rescued herself," said Montefeltro, lighting his pipe with a snap of his fingers, and shaking out his thumb as it were a match. "She used the mass of the Object as a feed for her transfer. When we were two hundred kilometers away from the Object, I detected a a Gripper Gate open within the very hold of our ship. Zallo explored, armed and fixed, upon death of course, but there she was, weaving a new dress for herself out of star stuff, sitting and smiling kindly in the same launch bay where the wayboat once rested."

Montefeltro then made a face that indicated he was cut off in mid-thought. His recollection slowed rather than halted, but whatever he meant to say, all that pushed past his lips was a sudden, "Ah!"

"What is it?"

"I have your report."

"My ... oh! You scanned the area of space?"

"Yes. I am sending the report to Fel's ticks. It is ... alarming."

Mún tilted his head, as if listening to some far-off sound, and the data that flowed before the miniature EtherCore processors of the lion's robotic ticks was now privy to him. Numbers and calculations tumbled about his brain and jostled with abstract visages. He saw the totality of the Hæl System from an extreme range, the outrageous orbits of its satellites represented as radiant lines, their distances represented in kilometers and Astronomical Units. The distance between Mún as an observer and the stellar system as a backdrop began to close, and new lines from either side of the small yellow dot that represented the star, Foss, blinked into existence. The new lines became circles and the circles enhanced themselves and grew into starling illustrations. Then, the ticks interpreting the data therein, the lighted line art was rendered out into three-dimensional imagery. Sinister things moved on through the silent vacuum of Hæl's seemingly preternaturally ebon space. Cape Series, Simba and Guggisberg Series colonies came from the prograde side of Foss, from where the Long Savanna spun in silence, away from her blighted sister colonies. The information revealed that out of ninety of the Cape's colonies, only twelve pushed on through the night, propelled by unseen forces. The Cape's twelve spun on behind the ruined toroidals of eighteen of Simba's, while leading the pack on this side of Foss came twenty-eight colonies of the Guggisberg variant. Then the imagery flashed, moving to the opposite side of Foss — Barbary Combine's side — where lumbered fifteen of the Batang Series, followed by seven Masai Mara, thirteen Manyara, and finally three of Seronera Series. There should have been ninety of each of these colony series, leaving five hundred and thirty-four colonies missing. Could so many have crumpled under the strain of their Bœzch infections? Mún thought it likely, and the pain of his failure to save them brought his hands to his face. They marched on as would the undead, tugging their forms through the ink and entropy on a course for Barbary Combine.

"I need to speak with everyone, immediately," Mún heard himself say through his fingers, and he felt strange then. His body grew light. He was lifting up and up, the sensation of rising dropping his hands to his lap as he slowly spun upward. He was leaving the sofa, leaving the library, the rabbit motifs laughing up at him while the hues of the wooden shelves and paneled walls faded and turned slowly to silken white.

The room was falling apart like domino pollen, blowing away from Mún in flocks and droves. The white surrounded him even before it became light. He rose up and up as if dead, Montefeltro's voice at first far behind him as he floated through the white ethereous nothingness, "It will do you no good, Mún ..." Then finishing up before him, the Librarian said, "As long as they remain enslaved, this crew will fail to fight well for you."

Somehow, bathed in effervescence and love, Mún knew he had been forwarded through Montefeltro's library to a place more thrilling, more achingly beautiful than any Tacit Realm filled up with Human dreaming. He had been passed on to Æsirisæ's own Quiet Place, and the startled young man was filled with a billion bells of lighted joy. "The Oshii Librarian speaks true, Felmún!" proclaimed the Ægeleif, her every word a symphony of truth glittering across the warmth of his cerebellum, far down in his sighing lion body.

Within this lighted, Nouveau chamber, an airy vault ten kilometers high, the open vine-woven columns revealed endless storms beyond the white shimmer of phantom-physical constructions. Gossamer syncopations swirled from unseen string ensembles, where the vamped tonality of musical syncopations was king, and sonorous rhythms lifted the spirit whilst dooming the mundane. There all the crew of the *Mare Hypatia*, the incapacitated, the injured, and the living, surrounded sublime Æsirisæ like an immortal Norse Pantheon attuned to the melody of lights. The righteous, hallow bell voice of Æsirisæ radiated through Mún as she said to him there, "The data is shared among us. We all see the approaching horde wreathed in myriad dooms! They come to kill us now. What will you do, O leader? What say you of emancipation? Liberate the sword-arms of your people and they will sing for you! What say you, Felmún? Become my Gylfinîr and together we will ride down on them! Angels in the black mists! Bring death to doom with me and together we will know a love cloaked in fire!" Mún stared up at her, his heart pounding a thousand kilometers below him, the intricate melodies sweeping over him as a syncopating wind — lights, hues of ash and bone, a melancholic joy that pursued and dominated the essence of one's hidden self as a lover to a friend: Mún's courage built up around him, an armor of radiance and sound, of elephant clouds and running leopards, of fading dementia, of the thrill of waiting to be born. He closed his eyes and made his answer.

Chapter Fourteen
Fall of the Damned

"Make me your Gylfinîr? Are you trying to bewitch me?"

The Ægeleif lowered her head, hiding exquisite features in the shadow of her own form. She trembled there, as if throwing off a great temptation. Æsirisæ said, just above a whisper, "If that is what it would take to move you to action, I confess from my heart I would bewitch you a thousand times or more. That is what my younger self would have done, and that is why my youth was wasted." She paused, becoming aware of how her own elemental passions could sway the Human conscience, and she clasped her hands over her face in a motion that was improper to her kind. She made an inhuman sound, as if she wept Christmas bells, and shouted Æincode data into the hall, clutching her fists to her side and revealing a grimace, an ire of restraint. She shouted, "Hypocrisy! Shall I enfeeble your mind as you have your peers and force you to release them from enslavement? Would you be any better a fighter than they?"

She rose up over him, bending light away from where they met upon the dais, but the young man remained embittered in her shadow, his defiance overt in the manner of an old man, wizened and weary, full of ire for the healthy. "I can't trust them!" Mún shouted in reply and gestured toward the pantheon of heroes before him, and though his venom spat towards seething Zallo, his air was one of suspicion for the lot. "They would murder my lion body, destroy our urgent mission on a whim of fright! Yes,

I was deformed by demons into the lion that leads my ghost! No, I am not another Bœzch demon! Yes, it was their intent to make me one of their own, but no! A hundred million times no! I am not theirs! I am my own monster! I am mankind's monster! And yet they — these fools would kill me and assure the enemy their victory just to tuck away their fear of what I might be! Babies and dolts! And you expect me to give them weapons unsupervised?"

Zallo bristled and moved forward, but he was held by Bacalhaus, who placed a hand upon the mercenary's chest, pushing him back in line and shaking his head. The great blue genie then turned away from his distant relation and strode across the white pavilion to Mún's avatar, falling to one knee before him, startling everyone present when he bowed his tattooed head and proclaimed, "You are right, and we have been fools. In my travels through the galaxy, millennia after millennia, I have witnessed few who have suffered as bizarrely as you, Mún Rafæl, and many more who have dealt badly with a far better hand. I will follow you with or without the Will of Æsirisæ driving me to, but it is true that I will fight better for you as a free man. I cannot predict my performance in the theater of battle otherwise. Free me — free all of us — and I personally will make certain that all here follow you willingly." He inclined his head towards Zallo, who stood shaking and pop-eyed. "*All* here," Bacalhaus repeat.

Mún stepped back and sighed. It was then, with the cool white of the hall upon his brow, and the arrested ambiance of pastel music and sonorous color exerting his senses, that he knew he was tired, more so, that he was at the end of his breath, and that he truly did not know if he could last to the end of the mission on his own. All the eyes of the Ægeleif's pantheon were upon him. Mún's legs were beneath him, but they were not his own. His aches were phantom aches, his pain and exhaustion mere circling ghosts of his Human trepidation. The lion body far below him, he knew, had maladies of its own, and those were true weights upon the flesh, despite his grand engineering. While Fel hurt, Mún could only imagine distress; while Mún suffered, Fel slept in fits; the one forced a feedback upon the other. The eyes of the crew that bore into Mún now, simple avatars though they were, they made the lion moan in exhaustion.

"Give us your answer, Felmún!" Æsirisæ loomed in wait.

"Would we be powerful together?" Staring past her, he seemed to be inquiring some invisible entity far off her shoulder.

She sensed a turning in him, the lion was rolling over, exposing the soft Human underbelly, where reason could seep in, and animal suspicion cast off. She was kind to him, appearing at first to ascend the dais, she instead grew small, drifting down to meet his gaze eye to eye. Softly, she said, "As Gylfinîr to Ægeleif, we will form a bond, you and I. Through this bond, upheld by the Skript that Ünderwrites, I shall pass before the eye of my sister Jeüdora that turns within you. Her strength and my strength, one links to the other; your strength and Fel's, one uplifts the other when they are too cruel alone. As long as we have an adequate supply of power, we four can convert our momentum into tumult and wrath!"

Mún blinked. "Adequate?"

Æsirisæ blinked as well, but through space, appearing behind Fawn Virgilis, the Vongallo sisters, and Montefeltro, sailing past them on unmoving feet, saying to

Mún, "The superstructure of each of these colonies is not enough mass to create a Gripper Gate from here back to Society. But it is enough to move around within the Hæl System."

Mún struck his own chest without meaning to, the excitement in him growing. "Merced the Miser and Emmott the Judge! Those are the two remaining higher demons before my brother! Can you pinpoint exactly where they are?"

"No," said Æsirisæ. "But your lion self can do this."

He paced a moment, then turned to face a lighted status board that he called up from the ether. He studied the shapes representing the approaching colonies, advancing the animation under several approach vectors, expanding and shrinking the areas of interest again and again. As he examined the map, all eyes in turn watched him, noting that the signs of trauma had left him again, for he dithered from deranged to confident as easily as a flower opens and closes from dusk to dawn. Mún pointed and said, "It probably won't be enough to destroy just the two demons. The Bœzch invaded the colonies long before they set up any control demons. We'll only sew confusion as the infected colonies closest to the demons wither and die. The rest will ... well, they'll probably attempt to link up with Barbary." He stopped and considered his thoughts, then added with a furrowed expression, "The rest of you will have to defend Barbary while we make the assault on Merced and Emmott."

Zallo could no longer hold back his opinion. Fighting past the Will that sought to bind his thoughts, he barked, "Defend? Ridiculous! If this is to be a battleground, then make it a trap! When the Bœzch attempt a landing, detonate Barbary Combine and murder them all at once!"

"No!" screamed Mún. "There's too much life left here! We've lost so many others! The whole point to being here, besides whatever the Ægeleif are mapping, was to preserve Earth's biosphere! EUDOLA ..."

"EUDOLA has Terran colonies everywhere in the Milky Way! Their mission can stand to lose a few!"

"No! What are we fighting for if nothing remains when we are finished?"

"Bah! We make our worlds within our minds!" Zallo scoffed, gesturing towards his own temple. "Idolizing the physical world is a waste of resources!"

Mún vanished and reappeared before Zallo, ending his brief leap through space in a shove that connected with the mercenary's chest, sending him onto his back. Mún stood over him, more like a frail ogre than a reprimanding father, saying to him, "These colonies are here to ensure that the diversity of Terran life flourishes forever! Not just in memory! Why are you here, Zallo? Why are we burdened with you, you damned mercenary-parasite!"

He raised his hand to hit him but was frozen in mid-strike by the voice of the Ægeleif. Æsirisæ said from her full height, "They cannot fight for you, Mún, no matter how you abuse them! You have made this an impossibility!"

Fawn Virgilis pulled at his side, followed by the Vongallo women, who also surrounded him with urgent expressions. "Free us, Mún, and we will serve you willingly!" said Fawn. "We will follow you! And your lion! But let us go!" said Vígdís and Védís.

Mún looked past them, to where Montefeltro stood silent but secure, a rabbit king frowning from his place upon the lighted knoll. "What of the *Mare Hypatia*'s guns?" Mún demanded. "She can easily kill a festering colony."

Montefeltro spread apart his hands and shook his head, saying, "Inoperable since the Bœzch General clung to the hull. It's an incompatibility problem between the ship's original AI pássware and my own. Bacalhaus and I will correct it eventually — when we figure out how."

Mún could take no more from them. Montefeltro's words ran past him and away, and everything came to him now as if from a terrible distance. He could only focus on those words spoken by Æsirisæ: "We four can convert our momentum into tumult and wrath!" We four. If the Ægeleif said it so, then was it so? Though they shared a single brain, were they two separate entities now? What was he outside his own body? And yet he could feel the space the lion occupied growing alongside him, pushing him to the boundaries of his cognizance, so that he lived like an interloper within his own mindscape. He began to realize, this was how the dementia crept up on him. He could feel the asymmetry of his brain. It would begin with aphasia — it had already — the rending of his ability to comprehend language, and he would fall like those Ærdent adults of his youth. And yet ... he turned and stared at Æsirisæ. He felt whole with her near.

In terror for his future, he rejected the scene then, pulling back from the crowd until the white of the great hall was a penlight far from his eyes, and then he was standing back on the river shoreline, Fel resting at his side, the Gylfinîr and the Ægeleif both watching him with anticipation.

Mún went to one knee. Placing his hands upon the lion's mane, he peered into those abstruse, reticent eyes and said, "You were so weak and weary when we started out, dragging yourself along the Long Savanna in fight after fight. But that was me dragging you down, wasn't it? What could you do without me? Can you show me?"

Fel shook his mane and roared a reply to the wind above, a roar that bore out from deep within his breast, where the eyes of an angel shared a space with his own flesh. Was this an acknowledgment, or just a dumb animal's cry, an involuntary Pavlovian response to attention? Mún felt a part of himself answer, like a quiet mumbling through a muddle of gloaming static, and he chose to draw away before he could decipher the meaning. He didn't need to understand. His divided subconscious said for him to listen to instinct, to trust in the feral. And so the lion was his own man.

Mún sat upon the damp grass, his telepresence pressing the cold and wet into his clothes. He repeated to himself: he was tired. "What am I becoming?"

"Separate," said Æsirisæ.

"Una Furtiva Lagrima," Mún replied through a whisper and a sigh.

Fawn Virgilis, sitting beside him, held her own face, her lips an O of astonishment. "Did you ...?"

"Yes," said Mún flatly. "'One furtive tear,' that's the oral pásscode. You're all free."

After a short time, on the opposite shore, straight ahead over the swollen river, Mún could see some of the crew gathering near Zallo's child, Fjorn, and his friend, Besha. Zallo was there, of course, and so was Alon. They were joined by the remaining Vongallo sister, and an argument was in play between them all. Mún could guess the subject of their fight. He did not need to focus Fel's engineered ears in their direction. If the man still wanted to kill the lion and his ghost, then at least it would be Zallo alone this time. Still, Fel would have to be quick. Zallo was an experienced warrior, and their earlier confrontation was won primarily to Mún's advantage on the *Mare Hypatia*.

He watched as Zallo pushed past his friends, and when the argument grew and they sought to persuade him over the shore, Alon and Zallo came to blows, the larger of the two easily felling the poet, knocking his cap from his head as he tumbled into the grass. Zallo stood over him. Mún could tell this was not the first fight in their long friendship. Alon did not get up, but sat there sulking and rubbing his new leg. Alon hurled insults up to the mercenary, and Zallo again came at him with his fists raised. Yet now the children moved between them. Whatever was said then by the young fighters, Fjorn and Besha, had a far greater impact upon the soul of Zallo than any argument made by his comrades.

As Alon brushed away the mud from his campsuit, the words spoken by the youths made everyone present halt in their places. The scene across the river did not go unseen by Fel, who at first only inclined his sleepy face in their direction, yet when the children rounded on the mustached mercenary, the lion stirred and sluggishly rose to his tired feet. He roared to the other side of the shoreline, and they grinned up at him in reply, the children nodding to Mún's animal half — an earnest agreement, a conspiracy between the three of them that not even the phantom young man was privy to. Mún continued to watch the space between them, with the lion roaring his blessing across the water, where the children smiled to him as a friend-in-arms, and in that space Mún saw a little-used window from the lion's hidden Quiet Place, where he chuffed his farewell to two small bodies that sailed weightless and free from an airlock; they drifted into the dead of space. The vision left him. Mún wondered at its authenticity. Had the children really threatened to kill themselves? As the group across the river moved on, the two warrior-children going hand-in-hand, Alon and Védís reluctantly leaving Zallo, Zallo alone turned away to wander into the fractal-wrought hillside, his shoulders drooping in shame.

The day drew on. The lion rested at the foot of the lighted carousel until the golden Charon lamps again dimmed to an evening shade and then to indigo night. His dreams were set aside this time, for through them crept that phantom friend, Mún, who paced and wondered at the clouds and fretted for the urgency of his mission. The Ægeleif left them alone to contemplate, moving herself into the hotel lobby using the trick of the Gylfinîr and passing through the walls in spirit fashion. When night fell, a call rang out from the lobby entrance — more of a feeling, a compulsion, than a sound — that gently pushed at the back of Mún's head, as if a ghostly finger curled, beckoning him forward. Mún shrugged his shoulders and walked the distance from Fel to the dimly-lit hotel, feeling the edges of the lion's personal AR network as he passed into the colony's Outhernet domain. He felt no restrictions on where he could travel. He had forgotten to inquire as to the whereabouts of the Barbary Combine's EtherCore personality, but suspected it may have gone into hiding when Dianthus invaded. But the call had not come from the colony's lost AI. Æsirisæ the Ægeleif wrapped in radiant silken white, Fawn Virgilis the Gylfinîr, armored in black and orange, her eyes concealed, and Védís Vongallo the Hiichiim Gird of the Gyl, her gray and black campsuit outlined by blue pinstripes of light: they waited for Mún amongst the delirious children, the ones who went mad from experiencing death after death.

The grand, expansive lobby, styled in that modern form of Art Nouveau opened up like a verdant nest surrounded in wrought iron ivy. The splendid furniture was pushed aside or requisitioned for the sick; the children were arranged in rows upon single mattresses absconded from hotel suites. This was the old familiar setting, Mún knew too well. Around him now were the open O mouths gasping for reason, the staring eyes fixed on multitudes of nothingness, the enfeebled cries of "Help!" that led a chain of mimicry around the great open split-level room. This was simple madness brought on through trauma and stress, but its effects were all too similar to the planet-wide dementia of Tenniel's Garden, the plague of Æsirisæ's birth. Seeing them stirred a childhood fear of Mún's. This was the thing he left behind, that he wished to never see again, and yet he feared it was a window to his own future. Only in the nearness of the Ægeleif did he feel the inklings of aphasia subside. He would need her closeness from here on if he were to finish his opus, the thing he was convinced more than all else was the crux to winning his war.

Mún said to Æsirisæ, "What happens now?"

"Retribution and woe," replied the crystal bell voice.

And all of his world turned white.

Over the deep black of Hæl System spun the plagued and wretched armada that followed on behind the yellow star, Foss. As Foss moved along her asteroid belt of stones and ice, orbiting the distant glimmer of bright blue Hæl Damiano, the largest and most deformed of the Batang

Series colonies crept onward towards Barbary Combine. The wretched colony surrounded itself with fourteen of its sister colonies, a ring of perversion that was the center of a succession of rings of colonies that included the seven Masai Mara, the thirteen Manyara, and the three remaining Seronera Series at the spearhead. They traveled on through the dark as glimmering specks against the alabaster illumination, like shooting stars wreathed in nightmares. Once, they were all populated worlds, more home to Human habitations than to animal kingdoms. They held no Barbary Combine forests or Long Savanna planes. These were the major urban centers of the system, and thus they fell the fastest when the Bœzch came to claim their souls. At the center of this group now, Batang One hosted a demon in its greatest city, and that demon dreamed of a lion. The tower where the dreamer laid his hideous head had once been a city hall, a pentagonal-shaped building eighty stories tall, with fluid lines in kinship with Antoni Gaudí's Casa Milà and garden balconies the size of ballrooms on every level. All was dead or diseased now. The colony itself was a Bœzch entity, a toroidal horror, a fantastically large dumb animal that spun its red chitinous material over every tree or creature that once lived there — absorbing their masses into its own — a dumb animal that infused every fractal replicator within the walls of the colony with the Bœzch ideal of life, so that the health of the colony itself was attacked as a cancer. Everything was rewritten and reborn.

Emmott the Judge whimpered and shook to life. His chamber was ill-lit, his only light source a wall torn asunder by chitinous growth. Diffused in gloom, the Charon lamps above his building were either extinguished or turned to a dusky green and indigo hue. He stirred on a nest of broken horns, collected as they were from the underlings he ravished at his Court of Bones. His entourage did not rise with him; Serfs and Generals slumbered within burgundy hives formed from the remains of their lesser brethren. The fat demon sweat and shuddered from the vision that haunted him, and in his grotesquery, he was more hideous still by the expression of woe upon his many-jowled face. As he lifted his head of curled horns from his pillow of red leather faces, his fat lips smacked under his vulture's nose and his neon moniker came aglow above his head. Lay Your Souls Underfoot and be Trampled by Righteous Spurs, spelled out the lighted words above him. He pulled his red coat around his trembling belly, saying aloud to no one within sight, "Merced? Merced, I dreamt a damnable thing once again, and I am sick for it. Merced! Merced, hear my thoughts! Sweet, good, and kind Merced. Merced, who is my only friend. Lovely man, speak and know my affections."

A far-off connection was made then, and within Emmott's mind he could feel the link between him and the other demon as they connected. Like Emmott, Merced sat within a crimson nest of bones, in a ruined city, within a diseased colony surrounded by an army of the loathsome, but he approached Barbary Combine from the opposite side of Foss than Emmott's armada. Their progress would be slow, taking a year before they could fully force a link with Barbary, for they would use the amniotic propulsion squirted out from the Skin of their transformed colonies, an arduous task that wore on the Bœzch therein. "What is it now, driveler?" said the mind of the demon, Merced, into Emmott's own. "After all this time and still you interrupt me when I am eating!"

Emmott was a low and paltry sniveler before his friend, and thus had been their relationship since the beginning. It pained the demon Judge to hurry his domineering comrade, so he would hurry him with feigned devotion: "But dear, glorious, sweet Merced, you are always eating ..."

"What do you want?" shouted Merced the Miser.

Emmott convulsed in mind and body, dropping his terrible white hands over his face. In a rush, he thought-spoke to his friend, saying, "To describe to you the dream that still lies fresh upon my fretful brow. The lion! I saw him more clearly than ever before! He's coming for us, Merced! Oh with such a terrible wrath this time! It isn't fair! Hünde said he was ours!"

"Wülvogarti is the name of our master, fool!" Merced's reprimanding ire was like a slap across Emmott's blackened teeth.

Emmott sniffed, shaking his jowls under his wig of horns. "Yes! And a good, strong name it is!"

Merced softened under the whimpers of the Judge, and said to his mind, "And aye, the dear leader decreed he was ours those many years ago, and though this Mún still fights us, it is a criminal act, for the property cannot rightfully hound the owner of the leash. It sickens me that even your idiot brain should suffer to witness the property lash out, even in dreams. How dare it! *How dare it!* Tell me, sad Emmott, what have you dreamt?"

Emmott continued, in a rush still, "It's the fool inside the beast I'm finding. Old Mún is growing weaker in his protections, and the closer we come to Barbary the more I see of him."

"The music? It does not lock you out?" asked Merced.

"At the present, no. But I think he is composing a new firewall."

Merced's disgust was evident, even if Emmott could not see his face. The Miser made a sound as if spitting up gristle and said, "Ridiculous. Music busies the thoughts within the brain and makes it difficult to reach through when the traffic therein is lighted with harmonies, but it is easy enough to break through with patience. What is the lion doing in this dream of yours?"

"At first I saw nothing of the great feline," said Emmott. "I saw the property, Mún, bent in that revolting slouch of his, sulking amongst a hive of maddened children. A good work that. Reminded me of Tenniel's Garden. But there also sat the Ægeleif and her witch, and the witch's bodyguard. They were haughty and repulsive in that manner we have known them for and I was sick at the sight of them."

Merced huffed across the great distance between their minds and interjected, "We shall have them soon. Remember, the right eye of Æsirisæ is mine, the left yours."

Emmott replied, "And I thank you for your swirling generosity, sweet Merced of the Miserable Feast, yet there is more to tell and tell it quickly I must, for I fear the battle comes to us!"

"Then tell!" shouted the Miser, returning to his impatient demeanor.

The Judge gulped and said at once, "In my mind I found the property on bended knee before the hated angel. She promised him absolution of a sort. 'Take my hand and repeat the Æincode to me,' said she, and her tongue spun such a twisted harmony as I cannot recall, but it had an immediate effect. The property found himself compelled to repeat the harmony, under an invisible strain, and with malice towards our kind, he called out to his other self, the lion that slumbered outside my vision. The lion returned the cry, and the ground of their chamber ripped and shook with a radiance that too was frightful to my eyes. In he walked, five times his normal height, his extra mass pulled from that place that the Ægeleif hold secret still. White and searing to the sight of those around him, the beast was no mere Gylfinîr! All fell prostrate before the lion, for a connection has been made, my sweet Merced! With the activation of the Skript, a terrible connection between the Ünderwritten elements and the lion, and it will stalk us even through our many protections! We must --"

A scream from Merced drew Emmott out from his delirium. "What! What is it, Merced!"

"He is here! He is here! Œlexasperon protect me!"

Static and pain flashed between the two demons. Through his cruel friend, Emmott heard a roar like a thousand kettle drums, then the sound of thunder through a heart's hollow chamber, a rending and squealing of elephantine terrors, and then a void, a nothingness that threatened to swallow him up had he not retreated deep into his own cognizance.

Emmott paced in a mad circle, fluttering his long fingers against his fat lips, sweating and crying and shouting, "Merced? My dear friend, answer me! Merced? Merced?"

Silence filled up Emmott's mind like a ballad of woe. His hearts thundered as an orchestra within him.

"Marcél?" Emmott whimpered.

The frightened Judge could stand by no longer. With great effort he shook away his petrification and took up the immense gavel by his throne. Blue flames came to life by his touch and the neck of the hammer extended like a telescope until the thing dwarfed him. Down he flung the flaming instrument and rattled the weave of bones at his feet. Creatures stirred in the gloom. Four Bœzch Generals, whose branches and horns seemed to be mere ornaments on the walls, lifted their crimson frames to join the call. Lesser Lieutenants and Serfs crowded up from the base of the throne, moving from that otherworldly place they held between dimensions, then expectantly turned all about, as if wondering where their target had escaped to.

They chittered in lugubrious protrusions of vocal simulations, chastising their leader for waking them for nothing. He halted their protestations with a thump from his gavel, holding his hand out to prep them, make them ready for — for what?

Mún felt so tiny in the presence of his body, accelerated as it was and flung out among the stars. They had run out across the chasm of space after Æsirisæ had opened a Gate and pulled them through; they stuttered across the void like a miniature *Mare Hypatia* affected under Dlaüt Drive, the Ægeleif feeding herself from ambient mass from Foss' unending river of asteroids and ice as big as moons. The young man, the Ægeleif, and the disembodied eye of Jeüdora whirled around the great radiant lion as mere sprits in the night, and together they were a flickering cometary object. They pushed on in the prograde direction that Foss took around Hæl, strobes of light popping about ahead and behind them, jump after jump, sailing ahead without moving. Fel's life support was in place and functioning with ease, but the rest of his systems were overloaded with whatever incantations worked on him through the Ægeleif. His size was unearthly, and the shimmer of the angelic beings lit him from tail to tooth with an undulating chemiluminescence so that all of his body seemed full up with winking stars atop a lamp-lit lake. His robotic ticks were blind, shutting themselves down in the confusion of the transformation, allowing the lion's inexplicable sense for the Bœzch and their once-Human leaders to guide them to the hearths of their enemies.

Though there was no need for movement, Fel ran his legs under him until they opened the final gate and his feet touched Bœzch-tainted ground. Invisibly, Mún watched with great surprise as they appeared at the foot of a blighted tower within a colony that, the lion's intuition told him, was Simba Eighteen. The tower stood at the edge of a city that crawled with the red and black vines of the Bœzch plague. Dying Charon lamps flicked purple and blue behind oily gray clouds, which the tower wore upon its highest story like a crown of fog, and in the Gaudi Nouveau fashion of the times, the planned artfulness of the building wove itself into the Bœzch tendrils so that the whole of the structure seemed to teeter like a scarecrow overgrown by its field, but there was a melancholic life to it, and the scarecrow tower took on the sad, demented state of an old man who looked about his room and wondered how he got there.

Fel roared once to the fog above, Æsirisæ whispered to him, "My brethren," and with a flash they were up the tower, within the chamber of Merced the Miser, and there upon his wretched dining table. The lion did not stop. He did not seem to see the chewed and regurgitated horrors at his feet. He clung to instinct, and when the long, frail foe was sighted, he leapt straight for the astonished face. "He is here! He is here! Œlexasperon protect me!" Merced cried out to no one.

In the hours that followed, Mún could little recall just how the demon Merced had met his end. He remembered the flash of white, the blur of action, the semblance of chattering voices asking for his attention elsewhere, while the demon's blood detonated at the lion's touch.

Were they only memories of conversations? Where did the sounds that pursued him come from? Another strobe from the opening of a Gate and they were returned to the empty vacuum of Hæl System. Blighted colonies on the march to Barbary all seemed to shutter with the rending of space-time, the local area rippling out from Simba Eighteen, which spun apart with the death of its master. Several other colonies, but certainly not all, followed Simba to its end, at least twenty of each type unraveling like tread from a shredded tire. Mún's eyes would not close here; he saw the Gates open and close ahead and behind, Grip Points pulling him and Fel forward and flexing them through invisible openings, space bending space like a hand bending at the elbow to touch the shoulder. Again and again Mún felt Æsirisæ form the calculations, steal the mass, and make the Gate, always following the lion's nose. There flew past them yellow Foss and there went Barbary Combine. Flash and flash, rattle and jump, the lion's feet again unconsciously running upon nothing more than the road made from his desire to slay the wicked.

How long had they traveled, Mún could not say, and yet here they were at the head of the second armada, the lion pointing them onward to Batang One. He recalled his last moments on Barbary Combine, and the plans that were made and the farewells that were passed between friends.

They were his friends, he realized now, for if he could not be their master, then he must be their equal.

Mún remembered standing near the transformed behemoth of his other self. There were blazing serendipitous tides, tendrils of truth and conviction that passed between his lion self and the Ægeleif within him and the Ægeleif that
stood over him, and in the air and in the stars, however far they stood from him. He knew not what it all meant, and Æsirisæ could feel his doubt, doubts which she cooled with a glance. The others came through the door then — the warrior children, Fjorn and Besha, who both took a seat in one of the comfortable lobby sofas, staring hard at the wonder that flowed and shifted in radiant beams within the grand expanse of the room. Silence fell over the afflicted who still rested within their makeshift ward, for a soothing presence saturated the atmosphere of the place. Soon there was a rattle from the entrance, footsteps on broken glass still upswept from the months of disasters. It was Alon, with Bacalhaus in tow. They nodded to the whole of the group, their toothsome smiles snatching away any remaining gloom. "There has been a development," said the blue, tattooed genie, and he demonstrated what he meant by stepping aside as if this were a theater, and the spectacle that approached was the grandest show of all.

Under the vine-covered archway strode five figures: the man was Zallo, who seemed to have recovered his old swagger, and with him were two crimson red lions, walking in at a leisurely pace with the recognizable markings of Fel's own biomechanics. Not far behind them, tiptoeing forward in whimsically small steps, two diminutive humanoids the size of children, but with the skittish manner

300

of laboratory prisoners, checked their forward momentum with both suspicion and interest.

"Hvitt! Rost!" shouted Mún with sudden recognition and delight, for he knew the little men immediately.

They looked past him, both looking very interested in the Ægeleif, the Gylfinîr and the Gird of Gyl guard, until Zallo, stabbing with his thumb in the direction of Mún's avatar, said to them, "All right, you imps, Mún's here. He wants to say hello to you."

At first, the one with the rounder head, the one called Rost, stared uncomprehending up at Zallo, but then the other, Hvitt, took out two small devices the size and shape of clothespins, and clipped one each upon their tiny button noses. They mastered these with some consternation, but once they were properly affixed they both saw Mún fully and each gave a shout. "Our dreary friend! He's made a return! Just as we thought! We're so clever." But when they caught the great outline of the lion transformed, they raised their eyes to the tops of his electric mane and dropped their wizened jaws agape. "What have you done to yourself?" shouted Hvitt, the more emaciated of the two.

Mún waved to everyone present, saying, "It is my pleasure to introduce my fellow engineers, the Tishbyts, Misters Hvitt and Rost." He added, as he watched their movement around Fel, "I had forgotten you two completely."

Fel sat upon his haunches, looking far off through the walls of the building, ignoring everything around him. All seemed new to him, every minute crashing into him as if he were reborn between the atoms with every momentary fluctuation of wind or dust. While Fel looked on, Hvitt prodded at his legs with an egg-shaped device while Rost sent up a number of robotic probes from his belt. The one-eyed probes circled the lion from on high, but still Fel only looked away. "As you were meant to," said Rost. "You were supposed to forget about *you*, too, but we see that that is still a recurring glitch."

Zallo interrupted from the door, raising his voice and gesturing from the Tishbyts to the red lions. "We found them coming from the direction of Barbary One, riding these two ... things."

Hvitt corrected him, perturbed, "They are not mere 'things,' oh no, but a part of your salvation, and there are three hundred more of them waiting under our house." The little Tishbyt retrieved his probes from around the lion's face and beard and said to Mún, "Manticore Project remains complete, Mr. Rafæl."

Mún was watching the light fall across the backs of the red lions, uncomprehending as to the meaning of Hvitt's proclamation, but then a memory of himself crept quietly through the shadowed alleyways of Long Savanna's lone city, Aza Nairobi. There he saw himself as a Human. A full year before the Bœzch attacked, Mún made contact with Long Savanna's resistance movement. This was why he chose this colony, this most remote star system. While in college, his new talent, pásscoding, came too easily to him, and his mind wandered too often back to the war he once waged with his brother on Tenniel's Garden. He fell into a group of Tishbyts, and perhaps it was because he fought with Hünde his entire life that the peace of University wore on him. He needed a new fight. He traveled to Hæl System on a duplicitous contract, one part zoological intern, one part secret mercenary. Luti came with him, unaware of the factious friends he made.

Per the Tishbyt instructions, one night Mún set out alone in Aza Nairobi, found the hidden entrance behind the public garden, and pulling his cloak from his face, there he greeted his two Tishbyt comrades and set about his plans to transform the colony's wildlife into a weapons system, to be used against the aggressive larger colonies. Mún smiled at a reflection of himself in his memory. He turned from the lions and said to the room, "After the Bœzch changed me, it was to Hvitt and Rost I went. They infused my lion body with the Manticore biomechanics we developed together — well, they developed the weapons and defenses. I developed the pásscode macros right before my transformation. Before we erased my mind, we decided that it would be safer if our lion cloning center were relocated to a colony with fewer Humans, fewer thinking minds. The Bœzch seem to have a difficult time detecting Tishbyt thoughts, so Barbary was made our rendezvous point."

"For what?" said Alon.

"Hmm?" Mún replied.

Zallo continued for his friend, "What were you rendezvousing for?" He rounded on Mún without pause, not giving him time to change subjects with any coherence. "And where the hell did you befriend Tishbyts? They're Ægeleif creations! Elfin helpers to the angelic, not the monstrous!"

"We are free agents, of course," said Hvitt.

"What?" Zallo barked.

Hvitt continued: "We were meant to be Æsirisæ's servants, but when she was censured by the Ægeleif, we were let go, and so we followed a work program to Hæl System under an EUDOLA contract. When the more populated colonies began abusing the smaller ones, we became disgusted with Human arrogance. We decided to aid Long Savanna, and so we recruited talented students like Mr. Ræl for our Manticore Project."

All eyes turned to Fawn Virgilis, who flushed pink under her headscarf. "I wasn't informed of Tishbyts being granted autonomy," whispered Fawn.

"What?" Zallo repeat.

Hvitt pointed to Zallo with his thumb, saying, "He's a thick one."

"As black pudding," added Rost.

Fjorn laughed as Besha bent to kiss his forehead.

Æsirisæ looked on contented, for there was camaraderie in their bullying.

Mún explained, pointing to where the red lions lay, "We were to rendezvous for them, of course! Three hundred lion clones finally complete, biomechanically rebuilt and ready for fighting! Let's see if the Bœzch can defend themselves against an army they can't see coming!"

Bacalhaus broke the remaining tension and gave an uncharacteristic whoop, shouting to the Tishbyts, "Three cheers for the little men and their ghost of a friend!

As was typical of their ilk, the skittish little men jumped with fright at the unexpected sound and fell into silence, sighing at their shoes.

Zallo was a model of his kind as well; ever the mercenary, he ranted, "You're cheering a man who was remade by demons and goblins!"

Bacalhaus slapped Zallo across the back — not all too cordially — and roared, "And a damn fine job they did! If only you could be so useful!" Then, spinning about to the whole group, the grinning blue man gestured from one face to the next, beginning with Fawn Virgilis and ending with Mún and said, "Above us we have our friend

Montefeltro, who has literally become a one-man fighting ship, and who tells me his guns should be ready soon — he corrects me, *soonish*; before us we have our friends Fel and Mún, whose duplicitous mind alone is a calamity to our foe; we have the strength of the lion, which we have seen tested, now made into a Gylfinîr of sorts; we have a mighty Ægeleif, who is sworn to love us; and now we have an army of engineered felines. All this, combined with the finest mercenary force that ever tromped their boots through the insurgencies of this age! I ask only: where do we go from here?"

"We go to Hell," said Æsirisæ, her gaze cold upon them. "You are jovial and you will need your joviality. You will need all the joy and humor and pleasantness that life has laid down at you, for the hardest mountain comes tumbling down at our feet, and we are only at its footstep. If I could show you the horrors I have seen though Jeüdora, or the Hells I have tread, you would cling to your mirth. But do. Take with you your courage! For I nearly lost mine! When I saw the Bœzch homeworld, the shock of umber howls, ringing with slow clarity like the sound of a rattled bell, turned into primary colors, became wavelengths of dread! I saw the sound of my own name shouted out over the red sky in hues of echoes! Bœzch Übor is not a world for the pondering mind. We must access its shores without aid of our thinking vessel. Tell me, Mún, do you know my meaning?"

Mún met the stare of his lion self, and they both looked to the Ægeleif as if in confirmation. The lion chuffed. The angel smiled. The ghost sighed. "I have an idea," said Mún.

Until she spoke, his plan had not been to leap across space unprotected. Mún wanted to use Montefeltro as transport across the void. But Æsirisæ convinced them that the *Mare Hypatia* could serve them in another capacity — just as urgent as this — and so Mún and the lion now found themselves agreeing to leap across the heavens.

Stepping out from a Gripper Gate within the very chamber of Emmott the Judge, there was a moment of pause as the Bœzch Generals and Serfs within the blighted room struggled to locate the presence of hidden minds, and Fel adjusted his augmented senses from the chasm of space to the closeness of the room. In that brief instant, Emmott's rotund lips flapped in terror, for only he could see and hear with mortal eyes and ears the flash of light and the tear of the sound barrier that accompanied a Gripper Gate opening. Several Serfs tore through the vacuum of the Gate and shot out behind the lion, falling through the blackness Fel had just come from. The Gate closed. Emmott quaked and pointed, screaming high and long, a fat falsetto in the height of his cadenza, "Save me! Save me from the property!"

In the manner of a nimble fencer's wrist, they twisted up about the shining feline who towered head-to-head with the tallest of the Generals. Eight Generals, thirty Serfs, a dozen Lieutenants skittered along the rotten floorboards and chitinous walls, trying to hook their horns and hands into him, but he slipped off them, his radiant white frame now six meters in height, electrifying his attackers and sending them crumbling to the floor in heaps that careened between dimensions, and flickered and died in one reality or another. The living fought on, attempting no new tactics except to call in reinforcements. Scores more Lieutenants surged up the open hall, urged on by the

Generals who kept a pace back, but this new wave was pounded to splinters as the lion used his full weight against them, slamming them against every surface, using his massive forequarters as a battering ram.

From the top of the nest of bones, ten meters from the center of battle, Emmott stood with his flaming gavel, petrified and unable to wield the power embedded in him. His black eyes moved between his allies and the angelic cat, his deranged mind weighing the possibilities of survival; to-and-fro, to-and-fro went his panic, his cowardice and loneliness tipping the judicial scales within him this way and that until the growing pile of bodies stood as a thumb upon the scale; "Spare me!" he called out to Fel and the man within him, "Mún! Mún, I can feel you in there still! And Emméte! That was my name before I was Emmott! I am no demon! Hear me, Mún! Save me! Spare me! I am a victim of the Bœzch in much the same way as you! Spare me and I will tell you how to kill Œlexasperon!"

But the lion seemed not to hear him, and Mún, if he listened then, gave no sign. Two Generals stepped forward from the ring of eight and approached the Judge from behind. The remaining six moved on to face the lion, yet the first two had only interest in their traitorous leader. One reached for Emmott, but the demon's powers were still greater than his charges. Down came the gavel, and the colossal Bœzh horror was smashed as easily as a tree of balsa under a flaming avalanche. The other Generals stopped their advance against the lion and turned toward their betrayer. Up the swollen nest they moved, slowly sizing up their prize, seeking a way though the flailing hammer while behind them Fel continued to work his way through the swarm.

"Mún! Mún! Remember me! Remember your friend, little And Emméte? I was always good to you, Mún. I always tried to protect you from your brother! I tried to make the others behave! I tried to help you! Please, Mún, don't let them have me!"

The gavel swung and swung while the lion crunched and decimated. Two more Generals were reduced to cinders under the weight of the hammer. Eighteen more Serfs and six more Lieutenants were trampled and pulled apart by tooth and paw. Still the lion gave Emmott no sign of reproach. Emmott grew more desperate, his blubbering more unintelligible. Again he pleaded to the man within the cat, "Œlexasperon! Go to him! Kill him and you end this, Mún! He is too heavy to fly from the surface of Bosh Übor, and only when the mass of Bram is close to him can he finally use his Ægeleif to make a Grip Point to Society! Spare me and fly to Bosh Übor! Kill Œlexasperon while he remains grounded, but save me! Save me! Save me! Save me! *Save me!*"

There, in the midst of his circle growing smaller, the Generals crowding in on him and fearing his hammer less and less, then did Emmott see the man he once called his property. With the dead smoldering around him, with no more Bœzch coming up the hall to attack him, then did the lion finally sit upon his haunches and watch with morbid fascination as the demon was beset by his own troupe. That was the moment he saw the young man, Mún, appear, cradled in the arms of the Ægeleif, Æsirisæ. Their eyes collided over the din of destruction. The gaze tore the demon down. He could see it on the face of the phantom young man. He only wanted to watch the demon die. The benighted hands of the Generals clasped Emmott's skull. He cried out. A massive Gripper Gate flashed up from nowhere, tearing out the skyward walls of the tower, syphoning all the mass of the fleet of blighted colonies. In that last moment before Emmott was burned into entrails, galvanized into lighted geometries, remade and unmade, blown into stardust and consumed, he saw the lion fly to Bosh Übor, fly on to Œlexasperon, fly on to doom.

Lambent and scintillating, the Gate heralded itself up, a staff and a banner all in one, then drawing itself in in stupendous inhalation, it withered away and away and away.

Chapter Fifteen
Hell

"Have you ever wondered," said Æsirisæ's voice in his ear, "why Tacit Reality feels the way it does? Words spoken in TR are like fairy wisps of familiarity to us; the skies we make feel like strands of our own birth, fronds of memory and belief that should have no place in a breeze or a color, or in a manufactured realm. But they do. Everything in Tacit Reality rings with a closeness, the kind that is lost from your real life the moment you cross through a Gripper Gate. I've explained to you, dear Mún, what happens when you pass through a Gate farther than four lightyears, that you become permanently abandoned to an alien universe that is in every way like your own, except perhaps a particle is somewhere it shouldn't be, or a star you shall never find burns hotter in this universe than in your place of birth. So much displacement, so much loss and abandonment felt at every turn. It haunts every member of Windsor Society. How do they not go mad trying to find the thing that is twitching at their subconscious, the feeling of wrongness?

"Listen, my dear: Tacit Reality is written from a memory that each of you carries in the patterns of your brains, the true memory of the universe of your birth. Thus, no matter how strange or unnatural every world thereafter may feel, you can fall back into your Quiet Place and be surrounded with the firmament of the familiar."

Mún's avatar pulled back from the voice in his hear, from the glimmering white of the Gate transfer, and reeled as the lion groaned, for they had stepped into a furnace. He was about to say, "I have no Quiet Place," but he was struck dumb by the land into which they trespassed, and he gasped instead, "What is this?"

"Bosh Übor," Æsirisæ said as she moved to shield him from the world. It was too late. He had seen the hellscape, and with it came the fear and horror. Argon, sulfur, and carbon dioxide gales drifted through peals of black lightning; the raw red and umber sky stained the gray-black ground from kilometers around, and everywhere the vision and presence of dead souls trapped in their final moments of horror drifted about them as abhorrent seeds in a mephitic wind. The ground was composed of an alien ceramic, resistant to the terrible heat, packed and molded like kilometer-square Mayan tiles, with burning rock for grout. Distant volcanoes rose up with plumes that gathered together in hypnagogic rows of *Vesica piscis* haloes. Here was a metal cathedral before them, beneath the overlapping haloes of fire and ash, a thing that curved itself up in the manner of a stolen smile. Radiant and sure, the lion and the angel. Diminished and broken, the phantom young man. All stood atop a high platform of some other structure, a vent or chimney that rose a quarter kilometer from the blackened surface in a line with a row of several hundred of the same type of edifice. These telescoping cylinders were steeped in the pestilential growths of the Bœzch, and whatever they had once been to some long-consumed civilization, they now only served as a thousand-kilometer-long wall that surrounded the court of the upturned snake of a fortress, the smile that grimaced down at them from so far off.

Something stirred at that great distance. There was a sudden recognition of danger — that they as intruders were the danger. Mún bent his head and shook the feeling away, turned on his musical firewall, accessing the beginning of the opus he composed in the fractal valley on Barbary Combine. Distress trickled around the firewall, roughly cutting along the sides as if Mún's barrier of sound had been an ice cutter, and he reeled and convulsed just as if he had come upon a great wall of frost. He looked up, wondering what his other self felt. Did the Ægeleif feel it, too? Neither angel nor beast moved; both watched the strange cylinder of smoke that had come alive at the base of the smile. Doubled over, Mún tried to focus ahead but found himself compelled to watch the sky. Two spheres appeared directly above them: one dark and looming, the size of an elephant behind the thick red fog, the other much smaller and as bright as the Sun when seen from Earth. He understood these to be Bram, the seat of Jeüdora, and Étienne the orange star that Bram circled as it marched onward to devour this unappetizing lump, Bosh Übor.

Æsirisæ called Mún's attention to her without having to ask for it. He pulled his eyes down from the heavens to look upon the approaching tornado.

Through the lion's augmented eyes he could see that it held all the shape of a unicorn, but none of the majesty. Thirty meters in height, it was equine in structure, red in color, fossilized in texture, having the fore and hindquarters of a horse, but where there should have been a horse's muzzle there was instead a single horn that formed the whole of the head. No eyes, no mouth, but down in the throat was fixed a demon, locked and buckled to a mechanized neck — a wolf-headed satyr, bronzed and branded in flames and hatred, his brother in damnation. The satyr cried out in radio bursts, "I see you, Mún! You can hide from my master but not from me! I will have you! Wülvogarti comes to brutalize his property!"

The lion gave a tremendous, undulating roar that seemed to crash on and on like a wave, his ferocity tantamount to the sweeping cyclone. His body changed again, his armor separating itself from his frame, hovering up inches from him — he was exposed to this world's elements but he did not die. Mún saw the Ægeleif dwindle in size by a meter at least, and what she lost, the feline added to his own body. He was a black thing, black as emptiness, and to look into his body was to see into an event horizon where a single starlight, the eye of Jeüdora, shined out to touch her sister angel. The white, radiant fur shifted and spun around Fel's expanding frame, becoming a kind of anti-Casimir field that preserved his remaining mortal properties from the planet's atmosphere. Now seven meters in height, the shining cat moved on, leaping down upon the searing ground and charging towards his enemy. Mún found himself dragged from his fetal crouch and borne along with the sweep of action with his head in his stomach, the fear in him a sickness and an earthquake in one. Æsirisæ gathered the phantom young man up in her arms as she ran with the lion. She said to him then, "This fight is not for you, little Mún. Your mind will not survive this unprotected." She increased her pace to match the gait of the lion, the two armies of giants diminishing the emptiness between them. Her cadence sped up with her stride and she continued in a rush, saying, "As we traveled, I prepared a Quiet Place within me that is formed of your memory of your favorite home! Go there now! As the lion is my equal, you are now our Gylfinîr! So, go! Make a complex music to save us all, Gylfinîr, and stay far from the sounds of mayhem!" At that last word "mayhem" she raised a short sword of lightning and took Mún's avatar in her free hand as easily as she would a paper bird, folding him up like origami, his view of the world growing smaller, his heart growing lighter — but before the hellscape faded from his eyes, he took in one last glimpse of the smiling structure, seeing that it was actually a full halo of some structure, its upper portions lost in the red and umber clouds that hung low into the vaulted plumes of fire. A citadel and a crown and a prison: there within its innermost point hung the still-radiant Ægeleif, Jeüdora, she with the missing eye. The foes clashed beneath her, and Mún lost his place among them.

He arrived in a hodgepodge twentieth-century city. He was excited, for the anticipation of his birth, eight thousand years hence, hung in the air all about him, and wherever he moved he filled up the space prematurely, a lone block of cloth from some future quilt. It was any city he had studied and many specific places in one central area. There was the Gothic clock tower, called Big Ben, at the North side of the queen's Palace that sat surrounded by the shop-lined gondola waterways of the Venetian Canals, and the great Art Deco suspension bridge called the Golden Gate (more orange than golden, he noted) where he drove a black Model T with a handkerchief over his mouth, and after he parked his car near spotted horses and Italian roadsters in the Modern shadow of the Empire State Building, he took the red cable car from bronze and ornamented Grand Central Station to Palais Garnier, the Opéra de Paris.
Up the Rococo Grand Staircase he would go, turning left or right up the bisected steps and then down, and under the dramatic facades of Greek mythologies, he would find his way into the theatre under the six-ton chandelier. He had with him an orchestra of ghosts, mere

minor AI from the structure of the Quiet Place, and he as their Phantom would conduct what he did not know of music, for he was no musician. He would take his will and give it to his spirit men and ask them to hack and combine snippets here and whole lines there of the *Cold Song*, *Boléro*, and *Una Furtiva Lagrima*. He would take this jumble and pull up his holographic status boards from the air around him, distorting and reverberating and flanging and sending it off ... to where? Where was he? The nights and days, they came together and in his repetition he forget where he was, who he was, why he made the music. Couldn't he mix more than just these three songs? He couldn't remember.

At night he would sleep in a Tudor loft over a frozen bay and wonder how he got here until sleep claimed him. But always the dreams came. He dreamed his hunger was sustained by the flesh of stars; he heard the sounds of animal fighting; he felt the pain that felt like his pain, and he fought a compulsion to run into the cobblestone streets and scream and terrorize the unliving tourists who frequented the shops outside his home.

Often, when he took his morning coffee and chocolate by the window of his favorite bistro, and looked out at the puffins playing and gliding and dying by the cliff sides, the faces of some unknown past would rise up and haunt his reflection. Three gray faces like his own, a blue man, two whites, and a black who was now a ship? Did he know the significance, that mired in the tribulations of their own war, they had forgotten him to the pitch of space? Only the Gylfinîr thought of him now, for a year had passed and still the dreams of animal fighting made him rise in terror. What did she think of him and when? She wondered of him and his better angels as she herself rose to battle alongside her Ascended friends, both Human and red lion alike. Fawn Virgilis pressed her hands to those eyes she hid behind her cloth whenever Montefeltro reported another victory to her.

Montefeltro had been a rabbit king in his library burrow, but now he was majesty of space. When the corrupted colonies first pushed on to meet Barbary Combine, despite the loss of their demon leaders, Montefeltro lanced them one by one with the restoration of *Mare Hypatia*'s cannons. He was confident and alive as he sat within his Tacit Reality library, stirring his own coffee and smiling at his power. In went the sugar, and another blighted colony was torn asunder. Around swirled the cream, and two more buckled under the strain of his fractal cannons. But the enemy was persistent. There was more to be done.

Having abandoned their doomed transports, the Bœzch hurled themselves into the night and struck Barbary Combine bodily, one by one and often in the hundreds. The battle drew on just as it did upon Bosh Übor. Just as it did the months and years to come.

Fawn Virgilis lost her thoughts in the night.

Mún Rafæl lost himself to his music.

Sometimes as Mún hurried through the narrower streets, moving past horse stables and necktied business men with digital wristwatches, he would pass a baroque building that would make him hurry, or pull his feet in closer as his slipped by its gas and electric-lamp-lit double door. In the darkness above the archway where moths pooled in tiny tornados, he could just make out a crest, but in fear he would recoil from examining it, for the sounds of elephantine hooves and maddening roars rattled the hinges. He fled from its marbled steps, out into the amber night lights, and lost himself further in the potpourri city, lost himself to darkness, lost himself to thoughts.

Could he think on his friends? Could he think on the fate of Zallo Frautmorgan, who, when cut off from his companions in the worst of the fighting, was driven into an isolated valley under the mountaintops of Barbary Five? For days his friends Alon and Bacalhaus tried to reach him, plunging through a regiment of Lieutenants in their beetle suits, a company of red lions burning the path forward. Desperately they sought him, and he stood his ground for as long as he could, making a circle of fractalwire fire under the valley walls, the sheer cliffs an impossible climb even for his beetle suit. He had found the iron chamber where Dianthus once experimented upon her hellhounds and other grotesqueries, and set he fire to its remaining horrors. But his attack was a signal to the enemy, and they climbed into the valley to meet him by the dozens. He made his peace then. Not with Mún, whose name he called out once, laughing as he shot on, "Mún! Mún, wherever you are, be dead before me, at least be so good as that! Have a courtesy now!" Perhaps he did not mean it, but it felt good to say out loud. It was the same as Mún saying to himself that everything would be all right.

Could Mún know of the tearful goodbye between a father and his three children? There they last saw him in their virtual Quiet Place, he stood on a pier in his spine, setting them weeping upon a little boat and pushing them off with a favorite pony. He waved to them in the fog, a big and powerful man made tiny on the creaking virtual dock. The Bœzch rushed closer in the real-world canyon, though torn asunder they were by Zallo's fury, both his armored hands a blaze of ammunition; the horrors pushed closer with every death; Zallo's comrades called to him to resist a little longer. They were so close to him now.

Could Mún see Zallo's spine eject from his body, to be encapsulated within a Brummagarti escape pod that launched the souls of his three children high over the heads of the Bœzch? Down the pugnacious man went, and though they had him pinned, they had not his mind or body. A grin and a silent gesture, and the self-destruction of the beetle suit blew back the seven Lieutenants who held him down, tearing them apart as Zallo blistered, burned, and winked from life.

Mún could not know.

As the thirty red lions broke through the remaining Bœzch Lieutenants, Alon paused over the smoking crater that once bore the weight of his friend. They had been comrades for centuries, now there was only the canister that bore the precious cargo. Alon cradled the escape pod in the arms of his beetle suit, connected his personal Outhernetwork to it, and somewhere within his own Quiet Place, within a grand restaurant — a smoky, exotic bistro eight stories tall — Alon stepped down from the open stage and microphone where he composed his silly ballads about war and love. He made his excuses to his patrons, all of them small dogs in black casual attire, and walked out to the street where the sidewalk ended in a little jetty. A tiny boat bearing three crying children and a gray pony, bobbed lonely and dour in the fog that carried them to his shore. They wept together. They moved into the restaurant hands linked and heads down.

Mún would never know.

There was no known time here in Mún's city, for it was a mere memory, a patchwork digest of every decade from nineteen hundred to two thousand of the old Earth Christian era. Eight and sixteen, thirty-five and seventy-millimeter motion picture projector films: his father had collected so many reproductions from that time. All of it thrilled Mún, this record of a time before him; it filled him with the anticipation that a child feels before his birthday, a dithering excitement for the absence of himself and the expectation of knowing that he would someday fill up the empty space that whispered his name. He wished to walk those lanes of apprehension. He wanted so very much to wear a thin necktie in that time, to walk through diesel fumes under neon-lit advertisements, ads for circuit-based electronics, for war bonds, for red-labeled beverages in tin cans; he wanted to carouse at nightclubs with all the urban tribes, the punks and flappers, zoot suit rioters, gangsters and gays, mods and Goths and beatniks; he wanted to feel inorganic plastics, to know the many uses of petrol. All the myriad urban things that happened before his birth so long ago, recorded forever in those precious films. The universe should have made a place for him then as much as now. Why did his father collect so many reels of this particular century when he could have indulged in eighty others? Because this was the first century of talking film.

Months after Zallo's death, Mún was affected by a strange and implacable gloominess. It began as not his own, but as a signal lifted up to him and sent thousands of AU his way when Fawn, his fellow Gylfinîr, heaved a heavy radio sigh to the wind. In Mún's dispassion, his composition suffered, and at times the rattle of desperate battle grew louder than his music. He worried then. "I need a change of scene," he said out loud before his orchestra, a statement that felt more like a wish. His spirit players paused a moment while their conductor composed himself instead of his music. When he said the words, all turned to his attention, for it was his world, and it was always listening. Like everything here, his words felt as if they were an extension of his will, so much so that upon the last utterance of the unexpressed final e in "scene" he heard somewhere in the city the sound of something falling into place, a great thud of mortar and brick and glass. Somewhere, a new building waited for him.

One night the sound from the forbidden door carried all the way to his window by the frozen bay and into his dreams. He ran from his bed, forcing himself outside, shivering, barefoot in his vest and slacks. He sat miserable and freezing with the puffins nested in the rocks down from his loft, until he was mothered by the beautiful birds, and they brought him a proper pair of pointed boots and a double-breasted coat with silver lion head buttons. A storm burst upon him then, and the birds bowed to him and told him he must go. They pointed to the place in the black and gray firmament where clouds in the shapes of lions and unicorns and giants hurled lighting against each other and shouted in thunderclaps. Again, Mún lifted himself and ran, moving on into the smallest lanes of the city, over the Rialto and across Trafalgar Square, where, falling on his face in a puddle before some Argentinean avenue, his ears lifted him, braced as they were on a drifting melody.

The club building was new to the street, though it looked like one of those dingy, well-used structures, the brick and mortar kind that was all that he wanted from the old film reels. Once through the squalid, fluorescent entryway, the young man was lost among mohawks and filigree spikes, colored hair and eye shadow, and though he was thrilled, he knew not why, for his reason for being there was as far from him as the place this city was based upon.

A sound entered him. Some lyric he could not understand. A singer projected upon the wall had the bluest eyes — as blue and crystalline as his, though she was no Hiichiim woman. What was she singing? It sounded like, *"Hitherto to your hither side, I couldn't tell your head's so deep ..."* Electric guitars folded in upon themselves, sometimes droning and heavy, but always shimmering, like cannonballs lobbed into a glittering well. On and on she repeated, each time a variation on the melodic style, *"Hitherto to your hither side, I couldn't tell your head's so deep ..."* If that is what she sang, he could not tell, but he was pleased to accept it as it could have been, to simply bask in what it meant to him, that he should be hitherto his own hither side, hitherto his hidden side ....

He stood with his back to a wall and took in the pulse from a meter-tall subwoofer, trying to drown out the storm that raged offshore. That was when she pushed up against him, the familiar girl. Recognition should have seared him, but only left him uncomfortable. She, too, held him at a distance, and there were many leagues more within her amber ale eyes.

She grew impatient with herself, looking this way and that as she beckoned to something in her small black handbag. A smell of gardenia and vanilla drifted on and upward. He leaned to the left, discreetly peeping into her bag, but when the tempo around them changed from ethereal to raucous, they were separated by a swaying company of clove-choked vampires and driven into the streets by the swell of velvet bodies.

Out in the sepia night, he followed her and she pretended not to see. They both sensed their familiarity, though neither knew why. They were blank and new, even to themselves. Their paths secret and winding, they took turns sneaking up on each other, going through magazine stands and telegraph windows near parked locomotives, the boiler steam hiding them from the thunder above, their lonely footsteps taking them through filmstrip memories of yellow cabs, burger bars, used book shops, all-night grocers, the zoo.

At the animal park, they sat hand in hand on a green park bench within the entrance to the great cat exhibit, saying nothing, each trying to catch a memory from the fog-drunk stars. The exhibit was more than a spectacle. There were no bars, and having a quality more like those grassy plains that Mún remembered from some long Savanna, and like those open fields that Luti recalled from flat films flickering in an Ærdent basement, they both felt as if this place was where their two memories stitched themselves together as one. With the hanging yellow incandescents above their bench like the body of the leopard between their lion selves, this wholeness comforted them. The two of them were alone with the big cats keeping the wolves away. There were five lions: two males, the rest females lying three meters apart each, like markers for a future wall. Beyond the lions, the leopards draped themselves in thorny acacias around purring piles of ocelots, servals, and cheetahs. Together, the smaller cats made a great music all their own, while the larger kings and queens kept their silence. The thump of cheetah purrs seemed to vibrate the bench beneath the young lovers. Another memory was accessed and added to this Quiet Place — the recollection of when music became their second greatest joy, superseded only by their love of nocturnal predators. It was the sound of the thump, thump, thumping of the cheetahs' exhalations, first heard in those millennia-aged films, that made eight-year-old Mún run from their secret basement theater, across the empty stones, and to his father's music shop. He spent that day attempting to reproduce the sound of the thumping purr with a simple acoustic guitar, while little Luti scraped a small drum with a brush she took from her mother's dresser.

"I still drum," she said to him on the green bench. "Still play them. Want to hear?"

He stood and held out his hand, "Please."

She did not take it, but watched the vortex above and how it met with the fog below, the fog that crept up on all sides, and stalked the raindrops that were hostages to anticipation. The cats became still. Luti rose and shook her head to him, starting into a run, saying, "Let's go to our homes and each dream of nothing, and in the morning we'll find each other."

He started after her and called out, "But where? When?"

"I'll bring my drum to the opera!" And she was out the main gate and away from him.

By the time the morning came, he was running again, for he felt heavy hands, red yet invisible, somewhere above his head, far out into space. These hands and their long, terrible fingertips were only repelled by his music. They would come down out of the clouds, day or night, and seek to congeal a meter above him, trying to reach through his temples and crush him to stardust. Yet the music disturbed the firmament above, dispersing the clouds before the red hands could form, and in the days when his breast swelled with the best of his talents, the clouds would be torn asunder by humid, white storms that raised spikes of lighting, firing towards the heavens like cheering swordsmen and gaping lion maws.

Today was such a day when the red fingertips covered all of the hodgepodge city, causing all the phantom inhabitants to shudder and whisper their doom to each other as trolley cars carried Mún over the cement hills to work. The streets were trafficked with fender-blistered sedans, perturbed horses and two-wheeled scooters, electric cars and accidents, and everywhere he saw the population was distress. When the thunder crashed down upon them, windows shattered in the highest buildings, alerting those at the top stories to the fight from outer space.

Demons and angels and beasts clashed above them all, and all the horizon was a tumult of fire, lightning, and oaths. Mún found his way through the panicked streets to his opera. Looking up once, he spied wolfish black eyes following him from the other side of the heavens. Endless pools of hate from the depths of the farthest black hole whirled down at him and told him he could not hide. He bent his face away from the vision and pushed through the gilded doors, running and leaping up steps, every footfall drowned in thunder cracks. As he pounded his heels through the bronzed Beaux-Arts halls, the focal point of clamor shifted from above him to ahead of him. Drumfire echoed and reverberated and became actual drumming, for there upon the four-hundred-man stage of the Palais Garnier was Luti and fourscore of drums. The drums were the Oshii Librarian kind, he knew, the type called taiko. The heads of the two-meter-tall drums were flat and rope-tuned, the blue-robed drummers attacking them with a single man to each drum, a stick in each hand. The drummers were accompanied by phantoms bearing small flutes, the one setting the tempo for the other; they shook back the skies from the black demon eyes.

Cannonade, calamity, explosions under the six-ton chandelier, harmonious barrages set in time to sonorous taunts and shouts — Mún smiled up at the stage from the orchestra pit and finally knew relief. He knew that the music itself, once aired, once shook out like wet linen, dried and sent aloft at the first wayward gale, became a thing called pásscoding for a great firewall against probing minds, but until now he had forgotten what any of it truly meant. He thought of the puffins that brought him his clothes. Was this place real?

He mused to himself, *What are pásscodes?* He remembered: *they're a series of macros that I write — macros identical to musical notation — that activate or dismiss computer applications utilized by EtherCore entities or biomechanical brains.* What was this city? A memory, certainly. A wondrous memory of a time long before his own. But was there no other meaning beyond this? What figures loomed in the cumulous stratosphere and roared and hurled lighting to the black-eyed thing with the long, terrible fingers? He had become a child who accepts his meat and potatoes, but makes no correlation between them and an animal or a mound of soil. Yet, even without the relevance, Mún knew they had won another day for themselves and for the giants in the clouds.

Another thought occurred to him then: why was dead Luti here with him?

Because the theory of her is gone from my world. The theory of me is gone from hers. But what if our memories of each other became a hypothesis that needed to be proven by the one being that observed us? If that one being sees us both, then it is a paradox, and so that person has always been our constant observer. What do two codependent theories do when they can no longer be observed together, but still be remembered together? Is this how a tiny universe proves our two hypotheses, by stitching them together over a bridge of two memories?

But why is she here?

Because I made a wish that she'd be in my pretend city ... or am I in her city?

Mún blinked.

I'm going mad.

And he named the city Paradox.

They spent the many months ahead always together. At night, when they lay awake as man and woman, they would hum the day's melodies in between their moments of embrace. It was always just a moment, very brief, for they would soon pull away, the one looking at the other as if remembering a death, both dreading some necrophilic spell had been cast there in Mún's bed overlooking the frozen bay. Both were struck with a memory of the death of the other. But this memory was a vague recollection. It was a weightless, formless thing, a shadow and blur. The fear never lasted, and they soon forgot whatever vague recollection it was that passed between them.

During the daytime, they would ride the trolley together through Paradox City, racing to beat the cloud demon before his fingers bore down on them again, and always they passed by the door with the hidden crest, and always they shared a shudder at the sounds from behind that portal. This was their time together, day after day, four years moving by them without any understanding of chronological order. Their movements through time seemed out of step with linear motion. If they passed a location and it was their first time through those narrow avenues, they would still feel the imprint of themselves there: a bakery, a newspaper printer, a shop of fishmongers juggling flesh from the sea, they knew every boulevard was tailored to them. They could not stop to contemplate the mystery of this. Contemplation felt forbidden to them. They were only to compose and play, sleep, and eat, dance and hide.

One thing changed the day Luti first released her drumming. Whether it was a consequence of the Devil losing his grip upon the sky, or a final infection before he was driven out, wolves began filling up the dark corridors of those parts of the city that felt most like an unfinished patchwork. They were huge, hulking creatures, mangy, unnatural dog soldiers that slinked from the animal park when the lions and leopards were at rest. Now they grew in numbers, becoming bolder as the years wore away, stalking the citizenry with increasing belligerence. It was common now to see people fight for their virtual lives from the very bars of the trolleys they clung to. Mún and Luti knew they were the targets of the beasts. The soulless citizens understood this, too. When the wolves surrounded the couple as they dashed from cafe to trolley to home, Tacit Reality policemen in their tall black helmets would throw themselves into the maws of the monsters, beating them back with bullets and clubs. Clear days were worse than stormy nights, for the showers of blood were thickest when the rains were away.

One night, more than four years after their first meeting in the club under the shimmering guitars and crystal blue eyes, they showered together, washing away the wolves' blood, still hearing the heartbeat of the taiko in their inner ears. Mún pressed up against her breasts and rolled his head upon her neck, asking, "I think I had brothers once, have you any brothers?"

"I have you," she said.

"You do ..." He moved to his knees and kissed her once upon the belly.

"What were they like?"

Leaning back into the curtain, he stared at his hands for a time before he raised his eyes and admired her. Distantly, he said, "One was dead. One was angry."

"The dead one, was he angry?"

"No, he was dead. But when he was alive he was very pleasant."

She sat with him in the stream of water. Facing him, she asked, with an uneasy sort of glimmer, her old fierceness spilling up over them both, "And the angry one?"

"He's still out there. Still so very mad at me."

"Why? What did you do?" She seemed to be recalling something — an old emotion, a hint of bitterness shared between them.

Mún felt it, too, for it was always a point that when one waded neck deep though a strong emotion, the other would soon come swimming after. "I wouldn't let him own me. He's a bully, so he has to own someone. You see, when they decide they own you, the bully sees that as a right. When you say no to them, when you defeat them or reprimand them, their brittle brains tell them that you have stolen from them. A constitutional right has been swindled from under them, a joyous privilege is gone and taken by you, the cruel and evil thief. They were entitled to have you, how dare you decide otherwise. Prepare for righteous war."

He grew cold and robotically considered his own words. Finally, he said, "And the more you love freedom, the more they want to break you. He's a broken thing."

"We're all broken things," she said without feeling.

A shadow passed over his eyes. "He's more so, because he's still a child."

"Children are broken?"

Mún's analytical side crept up on him then. He startled himself for a moment, for it was so long since the last time he felt it near. All the way back to when he was first ... first what? He tried to remember but all he heard now was the roar of a lion, and he assumed it was a recollection of the storms above or the beasts of the animal park, or the fury from behind the feared door. His mind worked behind his eyes, filing through the possible answers, until the cabinet marked "whimsy" called out to him, and he opened up his mind to open his mouth and said, "All children are broken people, and the process of growing up is the process of repair."

Luti liked this side of him. She teased him with another question, hoping to continue down the path. She asked him, "We're grown-ups now. Are we fixed?"

His reply was quick, sure-footed, the old confident Mún: "No. Once you grow up, you long to be broken again."

"That's a sad state."

"The saddest."

She raised her eyes up to the falling water, using her own analytical mind to make sense out of her environment. She focused on the thing that always bothered her here. The ethereal feeling behind the droplets, there was a dreamlike quality she could never place. "Mún," she said, "Where are we? I feel like I walked into a dream."

"In Paradox City," he replied without thinking.

"*Where* is the City?"

He shook his hand before her, as if her words were written in chalk upon a blackboard. "Never mind. Never ever mind that. Listen: I think that devil in the clouds is my brother."

"I've been wondering about that."

"You felt it, too?"

She reached into the warm water around them and beamed, taking hold of him, "I feel everything you feel."

He dithered, shaking her off, breathing, "Can you see and hear everything I do, too?"

"No. Don't be silly."

"Then I should tell you," Mún whispered conspiratorially. "A wolf told me the demon was my brother."

"What? When?" Her surprise was not genuine.

"Two days ago ... I think. Or maybe it hasn't happened yet. I went to a flower shop to buy you something nice, and when I tried to leave, the shop was surrounded by the fiercest pack yet. The shopkeeper summoned the police and they gunned my way out. One dying wolf caught my shoe in his mouth, and when I kicked him away, he spat at me and said, 'Deny your savior, put a gun to your temple and head straight to hell to claim your prize!'"

There was silence between them for a while; both stared into the eyes of the other between the curtains of water. She broke the quiet with a smirk, asking, "What kind of flower did you get me?"

"A gardenia."

"My favorite!"

"I know."

Then she questioned him, and it was an honest query, "What did he mean by, 'Your savior'?"

"I asked him that. He said, 'Wülvogarti.'"

"Was ... that your brother?"

"It doesn't seem like it should be ... does it?"

Silence for a time again.

Luti begged, "Is that all he said?"

Mún reached for the spigot and the water ceased to fall. Toweling himself dry, he said between beats, "Yes. Another policeman killed him completely after that."

Luti stayed dripping as the water drained about her thighs. "Why do you think that's your brother's name?"

"It sounds angry."

She stood and danced from the room, full of brilliant thoughts and unsettled compulsions. "Let's trap one," she sang. "Tomorrow!"

He chased after her with a fresh towel. "A wolf? How?"

He caught up with her at the balcony that overhung the city side of his flat. They leaned together naked and glimmering under the patchwork moon, drawing the towel around them for warmth. She pointed to the lighted theater marquee five blocks away, to the dark smudges that fought with the lean stickmen in tall back helmets. Gunshots were common below, as were howls and shouts. They were tired from the days tribulations, one part banging out the music that would save their souls, one part running from wolves between cars and music halls. Both felt caged in fog, for everything between them was a blur, freedom was an empty space between terrors.

She waved to the police call box below the marquee and said, "There are guns there for us. The constables set them aside in case they can't get to us soon enough. We'll hunt with one of those."

He squinted at the blackened city, saying more to it than to her, "What kind of guns?"

"Bullet projectile."

"That'll do, won't it?"

"Unless it all goes wrong."

How had it gone wrong? It was terribly clear from the start. The wolves had been watching the red call box since it first appeared. And who had placed it there? Like programmed things — and perhaps that is what they were — the wolves swarmed to the box from every part of the city. At first the police guided Luti and Mún safely to the place within, where automatic pistols were kept in drawers labeled BOY and GIRL, cautioning them that this wasn't the job of the two lovers to protect themselves. They should continue on their daily course and let the police do the fighting while they made their music. But they couldn't get the police to question a wolf, they only wanted to kill, said it was their duty to do just that and nothing more. So the young man and woman fell into folly.

Now they clung to their coats as they clung to their lives, tearing through alleyways while police and citizen avatars poured into the streets from every building, failing at every block to fend off the tsunami of snapping canines from the fleeing lovers.

The weapons in the box were useless, mere wooden toys left by some trickster, and now as they legged it through oiled pools under neon lights, it occurred to Luti that she knew not how the idea of the police box first struck her. The notion had come from somewhere. Mún admitted that he, too, had some inkling of the concept the same moment she suggested it. They knew now that they had been duped, that the rain itself had misted down from the deep black eyes and red fingertips that lurked behind the clouds, a penetrating rain that seeped into the skin, rode the current through the heart, up and up, stopping only to nest in the neurons of the brain. Their scalps itched from the crawling rain. Their hearts beat in their throats as they ran in circles through infinite alleyways.

Corralled, they came to the door. A thousand mongrel maws swept in at every side, the beaten citizens a thinning wall of grimacing teeth and screams between them. Before them, the press of the wolves, behind them, the door from which sounds of battle issued still. "This is what they want! This is what they wanted all along!" shouted Mún over the clashing cacophonies.

"Listen!" Replied Luti, her back to the darkened door.

The sound was a new and thumping music, indifferent to melody, it focused on force. It came from the wolves, a chorus, a chant, an evil wish: "In! To Wülvogarti! Out! The little lions! In! To Wülvogarti! Out! The little lions! Out! Out! In! To Wülvogarti! Out! The little lions! Out! Out! Out, out, out!"

With every cry of "out" the hulking things tore away a row of citizens with a swipe of their fangs, as easily as if they had been crumbs upon their whiskers. The lovers checked themselves again. The weapons from the police box were indeed useless, their circle of protection shrunk before them, there was nowhere to go but through the dreaded door. They held hands as they held their breath. Together they would go through. Together they stopped before they leapt. They looked upon the hidden crest over the arch of the portal, and they both laughed, part from frustration, part from the memories of dread that that image carried with it. It was the Society Seal of the Great Windsor Temporality, that vast government of worlds that ruled the majority of the Human Universe. On one side a lion, on the other a unicorn, between them the heraldic crown they fought over.

Mún pointed to the seal.

A church bell rang within their ears, and all their memory came galloping back to them. This *was* a pretend city, a Tacit Reality construction built in an instant by Æsirisæ. Beyond that door was reality, where a lion in two different dimensions fought a demented unicorn over an angel under a crown. But was Paradox City located in Fel's biomechanical spine or in Luti's feline body, the lioness Nova? Did it span over both, yawning across the thaumatropical dimensions?

Luti shook her head and stared at the door. "We can't go through!"

"Yes!" he shouted over the tumult. "This is why we're here! We must continue to make the music!"

Luti braced herself a moment and closed her eyes. She stiffened her back and said, "I'll go through."

All of Mún's body shook as he replied, "What? No! Through that door is reality! If you fall between Fel and the demons, you'll be devoured!"

"It's not just Fel. My Nova is there, too!"
"Your Nova?"

She moved close to his face, taking him by the collar, saying, "My lion body, the one you see as a leopard. Our realities have merged. Like when we called each other with the eye of Jeüdora. But this time ... it's Æsirisæ. We're in a Quiet Place she's made just for us. Both Æsirisæs: one from my universe and one from yours. If I go through, I'll see your Fel as a leopard fighting alongside my Nova in my universe. That's why it's me who should go. It's you who turns the music into a coded firewall protecting both our lion minds. If I go, at least one version of Wülvogarti will vanish and at least half of the wolves with me! You'll have a fighting chance then!"

Mún, exasperated by her logic, clutched his temples and cried, "You don't know that! You were wrong about the police box! You could be wrong about this too!"

"I was tricked!" she shouted. "But not this! This is clear to me! Wülvogarti can't fight and maintain these wolves. He must be aching to stop. He'll stop them if he sees me. I know it. I know him! We both do!"

He was losing her again. In his imagination, he could see her when she fell into stardust, dissipating like a love letter over reticent flames. He was weak and begged, his voice becoming small, "You can't die again!"

"And neither can you! Remember the mantra: we must go on, we have to go on! Now let me go and I'll see you when this is done!"

Screams from behind him. A citizen avatar with a torn neck fell onto Mún's back and bounced to the ground. Spattered in blood, he stared from the corpse to the growing pile of dead around them and wept. He had finally had enough. "This will never end!"

She sobbed with him, her own end reached: an end to patience, exhaustion, mental deterioration. Though each was a ghost in the other's universe, she had experienced all the same challenges. In her universe, Zallo tried to kill her as well; in her world, she had tried to save the elephants from sliding into the abyss; she followed the leopard through Æsirisæ's Gate; like Mún, she killed the crew of the *Mare Hypatia* when they mutinied, saved the children from Ambros and Dianthus, and she walked the long dark chambers of the Ouroboros Object. They were identical beings in everything but their talents. Same passions, same hates, same creeping depressions, same bouts of arrogance, same orgiastic love of free creatures unhindered by civilization, same enemies — all their lives, always, always the same damn deranged enemies. She touched his face once more, kissed him quietly and said, "No matter the space between us, I'll have you again."

He tried to move between her and the door. She kicked him aside, more a push with her foot than an attack, but he spun away nonetheless, falling into the arms of those bleeding citizens nearest. And her hand was upon the latch. And she didn't look at him again. And she was through. The door swung behind her. All of Hell splayed out before her.

Chapter Sixteen
Ascent of the Blessed

Under the heat of *Vesica piscis* haloes, the alien cathedral still shook from battle. Nearly five years of craters and scars stripped the metal and ceramic from the burning foundations. Luti arrived directly under the immense crown where Great Jeüdora had come down from her prison to pierce the many hearts of the unicorn. Above them, the terrible orb of the brown dwarf, Bram, churned her hot ammonia clouds from horizon to horizon. The ground undulated constantly, not just from Wülvogarti's blows upon the spine of the miserable, felled Ægeleif, Æsirisæ, or the strikes upon him by the mystical leopard at one side of him and the shining lioness at the other; these quakes rippled forth as Bram's gravity pulled the planet slowly into its maw, lapping up the atmosphere and mass with all the hunger the physical universe allowed.

Œlexasperon, for all his horrific might, lay dying at the hands of the angelic. All these terrible years, they had concentrated their attacks solely upon the Bœzch Emperor, leaving themselves prone to Wülvogarti, who long ago unleashed himself from his master's neck and marked his fury upon the divine invaders. On what did they sustain themselves? There was no meat here. There was no rest, no place or time to lie down and recover. For the demons, there was their otherworldly stream of energy, which they imbibed in great laps, though it did not refresh them as greatly as did mortal cognizance. For the lioness, who stood somewhere in godhood between Gylfinîr and Ægeleif, and for the Ægeleifs themselves, there was the mass of Bram bearing down upon them all, and as it grew nearer their droughts grew as well. But for the leopard, this cosmic glitch, there was no explanation Luti could fathom, for thinking on it was like an insect attempting to comprehend the stars above. She only knew its name: Paradox.

The demon, Wülvogarti, spied Luti's tiny avatar standing mesmerized among the flaming rubble, and shrugging his shoulders free of the cats, he released broken Æsirisæ from his hands and strode with damning confidence to her. The leopard and the lioness were shook loose only for a moment. Turning together, they collided into the demon's back, attempting to drag him down, but he moved on, grinning down at Luti's avatar in Augmented Reality. The wolf-faced satyr, fifteen meters of unforgiving flame and red biomechanized muscle, thudded hoof over hoof toward her, his words lashing forth in cinders as he said, "There she is! Little whore of the property! There she is! My wolves smoked you out! There she is -- "

"Demon, a tha -- — • — - !" thundered Jeüdora in her angel speak.

Lightning arced from her body to his, blasting his gargantuan frame so that he skidded and rolled a hundred meters across the sulphuric ground, under the planet-swollen horizon. Nova and the leopard, too, flung apart, though they rolled and returned to their feet merely a few meters apart. Luti saw that Jeüdora left the stupendous unicorn to bleed out through this dimension and that, its single broken horn jumping though segments of time, stuttering and strobing its body as if it were a player from a silent film. She carried dying Æsirisæ in her left arm. Luti could see that the younger of the two Ægeleif was split at her collar, and light and stardust shimmered from the tear.

Could an Ægeleif actually die? Luti had not thought it possible, yet she had not the time to think on it. Wülvogarti was up and careening back at them, the great divine cats rising immediately to meet him. Jeüdora glanced up once with her one silvery eye, then looked back at Luti and shouted in her temple bell lilt, "These sights are not for you! Quickly! Hide within me, frail spirit! I shall pluck you up safely and into a memory!"

She saw a radiant hand the length of her own virtual body reach out for her. Darkness. She opened a new door.

Little Luti Casanova was nine years old when her home on Tenniel's Garden succumbed to dementia. She was there now, walking through her memories and young Mún's door. The boy was as exhausted as she, and as he laid his head down to sleep, she stared out his bedroom window, past the slumbering katee hives to the hilltops in the distance, where she knew a smaller Ærdent village sat fixed at the lip of a green caldera. She was unable to sleep at her own home. Her parents, both Ærdent naturalists, had succumbed to the madness. She knew she had lost them to the disease. In their place sat wretched things, mere ghosts of flesh, broken recordings of gentle people. She wept quietly, trying to focus on her own future with Mún and his mother.

Her thoughts brought her to Mother Rafæl, who was resilient from the start and showed no signs of dementia. Mother Rafæl's pain was only for her sons: one kind but independent, one dead at her own hands, one gone to a madness all his own since birth. That poor, guilt-wrought woman — guilt she felt for bringing into the world such a gnashing brute as Hünde, guilt she knew for ending Paölo's torment, guilt, guilt, guilt upon her for Mún's sacrifices.

And yet Luti could not hate her. She understood her. They were each as trapped as the other, Human animals ensnared in consecutive crises that loomed as large as Tenniel's Alice in the distance, and for which they could do nothing but wave courteously, gesture rudely, or stand defiant as doom approached them. They were dancing, dying melancholy things.

Luti leaned towards the window. The scene was changing. At first she thought it was a mirage of the night. How could the tiny pin lights of the far-off village grow so bright? The color was wrong, too. Despite their vows of Luddism, the Ærdents of Tenniel's Garden still used modern lighting, which cast a blue hue that reached into yellow as the evening approached. But the lights that flickered and spread out all over the far-off town were bright orange.

Fire?

Luti looked to sleeping Mún, so peaceful upon his pillow, then glanced back to the Jack-o'-Lantern like grin that widened under the hillside. She moved from his bedside, peeled open the shuttered door to his room, and ran down the dark-paneled hall, light-footed and fleet. She took the latch of the door at the end if the hall but did not open it. She pressed her body to the wall, siding her cheek up to a crack in the hinges. Light and voices squeezed through to Luti's spying ear.

"Mother, let me through," said young Hünde on the other side.

"Get out! Here, take these and go. Just don't show yourself to me." It was Mún's mother who replied.

Luti pressed her eye up to a split in the doorjamb. Light trickled in from the other side. In darkness and in silence she held her breath and watched from her hiding place. She saw Hünde, his school uniform blackened from fire, his face and ash-colored hair wiped clean. He was holding a set of neatly folded clothes, lifting them with a kind of awkward contempt. "It doesn't matter," said Hünde, trading off his befuddlement for increased anger. "It's not as if you ever mattered. I'll do as I please. Emméte! Marcél! Come here!"

Two boys walked in with trepidation through the front door. Peeping from her dark corridor, Luti recognized them both, one thin and vain, the other fat and with eyes that darted about as they sought protection and comfort from any source. They dragged a heavy object between them. Neither wanted the hatchet in his hands. They passed it back and forth, failing to conceal the cowardice that also moved between them. Hünde dropped the bundle of clothes and took the axe from them, jerking it away with frustration, and once in his grasp, his minions silently fretting they were fools, for they realized that the power they handed over to their leader could cut any which way he chose.

His mother pushed away from him, weeping, "What are you -- ?"

He caught her by the arm and pushed her down, his strength grotesquely masculine for a boy of ten years, "Is this the axe that Mún used on Paölo?"

"No!"

"It is!"

"You know that it was me!" She screamed and pulled at him, "You know that Mún was only saving me from the council!"

"Shut up, woman! That's why I'm going to chop him! I'm not giving him one more reason to keep you all smug to himself! I was here first!"

Hünde paused then, his breast rising and falling in tremulous waves. His face changed, the line of his mouth going straight, an expression he often took when he was considering possibilities. Luti pressed her eye closer to her split in the door.

"Marcél, go in that room and kill my brother," said Hünde. Luti turned her head about, searching for anything she could use as a weapon.

"Me? Why me?" Marcél whined.

"Because you're weak and you make me sick with it!" shouted Hünde.

"But Emméte is weaker! I helped you set the fires when he only cried!"

Fat Emméte, who was two years older than the other boys, seemed to be calculating something behind his eyes, for his pupils went up in his head between pauses as if he weighed his options. He sputtered, "I'm not! I just don't see why we don't take what we want and just go! We should leave them all!"

Hünde slapped at them both, striking them about the shoulders and neck. "Shut up, the both of you! Where's Dyana? She'll do it! She does anything I ask!"

"She's looting with the twins," Marcél said, humiliated.

Emméte tugged at Hünde's sleeve, ever the child. "Let's go, Hünde. Taum's ready to burn everything here. He's going to start any minute."

Hünde readied his free hand to deliver more abuse. A scream and a push, and his mother leapt on his back, tumbling with him to the polished wood floor.

"Get off me!" cried Hünde, struggling to buck her away, but she slapped and slapped and slapped his face until, out of his mind with rage, he struck back with

342

whatever was in his hands. The struggling ceased. Hünde sat up and scrambled back upon his knees, pushing the dying woman away from him, the axe embedded in her neck, the blood that pooled beneath her flooding the boards. She did not scream with the fatal blow. She looked to be drifting upon a red river, her eyes serenely moving past the ceiling, up through the nighted clouds, to the face of massive Alice, where the baby Æsirisæ faded through a womb of lightning, calling her to rest by her side.

Hünde kicked away from her one more feeble time, his eyes fixed upon her, not seeing what he we seeing, but looking on some event he always knew was coming but until then doubted the possibility. His cheeks pale with disbelief, then crimson with anger, he crawled on his palms to her still-lovely face and screamed, "Now, look! You've done it! You've done it!"

"She's bleeding all over," wailed Emméte, his face also waxing from pale and crimson, but from fear and disgust instead of Hünde's more visceral despair. From the darkened door, behind which Luti steadied herself to lunge through, and having found nothing to fight with, she carefully watched the scene even through her panic. Though only nine, her instincts were analytical, mature, her poise allowing her to pick her targets in time that was slowed down within her mind. The axe — she would watch for the axe. If she could spring quickly and kick Hünde while he still kneeled by his mother, she might be able to rush past him and into the other two boys.

Luti coiled. The door would swing away from her, and for this she was relieved. Slowly, silently she turned the latch, closing her eyes, her ankles tensing up, reading a release of energy and speed. Drawn back, a cool hand touched her arm. Startled but not alarmed, she saw Mún was with her. His face was drawn down and tear-streaked. He waved for her to wait, handing her two wooden table legs torn from his nightstand. He clutched an identical pair of weapons for himself. They made ready to rush together.

On the other side of the door, Hünde stared up at the other two boys for a beat. He shrieked, the sound a gibbering moniker for his anguish, his empathy forever on sabbatical from him, and now like a howling hermit released from solitude, with even his suffering volatile and broken, he ripped the axe from his mother's body and flung it at his lackeys, splattering the pair but missing them by a meter. He screamed, "This is what happens to the weak!"

Somewhere far off, Luti heard drums begin. Mún counted under his breath.

The lackeys did not run. Defeated and petrified all at once, they watched their leader as he mourned and hated.

"Hünde ..." one of them whimpered.

"Shut up!"

"You said your mother couldn't die."

"I said shut up!"

"You said she used to be a Gylfinîr! You said she couldn't die!"

"Look at her!" he snapped. "So small now. All that power, and she gave it up to live in the mud here. She once walked alongside angels. Angels! I could have been the son and heir of a house of real power in Society. But she was weak, and she married a stupid musician who didn't even believe in his own shitty cult in the end. Because of her ... because of her, I was born so far away from my life."

Emméte moved to cover the corpse with a quilt from a rocking chair.

Hünde threw it aside. "Don't! I want to watch her."

Marcél shouted out.

Forward sprang Mún and Luti, wielding their broken sticks. Hünde was clubbed across the temple by his brother while the lackeys, turning to flee, were beaten across their backs by the vengeful girl. The two boys ran out into the sett stone streets, screaming and whimpering for their lives while the girl hit at them. Inside, Hünde held his head only for a moment, and only after he flipped Mún over his shoulder and through the bay window that overlooked the front porch. Down crashed Mún, colored glass bursting around him, sheets as big as his torso slashing him. Hünde collected his senses, looked for the axe and found it embedded in the wood and plaster around the door frame of the main entryway. He leapt to it, forgetting his dead mother and all else but his rage. Finding it stuck, he pulled at it with all his fury, only to snap the blade free. He stared at the frayed handle unbelieving, then turned to find bleeding Mún rolling up at him with his two clubs. Up came Hünde's foot, catching Mún in the chest, pushing him down and back a meter, tumbling him over the porch and onto the sett stones.

The two lackeys were gone, having run off to find their friends, Luti chasing after them, she becoming the screaming banshee that would forever hound them within their minds, even when, years later, they themselves would transform into the damned. Only Mún remained to fight his brother, though he did not face him alone. There within his inner ear he heard taiko drums thundering, and strange visions thundered along with them. Down the street, an orangish hue began to shimmer up the edges of the horizon, and now he could see them as the fire welled and spread from house to house – shadows of people: the mad, the dying, and the children who fought among them. But there was something else intruding. As Hünde came at him and

Mún responded with blunted swings of his own, his vision doubled up so that he was seeing not just this moment, but a moment somewhere far off in his future where a lion and a leopard tore at the haunches of a demon trapped in Hell while an angel struck out from the fore. Down the boy went as Hünde cracked him with his axe handle, down the lion went as Wülvogarti clubbed him with iron fists. The leopard sprang and so did Luti, both distracting either Hünde in the hellish village or Wülvogarti in Hell. Whenever the leopard and the girl were driven back, white lightning flashed from an ethereal eye deep within the lion and in Mún; they were on their feet again, bipedal and four-legged, both sustained by forces outside their bodies, both listening to the drumming, drumming, drumming that beat away invisible fingertips. Invisible Bœzch fingers yet clawed forth from the last spurting remains of Œlexasperonto cool their temples and butt at his sinuses, relentlessly seeking to tear the minds of the lion and boy in twain.

For Luti and her lion, Nova, it was the same as it was for Mún and his Fel. Here within Jeüdora's Tacit Reality memory of their youth, where their two universes combined into one, the boy and the girl joined under the flames of their ruined village against a boy who would someday be a demon. They held this as a memory as surely as they acted it out in the present. While in the present, in two separate realities, the two lions gave their last strength against the demon man. In both realities as in the past memory, they battled on until they wore the monster down. Over and over Hünde and Wülvogarti destroyed Mún's and Fel's and Luti's and Nova's bodies. Over and over they returned to life, again and again, until Hünde collapsed upon the sett stones, exhausted, backlight by the burning village, whimpering for an end. Hünde could see it then — he could see himself at the edge of the village hellscape as a man, as his future demon self. They made eye contact, he and himself. He saw himself fall, saw his strength bleed out from his ultimate future, but only thought, *I can prevent that. That's not me. I can win. I will be better.* Then both realities of Wülvogarti fell on their backs, upon the ground of the burning Bosh Übor fortress, as Bosh Übor itself, in both realities, was torn to splinters and swallowed up by Bram.

The sky above Tenniel's Garden was black and with few stars: only mighty Alice, so red and purple, a face of a Queen of Hearts bloated up into a super Mars, with pink streaked clouds whirling around the point of light like a royal mouth that spelled out Æsirisæ's birth in letters of doom.

The sky above Bosh Übor was vanishing into Bram's upper atmosphere, the huge million-year storms whipping up the matter from horizon to horizon.

In the Paradox memory reality, a new light glinted in the midnight sky over Tenniel's Garden, a resplendent fairy light that grew and grew, becoming a plume of anti-Casimir exhaust from what could only have been a spacecraft. As it crept nearer and set down at the end of the village path, well away from the flames and madness, it looked all the more like an upright tombstone twenty meters tall.

In the future of ruined Bosh Übor, light also glinted above the lion and the leopard where they lay. The light here was not up in the sky, for ground was soon becoming sky, but upon the disintegrating firmament where one Ægeleif held another in her arms.

Luti and Mún moved away from gasping, bleeding Hünde and abandoned him over the sett stones. Nova and her leopard in one world, and Fel and his leopard in another, kicked away the ruined, vivisected husk of their Wülvogartis, fading as it was from this world to that out if synch with its own dying, and together and apart all in one, they moved through the sulphuric winds to the wistfully divine women.

From the tombstone-shaped ship, there extended a ramp, from which two small men, Tishbyt Engineers in their gray-and-white-striped campsuits, cautiously toed the road at the end of the burning village. They waved with unease to the boy and the girl as the children supported each other, one limping and the other dragging their limbs. One of the little men said, shaking his queer head in distress when he saw the condition of the children and their world, "Children! Greetings, and our many sympathies. There has been a blind birth on the planet which your moon orbits. I am Hvitt, and this is Rost. We were the first to detect the unfortunate, and there are more Society Grippperships on the way. Tell us, have many succumbed to the blind birth sickness? Is there madness here?"

Child Luti and Mún said nothing, just held each other up and dragging themselves past the Tishbyts, pausing only once to stare at the house where the body of Mún's mother roared up in flames. Then up the ramp and into the ship they went, where they continued to wind its narrow halls until they curled in an acceleration couch together and closed their eyes.

"Go. Let's just go," said the boy, Mún.

Before Nova and Fel in their adjacent universes, light poured forth from Jeüdora, even as all the world's light from the orange dwarf star Étienne was blotted out by

the all-devouring shadow of Bram. Jeüdora cradled dying
Æsirisæ in her lap in as much the same fashion as
Michelangelo's Pietà, where a mother held her son, the two
figures in the statue locked in marble as the Ægeleif were
locked in grief. Said Jeüdora, electricity still pouring forth
from her missing eye, "It is time we exited here, my lion
friend, though our beloved Æsirisæ will remain. No
Ægeleif has ever died before this hour, and I know not what
the repercussions will be except this: she will go out with
as great a flame as the one she made upon birth. Come.
Bosh Übor is being swallowed and this ground will not last
beneath us, but with Æsirisæ's life, Bram also shall pass.
Come!"

Jeüdora's Gripper Gate came up. Fel's and Nova's
and Paradox's paws touched Æsisrsæ once in both the twin
realities; Jeüdora's lips touched her forehead; Æsirisæ
smiled and closed her eyes. But for the lone Ægeleif, Bosh
Übor was abandoned.

Within the paradoxical memory, Hünde sat battered
and aching at the end of the street. His gang approached,
feeling victorious but scared, but they could not see what
Hünd was staring at. A connection had been made, one
that would not close. When Jeüdora made this Quiet Place,
The memory of Mún's past was borrowed, not replicated,
and so the last whispers of dead Œlexasperon bled out from
him and urged the boy Hünde to come to him, to come to
Hæl System, to make this future not his own, but to be the
victor, and never fail him as this other Wülvogarti. Hünde
saw his future demon body twitching its last, the ground
around the colossus disintegrating, until a lift and kick of
sucking vortex, and dead and dying Wülvogarti tumbled on
into the maw of Bram, vanishing into a black and red
hurricane eye. Hünde saw this, and though it terrified him,

it also enraged him as easily as everything else. He said to himself, "I will be better when it's my turn."

The Tishbyt ship lifted off with little Mún and Luti. Except for the bully gang who roamed and pillaged there until the next rescue ship arrived, Tenniel's Garden was abandoned.

Æsirisæ died in a Phoenix inferno that pushed Bram into ignition, and now one star orbited another where once a brown dwarf orbited a wandering sun.

Æsirisæ was born and came down to Tenniel's Garden to meet the charred villages and stare in wonderment and shame at the wreckage wrought by madness and children.

So it would always go, the one feeding the other, only rising in tempo over the years like dreaded *Boléro*, crash-diving at the end like *Una Furtiva Lagrima's* climax, marching along with the *Cold Song*'s slump-shouldered hike. But always Æsirisæ would look to her future to misremember rather than forget her past. Always she would hear drums that led the beat of her footfalls.

Jeüdora could not get close enough to use the mass of any of Hæl System's stars, now four in number. She could not creep near enough and survive the heat to make a Gate back to Society. Only a gas giant or a failed star would do. Thus Montefeltro had to gather many ships to build an engine train large enough to propel all of Barbary Combine via Dlaüt Drive out of the Hæl System. The task had been none too difficult as it happened. All of the ships that had attempted to evacuate the colonies left records of their path through the empty system. His own ship body, the *Mare Hypatia*, was unscathed from the final war on the Bœzch, his mind was clear with purpose, and his heart was fresh with the joy of victory. The ships he found were usually vacant, their doors opened to space and their occupants lost to the black vacuum all around them. More madness, a symptom of steering too close to injured Jeüdora when the Bœzch first pulled her down from her seat on Bram. The ships, sixty-eight in total, had intact EtherCore personalities, though they were in emergency suspension, and it took far too much of Montefeltro's time to coax them back into existing. He was an expert at this, for like a king he commanded them awake, and like a rabbit he tricked them from hiding.

All ships but his *Mare Hypatia* fit themselves into the central spoke of the great Barbary Combine colony and acted as propulsion. All but *Mare Hypatia* did this, for *Mare Hypatia* gave herself up only for Long Savanna Colony, which led the group ten thousand kilometers ahead.

No one lived upon the Savanna colony besides the lion, Fel, and the Ægeleif Jeüdora, who sustained him with dreams; in Luti's reality, it was Nova and another Jeüdora who passed over the Long Savanna's grasses; and at the intersection of both these universes, there walked the lone leopard, Paradox in both name and function.

Fel was not as large as he had been during his terrible five-year ordeal upon Bosh Übor, and whatever power was given to him by Æsirisæ diminished when Bram ignited into a star. Now at rest, did the lion know that, somewhere near his spine, somewhere near Nova's, *somewhen* over the body of Paradox, the young man and woman returned to a quiet place called Paradox City? How could Fel understand that his dreams of Mún dancing with his love in twentieth-century apartments overlooking frozen puffin bays was an intersection of two universes. A gift to him and Luti from Jeüdora, the phantom lovers would visit with their lion selves whenever their great cats dreamed alone. Into the virtual wild animal park at the center of the city, Fel and Nova would come together as dream stuff and circle and greet their Human halves, the four of them running together in the Tacit Realty night.

By this time, years after the end of the Bœzch, there were new dramas brewing within Barbary Combine, but they were Human dramas now, and without the theater of world-destroying monsters. Fawn Virgilis, Alon, Bacalhaus, the Vongallo sisters, Zallo's children, or the Tishbyts and their few surviving lions: whether any of the new colonists of Barbary Combine squabbled over where Jeüdora and Montefeltro guided them, it was of little concern to Mún or Fel, or Luti or Nova.

Could either of the lovers see the stars that circled the great single-eye galaxy that peered down at them when their lonely colony fleet exited the black curtain surrounding Hæl System? Could they care even if they understood? Perhaps either Luti or Mún shared the relief the rest of their friends felt when Hæl was finally behind them. They did know. They did see the galaxy ahead of them, and when the two lovers watched their Tacit Reality sky shift to match the real night sky, when they watched the fleet follow the teardrop clusters all the way up to the galaxy eye, they held hands and rested upon each others' shoulders and whispered to their lion bodies lounging contentedly in the their separate universes on Long Savanna grasses — they whispered and thanked Æsirisæ, wherever she was, and hoped that this will never end.

MAPS

Hæl Tripple Star System
(Euphön Diversity of Life Authority)

Main Star: Hæl Damiano (O Class, Blue Hypergiant)
Distance from Sol System: Approximately 30,000,000,000 LY
Mass: 148.297 sol
Radius: 77.055 sol
Luminosity: 73,744 L
Claimed by: Euphön Diversity of Life Authority (EUDOLA, Windsor Temporality Vested Cosmopolitan Fellowship)

Orbital Bodies (6): Hæl I (Dwarf Planet, Vacuum), Hæl II (Dwarf Planet, Vacuum), Hæl III (Dwarf Planet, Asteroid Belt),
Hæl IV (G Type Yellow Star Named "Foss," Planetoid Hæl IVa, Hyper-Kuiper Size Asteroid Belt, and EUDOLA Colonies),
Hæl V (Planet Named "Bosch Übor," Inhospitable), Hæl VI (K Type Orange Dwarf Star Named "Étienne," and
Inhospitable Brown Dwarf Named "Bram" (System's Grip Point, Seat of Ægeleif Entity Jeûdora)).

Planet of Interest: Hæl V (Bosch Übor)

Distance from Hæl Damiano: 811,126,034,650 km (5,422.04 AU)

Radius: 6,866 km

Gravity: 1.07 G

Orbit Period: 26,423.76 years

Rotation: 26 hrs

Surface Temperature: 731 K (Since Thaw)

Atmosphere: 60 atm (CO2 87%, SO2 12.4%, H2O .6%), Inhospitable

Moons: 2 (Pawn, The Follower)

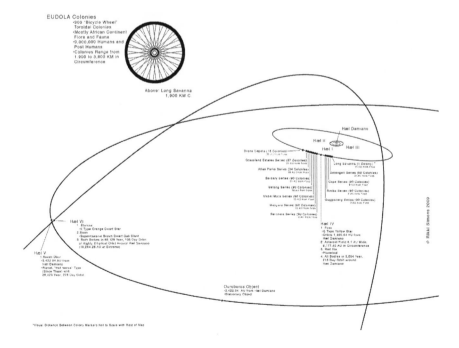

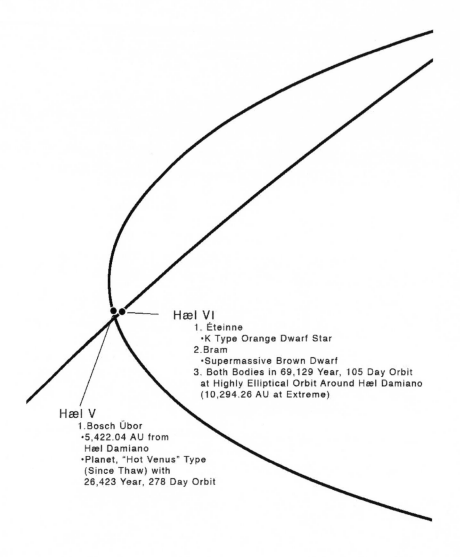

Hæl VI
1. Éteinne
   • K Type Orange Dwarf Star
2. Bram
   • Supermassive Brown Dwarf
3. Both Bodies in 69,129 Year, 105 Day Orbit
   at Highly Elliptical Orbit Around Hæl Damiano
   (10,294.26 AU at Extreme)

Hæl V
1. Bosch Übor
   • 5,422.04 AU from
     Hæl Damiano
   • Planet, "Hot Venus" Type
     (Since Thaw) with
     26,423 Year, 278 Day Orbit

*Visual Distance Between Colony Markers Not to Scale with Rest of Map

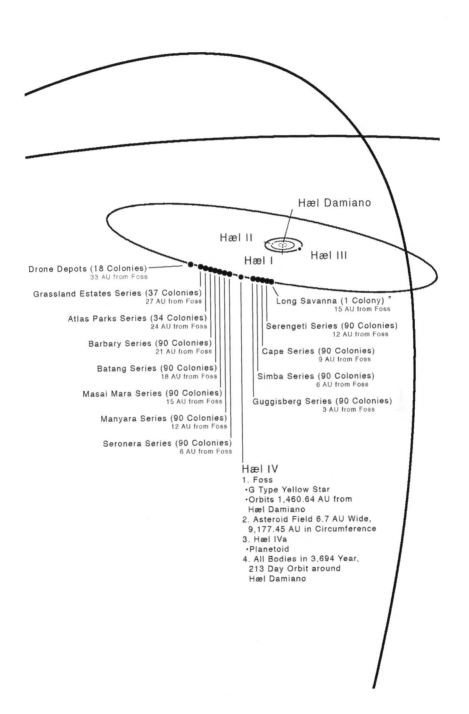

Hæl Damiano

Hæl II

Hæl III

Hæl I

Drone Depots (18 Colonies)
33 AU from Foss

Grassland Estates Series (37 Colonies)
27 AU from Foss

Atlas Parks Series (34 Colonies)
24 AU from Foss

Barbary Series (90 Colonies)
21 AU from Foss

Batang Series (90 Colonies)
18 AU from Foss

Masai Mara Series (90 Colonies)
15 AU from Foss

Manyara Series (90 Colonies)
12 AU from Foss

Seronera Series (90 Colonies)
6 AU from Foss

Long Savanna (1 Colony) *
15 AU from Foss

Serengeti Series (90 Colonies)
12 AU from Foss

Cape Series (90 Colonies)
9 AU from Foss

Simba Series (90 Colonies)
6 AU from Foss

Guggisberg Series (90 Colonies)
3 AU from Foss

Hæl IV
1. Foss
 •G Type Yellow Star
 •Orbits 1,460.64 AU from
  Hæl Damiano
2. Asteroid Field 6.7 AU Wide,
   9,177.45 AU in Circumference
3. Hæl IVa
 •Planetoid
4. All Bodies in 3,694 Year,
   213 Day Orbit around
   Hæl Damiano

GALLERY

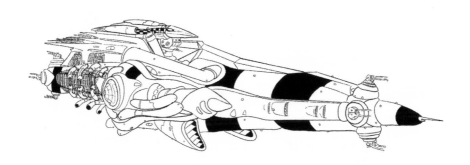

Rikki Simons is a voice actor, writer and artist, mostly known for his performance as the voice of GIR on Invader ZIM. He lives in Los Angeles with his wife, the illustrator, Tavisha and dreams of having lots more cats.

Nikkitikki | Tavicat

tavicat.com

Made in the USA
Middletown, DE
10 November 2020

Made in the USA
Middletown, DE
10 November 2020